ALSO BY MICHAEL FRANK

The Mighty Franks

What Is Missing

What Is Missing

MICHAEL FRANK

Farrar, Straus and Giroux   New York

Farrar, Straus and Giroux
120 Broadway, New York 10271

Printed in the United States of America
First edition, 2019

Library of Congress Cataloging-in-Publication Data
Names: Frank, Michael, [date] author.
Title: What is missing / Michael Frank.
Description: First edition. | New York : Farrar, Straus and Giroux, 2019.
Identifiers: LCCN 2018059643 | ISBN 9780374298388 (hardcover)
Subjects: LCSH: Domestic fiction.
Classification: LCC PS3606.R3834 F47 2019 | DDC 813/.6—dc23
LC record available at https://lccn.loc.gov/2018059643

Designed by Jonathan D. Lippincott

Our books may be purchased in bulk for promotional, educational, or business
use. Please contact your local bookseller or the Macmillan Corporate and
Premium Sales Department at 1-800-221-7945, extension 5442, or by e-mail at
MacmillanSpecialMarkets@macmillan.com.

www.fsgbooks.com
www.twitter.com/fsgbooks • www.facebook.com/fsgbooks

10   9   8   7   6   5   4   3   2   1

For JAS

and from her

LFF

and from them

CFF

Eccoci qua

Wherever I am
I am what is missing.
—Mark Strand, "Keeping Things Whole"

What Is Missing

I thought I knew you. Then I learned that I did not. I thought I knew myself. I now know I have a lot more to learn.

If I start to speak about the drugs, the drink, my mind, the way my emotions were stirred by everything that I discovered in the middle of that brutal night, I'll try to explain myself, and I can't do that, not now.

Nor can I see you right now, or speak to you. I have to go away. Please don't come find me. Please.

Ten Months Earlier

A ndrew Weissman's heart was pounding. He heard it, the roar and
pulse of it, in his ears. He could almost feel the blood juicing
through his body, propelling him forward. When he realized that
there were only three more bridges before he had to turn away from the
Arno, he made one last push. He dug down into himself, past the fatigue,
past the thirst and the heat, to see what he could find. He shot forward, a
body hurtling through time, slicing through the soupy air, flying.

After the second bridge he began to slow down, and the sweat came
up profusely. Somehow his body knew, as he was closing in on the end of
a run, that it was okay to cut free, to liquefy. When he reached the last
bridge, he slowed down even further, relaxing into an easy jog that carried
him all the way into the lobby of a palazzo on the left-hand side of the via
Tornabuoni. Just as the elevator door was about to close, he slipped in.

A woman stood in the corner of the cab. She had long spilling golden
hair and skin so translucent that it might have been made of paper. She
was holding a large padded envelope, its flap ripped open. On top of
the envelope were the first of what appeared to be a thick stack of typewritten pages. Her eyes were racing across the print on them at a fierce,
unbroken pace.

In his saturated shirt and shorts Andrew sank into the opposite corner and watched her. She didn't once look up from the page, not even
when the door opened again upstairs. She continued to read as she
stepped out of the elevator.

A sheet slipped out of her grasp and floated to the ground.

"Wait," Andrew said.

She stopped and blinked at him, came into focus. He picked up the fallen paper and handed it to her.

"Thank you," she said, then she set off toward her room, which was in the opposite direction of his. The air she had disturbed held her scent in it.

Andrew showered, then pulled on his jeans and T-shirt. He glanced at the list his father had left on the table between their two beds, with his suggestions for sites that Andrew might visit that morning. He folded the list in half and tucked it into the drawer, grabbed his camera, and headed for the sitting room, which had quickly become his private hangout at the Pensione Ricci.

Seldom used during the day, it was furnished with several constellations of deep sofas and chairs. A dark tapestry covered one wall. Large bright paintings of imaginary landscapes hung on two of the others. On the fourth a pair of long windows opened onto the via Tornabuoni, five floors below.

Andrew headed for the windows. He preferred the one on the left, with its open view up and down the street. He folded back the shutters and fastened them against the exterior of the building. Then he leaned on the windowsill and began to frame his first shot of the day.

Only then did he become aware that he wasn't alone. The woman from the elevator was sitting at a desk at the other end of the room, reading from, it seemed, more of the typewritten pages that she had been carrying before. Again her eyes were racing; again she didn't realize that she was being watched.

Andrew loved to take pictures of people reading. He loved the way readers were having a private experience that he could observe, and photograph, without being observed back. Slowly he angled his camera in her direction.

Without looking up from the page she said, "You might at least ask me to smile."

Andrew lowered the camera abruptly. He blushed. "People don't usually smile while they're reading."

"I do." She looked up. "When something delights me."

"You weren't smiling just now."

"No"—she sat back in her chair—"I wasn't."

"I'm sorry. I didn't mean to interrupt. Or to—offend you. I just—it's just what I do. Take pictures."

She studied him for a moment. "I've seen you before in here. Staring out the window."

"Not just staring. Shooting the street. It's part of a project I'm working on. I like to find patterns, repetitions. It's how I get to know an unfamiliar place."

"This is how you spend your days."

"When my father's out."

She looked as if she wanted to know more.

"Giving lectures. He's presenting at a medical conference here."

"Your father doesn't like you to go out without him?"

"He wants me to. It's just that sometimes I get tired of seeing the things he likes to see."

"What things are those?"

Andrew recited a list: the David, the Medici tombs, the Uffizi, the Baptistery doors, the Duomo. Other sites and countless artworks that had sped by in a blur went unmentioned because he no longer remembered their names.

"You've been a thorough tourist."

"My father likes to see everything. Everything interests him."

"But not you."

Andrew shrugged.

She tilted her head. "What do you think about when you look at these things? The David, the Medici tombs, and so on?"

"I feel like there's going to be a test."

"That's too bad. When it comes to buildings or sculptures, it's best if you feel—wonder. Otherwise, why bother going?"

"That's why I don't if I don't have to."

She nodded, then returned to her reading. Had he said something stupid, or had the conversation just petered out sooner than he would have liked? Either way, he got the message. He looked out the window and raised his camera. But he quickly lowered it again to watch her. She was reading even more rapidly now, her eyes speeding across the page urgently, anxiously. The troubled look on her face made her even more beautiful somehow.

Andrew forced himself to return his attention to the street below. A man in a straw hat was looking in a shop window where the mannequin was wearing virtually the identical straw hat. Andrew framed a shot and pressed the shutter.

"How about a walk?" she said. She was stacking up the pages, tapping them against the desk to even them out.

"But I don't even know your name."

"Will that help you to decide?"

"It just seems—proper."

Lines appeared in her forehead. "My name is Costanza."

"I'm Andrew."

"There. Everything's *proper* now, yes?"

Her hat was made of straw, like the one in the window. Its white band matched her dress. Her dress was linen, and it pulled across her breasts as she walked. It was hard for Andrew to take his eyes off those shapes.

"So you're in Florence by yourself," he half said and half asked as they set off up the via Tornabuoni.

"What gives you that idea?"

"You were alone in the elevator. And in the sitting room."

"My companion could be . . . attending a professional conference, like your father."

"Then they might know each other."

"They might be colleagues. Friends."

"Or enemies."

"Why enemies?"

"Lots of my father's colleagues are his enemies. He has very strong ideas about his work. And his kind of medicine is very competitive."

"Why is that?"

"I think it partly has to do with money."

"Let me guess. He's a plastic surgeon."

Andrew shook his head.

"A psychiatrist who has invented a pill that makes people amiable."

"I don't think that would be very successful in New York. People might lose their identity along with their edge."

She laughed. "I give up."

"He helps older women have babies."

Andrew noticed her right eye twitch. How old was she, anyway? A faint latticework framed her eyes, fine as mesh. That was all. His mother, Judith, was much more lined, and she had been dyeing her hair for eight years at least. His mother was forty-nine.

They were approaching the large open market near the church of San Lorenzo. Andrew and his father had walked along these same streets over the weekend, on their way to see the Medici tombs. The neighborhood had been in a Sunday slumber then; now it was alive with stalls selling tablecloths and leather goods, scarves and stationery, T-shirts and belts, watches, coral necklaces, mosaic picture frames—a daunting unbroken panorama of stuff.

About fifteen stalls in, Costanza angled to the right and led Andrew to a building covered by a large glass roof that stood behind the market stalls.

"What is this place?" he asked as they walked up the stairs.

"The Mercato Centrale. It's not on your father's list."

The way she pronounced Mercato Centrale suggested that she spoke Italian, or was Italian. Yet her English was perfect and had only a trace of an accent.

Andrew could have looked for hours at the meat cases alone. They were filled with things that were still half the creatures they had recently been. There were boars' flanks covered in damp gleaming fur, chickens with untouched faces connected by plucked bodies to limp clawed feet. Pheasants were feathered, more asleep than dead. Cows were in possession of their heads, pigs their snouts. There were slack tongues, looping intestines, accordion ribs, and pink spongy brains. Andrew raised his camera, but he couldn't find a way *in*.

Costanza led him around to the fruits and vegetables. They too let him know how they'd started on this earth. The oranges had leaves attached to them, the garlic their stems. There were berries he didn't recognize—*di bosco* she called them, "of the woods"; they were small, blush colored, covered with little freckles and bumps.

The mushrooms were brown and wrinkled. They looked leathered like an old man's skin and gave off a smoky, rich, strange smell. "When I was a girl," she told Andrew, "we used to visit my grandfather in Tuscany. After he retired he bought a small farm there. He used to hunt for his own mushrooms and dry them on special racks."

She leaned forward, closed her eyes, and inhaled. The scent evidently took her somewhere pleasant, somewhere far away.

Afterward she exchanged a few words with the vendor, who tossed several handfuls of mushrooms on the scale. "Is there a scent that takes you back?" she asked Andrew.

He shrugged. "I don't think so."

"That's because you haven't lost anything yet. You're still too young."

He couldn't decide if she was insulting him or challenging him. "I'm not *that* young, you know. And I've lost a few things."

"How old are you, anyway, Andrew? Eighteen?"

"In February."

"And do you want to tell me what it is you've lost?"

What hadn't he lost, really? His nuclear family, with the divorce. His grandmother, who died when he was nine. His brother, who vanished at the beginning of the summer—actually months, many months, before. His girlfriend, who broke up with him at the end of the school year.

He couldn't say all this to *her*, so he went for what felt like the simplest of the three. "Well, my parents are divorced."

"I surmised. You're traveling alone with your father. You don't seem like a boy who has no mother."

"I don't get how you can tell that."

"Just a feeling. I don't have a father myself. He died when I was fourteen."

"What did he die of?"

She thought for a moment, then said, "He killed himself."

Andrew had no idea how to respond to that.

"It's okay to say nothing. Sometimes nothing is best."

So he said nothing. Until they were nearly back at the meat counter.

"Can I ask if you're Italian or if you just speak it really well?"

"I'm Italian on my mother's side, American on my father's. My mother's father was the man who dried his own mushrooms. My grandparents' house is the house that is gone. Everyone's dead now except my mother, who lives in the north, near Genoa. And, yes, I'm here in Florence on my own." She paused. "Have I foreseen most of your questions?"

"I guess." Andrew's eyes drifted down to the gold band on her finger.

As soon as they rejoined the crowd outside, Costanza glanced at her watch and told Andrew that she was late for a lunch appointment. The hat went back up; a pair of dark glasses went on. He wondered if this had to do with his asking too many questions. In parting she said, "You can find your way back to home base?" He nodded. *Home base*: the words felt like a gift. She bestowed them, and then she was off.

As Costanza walked away from him, he took a series of photographs of her long white form, receding. Against the chaos of the market she looked like a cross between a goddess and a ghost.

⇌

Costanza's lunch date was with her husband, dead now almost a year to the day. She had decided that the best way to face Morton, newly resurrected a year after he'd been buried, was to take herself, and his words, somewhere public.

As she made her way toward a trattoria that was not far from the market, Costanza thought about how the Jews managed their grief. For a year they grieved, then they set their stone. It didn't mean they forgot. She was incapable of forgetting anyway. That was not her goal. She had something different in mind. Engaging with that young man, inviting him to go for a walk: it was all part of her plan, to force herself to do one thing every day that was completely unrelated to Morton. Only in the doing it didn't feel like an assignment. She had spoken to Andrew and remembered how much she liked talking to strangers.

Was it specific to this boy, or would it have been the same with anybody else? She had no idea, and she didn't care. She had done it; that was what mattered.

Costanza ordered a *quartino* of red wine and drank several sips thirstily. She saw that she had been anticipating the anniversary with more anxiety than she realized. She had invested its ceremonial quality with meaning. And so, clearly, had they.

They: Morton and his brother Howard. Morton and his minions. Morton and his army of helpers: the agents, the editors, the lawyers, the producers, the accountants, the financial advisers, his assistant Ivan, and, later on, the doctors, the nurses, the physical therapists, the acupuncturists and alternative healers, each of whom came into his life with a notion as to how the Great Writer should present his work, care for his body, organize his time, understand his psyche, guard his literary legacy, and—finally—die. For someone who was fundamentally so private, in his later years Morton surrounded himself with an awful lot of people who had an awful lot of responsibility for his affairs.

Howard, as Morton's executor, might have sent the package, but it was impossible to know who ultimately was behind the appearance of Morton's diary a year after he died. Most likely it was Morton himself. The gesture had his mark, his flourish, on it. His theater. The theater of Morton, with a surprise fourth act, or epilogue. A few words from the author, spoken—"spoken"—from the grave.

A few? The manuscript ran to more than five hundred pages. And it covered only six years, from the period just before they met through the month before the end. Nathan Wolf, Morton's agent, had already shown it to Morton's longtime editor at Magellan, Howard wrote, and she was hardly alone in feeling that nothing this gritty, intimate, and unexpected had been written by a leading American man of letters in decades—if ever. The story of Morton Sarnoff's return to the whirl of life, after more than a decade in rural retreat: it was going to be a sensation that would rekindle interest in Morton's earlier work, change the way the last novel was read, and translate into a lot of hard cold cash besides.

Costanza was not entirely surprised to learn from Howard that Morton had left the rights to these diaries to him—another clever gesture on Morton's part, since he knew that his brother needed money, and a good deal of it, to free himself from his unhappy marriage. She *was* surprised, and also hurt, to discover that what she felt about them didn't matter, to Morton or any of the others: the diaries were clearly being sent to her as a courtesy, so that she could make peace (or not) with whatever she found in them before they were published.

Howard didn't put it like that, of course. He said, instead, that he was so excited to be able to share this wonderful news with her. He hoped she would let him know what she thought, he couldn't wait to hear from her, and so on. Boilerplate through which she could detect his gloating: finally, for once, he was in charge.

She had not known that Morton kept a diary; she hadn't even suspected. She thought that what he was writing in those large hardbound ledger books were notes and ideas, sketches for his next (he sometimes wryly referred to it as his last) novel. That was what he had told her when she asked, and she had believed him.

Morton had not lied exactly. Just as he had answered her that day, the first pages contained miscellaneous unrelated scenes, sketches for possible characters, citations from books he was reading. Every so often he inserted notes from his doctors' appointments: "Grubman says it's the Coumadin that makes me bruise so easily." From Pam, his physical therapist: "Suck in my abdomen when I get up out of bed in the morning, it will help with the back. Always sleep with a bed pillow under the knees. Stretch, stretch, stretch."

Twenty-some pages in, a different kind of sentence erupted. "All these notes and fragments only confirm my emptiness," he said, apparently out of nowhere. "I'm writing here to avoid writing"—and he was off.

Back at the pensione, Costanza had read through the entries from the time before they met. She listened in, or so it felt, as Morton battled his black moods and worried whether his return to the city had been a mistake. She watched him agonize over his writer's block; she saw him fight, then quickly make up, with an old editor friend; and she saw him struggle with Howard, who kept trying—and failing—to get him to go out into the world.

Then she came to that April:

> A remarkable astonishing thing has happened: Howard, for once in his life, was actually *right* about something.
>
> On his last visit into town my brother apparently noticed an invitation to one of Nathan's book parties on my desk. I haven't gone to those things in years. Howard—the sneak—made a mental note and then simply appeared here last night at five.

This was as far as she had read. Now, after taking another sip of wine, she continued:

The party was down in the Village, at that place run by the Italian department at NYU—I'd been to a lecture there about Moravia a few lifetimes ago. There was a spread of Chiantis and cheeses I would have loved at least to sample; instead I stuck to a glass of bubbly water and some nutritionist-sanctioned carrot sticks.

At one point Nathan, very likely egged on by Howard, came up to me and said, "You know there's someone here you might be interested to meet."

"Oh," I said. "Why is that?"

"Because she's interesting."

He gestured toward the drinks table. "She's standing just over there."

Interesting is not the first word I would have used to describe this woman. I would have said, She is striking. Unusually striking. Very refined features, golden hair, eyes with focus and clarity. Lips pale and slightly chapped, maybe from being bitten or gnawed at. A good body, though this I had to deduce, since it was hidden under a skirt and big full sweater. Too much of both, the sweater especially.

That was interesting: a beauty who hides her beauty in yards of fabric. The opposite of all those leggy black-clad publishing girls.

"Costanza translates from English into Italian," Nathan said. "Maybe we can convince her to take on your next book," he said, "which will be done when . . . ?"

"When it's done," she offered kindly.

We fell into some very natural talk. I discovered that she is half-Italian, half-American. She grew up there, not here. The American father is dead, the Italian mother, she said, is "very much alive."

An American father, but an Italian last name? "After my father died," she said, "my mother changed my last name to hers. A bit peculiar, until you know the story."

It may have been the voice, with its slight softening old-world accent. Those sparkling green eyes. The slightly stiff way she carried herself. That intriguing reserve. It was hard for me to take my own eyes off her.

These pages disconcerted Costanza. She could think of many reasons why. Discovering that she had been observed—studied—like this was unsettling. Then there was hearing Morton's voice again, which made him seem so alive. And the way the diary allowed her to go back in time, yet bring with her everything she knew that followed. She could think of no other circumstance in her life where she'd been able to do that. Maybe in dreams. Only in dreams.

She remembered that first conversation, though not in such detail. She had just moved to New York. It had been another of her sudden impulses, but within weeks she had received assignments for two books to translate. She had rented an apartment in the East Village and she had begun to go out. She had found Morton to be magnetic; trim and with abundant silver hair, he had eyes that even on that first meeting ranged from icy to inky blue. Later on she would be able to read his moods, to predict the imminent return of the black feelings he wrote about, or his anger, merely by noting a subtle shift in those eyes. He spoke confidently, as though no person (no woman, no man either) could possibly be immune to his attention, once he had turned it on. Yet his demeanor had a quality of respect to it too. A modesty. The slant of his questions suggested he was genuinely interested in hearing what she had to say. She didn't often meet men like that. Not men her age, Italian or American. He reminded her of her father. He had a similar touch of old-fashioned decorum. And hauntedness.

Eventually she would learn that this Morton was still much under the influence of his illness and his unsettled life. In time a more autocratic, more complicated Morton, a steelier and colder Morton, would emerge.

She was surprised to receive a phone call from him the next morning. It took her several minutes to realize that he was interested in her in *that* way. Her cousin Cristina always used to tell her that she was unaware of the effect she had on men.

April 25th
Well, it wasn't as easy as I thought. After a little stab at holding back, I simply called and asked her out. And do you know what she answered: Why?

Why? It never occurred to me that I would have to explain (it's funny how unused I have become to people other than

Howard asking me simple questions like Why?). Because I found you intriguing, I said. Because I went back to Natalia Ginzburg as you recommended, and liked a lot of what I read. Because I thought we could, I don't know, talk. It came out more like "I dunno"; I sounded like I was seventeen.

At her end of the phone: a long excruciating silence.

To be doing this at my age. To be *feeling* this.

Then she said, All right.

On Thursday I picked her up at her apartment in the East Village. Old kilims, a sofa covered with a printed Genoese fabric, a wall of thumbtacked drawings, quotations written out on three-by-five cards. "I'm experienced at improvising homes for myself," she said. "It's the flip side of a wandering spirit."

Even though she grew up near Genoa, she spent summers in Tuscany, where her grandfather had an old farmhouse. Her summers were a mixture of country and "town" (imagine thinking of Florence as a town), where she used to stay in a pensione with her father and spend the weekend looking at paintings and sculpture.

She said that she was drawn to the backgrounds of those pictures, the fantastical roads and cities that hover in the distance of religious paintings and certain portraits. Most people think of them as an afterthought, she said, but for her they were the main attraction. I asked if that was connected to her wandering spirit, and she said that she hadn't put that together before. I said, "But it's so apparent."

I loved watching her think. It made her more radiant, if that's possible.

She said that whenever she goes to a notable place—a ruin, a monument—she always turns away from it, to see the secondary view. In great houses she likes the kitchens and attics best. She's captivated by the provenance of paintings, footnotes in biographies. Her favorite part of a menu is the side dishes; on trains she prefers to ride facing backward.

"I prefer to ride forward," I said. "That way, I can fool myself into believing I know what lies ahead in life."

"So that's what I've been doing wrong all these years!"

I laughed. She laughed. Then I asked if she was seeing anyone romantically.

"Not at the moment. What about you?"

"That depends." I held her eye.

"On what?"

"On you."

Costanza knew she was right to limit her reading. She had not
brought more pages with her, and she was glad.

⇌

By the time Andrew found his way back to the pensione, it was past
three o'clock, easily the latest he had stayed out on his own since he
and Henry had come to Florence. As soon as he stepped onto the via
Tornabuoni, he saw his father standing in front of the palazzo, looking
up and down the street impatiently.

The central feature that father and son shared was their thick hair,
peppered now with gray in Henry's case, a deep chestnut in Andrew's.
Most everything else about them was different. Andrew was a tall,
spider-limbed boy whose imperfect complexion upholstered the bones
of what in a few years seemed likely to be a handsome, possibly even
notably handsome, face. Henry by contrast had a wide forehead, sharp,
miss-nothing eyes, and a thick beard topped by a beak of a nose that
looked as though its maker had been called away to a more important
job halfway through; yet he was the sort of man people invariably noticed, mainly on account of his unbridled vitality. He was a pot on a
constant flame, sometimes simmering, sometimes bubbling, or bubbling
over. Some people found Henry's vitality contagious, some people were
oppressed by it, but no one responded to him with indifference.

Henry had changed out of his lecturing jacket and tie and was wearing a pair of khakis, a dark blue shirt, and comfortable shoes. His hurrying shoes, Andrew thought of them. Wearing his hurrying shoes while
having to stand still put Henry's mind and body in torqued conflict. Often the very sight of those shoes would cause Andrew himself to hurry.
But not at the moment. At the moment Andrew decided to take a picture
of his father. Calmly he turned on his camera and zoomed in on Henry's

face, where a scowl was implanted in his dense beard. Andrew captured the scowl—three times—then walked across the street and tapped his father on the shoulder.

"*There* you are. I've been worried. You're turning into your mother, Andrew. She was perennially late, especially near the end."

The end: as though she had died.

"You keep encouraging me to go out"—Andrew shrugged—"so I went out."

Henry frowned. "Day after day I leave you suggestions, and day after day all you do is go for a run and sit there in the pensione. I accept that you're not much of an adventurer. That's more Justin's thing."

Nearly every time Justin's name came up, Henry's face darkened. He behaved as though traveling without Justin were like traveling without a limb.

Andrew was relieved that Henry didn't ask where he'd been.

"Have you eaten?"

Andrew nodded. "But I can sit with you."

"Angelo made me a sandwich," Henry said, his vexation receding. "Things are opening again in a few minutes—I know you've been wanting to go see the Fra Angelicos at San Marco. What do you say to heading over that way? And afterward I thought we might look for some shirts. I know how you like your Italian shirts."

Andrew had never said a word about wanting to see the Fra Angelicos at San Marco; he didn't even know what they were. And it was Justin who liked Italian shirts—it was Justin who liked *things*.

"Sounds good," Andrew said, because sometimes it was simply easier to agree.

For the second time that day Andrew headed up the via Tornabuoni. He didn't walk alongside his father, as he had with Costanza, but behind him. Henry, in his hurrying shoes, wasn't interested in the experience of getting from one place to another. He wasn't interested in the shop fronts, the street life, the light, the language. He was interested in getting where he was going, fast.

He was also interested in being prepared when he got there, and preparing Andrew in turn. Henry was a devourer of guidebooks (still!) and books on travel, history, architecture, and art, and as they headed to San Marco, he asked and answered his own questions in a rapid-fire staccato delivery, first into the air alongside him and then, when he re-alized Andrew was lagging behind, back over his shoulder: "—Patron? Cosimo il Vecchio. Architect? Michelozzo. Period of transformation of buildings? Fifteen years from 1437 forward. Special feature? First pub-lic library in Europe. Most famous prior? Savonarola, and we know what came of him. Most famous friar-painters? Fra Bartolomeo and Fra Angelico. Better of the two?"

When Andrew didn't answer, Henry turned around. "Well?"

"This feels like a class, Dad. You want to be my teacher? Wouldn't you say I have enough of those already in my life?"

"I want to be a student. The truth is, if I could do it all over again . . ."

Andrew came to a standstill. Therefore so did Henry. Andrew looked at his father's face to see if he was serious. "You wouldn't be a doctor?"

Henry shrugged. "It could be this city," he said, gesturing. "It's so . . . infinite. It's so . . . what's that phrase of Justin's? It's so my way. Every-thing about it. The history. The art and architecture. So much began here, so much ingenuity, so many ideas. It makes me think, I don't know, of all the possibilities in life . . ."

Andrew was perplexed. "I can't imagine you as anything other than a doctor."

"Yes, but I can," Henry said. "Left to my own devices, I might have become a historian, or an art historian. I might have been a musician, who knows?"

"Dad, you're tone-deaf."

"I guess that's where Justin comes in. He expresses enough music for the rest of us."

Father and son resumed walking, this time more slowly and in silence. Andrew wondered whether something had gone badly at the conference that morning. His father not a doctor? Who (what) was his father if not a doctor?

When they reached San Marco, Henry opened his guidebook and consulted a map of the building. "The place to start is with the Fra An-gelicos upstairs," he said, sounding more like himself. "They're the main attraction, though I wouldn't mind seeing Savonarola's hair shirt. A piece of underwear five hundred years old. How crazy is that?"

The largest Fra Angelico *Annunciation* was waiting for them right at the top of the stairs. On the left-hand side of the fresco an angel,

having alighted on a colonnaded portico, was lowering himself into a
gentle bow, his arms crossed elegantly in front of his chest. With his
bent knee and his wings still up, it seemed clear that he had just arrived. Fra Angelico had chosen to paint the moment just before the angel was to deliver the news to Mary, who was sitting on a sturdy wooden
stool, her own arms crossed in front of her plain tunic, her face in
meticulous three-quarter view.

"Can you imagine what it must have felt like to be able to come and
tell this woman that she was pregnant, and pregnant with *this* of all
babies?" Henry said. "I think it's brilliant the way he draws us into the
angel's mind."

To Andrew the angel looked blank, impassive. A messenger, not much
more. He thought that Mary was deeper. She appeared to be both
worried and curious, as if she knew something significant was about to
happen to her.

They moved on to the dormitory and began to tour the monks' cells,
each of which had its own small private fresco. There were more than
forty of these paintings, which seemed to hover on the white plaster
walls like projections, or dreams. The rooms appealed to Andrew. He
would have liked to be left alone in one of them for just an hour, or half
an hour; but Henry, consulting his book, was rattling off the subjects
and the probable painters of each fresco, his pace picking up giddily
until they came to another *Annunciation*.

In this version Mary was on her knees, and the angel was standing
and looking down on her. The painting gave off a visceral sense of waiting. And it slowed Henry down. Very little slowed Henry down.

Andrew studied his father studying the fresco. "I guess you can
relate."

Henry looked at him.

"You're like the angel. You get to tell women they're pregnant."

Henry glanced at the painting, then back at his son. "I don't just
tell them they're pregnant. I *make* them pregnant."

Andrew let out a long, though nearly silent, sigh. A private sigh.

Henry trailed out of the cubicle and into the hallway, and Andrew
trailed after him. Standing ahead of them in the corridor, looking into
one of the monks' cells and intensely studying a painting, was Costanza.

Andrew felt his heart twist. With her linen and her pale skin and golden hair, she looked like a modern variation on one of the Marys in the frescoes. Henry was charging directly toward her, oblivious; Andrew was several steps behind. Just as she was about to turn forward, Andrew quickly unhooked the red velvet rope that limited access to the cells and darted inside one of them.

The next thing Andrew knew there was a loud clunk. From the sound of it, Henry had plowed right into her, and something had tumbled to the ground.

"*Mi scusi.* I didn't see you. I was—"

"In a rush, apparently."

Andrew peered around the edge of the wall. Henry had bent down to collect a small bag that had gone flying.

"I hope it's not broken," Henry said.

"My shoulder?"

"Your package." Henry handed it to her. "Please tell me it's not fragile."

"It's a book." She took it out of its bag and examined it.

Henry glanced at the title: *Lives of the Artists.* "Vasari seems to think Fra Angelico was some kind of saint, crying when he started in on a crucifixion. He brings out the preacher in him—all that talk about painters who paint holy subjects needing to be holy themselves."

"You disagree?" she asked.

"I don't agree or disagree. It's just not what I look for in pictures. I look for technique, psychology, drama. Subjects that are translatable beyond the stories they depict. I think that's what makes a great painting. Universality, applicability. Religion, by itself, leaves me cold."

He was actually saying all this to someone he didn't know—to *her?*

She didn't seem fazed: "All religion?"

"All." He paused. "I'm sorry if I offend you."

"I don't offend so easily. I like people with opinions."

He hadn't even noticed that Andrew was missing.

"Forgive me," she said. "But I feel as though I've seen you somewhere before."

"Well, I've been in Florence almost a week," Henry said, as though that were sufficient. "I'm staying at the Pensione Ricci."

"That explains it," she said, tucking the book under her arm. "Well, perhaps I'll see you at home base."

Henry got a *home base* too?

"So you're also staying there? At the Ricci?"

She nodded.

"The terrace is a nice place to have a drink," Henry said.

"One of the nicest in all of Florence."

"It's particularly lovely around seven o'clock."

"Yes, it is."

"Maybe our paths will cross there this evening."

"Maybe they will."

Andrew pulled back from the doorway. After two beats Costanza walked by the opening to the cell in which he had been hiding. Even in profile he could see that her face had light in it. Light that, it appeared, this brief encounter with Henry had brought on.

Andrew waited a moment, then rejoined his father, who was staring ruminatively off into space.

Henry looked up and smiled. "It's such a fine afternoon. Let's go spend some time out in it."

Henry and Andrew wheeled past the Duomo and Orsanmichele, through the straw market and across the Ponte Vecchio, where windows full of gold captured and deepened the late-afternoon sunlight and looked like the embers of dozens of tiny, slowly fading fires. Their fires were fading; Henry's was picking up. They'd been here, or in a place similar to here, before. Henry, buoyant. Henry fueled by an almost manic energy, which was high and rising higher, along with the stack of shirts that, as soon as they'd found the shop he'd been looking for, he had piled up on the counter. Six or eight were in Henry's stack, the same number set aside for Justin. Andrew had half-heartedly picked out a single one. Pale blue. He didn't need or want it particularly, but he knew it was prudent to take part.

Andrew's choice disappointed Henry. "My son here needs color," he said to a compact gray-haired man, Signor Zubarelli himself. "He needs pattern. He needs *help*." Henry waved his hand at a blue-and-yellow-checked shirt. "Let's see one of those." To Andrew he said, "Humor me. Put down your camera for a moment and try it on."

In the dressing room, as Andrew changed into the shirt, he had a fleeting glimpse of how his life might look to someone who regarded it from the outside, someone who was not yoked and bound into it: here was a young man being shown the world by a father who wanted him to know things and experience things and have things, and all that he, the son, could do was chafe at his confinement and dream of his escape.

But to see Andrew in such a light was to have no real idea what it was like to be alone with Henry for these long, unbroken stretches. To be alone with Henry . . . to be alone with Henry meant being awakened at two in the morning whenever he felt a need to vent. It meant having the imperfections of your admittedly imperfect mother raked over for the thousandth time while you listened to a pretty much idealized view of your older brother. It meant being found wanting for not having an opinion about fifteenth-century religious frescoes. It meant having to anticipate, and provide ballast for, his mood swings. It meant having the spontaneity hurried out of you when Henry was feeling up and your independence squashed when he was down. It meant having your girlfriend (well, your former girlfriend) treated as a non-person. It meant knowing his love, yes, but it meant knowing that love to be sometimes consuming and selfish—self-interested.

Andrew stepped out of the dressing room. "I feel like I'm wearing a tablecloth. And the sleeves are too short."

Henry pulled back the collar and looked at a label. "Equal to fifteen and a half, thirty-five, American, si?" When Zubarelli nodded, Henry said, "Arms can't grow a full size in three months."

Zubarelli measured Andrew's arms. Apparently they could.

Alas, nothing other than solid blue or solid white was in stock in Andrew's size, Zubarelli reported after consulting his inventory; if Henry could be patient, he added, a shirt could be made up. But Henry could not be patient.

"Dad, it's all right," Andrew said from back in the dressing room. "The blue one is all I want."

"You could find that at Bloomingdale's."

"Bloomingdale's serves its purpose," said a voice from across the room.

Andrew, rejoining his father, saw that the voice belonged to a tall man in an impeccable linen summer suit, a white linen shirt that was surprisingly crisp for so late on a summer afternoon, and a delicately patterned orange silk tie.

"Isaac," said Henry. "What are you doing here?"

"The same thing you are, Henry."

"But how do you know about Zubarelli?"

"Zubarelli is *known*. And Zubarelli and I"—Isaac nodded in the direction of the proprietor—"go way back." Andrew watched this man take in Henry's stack of shirts with a quick if subtle glance. "Though of course mine are made for me." Isaac gestured upward with one hand to indicate—it seemed—his height.

In his other hand he was holding a shopping bag. Two shirts were in it. One was pale blue, like Andrew's. The other was gray with thin white stripes.

Henry put his palm on Andrew's shoulder. "This is my son Andrew. Andrew, this is my—colleague, Isaac Schoenfeld."

Schoenfeld gave Andrew a nod so princely it looked like a bow. Everything about the man seemed formal, almost regal. His clothes, his speech, his elegantly formed face. "This is the second one?"

Henry nodded. "Justin's at college, doing a composition intensive."

Schoenfeld gave Andrew a slow evaluative look. "Seventeen and a half, yes?"

"Actually, it's just a third," said Andrew.

"A mathematician," Schoenfeld said dryly.

"Math is more his brother's specialty," Henry said. Then: "What brings you to Florence, Isaac? Other than shirts."

"Eileen and I are on our way to visit friends at a villa in the Marche. Florence is a nice point of transition. And I was able to hear a very interesting medical talk today besides."

"Really? Whose?"

"Yours, of course." To Andrew, Schoenfeld said, "Your father is a gifted speaker. He never loses his audience's attention. I myself have never been very good at lecturing. I'm too shy."

"You sell yourself short, Isaac."

"The presentation was really very well done, Henry. Even without that lively PowerPoint, a layman might have understood." Schoenfeld took a pair of dark glasses out of his breast pocket. "How much longer are you in Italy?"

"The conference finishes on Friday. Then we're driving through Tuscany."

"Ah, a working vacation. I suppose there are still some corners of Tuscany worth exploring—up near Volterra maybe, where things get a little ragged and wild." Schoenfeld placed the glasses onto his well-shaped nose. "Nice to see you again," he said to Andrew. "Happy shopping, gentlemen," he added, and was off.

See you again? Andrew looked to Henry for an explanation, but Henry was busy handing his credit card to Zubarelli. Henry seemed to have forgotten all about Andrew's boring, Bloomingdale's choice of a shirt. In brooding silence he waited for his receipt.

Andrew watched this Schoenfeld through the window. When he stopped at the corner to allow a car to drive by, Andrew stepped closer, raised his camera, and framed a shot. As he was about to press the shutter, Schoenfeld turned back and looked in Andrew's direction. It was as though he sensed that he was about to be photographed. Elongating his already long torso, he almost seemed to pose. After Andrew took the picture, Schoenfeld nodded at him, then moved on.

Andrew walked back to his father. "What did he mean about seeing me *again?*"

Henry hesitated. "He met you when you were small. Isaac and your mother and I used to be—closer."

Henry didn't say anything else until he and Andrew were in the street. "I can't abide that man. Shirts specially made. Friends at a villa. Who specifies *villa?* And *working vacation*—he made it sound like I was a traveling salesman. He called me a verbose simpleton who pours out language that even an imbecile can understand."

"I heard him call you a 'gifted speaker.'"

Henry slowed down for a moment, then turned to Andrew. "I appreciate your trying to make me feel better, Andrew. Really I do. But—no. Schoenfeld is pretentious and patronizing—to *me.*"

The sun, lowering in the sky, was sending out long golden fingers of light that tapped the surface of the river and set it sparkling. "It looks like we're going to have a dramatic sunset," Henry continued. "Why don't we head back to the pensione and have a drink on the terrace? Angelo could bring us a bowl of those funny potato chips they serve, the ones that nestle together like poker chips."

The ones that nestle together like poker chips. A tiny coaxing detail, the sort of enticement you'd offer a child, like a lollipop after a checkup. Henry could have just said *Pringles.* They'd talked about how odd it was that they were served in all the bars in Florence.

"It's so nice being out," said Andrew. "Let's go sit in a piazza."

"But the terrace is up high—it's bound to attract a breeze. And those views."

Andrew persisted. "Isn't Santo Spirito near here, the one without the façade? Didn't you say it was your favorite church? I'd really like to take some pictures over there, see how the light hits it as the sun is going down."

Henry's glance lingered on the lowering sun, the coloring sky.

"Santo Spirito it is then," he said with a sigh.

⇒

The next morning when Andrew appeared at the door to the *salone*, Costanza was again sitting at the desk, again reading through a stack of typewritten pages. Her face looked less worried, somewhat less worried, than it had the day before.

He stepped on the dry parquet. It creaked. He took another step, produced another creak.

With her finger holding her place, Costanza glanced at his damp hair. "Back from a run?"

He shook his head. "Just a late shower. I didn't sleep very well."

"Insomnia can be a beast."

"It wasn't *my* insomnia. It was my father's. He gets up in the middle of the night and wants to talk."

"That doesn't sound like much fun," Costanza said.

Andrew approached the window. He raised and lowered his camera. Nothing on the street engaged him.

Every minute or so she turned another page. Generally there was something soothing about the way paper sounded as it was shifted from one place to another. Yet the expression on Costanza's face was once again the opposite of soothed. Whatever she was reading was now causing her eyes to narrow. She read a few more pages, then sat back and rubbed her neck.

"What time does your father finish today?"

"Sometime after four I think. But he always stays to answer questions."

"So you're free for a while?"

Andrew nodded.

"Have you seen the other David?"

"The other David?"

"By Donatello. It's in the Bargello."

Her dress was pale green this time, and her hair was pulled into a loose ponytail that fell down the center of her back. Her hat was the same and her oval sunglasses were the same, and the warm sunlight brought out her scent, which was something floral and floated off her as she moved.

They reached the narrow, shadowy via Condotta, walking the whole time in silence. As the sidewalk could accommodate only one of them, Andrew fell back and studied her from behind. He noticed the way she walked, how her hips, rising and falling, caused her body to swing back and forth gently on an invisible axis as she made her way down the crowded street. He noticed too how remote she was, how withdrawn.

Stepping into the street so that he could walk alongside her, he said, "You're kind of quiet this morning."

She hesitated for a moment before saying, "I suppose I'm wondering why you hid from me yesterday at San Marco."

Andrew's face reddened.

"I glimpsed you out of the corner of my eye as I was walking out, after I spoke to your father. You looked . . . tortured."

Andrew buried his hands in his pockets. "How did you know he was my father?"

"He mentioned the pensione. And something about him reminded me of you."

This, when he tried so hard to be different from Henry.

"I wasn't hiding from *you*."

She lowered her sunglasses and gave him a look.

Reddening, now flushing, burning. How was it possible for skin to have a mind, or behavior, of its own?

"The thing is," he said, "I was so glad—I was so glad to have some-thing . . . for myself."

Costanza pushed her sunglasses back up in front of her eyes. "I get that," she said.

Upstairs at the Bargello not one but two Donatello Davids were on dis-play, the early statue in marble, stiff and with oddly blank eyes, the later one in bronze. It was the bronze David that Costanza had brought him to see. Donatello's version wasn't like the Michelangelo David, the one even the laziest of tourists flocked to. He wasn't mighty, but soft and beautiful, in an almost feminine way. He stood with his left hand on his hip, which was cocked. This David wasn't about to kill but had already killed. Even though his left foot was planted squarely on Goliath's severed head, he looked young and vulnerable. He wore a floppy hat and leather boots but was otherwise naked; locks of hair wound out from under the hat and onto his shoulders. From behind it wasn't at all clear if he was a boy or a girl or some amalgam of the two. The statue may have been made out of bronze, but his body seemed pliable, alive in its stillness, and quietly sensual. A youthful, ambigu-ously gendered, sexy Old Testament hero? It made no sense, and the feelings the statue stirred in Andrew unsettled and confused him. But then many things he felt around Costanza unsettled and confused him.

"The first thing most people say is that it marked the return to the classical nude," Costanza said. "But that's not what I think about when I look at it. I think that, when you finally slay your demon, you ought to appear more—more rattled, to say the least."

"Whereas he seems so calm."

She stepped closer. "Maybe it's because he's so young and doesn't understand that even after you do away with your demons, they can go on living inside of you."

"You don't have to be old to understand that," Andrew said.

Costanza circled the statue. "Do you want to tell me about her?"

He gave her a confused look.

"A simple guess," she said with a shrug.

Did he want to tell her? He wasn't sure. "Her name is Charlotte," he said experimentally. "For Charlotte Brontë. She's a year ahead of me

at school. Her parents are English professors, and they live on the Upper West Side."

Costanza nodded. The nod was like a floodgate lifting. It came
pouring out of him. The sister, who was named Emily. The dog, Bran-
well, and Anne, the bird, a parrot they kept in a brass cage. The books,
everywhere. Four, five thousand of them, probably, on shelves, on tables,
in the dining room, the hall, the living room. The living room with its
peculiar arrangement of furniture, six comfortable armchairs in a circle: four for family, two for guests. They lived in those chairs. They ate
in them, they napped in them, mostly they read in them. Which was
what he and Charlotte did the first time they had what you might call
a date. After thinking about it for months, he asked her if she wanted
to go see a movie. She said she didn't like movies that much. He asked
her if she would like to go for a walk. She said she got enough exercise
on the swim team, which was where they had met. Instead she invited
him over to read.

"Very romantic," said Costanza.

"Well, not at that point it wasn't."

"No, I mean it. The books. The parrot." Her eyes sparkled with
interest.

"I don't think anyone said more than three words the whole night.
Oh, her mother offered me a cookie. It was like biting into cement.
Anne, the parrot, said, 'Don't eat the cookie! Don't eat the cookie!'
Afterward Charlotte asked if I would like to see her room. Her parents
didn't even look up from the page. We got up and walked down a long
narrow hall and we went into her room and we . . . talked."

Costanza widened her eyes. Instead of continuing, though, Andrew
simply blushed again.

"That's the whole story?"

He sighed. "For nine, almost ten months everything was okay, actually everything was *great*, between us. At least from my point of view.
Then last week, just before I came here, we went for a walk in Central
Park, and she told me she couldn't see continuing to go out with me
after she left for college. Even though we still had the summer ahead of
us, she felt it was time to—to be free."

Costanza considered for a moment. "She was afraid."

"Of what?"

"What she felt for you."

"How do you know?"

"Because I was once an eighteen-year-old girl, myself."

"I really cared for her. I even grew to like that stupid squawking bird."

Andrew's eyes had begun to sting. He averted them from Costanza.

"Birds have no business living in New York apartments," she said. "A double cage is too heavy-handed a metaphor for my taste."

He was on some sort of unprecedented automatic pilot: all this talk, all this feeling, all of it told and shown to someone he scarcely knew. He hadn't even told his father what had happened with Charlotte.

Andrew and Costanza headed toward a pair of wooden chairs. Surrounded by statues frozen on their plinths and pedestals, they sat for a few moments in silence, then Costanza reached into her purse. "I almost forgot, I have something for you." She gave Andrew a small bag, the bag from the day before, the one Henry had knocked out of her grasp. The one with the book, the Vasari.

She'd repaired its dust jacket with a piece of clear tape.

"Thank you."

"I thought it might make Florence come more alive for you."

You make Florence come alive for me.

The sentence flashed in his head, then fizzled out.

He opened the book. Touching the book that she had just touched was a little like touching her.

He came to the chapter on Donatello and scanned a few paragraphs. The skimming redirected his mind.

"It says—it says here that when Donatello was working on a sculpture for the front of the campanile at the Duomo, he liked to talk to the marble. He said, 'Speak, damn you, speak!'—to the stone. Do you really believe that?"

"I don't really believe that, no. But it does capture the essential puzzle of this whole room, which is how to get inanimate materials to tell a story."

Andrew studied her for a moment. "I think that's your puzzle too."

Costanza's head fell to an angle. "You think of me as inanimate?"

"Not at all." Andrew blushed. "What I mean is . . . I mean you want to hear my stories, but yours . . ."

She looked confused.

"Yesterday, for example, you were married, but today you're not." He indicated her hand, which was ringless.

She looked down. "Isn't it more accurate to say that yesterday I was wearing a wedding ring?"

He shrugged. "I guess."

She rubbed her ring finger. "Andrew, you have to understand. In Europe we're raised differently. There's much more indirectness, much more . . . discretion."

"So you're *not* married?"

"What if I were to tell you that my husband is dead, but I sometimes still feel married to him?"

He thought for a moment. "I suppose I'd understand that."

Privately he wondered how long her husband had been dead, and whether they'd been in love, and stayed in love, unlike his parents, and if they'd had children, and what their children were like; but something told him that he had asked enough questions for the moment.

She lifted her wrist, turned her watch around. "It looks like it's nearing time for lunch."

He was crestfallen. "You have another lunch date today?"

"Yes. With you." She slipped her arm through his.

The restaurant Costanza took Andrew to was on a side street deep into the Oltrarno, in a cool, slightly musty room with exposed beams and thick plaster walls. The tables were of uncovered plain wood. When they sat down across from each other, Andrew became aware of a brief pause in the conversation as the people at the table next to them tried to work out, or so he conjectured, the connection between this elegant European woman and this long-haired American kid.

The waiter put a name to it. He brought them half a liter of wine and poured her a glass. *"Anche per tuo figlio?"*

She indicated yes. The waiter filled Andrew's glass, then went away.

"He asked if your 'son' wanted wine too, didn't he?"

"Tuscans are very frugal," Costanza said. "They don't like to waste."

Andrew's hand circled around his glass. He took a sip of the wine. It was red, and sharp. He drank it, but it bit him.

She too sipped. "Well, it tastes real anyway. Like the food here. Will you let me order for you?"

The waiter came back and rattled off the dishes of the day. "What's good today are the fusilli with zucchini and tiny tomatoes. Light, for the summer. We'll have that, and then we'll see what we feel like afterward. It's the way here."

Andrew lifted his wineglass but did not drink from it. "Is it the way here for people to make quick assumptions?"

"It can be, yes."

"You're too young to have a son my age."

She did the math. "Not necessarily."

"Is it okay if I ask how old you are?"

"Andrew, you ask so many questions. It's very—"

"American. I know. But maybe you're just becoming less European."

"In the last day and a half, after nearly seven years in New York? I don't think so."

It had not occurred to him before to ask where her actual home was. "You live in the city too?"

"*The* city—yes. It would appear that you and I are neighbors."

He sensed a tightening in the atmosphere. He believed that it meant *some*thing that she spoke to him the way she did, so coyly and so—what was it?—playfully? He could feel it deep inside his body. He felt it without entirely understanding it, but he wanted it to continue.

"And . . . and *do* you have kids?"

The sparkle in Costanza's eyes dimmed. "I wanted to, but it wasn't meant to be."

The waiter appeared. He set two steaming bowls of fusilli in front of them. Costanza reorganized hers with her fork, folding the vegetables in more evenly and helping the pasta to cool.

"I think my mother might have liked to try for a girl, but that wasn't meant to be either," Andrew said, to break the silence.

"Because of the divorce?"

Andrew shrugged.

"Was it bitter?"

"*She* wasn't bitter. Not about leaving."

"There must have been someone else then."

Andrew nodded. "You understand a lot."

"The truth is, I understand very little. But I'm good at surmising." She ate a bite of pasta. "Is this the man she's married to now?"

"Charlie. My stepfather."

"What do you think of him?"

"At the beginning I didn't like him at all. I thought he was the reason she left. Later I realized that the marriage would have ended anyway. At least that's what my mother wanted me to believe."

"What do *you* believe?"

Andrew thought for a moment. "I was only eleven then. In those days when my parents fought or wanted to have a serious talk, they would go down to the street and get into our car, so I'm sure I missed a lot." He paused. "I'm not sure why, but I've always wanted to *know*. What happened, what went wrong. Justin, my brother, couldn't care less. I've tried asking him because he's older and should remember more, but he says the past is the past."

"People tend to fall into two groups. Those who feel the past on them always, like a shadow, and those who are free."

"You belong to the first group, don't you?"

"I think we both do."

They finished their pasta in silence. As the tables flanking them began to empty, the balance of the sounds in the room changed, and Andrew found himself listening to a table behind him, a distant table where someone was laughing, then speaking at a rapid-fire pace. He cocked his head. He knew that laugh; he knew that pace; he knew that voice.

When the waiter returned to see if they wanted anything else to eat, Andrew said no. So did Costanza. She asked for the check, which the waiter brought and which she paid.

Costanza watched Andrew, watched him listening, then looked over his shoulder.

"It's my father, isn't it? With his students?"

She nodded. "Florence can be an awfully small town sometimes."

Andrew turned around himself, just enough to see. He sighed. "I should probably say hello."

He stood up and took in the whole scene now. Henry was sitting at a long table in the back of the restaurant, flanked and faced by eight young people. Eight pairs of eyes were on Henry, eight heads were bobbing as he spoke, nodding and absorbing. And laughing. A young woman was taking notes, her hand moving agilely across a gridded notebook. A man opposite Henry was holding out a microcassette tape recorder, capturing his every word.

Andrew took several strides forward and into his father's bubble. Costanza dropped a few bills on the table, then followed.

"Hey, Dad."

Henry, being midsentence, continued to address his audience even as he looked first at Andrew, then at Costanza. Then his expression, professorial and authoritative, dissolved into confusion.

After a few seconds Henry's language caught up with his face. *"Andrew?"* But possessing a highly developed public persona, Henry quickly recovered. He stood up. *"Ragazzi,"* he said, sweeping his hand in Andrew's direction, "this is my son Andrew. And this—this is—"

"Costanza," Andrew said.

Henry studied her intensely, with eyes that sought an answer to the mystery of her connection to his son. They sought—and they failed.

Costanza seemed to bask in Henry's confusion for a beat longer than was necessary. "Please don't let us interrupt your lunch," she said. "We were just leaving."

"But—but won't you stay and join us for a coffee?"

A coffee and not just *coffee*: Andrew sensed that his father had tailored his phrasing just for her.

"It's the least I can offer," Henry added, "after having missed our drink the other night."

"I wasn't sure that was an invitation," Costanza said.

"It was." Henry gave Andrew a rapid penetrating glance. "Won't you join us now? Just for a moment?"

It was her turn to look at Andrew. His discomfort was stamped on his face.

"Some other time maybe." She turned to go.

"This evening then? At seven? On the terrace at the Ricci—for prosecco, if you care for it?"

She glanced at Andrew. "The appointment is for all of us?"

"All of us, naturally." Henry was speaking to Costanza, but his eyes were on his son.

For the first time in days, Henry did not hurry. Instead he slowly made his way to the Boboli Gardens, and there amid the moss-tipped statues and murky fountains he tried to figure out when his sons had begun not just to drift away from him but to drift away from his understanding of them, which was something altogether different.

He remembered a phone call that came for Justin when he was home over spring break, from one of his music professors, or maybe TAs: David. Justin took the call in his room, and when he came out again, his eyes were red and puffy. He said that this professor, or TA, David, had felt Justin's recent performance was not as good as it should have been. The playing was too restrained. Too cautious. Just repeating these words had made Justin tear up again.

Then after Henry had planned their summer trip and bought the plane tickets, this same David, according to Justin, felt that he should stay at Bard over the summer and do that composition course. Justin followed David's advice rather than travel with his father to Europe, as he had each summer in the past four years.

David felt he needed a better violin.

David felt he shouldn't lift weights at the gym more than once a week, as they could deform his arms.

David said to watch out for scalding water should he ever wash the dishes. Better: use rubber gloves.

David was a vegetarian, David believed vegetarianism was good for violinists.

David—it came to Henry in a flash of insight—might possibly be something more to Justin than merely his TA.

Once Henry allowed that thought to form in his mind, so many other things fell into place. Justin's lack of a girlfriend since he started at Bard. The curiously intense friendship he had had with a cello player he had met at music camp the summer between his junior and senior year in high school, and spilling into the fall afterward, when every night he was on the phone to this kid—Carter?—for hours after dinner, until, abruptly, the calls stopped. His total lack of interest in sports (but did that matter, or was that an outdated kind of thinking?). Yet he *had* had a girlfriend his senior year, or half of senior year. The redheaded one with a nose ring; Henry had already forgotten her name.

When Henry paused to think about it, to think that Justin might be drawn to boys, or girls and boys both, he decided he didn't care. Mostly he didn't care. What he cared about more was the not knowing— the hiding, and being hidden from.

And Justin was the son he thought he knew better. Andrew was the cryptic one. All that photographing, all that quiet observing and secret tallying up that Andrew did. Those long solitary runs he took. Everything about him was withheld, inward. Like Judith when she went into one of her moods. Even that dreary girl he brought home, the one with the stringy hair and glasses—she was so shy she might as well have been mute. The one time Andrew left the room she took a book out of her bag and buried herself in it. What about her could possibly have attracted his son? What about her could possibly have caused the pounds to melt off him after something between them went awry?

Henry saw this by accident a week earlier, through a crack in Andrew's bedroom door. Henry was walking down the hall and happened to glance up. Andrew was changing his shirt, and his upper body looked gaunt. At the time Henry had thought it was all the running. Or the pressure of high school, which in Manhattan, in this generation, was just insane. Or some new body-obsessed teen style—the concave torso—he'd failed to track, like the brims on baseball caps tipped to one side or pants being worn low to show off a brand of underwear. Now he felt that he had again missed, again misunderstood. Andrew must have been so distressed by this girl that he had stopped eating.

Suddenly Henry was noticing all kinds of things about Andrew. In just the last two days alone Andrew had caused Henry to rethink what he knew about his younger son. Henry could walk across every single inch of the Boboli Gardens and not get over how Andrew seemed to have made sure, and quite deftly too, that Henry didn't end up meeting Costanza for a drink the night before on the terrace of the Ricci. He had *finessed*. But why? Could he possibly care for this woman in *that* way? Andrew?

Then he appeared with her at lunch. Andrew had had lunch with the remarkable-looking woman Henry had spoken to in San Marco and thought about more than once since.

Henry didn't know if it was the red wine or the heat, which, as he aged, he tolerated less and less, but he began to feel woozy. A splintered but still serviceable park bench fortunately stood nearby, and he landed on it with a weary thud. Damp and ruddy faced, Henry sat stroking his itchy beard as he looked out at the gardens.

He had invested so much in being the boys' father—a lot when they were small, a lot certainly for a man of his generation who worked as hard as he did, and a lot more after Judith left him. He knew what people thought. Judith had articulated it a number of times, and with resentment: he had filled the hole she left with the boys. He had turned them into his companions. He bought them subscriptions to the opera and the philharmonic. He traveled with them. He didn't conceal from them the contents of his mind or the gradations of his temperament. Henry contended that such openness promoted honesty and friendship between fathers and sons. Real honesty and real friendship, both utterly unlike what he had with his own father . . . and both, he was beginning to see, not quite what he thought they were.

"You simply take up too much air"—Judith again, still audible after all these years. "You're so busy being Henry, Henry, that you don't leave room for the boys, any of us, to put forward our own notions or ideas. And the worst part is that it's unconscious. It's simply the way you're made."

He had never really been able to hear those words before. Take up too much air? Simply the way he was made? Those were the kinds of things he said, and thought, about his own father. But Leopold was a finished project, long ago fully baked. Surely he instead was more pliable than that. Surely he could still learn. Surely he could leave room for the boys to surprise him—and not only the boys. Life, generally. Surely, if he slowed down, if he paid closer attention, if he tried to take up less air, really tried, surely he could still surprise himself.

꜀

Groggy from the food, the unaccustomed wine, and his long hot afternoon, Andrew had succumbed so completely to a sticky summer nap that when he woke up, he wasn't sure where he was. Slowly and through half-shuttered eyes he took in the mirror, the chandelier, the desk where his computer stood closed, and finally the window and its view of the hills of Bellosguardo, which were at that moment washed with a soft orange light.

Andrew realized that the color meant that the sun was starting to go down. He was lying in his bed at the Pensione Ricci, and the sound he was hearing, footsteps coming into contact with dry parquet, was being produced by his father, who was tiptoeing around in his bare feet, getting ready to meet Costanza for a drink.

Henry removed the towel that had been tucked around his waist and used it to dry his body, his hair, the skin behind his ears. Even though they shared a room when they traveled, it had been a while since Andrew had seen his father naked. Previously when Henry had gotten dressed in front of him, Andrew had averted his eyes or picked up a book or his phone. Now he looked at his father's unclothed self as though it held a key to his character: the flesh as commentary. What did it say? Superficially at least that Henry had been enjoying his long lunches a little too much: he was probably ten pounds overweight. And that his body wore a haze of dark hair, which was more ubiquitous than Andrew recalled. And that time was knitting some gray or white strands into the thatch on his chest and the smaller, contained field around his penis. And that his penis, which Andrew first remembered seeing when he was five or six years old, when it struck him as a supersized, imponderable, and somewhat terrifying thing, a thing belonging to a giant, not a man, was from his more grown-up perspective no longer quite so large after all. Yet Henry-the-body was greater than the sum of its component parts and made an impression that was similar to the one made by Henry-the-man: he was a being of stature, a life force undiminished by the imperfections of his corporeal self.

A lot of this had to do with the way Henry moved. Even impeded by his efforts to be quiet, Henry *aggressed* into his clothes. He didn't step so much as lunge into his gray shorts. Khaki pants and socks (beige with tiny blue dots) followed. Then came one of the new Zubarelli shirts. First Henry held up to the mirror one that was boldly striped and highly colored, then another that was a more sedate blue check. Finally he settled on a plain white one. Like a pedestal under a statue, its purity offset his Roman head with its imperially wayward nose, newly trimmed beard, and enigmatic smile.

Henry's smile didn't last long. After he buttoned his shirt cuffs, then reconsidered, unbuttoned them and casually rolled them up, he took one last look in the mirror, where he saw Andrew. As he pivoted around, his entire demeanor changed. He made his way to Andrew's bed, where he bent over and put a hand on his son's forehead. "I thought maybe you weren't feeling well, Andy," he said, using a nickname that had been retired around the time of the divorce. "You've been sleeping ever since I got back this afternoon."

Henry's body gave off a scent that was more than just soap. Something new and fragrant, half-sweet and half-spicy. It rose up into Andrew's nostrils and made them itch. "I think you may have a little fever," Henry added solicitously. "Do you want me to get you some aspirin?"

Andrew shook his head no.

"You can take it easy tonight if you like. I'll have Angelo send you up a tray."

"It's kind of early for dinner."

"I was thinking about later."

"I'm just tired. I got too much sun today." What was that line from *Hamlet*? They'd read it that spring in honors English. "I am too much in the sun." A play on words. *Sun* and *son*. Too much in the son: Andrew was pretty sure that was why the clouds were hanging on him.

He pushed back the blanket.

Henry understood what the gesture meant and glanced at the ever-more-orange sky. "I guess I'll meet you upstairs," he said forlornly.

As though Henry had a right to be forlorn. She was *his* friend. She had taken *him* to smell the mushrooms and to see the two Donatellos and to lunch afterward.

At the door Henry took one last look at Andrew. The look echoed the one he'd given him in the restaurant. Henry was mystified.

Costanza sat at her favorite table in the far corner of the terrace. Her face was tilted toward the sun, eyes closed. For as long as she could remember twilight had been her favorite time of day. At twilight she felt a shift in herself, a lightening that washed through her as she recognized that the imperfections of the day, whatever burdens or preoccupations she had too readily given herself to, were suspended. Often, when she was working on a translation, after twilight she would sit back down at her desk for a second stint. When she and Morton had been in conflict, she had found it helpful to go away during twilight, since afterward whatever had come up between them felt less fierce. And when Morton was dying, if she arranged to take a break as the sun was going down, she returned to him with more equanimity afterward.

But sitting on the terrace at the Pensione Ricci wasn't just about making the transition from one part of the day, or state of mind, to another; it was about connecting—reconnecting—to some of the most cherished moments of her childhood, when she and her father used to come to the pensione, just the two of them together, for a long weekend or sometimes for a week at a time. They came to sightsee and to look at art—she attributed her lifelong love of painting and sculpture to these trips—or because her father had, or (she later speculated) had trumped up, something he needed to dig out of a local archive, and every evening, no matter what their plans were, they began on the terrace at the Ricci, at the very table where she was sitting, or whatever its equivalent was twenty-five years ago. Away from Genoa, Alan was more buoyant, more *present*. Maybe that was because Florence brought back certain happy memories to him. Florence was where, studying during his junior year in college, he met and fell in love with Maria Rosaria (she too was studying there; the language lessons they began to exchange inspired her to become an English teacher . . . and years afterward his wife). Florence was where he decided to study Renaissance history, and Florence was where, in one of the student rooms on the top floor of the Ricci, he later lived for almost two years while he was doing research for his thesis. That was back in the time when Signora Ricci was still alive, back when an impecunious German baroness sat in the lobby typing the Signora's correspondence, back when there were no bathrooms on the top floor, and if he had to pee in the middle of the night, her father delighted in telling her, he was expected to use a chamber pot. The top floor of the Ricci was just under the terrace. For all Costanza knew, she was sitting, at that very moment, above the room where her father had lived and studied and written in the years before he married her mother, before he went to battle against the depression that seized him around Costanza's tenth birthday, before he tried to take his life the first time, before he succeeded the time after that . . .

Costanza knew it was a kind of magical thinking, but every time she returned to Florence and to the Pensione Ricci, she thought she would find her father there, or manage to awaken him from the dead, or if not exactly awaken him, awaken a new memory of him, though fewer and fewer of these came over the years; but that didn't discourage her from returning, hoping again for a glimpse of his long, narrow face with its sharp cheekbones softening into inky circles that wreathed his sad, distant, deep-sea eyes. She came to Florence when she got her first big translating job. She came to Florence not long after she married Morton, and on several other occasions afterward, with him and on her own. She had come now that he was gone a year.

Costanza opened her eyes and squinted in the still-bright sunlight. It took her a moment to focus and recognize the figure who was heading toward her. Henry Weissman, in a brilliant white shirt, the tendrils of his hair still damp from a shower, wasn't walking so much as striding across the terrace. He was so . . . vigorous. She felt his vigor in San Marco and again in the restaurant. She felt it in the way he moved, the way he spoke, even in the emphatic way he dropped himself into the chair opposite her.

"I didn't mean to interrupt your—meditating?"

"Thinking. Remembering."

He gave her a look.

"I was thinking about my father. This terrace was one of his favorite places in the world."

Henry looked at the flowering vines, the tables and chairs, the view. "I can see why."

"It wasn't just the beauty. It was a kind of retreat for him. An escape."

"The way it is for you?"

"It's different. I come here to . . . to check in with myself. With my past."

Angelo appeared with the prosecco, which he set on a low table at Costanza's knee. Henry told him he would prefer to open the bottle himself. He did, and nimbly. "What shall we toast? Chance meetings?"

"That seems fitting." She accepted a glass from him. "Though to be perfectly honest, Dr. Weissman—"

"Henry."

"*Henry*. I know who you are. Well, what you do. Two years ago, we came this close to meeting."

Henry looked puzzled.

"While my husband was still well, he and I put together the names of several physicians in your field. People we intended to consult. But we only got as far as the first one."

"Oh? And who was that, if you don't mind my asking?"

"A Dr. . . . . Schoenberg, I believe."

"Schoen*feld*. Isaac Schoenfeld," Henry said rapidly. "What did you think of him?"

Morton—Costanza remembered clearly—said that he failed to take them in. As people apart from their medical situation, Morton meant. He expected everyone, even his doctors, to engage with him, to be charmed or confused or affronted by him. Clearly that was not this Dr. Schoenfeld's way. But the real problem, she knew even at the time, was that Morton wanted the doctor to convince him to have a child, and that wasn't his responsibility. Any physician's responsibility.

"He seemed perfectly professional," Costanza said neutrally. "The truth is, we never ended up going through with treatment of any kind, because soon afterward my husband decided that he wasn't interested in having a baby."

"That must have been very hard for you."

Hard? Devastating, more like. "It was. But now . . . now I'm afraid it's just another tedious story about another complicated marriage."

"Complicated, I believe. Tedious? Not likely."

Costanza took a sip from her prosecco. She didn't expect her little deflection to be caught so quickly. "Don't you feel that about your own story, sometimes? That you've lived it and relived it to the point that it has lost its freshness, even to you?"

"I might feel that way about *my* story, but something tells me that yours is a lot more interesting."

Costanza took this as flirtation, as she suspected it was intended. It felt stirring to dip her toe into the world of human desire again. And— why not?—to flirt back: "And you're basing that on . . ."

"Observation and intuition. I use both all the time in my work."

"I thought what you did was all-science, all-business."

Henry considered for a moment. There were ways he spoke about his work in public, and there were ways he thought, and much more rarely spoke, about it in private. His instinct told him that Costanza was someone he could—should—speak to candidly.

"It *is* all-science—all-business, if you like. But even I admit that there's something intangible, in some couples, that can contribute to their success. A mental state, a hardiness that is not just physical but spiritual—things that as long as they remain unquantifiable I can't talk about really. Except maybe in quiet conversations like this. But I'm aware of them. I'm aware that, at the beginning, I can often predict which couples will come out with a live birth in the end."

"Surely you never let any of this on, in your office."

"It would be unjust, if not unethical." He paused. "Fertility is its own world, its own country, with its own protocol, its own vocabulary, even its own psychology. People come to me to seek help for something that should be perfectly natural. Something their parents did with ease, their siblings and friends often do with ease. Something they never even think about, until they find themselves thinking about it ceaselessly. There is nothing equivalent in medicine really. The 'patient' is not exactly ill, but suffers enormously and often over a long period of time. I know all this, but I have to shut most of it out. I have to see the couple as bodies that produce eggs and sperm that have trouble meeting up as they should or implanting and growing when they do. I have to look at this most organic of processes in as many discrete pieces as I can. And sometimes I'm unable to discover what isn't working, but I treat the patient as though I know. I cannot do all this and take in people's yearning at the same time."

"So you put up a shield."

"There's such anguish. You cannot imagine." The shadow that crossed Costanza's face immediately caused Henry to add, "I'm sorry. Of course you can."

"Please don't apologize. The subject was once of considerable interest to me."

"But no longer?"

Costanza looked out over the red tile roofs that appeared to hold the terrace afloat, a raft on a roiled terra-cotta sea. "Not at the moment, no."

When Andrew stepped out onto the terrace, it took him a moment to locate Henry and Costanza. They were sitting at a remote table shielded by a thick leafy vine. Since the sun was setting behind them, Andrew saw them principally in silhouette. From the way they leaned toward each other, he could tell that they had made a connection. Of course they had made a connection. He had known they would as soon as they started talking in the restaurant—before. At San Marco, when Henry collided with her, they had spoken as equals, or anyway as two people who could be in balance with each other. Or interested in each other. Nevertheless, his stomach sank.

Andrew was a watcher, a photographer. Stealth came naturally to him. He retraced his steps and quietly inched toward the door that led back into the pensione. As soon as he was out of sight, he texted Henry to say that he wasn't feeling well after all. In his room Andrew brought his camera and computer to his bed, and he opened up the file titled "Charlotte." Even edited down, it contained maybe four or five hundred photographs altogether. Photographs—many of them—of Charlotte reading. Of Charlotte playing in Central Park with her neighbor's poodle. Of Charlotte half-giddy and half-terrified the day they went out to Coney Island and rode the Cyclone, clinging to each other like little kids. Of Charlotte at swim practice, her sleek blue suit showing off all her beautiful curves.

Of Charlotte out of that suit one day after practice, when her parents were out of town and Emily was at a sleepover and they went to bed for the first time, and she let him photograph her afterward in the late-afternoon light.

Andrew's hand drifted down to his jeans and went inside. Charlotte was on the screen in front of him, and when he closed his eyes, she was in his head. But when he started stroking, she began to retreat, as if he were looking at her through the wrong end of a telescope or trying to pin her down in a tangled dream. Charlotte retreated, but someone else came forward, walking in her linen, gesturing at that disconcerting naked David, lifting a forkful of her perfectly wound pasta to her perfectly formed lips.

Andrew's whole body went clammy. He removed his hand from his pants.

⇌

In bed the next morning, with the first coffee of the day sharpening her brain, Costanza went back in:

May 23rd
Our fifth dinner. She doesn't like me to call them dates. I say, "As long as we continue doing them, I don't care what you call them." "What is it that we are doing, anyway?" "I don't know

about *we*, but *I* am falling in love with you." "Why?" That again. "Why am I lovable to you? Why do you find me attractive?" She really appears not to understand. "Because your mind interests me, because your heart interests me, because your body . . ." This is why we have language: to make our feelings clear, yes? But mine surprises me by falling short. "Because when I'm with you I tingle. On the tip of my nose, on the back of my legs. Because I smell you even when I'm not around you. Because I want to slide my penis inside you and keep time from going forward and taking me closer to death."

So the last part I didn't say, though Howard said I should have. "Death and all that, it's a real turnoff, Morty—but the sex, go for it."

Before the evening was over she agreed to go away with me for the weekend. *This* weekend.

May 25th—Vermont

C. and I have just made love. She is lying in the bed across the room from me, asleep, her face buried in a nest of golden hair.

I, Morton Sarnoff, male of the species, age nearly sixty, survivor of myocardial infarction and triple-bypass surgery, can still make love. I am not done yet.

I can still come without having a heart attack. You don't know what a relief that is. You don't know what it's like to sit in an armchair and look out over a glassy pond and feel life starting up again.

I sat up with my back against the headboard. She faced me. She straddled me. Her skin is white *every*where. Except for her nipples, which are pink. And delicious. Salty. I took turns taking them into my mouth, circling each one with my tongue until they stiffened. At the same time so did I. I never thought I could again be this hard, this long. What was this about? It was about this woman. It was about the moment when we both let out our sounds.

And now I am here in this chair, looking out at this pond, and I am thinking, everything is going to be different now. I am going to be "knitted more closely into life." Yeats. Or did he say tightly? I'll take tightly.

I am trying to keep my mind from racing. I think that is
why I came to sit here and to write. Only my mind is still racing, and she seems to be wak—

May 26th
She woke up. I put away my notebook.

She got up and got dressed. I got dressed. The sex made us
a little more formal with each other, rather than the opposite
as you would think.

We went for a walk. She told me how much time she spent
in Tuscany as a girl, and in the hills of Liguria. Everything there,
everything in Italy, seems so much more connected to the
earth. The houses, the garden. Animals. Food. She said nothing tastes the same in America. And yet she lives here. Why?
Because in Italy she found that, after a point, she couldn't
breathe, she couldn't become what she thought she wanted to
be. To know herself, she said, she had to go away.

I said I thought I understood. I said I wished I had gone
away more when I was younger. It's funny how limited, in certain senses, my life has been. My travels have been more interior than anything else.

I asked her what she saw in her future. "That depends," she
said, quoting me to me, yet sounding very much like herself,
"on you."

Costanza remembered the specifics of *that* conversation well. How
couldn't she? It was one of the handful of moments in her life in which
she had been truly daring. She had said what she was feeling in the moment, and it had changed everything.

She didn't regret having taken that leap, but it was unlikely that
she would take a similar one ever again. Her marriage to Morton had
been too costly. It had swept her up, it had consumed her, and it had
left her—well, that was just the point. She didn't know where it left
her. Not, certainly, where she'd been before they married. It had left
her suspended; that much she knew. And now, just as she seemed ready
to suspend her suspension, Morton presented himself again. Reading
these pages of his reeled her in. The bed, the lovemaking, the walk in

the country . . . it was as though he had somehow guessed, how she certainly couldn't say, that a year after his death she would be ready to open her life up and, possibly, allow another man to come into it.

Had a man come into her life?

It was too soon to be entirely sure, but she was better at reading the early signs now. And Dr. Weissman—Henry—wasn't exactly shy about broadcasting them. After that text had arrived from Andrew, it was as if something in him had shifted, and he poured himself, truly poured himself, into the evening. He asked her about her family, and she told him, candidly though in brief, about her parents' difficult marriage and her father's depression and eventual suicide. She talked about her work as a translator, which he speculated likely had something to do with the impulse to help a mother and a father who were in so many senses so deeply foreign to each other understand each other. That was perceptive of him; she tucked that insight away for further review, since she had not put it together quite like that before. He asked her about Liguria and what she missed from her life there. And he asked her to tell him about Morton, at least to give him an outline of Morton.

She could feel Henry turning over her answers to his questions with the rigor of a diagnostician heightened by the avidity of a man who, he confided, was eager to open up his life again.

Did she by any chance feel the same way? he asked, after saying that.

Yes, she answered him. She did.

After they finished their prosecco, they fell into a restaurant near the pensione. Now it was Costanza's turn. She wanted to know about his lectures, about his work. Once he got started, he scarcely took a breath. But it wasn't his fault. She could have changed the direction of the conversation. Instead she egged him on, gripped.

Henry was a crusader. That much was clear. Helping infertile women—and men—find a way to have children was his life's mission. So many treatments were available that she was only remotely aware of, or barely understood. He named drugs and described procedures that had been developed to increase the chances of a pregnancy resulting in what Henry repeatedly called a *live birth*. Costanza kept circling around this term. She had never heard it before. *Stillbirth*, *nato morto*, its presumable inverse, yes. But *live birth*? She wondered how she would translate it into Italian. *Nato vivo*? That didn't seem right. She asked herself why he couldn't just say *a baby*. *A healthy baby*, maybe.

But she knew it wasn't merely Henry's terminology, Henry's language, that held her attention so closely. It was the idea; the prospect. A live birth, a baby, a healthy baby: however you phrased it, it was something she had yearned for during a painful interlude toward the end of her marriage to Morton.

Before they married, she and Morton had the Conversation. An astute reader of human nature, he had been the one to bring it up. He was open to the idea, he said. More disinclined than inclined, but open. He was not young; his life was established; marrying late, marrying at all, was bound to shake things up. That was good, he believed, at heart. If being married to her meant having a child with her, well, then he was willing to think about it.

She for her part had said truthfully, or at least truthfully at the time they spoke, that she never thought she would have children. Her own childhood had not been happy. Her mother had been unmaternal, self-absorbed, and severe. And although she felt deeply loved by her father, and deeply loved him in return, he was not, in the end, a successful example of a parent either, since with his suicide he broke what she considered to be the fundamental pact you enter into when you have a child, which is that you will stick around as long as you possibly can to help your child live her life.

There was something else. In the years after her father's suicide, when she was old enough and distanced enough to try to learn about the subject, she came across an alarming statistic: the children of people who succeed in taking their lives have a sixty percent higher possibility of suicide themselves. Her great-uncle, her father's uncle, made four attempts before dying of a heart attack at the age of sixty-four. Costanza herself had experienced some very dark periods, including one that she did not know how to talk about because it remained ambiguous even to her and therefore all the more disconcerting. The night her first adult relationship imploded after nearly three years, she went ahead with plans to attend a party in Testaccio at the home of one of her classmates' parents. A lot of wine was on hand, and she drank it liberally. The party spilled out onto the terrace, which was on the third floor of the building and overlooked a large, lushly planted interior courtyard. Costanza remembered only a few details of that evening. One was that the court-yard had an old lemon tree growing in it whose trunk was covered by a vine that produced a sweetly scented flower, possibly jasmine. The way the vine clung to that trunk made her think of the way she had gone on clinging to Stefano long after she should have cut herself loose. If she had, then perhaps she would not have found him in his office that afternoon, stretched out on his sagging old tweed couch, his pants down and his penis buried in the mouth of Anna Carini, whom Costanza had, up to that moment, considered her closest friend at the university. She remembered that clingy vine, and she remembered that she had still been wearing a Moroccan bracelet that Stefano had brought her from Fez, and she remembered thinking that she ought to have eaten something before she began drinking. She did *not* remember having written in her datebook, "Next to my father's death, this has been the worst day of my life"—which her mother, and not only her mother, took to be a sign of intentionality behind what happened that evening.

Certain facts were not in dispute: Costanza had drunk copiously, she had not eaten, and she was upset. She was not normally a clumsy person, but when she hoisted herself up on the parapet of the terrace, intending—as she maintained—to sit up on its little ledge, she mis-judged the energy required and missed the ledge completely.

If the lemon tree had not broken her fall, she would surely have died, and with her death she would likely have been categorized among that sixty percent. Instead she came away with a broken arm, a fractured hip, and a scattering of bruises from which she recovered during a mis-erable three-month convalescence at her mother's house in Recco.

Her mother, Maria Rosaria, believed that Costanza had tried to take her life; Costanza did not think that people killed themselves because relationships ended, or because they were married to, or the daughters of, difficult women, or because they lost their jobs, their boyfriends, or their way. People killed themselves because their minds were diseased, because their depression was intractable, because nothing and no one they were attached to in life was strong enough to keep them alive.

Costanza was nearly certain that she was not this sort of person or had this sort of mind. But her doubts were sufficient to keep her from telling this story to Morton, or anyone else. What she did tell him was that her feelings about having a baby changed, once they had.

They were four years into their marriage when one day she was on the subway heading uptown from her apartment, which she had been using as an office, when she gradually became aware of a little boy jabbering away on the seat across from her. Costanza looked up from her reading. She was not versed in estimating children's ages; he was maybe eighteen months old. He had skin the color of wheat bread. His hair was curled into tight whorled buds, his smile slightly askew. He did not stop talking for the whole ride uptown. Not a word of what he said was intelligible, but it was fluent and emotive, like some kind of foreign language she might once have understood but had now forgotten.

First he babbled his charming incoherence at the old lady sitting next to him, then at a hoodied teenager, and finally at Costanza. With Costanza he carried on a full conversation, answering all her questions and appearing to ask his own in return. It was translating of a different order: she wasn't translating so much as trying to decipher what the little boy was saying.

All this went on for several minutes, while his mother, sealed off by a pair of headphones, ignored her little boy.

Costanza realized then that a thorn had wedged itself into her heart. The thorn had been there for some time, but she had never been so acutely aware of it before. She was thirty-seven years old, riding the subway on a September evening with a *New York Review of Books* in her lap, and it devastated her to see this sunny little child reaching out to the world with his own strange language. She had a vision of taking him into her arms and at the next station, while his mother was still listening to her music, breaking into a run.

When she got off the train, her back was saturated with sweat.

At first she thought the moment on the subway was an anomaly. But then a few days later she was walking in Central Park. This time it was a little girl, unmistakably younger than the boy on the subway.

The child after that she saw at MoMA, a somber boy of seven or so with horn-rimmed glasses, who had wandered away from his school group and stood in front of a Mondrian, biting his thumbnail, baffled.

She found Morton one October night in his library, writing in one of his hardbound books—writing in his diary, she now understood. Bursting into tears, she told him she had completely misunderstood herself, and her life. She told him that she wanted to have a baby, after all.

He offered her a handkerchief—Morton being the sort of man who still carried handkerchiefs—and then, peering over his reading glasses, he said, "You know of course that this means we would have to share."

"Share?" she said, confused.

"Share our time with each other. Our lives would no longer be about us."

She felt weak. She dropped down in the chair across from him. "Have you thought about later, when we're older . . . ?"

"Later is sooner for me, Costanza. Later is *now*. I can see seventy from where I sit."

"The actual arithmetic is that you're closer to sixty, Morton. You do know that."

"And you know that if we have a child, you're likely to be her, or his, only parent for a much longer time than we will be parents together?" She merely listened as he went on, "People never really think about how much life changes when a child comes along. How much work is sacrificed. How much freedom is lost. You can no longer move so easily through time and space, or even *think* the way you used to, your mind is always on that marvelous but needy little creature."

"All this is so negative. So bleak."

"I think it's realistic. It's important to be realistic."

"You've never had children. How do you know it's even—even accurate?"

"I've observed, haven't I? My brother, my friends. And I've listened, I've read and imagined. Imagining is my occupation, after all."

"Imagining an experience is not the same as living it."

Now it was his turn to remain neutral. There was no hint, no flash, in his eye that transmitted what he was thinking.

"Obviously I haven't forgotten that you're older than I am, Morton. Only you're healthy now. You could live until our child grows up. Is in college even. It's not unreasonable. And I do truly believe that you and I could give—that our lives would only be—that we would live more fully if we could experience—"

Even as she said them, the words sounded rote to her, almost platitudinous, while the feeling behind them was anything but. "And besides—"

And besides, a thorn is lodged in my heart, and there are days when I am finding it difficult to breathe.

"And besides, this is what I want more than anything."

If this is what you want, then this is what you shall have.

She longed for him to say this one sentence, but he didn't. Instead he said, "Let's see what Grubman feels after my next checkup."

Grubman—Morton's physician—said there was no physical reason why Morton was unfit to be a father, and Morton let that do the deciding for him, for them. He never once came to her and said, "Let's have a baby together" or "Let's make our own family," phrases that Costanza, looking back, realized she probably ought to have heard before they plunged into the year that upended their lives.

Costanza looked down at the thick rubber-banded stack of Morton's remaining diary pages beside her. She found herself thinking about a story Morton had told her not long after they first met. He offered it as an anecdote, half-amusing, but also half not, that illustrated the centrality of writing in his life. One morning about two years before he moved into the city, Morton told her, Mrs. Gonzales, his housekeeper, heard a stray dog whining under the hydrangeas that bordered the back patio. She had just given birth to four tiny puppies. With Morton's permission Mrs. Gonzales made the new family a bed in the pantry. Morton kept reminding her that she should be putting out the word in the neighborhood that there would soon be four puppies, and a dog, who needed a permanent home, but Mrs. Gonzales forgot ("forgot"), or resisted. She wasn't the only person in the house who enjoyed their company either. Little by little Morton found himself drifting downstairs, first just to check on the puppies and then, as they grew more active, to play with them. More than once he took his favorite, which had a big black patch around her left eye like a raccoon, back up with him to his study, where he continued petting the creature, or playing with her, or just watching her . . . until one morning he glanced at the clock on his desk. It was past eleven forty-five, and he was nowhere close to the five hundred words that were his quota to produce every day before lunch. He called Mrs. Gonzales up from the kitchen, gave her the animal, and instructed her to find another home for the dogs by dinner.

That story said one thing to Costanza when she first heard it, and quite another now, circling back to it from a distance. It told her everything she needed to know about Morton's capacity for attachment to anything, or anyone, beyond his work. She should have paid closer attention; much closer.

She plucked a page out of the manuscript at random. Well, not entirely at random, but from the last quarter or so, which was where she suspected he would be writing about their—her—quest to become pregnant, thus the beginning of the end.

She had chosen accurately.

"I'm finding it harder and harder to fuck my own wife," he wrote. *Fuck? Wife?*

The act has become something burdensome to me. Costanza is off on this path, lost on this path. It's all about the day of the month, the twinges in her ovaries, the consistency of her mucus, her temperature. What happened to me? Us? What happened to all the rest of our lives? By some miraculous luck I've generally been able to perform (and that is the appropriate word too), but I know that this cannot go on forever. Already I'm not with her when I'm with her; nowhere near. I am elsewhere, in my fantasy life. This is not what I anticipated, in making this marriage. I no longer know what I anticipated. I was deluded; I fear that I was seduced by an idea about life (knit more tightly into *what* exactly?). Many mornings now I wake up and wonder, How did I become married, anyway? Costanza is a perfectly splendid woman, but she and I want such—

On page 40 she made his skin tingle, and he wanted to slide his penis inside her to forestall death; on page 400 their lovemaking had become burdensome to him and she was *a perfectly splendid woman.*

For the first time in more than a year Costanza was angry. She could feel this unfamiliar, almost oily sensation bubbling up in her. She could taste it. It came up out of her stomach and into her mouth. Now, all of a sudden, she wasn't so inclined to be tugged back into the World of Morton. She wasn't so curious after all, she realized, to hear Morton think aloud about how he decided not to go ahead with the fertility treatment. She didn't want to know how he justified denying her the experience she most desperately wanted in life. She didn't want to see how he reasoned his way out of their marriage and back into his selfish, rigid, arid cocoon. She didn't even particularly want to know what it felt like for him to know he was dying.

She couldn't very well strike out at dead Morton. All she could do was send him back to the past, where he belonged. She picked up the manuscript and shoved it into her suitcase and shoved the suitcase into the closet. She would return to it some other day.

Or maybe not.

She closed the closet door and stepped over to the window, which looked out onto the terrace and beyond. In the distance, across the familiar sea of red tile roofs, a woman was shaking a mop out on a terrace of her own; Costanza was convinced she could see grains of dust falling like snowflakes through the air. Closer up, on the leaves of the wisteria, she saw the delicately branching veins; she wouldn't have been surprised if a bud opened into a full purple flower before her eyes.

She turned away from the view and picked up her phone. She and Henry had exchanged numbers the night before. She brought up his and sent him a text asking if he was free to drink prosecco again that evening. On the terrace, at sunset.

Three Months Later

F all in New York. This was Henry Weissman's favorite pairing of time and place. His season, in his city, when the sky, scrubbed of its summer haze, seemed to mint an altogether new shade of blue. There was a clarified quality to the autumn light in New York that Henry could perceive even from bed, even as the sun was just making its way over the horizon. He thought of a story by Chekhov he'd once read in which a character's state of mind was likened to a house where all the old, broken, and dirty windows had their panes replaced with new glass. Henry had felt something similar several times in the past, but this fall the glass seemed cleaner and more transparent than it had in years.

All this drew Henry out of bed with more gusto than he had felt in weeks, but deep within himself he knew that the real reason his day felt hopeful was that he was having dinner with Costanza that night. He was seeing her for the first time since Florence, for the first time since they'd made love in her room at the Pensione Ricci.

He had replayed the night more than once in the past three months, revisiting it both for its intensity and its oddness and to convince himself that he had not dreamed it. At several points in the past three months he believed he had dreamed it, but this morning was not one of them. This morning he could clearly see them standing outside the door to her room at the pensione, kissing. Then whispering. "Henry, I'm afraid." "You don't need to be." "All this seems hasty. And I've been hasty before." "Before—with your husband?" "Not only him." "Yet if there's a feeling, a shared feeling?" She had her room key in her hand. She played with its stiff blue tassel for a moment, smoothing and ordering its fringe. Then she reached over and opened the door. They went inside. She turned toward him, and she began to shake. But she was not cold, it was impossible to be cold on that hot, heavy Florentine summer night. "Are you all right?" he had asked, and she had said, "Just hold me," and he had held her. She had continued to shake. Somehow they ended up at first sitting together, then lying alongside each other, on her bed. She continued to tremble even as he stroked her hair and ran his hand down her back. "We can just lie here," he said, "if that's what you prefer." She shook her head, then she sat up, took off her blouse, and unhooked her bra. Once she revealed herself to him, she stopped shaking. For a moment he just took her in. Then he kissed her neck, her shoulders, her chest. She unhooked his belt, unzipped his fly, and reached her hand into the depths of his crotch. She freed his cock, then swung around and took it into her mouth. The boldness of the gesture was as disconcerting as her trembling had been earlier. He would never have guessed that she would linger over the underside of his cock, licking and moistening it with her tongue until it began to quiver with such intense pleasure that he was afraid he was going to come in her mouth. He wouldn't have guessed that she would have known just when to pause to allow him to wrestle out of his pants and shorts and to undo her own skirt and surprisingly minute panties. He wouldn't have guessed that she would have directed his hand between her legs, either to give him guidance, or permission, or to show him just how saturated she was. He wouldn't have guessed that she would have said, "I want you inside me" with such clarity, or that she would have followed the remark with a long kiss behind which he felt . . . ardor. All that dance of conversation over drinks and dinner seemed to vanish into that one kiss.

Into that one kiss and the fuck that followed. And it was a fuck too, led by her. She drew Henry up over her, and when he was where she wanted him, she ran her hands through his chest hair and down until they circled his penis. She circled it as though she were meeting it and mastering it at the same time. She guided it into her, and only then did she let Henry take over. He started slowly, gingerly. He dipped in and out of her, bringing up still more of her juices. Then as he began, tentatively, to venture deeper, she took the lead again. She dug her palms into his backside, pressed her hands into it, and brought him close, she brought him so far into her that he didn't know where he was. He didn't know if he was inside her or she was inside him. Their crotches were joined, soaked; electric.

She came first. She tilted her head back and closed her eyes and let out a long, slow sound whose pitch rose and rose. He too closed his eyes. He was aware of her trembling again, not on the outside this time but, it seemed, at the innermost center of herself. Her trembling, her orgasm, brought him to his, with a rapid heart and a flash of sweat that glazed his entire body.

They did not speak for maybe ten minutes. Finally she said, "I don't know what that was."

"I'm not sure I do either."

To both of them sleep seemed like the easiest path forward.

Costanza slept with her hair spread out over her pillow like the petals of an exotic flower. That was the association that came to Henry when he woke up at three a.m., groggy and disoriented. Slowly his eyes adapted to the dim bluish light, and he took a deliberate inhalation of dried sweat and semen mingled with soap and perfume, and then he understood: he was in bed with Costanza. He had gone to bed with her some hours earlier, and now the whole city was wound down; surely all of the pensione (including Andrew, he thought in passing) was unconscious. But not Henry. Henry was conscious. He hoped he wasn't going to be awake until morning. He could not endure one of his hyperaware insomniac spells on this night of all nights.

When he looked over at the face on the pillow next to him, he thought, *Is this really possible?* It *was* possible. In his stomach, his balls, and his wildly speeding brain, Henry felt a kind of hope about his life that he had not felt since Judith left. No, before that. Way before that. Since he and Judith began.

Costanza's face, in sleep, was unreadable. He was grateful for that. Her unavailability—her sleep—was the only chance he had for returning to sleep himself. He rolled away from her, drew the covers up to his shoulders, and willed himself to stop thinking. Amazingly it worked.

When Henry woke up, Costanza was already out of bed, transferring folded clothes from a dresser drawer to a suitcase. She had put on a bathrobe and gathered her hair back off her face. If she'd had a shower, Henry hadn't heard her.

"Good morning," he said.

A strong yellow light was waiting to be freed from behind the shutters. Costanza opened them.

"Good morning."

Squinting, he made a gesture with his hand to convey *What's going on?*

"I'm sorry, but I need to get ready for my trip. I have a train to catch in two hours. My cousin Cristina is visiting from Munich this weekend. I haven't been home since I came to Italy. It was all organized—before."

Shoes now, into a different corner of the bag.

"That's it?"

She nodded.

He pulled himself up on his elbow. "We kiss each other the way we did, we *touch* each other the way we did, and you just want to *pack?*"

"I have a difficult few weeks ahead. My moth—"

"So we say nothing? Plan nothing?"

She handed him his pants. "I will write to you, Henry, and you will write to me. I'm not capable of more than that right now."

She didn't show him to the door, but she might as well have.

Henry, bewildered, pulled on his pants, then his shirt. At the door he stopped. "I can't leave without saying I have to see you again."

"You will."

Then she kissed him—on his cheek—to say goodbye.

And that was it. She did write, though. Not e-mail—letters. Her first one, sent from Recco, was waiting for him in New York when he returned from Tuscany. In it she suggested that he reply to her Fifth Avenue address; she said that, since she was not certain where she would be in the coming months, "it would be arranged" for whatever he sent to catch up with her. All her letters came without a stamp or a postmark; Henry assumed that it was "arranged" for them to travel between Italy and New York by FedEx or the equivalent and then messengered or even walked over to his apartment. He didn't know what to make of any of this. She had mentioned that her husband's secretary still had unfinished business with the estate. Maybe he had something to do with the way these letters arrived.

Costanza wrote to him about her time with her mother, which, as she predicted, had not been easy, and her visits elsewhere in Italy, to friends and relatives. He wrote her about the rest of his trip, his return to New York, the winding-down late-summer IVF cycles he was overseeing at the clinic. Underneath all of these circumstantial accounts, at Henry's end, was an eager curiosity that he had to tamp down. Exerting rare self-control, he had managed not to say outright what was on his mind. He even managed not to ask when she would be back in New York. It was obvious to Henry, even to Henry, that with Costanza it was better to hold back, to do less, where his innate tendency was to do more. And he had been rewarded for all this restraint. On Sunday evening he received a note, essentially *the* note he had been waiting for these past three months:

Henry, I'm here. Will you come to dinner tomorrow night at 8.00? Text only if you are not able to make it. There will be prosecco. C.

Henry glanced at his bedside clock. Between 6:15 a.m. and 8:00 p.m. there was a universe of time to be lived, thoughts to be tamed, work to be done.

Before Henry walked through the door of his medical building on York Avenue, he stopped, as was his habit, at the fruit vendor who set up his cart at the northwest corner of the intersection at Sixty-Ninth Street. After all these years the fellow recognized Henry and had bagged and ready for him a single green apple and a ripe, but not overly ripe, banana, Henry's customary breakfast, or first breakfast, which tided him over until Wanda, his assistant, sent out for scrambled eggs and dry wheat toast in the earliest break between appointments after 10:00 a.m.

On this morning, though, for the first time in a long time, Henry stopped in front of the cart and looked at the fruit and vegetables as if he had never seen them before. In the clean fall light, with the cars and trucks barreling past and a construction worker jackhammering asphalt, the fruit stand struck him as an almost surreal oasis that had somehow dropped out of the sky and landed in Manhattan. With its neatly banked, tightly packed mounds of oranges, apples, and lemons, its spikily crowned, sweet-smelling pineapples, its baskets of grapes and peaches, string beans and broccoli, its tiny transparent jewel boxes of raspberries and blueberries and gooseberries (gooseberries!), this improbable cornucopia reminded him of a European or Middle Eastern open-air market, sized down for a New York street corner. How did all this gorgeous fruit come to be here, and where did it go at night, and who was the fruit seller, with his rheumy eyes and incongruous straw hat and knowing smile, and why hadn't he ever encouraged Henry to expand his morning repertoire? He loved blueberries. And peaches too. And apricots, and oranges. He loved them, and this morning, he bought them all.

By his midmorning break, Henry had seen six patients, and he was flagging. His usually solid barricade was pitted. Starting with Julia Bergman, with her multiple miscarriages and her heartsick husband, Henry had been letting himself feel. That was a mistake. Not because a physician should be an automaton, but because when he let himself feel, he got involved, and when he got involved, he didn't think crisply, and when he didn't think crisply, he wasn't doing his job. There were hundreds (thousands) of them, but there was just one of him, and if he gave himself to even a handful of them, there would be little of him left at the end of the day. Yet here he was, at the beginning of a new fall cycle, full of all this unusual feeling. He felt for Julia. He felt for "Miss Brown," the actress who booked her appointments under a pseudonym and was raw and genuine beneath all her polish and secrecy. He even felt for Arlene Brookner, closing a business deal on two iPhones—and scared to death. He was more open to these people, to their quests and their anguish, than he could remember being in a long time. Yet nothing in his morning consultations set them so far apart from the women that had preceded them. They were no different; but he was.

After his last patient, Henry worked his way down his phone list. When he reached the end, it was already seven thirty. That left him no time to go home to shower or change his clothes. He had wanted to bring Costanza some kind of gift, but he had no time for that either. Then he realized he already had one.

Henry had the taxi leave him at Seventy-Ninth Street, three blocks from Costanza's building. It was seven minutes before eight. He had just enough time for a brief transition between his workday and the evening ahead.

Henry and his bag of fruit made their steady way along the limestone façades of Fifth Avenue. He moved slowly. It had been such a long time since he'd allowed his hope to rise in this way that he wasn't so eager to have it leveled off by reality. So he savored it. For four, five, then six luscious minutes he walked up Fifth Avenue, strolling past liveried doormen and dogwalkers airing packs of mismatched breeds. He noticed everything: the gleaming brass door handles, the discreet nameplates advertising the services of plastic surgeons and shrinks, the roof gardens overhead whose furred trees looked like feathers stuck into grand chapeaux, the spotless pavement—even the sidewalk in these blocks was scrubbed clean, by someone. New York was a city of parallel worlds, of unending hierarchies. There was always someone who had more money, more talent, more friends, more connections, a bigger apartment with a better view . . . but Henry was convinced that none of them, at that moment, felt as buoyant as he did, none felt deep within himself the tiny pod of anticipation that made it seem as though his feet weren't so much touching that impossibly clean sidewalk as levitating over it.

Her building had a plastic surgeon and *three* shrinks in offices on the ground floor. The gold on the doorman's livery was so bright it gleamed. In the elevator cab, which was tricked out with beveled mirrors, Henry tried not to look at his reflection, and succeeded. He tried not to feel his heartbeat, and failed.

On the eighth floor the doors opened, and he stepped into a foyer. To the left of the door was a small illuminated bell, but before he could press it the door was opened by a short man who had carefully trimmed salt-and-pepper hair and brown eyes. He was wearing gray trousers and a white shirt so close-fitting they seemed to have been sewn onto him.

"Good evening, Dr. Weissman. Please come in."

Henry followed the small man into a second, larger foyer.

"I'm Ivan, Mr. Sarnoff's assistant."

Mr. Sarnoff's assistant: as though the fellow hadn't been dead for more than a year.

"Mrs. Sarnoff asked me to say that she will be down in a few minutes."

After noting Henry's bag Ivan added, "May I take your . . . parcel?"

Henry handed it over. "It's fruit. You might want to put it in the fridge."

Ivan took the bag. "May I offer you a refreshment?"

"Sparkling water, if you have it."

Ivan guided Henry into the living room, then disappeared.

Where had Morton Sarnoff come up with Jeeves? His background was not so different from Henry's, as Henry was reminded when, after he returned from Italy, he spent some time reading up online: New Brunswick to Henry's Brooklyn; a coming of age in the 1950s to Henry's 1960s; Sarnoff's father a high school science teacher, which was arguably several modest socioeconomic steps above Henry's father the upholsterer—though cerebral Leopold Weissman was hardly summed up by his relationship to fabric and thread.

In the early 1990s, after publishing a book of stories and three novels, Sarnoff went into exile in Columbia County, where he lived in an isolated farmhouse. There was a lot of speculation about a stupendous case of writer's block, or a nervous breakdown following a brief tumultuous marriage to the Actress. He was increasingly described as "the reclusive Morton Sarnoff" ("Isolation is life too," he said in a rare interview he gave to a journalist who ambushed him at his local Price Chopper. "And so, for your information, is discipline"). Then, just after he turned fifty-eight, Sarnoff surprised his readers by publishing *The Life to Come*, a large multigenerational family novel. The book was an enormous success. It was adapted into a movie in which Meryl Streep, altering her hairstyle, costume, and voice, played the grandmother, the daughter, *and* the granddaughter. People went back and read the early work. The dough rolled in; Sarnoff returned to the city; he bought his lavish apartment; he had his heart attack and bypass surgery. He met Costanza, married her, separated from her, was diagnosed with pancreatic cancer, and then he died.

Henry wondered if there wasn't a sense of vengeance about the whole setup. The man who was almost never referred to without the adjective *Jewish* appended to his name, as in "the once-prolific Jewish novelist" or "Sarnoff, the tireless chronicler of Jewish family life," had planted himself right there in WASP central, in a building that a generation back probably wouldn't have allowed him to sit for a board interview. The Georgian furniture, the Chinese rugs, the dull safe paintings, the plush (though expertly done) upholstery, the general air of cultivation and arrival: What was being beaten down here? The toxic anti-Semitism that was a commonplace of his New Jersey childhood? The high school science-teacher father or the mother who died at thirty-seven of breast cancer? Or was it all simply one big midlife extravagant whim?

Henry had no idea. There was nothing wrong with living well, anyway. The man had a big talent and suddenly deep pockets. He had no kids, so he spent on the pad. Yet something about the dead man's apartment felt spooked, inhabited somehow—though not by Costanza, wherever she was.

Henry tried out three different chairs and couldn't sit still in any of them. He stepped over to the windows and looked out at the Met. The fountains were bubbling away. The façade was lit by a gentle ivory-colored light. He wondered if Sarnoff, looking out at this same view, had ever felt he had come as far as he could, in life. A duplex on Fifth Avenue; a half dozen esteemed books; fame; a stunning, intelligent wife: he had a lot. Yet he couldn't, he wouldn't, follow her to that next experience in the arc, the step that Henry, personally, believed was the one experience that finally grew a man up. He couldn't, he wouldn't, agree to father a child. He was too old, or too stuck, or too afraid, or too selfish, or too committed to his work, too *some*thing, and so he let this special woman go.

At the far end of the living room a pair of double doors stood slightly ajar. Henry approached, pushed them more fully open, and stepped inside: Sarnoff's study. In contrast to the order and understatement of the rest of the apartment, the place was in cluttered, even frenzied, disarray. There were two solid walls of bookshelves. On every horizontal surface, on the desk, on a low cupboard, even on several large patches of the floor, books, periodicals, and files rose in unruly stacks. The desk itself faced a wall, so that Sarnoff sat with his back to Fifth Avenue. On the wall behind the desk hung a bulletin board covered with notes, clippings, a calendar. The calendar was open to June of the previous year. June of the previous year was when Sarnoff had died.

"Nothing has been changed since he passed." Ivan was standing in the doorway, holding a tray with a glass and a small bottle of Perrier.

"I can see that."

"I just thought I'd mention it, in case you felt like touching anything."

"I'm not in the least interested in touching anything."

"This room says what he was like. The rest, out there"—Ivan glanced in the direction of the living room—"those are all things that were chosen by the British fellow who did that sort of job for him. But in here . . . it's like looking into his mind. I keep thinking someone will want to come photograph it, or take some notes."

If Jeeves was going to insist on making conversation, Henry would have to join in. "Did you work for Mr. Sarnoff a long time?"

"When he came back to New York, he needed a secretary, someone to organize the meals and goings-on here. In the country he had Mrs. Gonzales, but in New York, it was just Mr. Sarnoff and—all this. It was just around the time that the movie was being made. There were lots of appointments and interviews. People used to wait downstairs to photograph Ms. Streep, when she came up here to speak to him about the character she was playing. In this very room they had their conversations. Long conversations. She only drank bubbly water, like you. She didn't care what brand. She liked it with lemon. No ice. Never any ice."

"And you've stayed on ever since, even while Costanza—Mrs. Sarnoff—was away?"

He smiled. "She made a promise to Mr. Sarnoff. As long as she remains in the apartment, so can I."

Ivan glanced at Morton's desk. "Perhaps we should return to the living room?"

In the living room Ivan set the tray with the glass on a table next to an armchair. He poured the water. "Will there be anything else?"

"No, thank you."

Ivan left. Henry drank. The apartment was only eight floors up, but he couldn't detect any traffic from Fifth Avenue. He had no sense of being part of a large populated building either. Were the apartments of the super-rich always this quiet? What was the trick? Double-glazed windows, the thick carpet and heavily lined curtains, the absence of common walls? The place was muffled, plushly arrayed, a resplendent tomb.

"Henry."

There she was, finally, standing in the doorway.

He stood up and looked at her. She was dressed completely in black: pants, sweater, shoes. High-heeled shoes, which made her seem tall, precariously balanced, aloof.

He opened his arms. She hesitated before stepping into them. He would have liked to kiss her, but the signals, her stance, the whole atmosphere, seemed against.

"I'm sorry I kept you waiting."

She stepped over to a phone. A phone that was also an intercom. She pressed a button and asked for the prosecco. Then she sat down in a chair, one of a pair, that flanked the fireplace. Was its mate Sarnoff's once? Henry wondered if that's what she was thinking as he sat down across from her.

"So." It was difficult to find the right way in. "How are you?"

"Tired. I've been away a long time."

"Yes, you have."

"Distance confuses things."

She sent off her remarks like little toy boats on a pond, leaving them to find their own way in the prevailing breeze.

Henry's heart sank. This wasn't at all what he had imagined, or what he had hoped for.

Here was Ivan again, slinking in. He was carrying a tray with a silver ice bucket, the prosecco, and two glasses. A bowl of tiny olives. Small square linen napkins, folded like origami. He set the tray down on the table between their two chairs and reached for the bottle.

Henry gestured. "Let me do it, please."

Ivan glanced at Costanza. She nodded at him, and he withdrew.

"He was very attached to Morton. I haven't had the heart to help him move on. I will, eventually."

Henry had the prosecco open now. He poured two glasses, handed one to her, and picked up the other for himself. He raised his. "Maybe this will help."

"Help?"

"Help get us talking. Help make us feel less awkward."

"You *are* diving in, Henry."

"Well, naturally. I've been waiting for this evening, Costanza. I've been waiting—well, let's just say I've been waiting."

She sighed. "I'm finding a lot of things hard right now. You have to understand, or rather I should say, I wonder if you can understand, that this place, for me, is—"

"Oppressive?"

"Well, full of my recent past. Full of my recent past in a way that, just now, feels overwhelming. Do you know how it is when you go away, far away, especially for a long time, and think you have changed, then you return to the place you started out from, and it feels as though you never really left?"

"That makes sense," Henry said carefully.

He waited for her to continue speaking. He wanted her to continue speaking.

"There's so much you don't know about me, and the life I had here, the life that seems to be lying in wait for me here. It's a lot to look after Morton's . . . to care for all this—" She gestured at the large lavish room and left it at that.

"Yes, but what's in it for you?"

"That's just what I'm trying to figure out." She paused. Finally she looked him in the eye. "And not only that."

"So you *have* been thinking about me—about us?" The word felt like a minefield. But why?

"Of course."

The phone by her chair rang. Buzzed, rather. It was the intercom. She pressed a button. Ivan's voice came through saying that dinner was ready.

As though commanded, she stood up.

The dining room was on the other side of the foyer. Its double doors, previously closed, were standing open now to reveal a large dark table surrounded by chairs, fourteen of them, a conference room's worth of polished mahogany. A cloth had been spread over just the far end of the table, leaving most of it exposed. The two places set on the cloth were a fairly substantial distance apart, as they would have to have been across such an expanse.

Before she sat down Costanza noticed Henry's fruit, which Ivan had arranged in a large glass bowl. It stood on a sideboard, sweating, and in this context looking, Henry thought, faintly ridiculous.

"I haven't seen color like that since Italy."

"It's from Dr. Weissman."

She turned to Henry.

"I was on my way to work, and there was all this fruit . . ."

"It's beautiful." The warmth in her voice made her sound for the first time like herself. Or like the Costanza that Henry thought he knew.

She sat down. Henry sat down. Ivan poured the wine, then withdrew.

Costanza picked up her fork and examined the food in front of her. "Zucchini, avocado, cilantro. Morton always teased Ivan for copying the newest dish. A recipe would appear one day in the paper, the next on the table. Morton—" She stopped. "But you don't want to hear about this."

"I want to hear anything you want to tell me."

They ate for a few minutes in silence. Henry's mind had come to a standstill. He couldn't think of anything else to say. He couldn't remember when he last had nothing more to say. It was the room, the apartment. The somber dark walls, the guttering candles, the silver, the linen, the fussy food, the hovering manservant. And then there was Costanza: her detachment, her remoteness.

He tried a topic, any topic. "You wrote that you saw some old school friends."

"Less than I would have liked. Most everyone is married now, and busy."

"How did it go in the end with your mother?"

"It was challenging, as usual. I realized that I can't go back there to live—not full-time, anyway."

Henry took this, at least, as an encouraging sign. A small one. But first he had to decide whether he wanted, truly wanted, to be encouraged. Only how was he going to decide that over dinner in a mausoleum?

Costanza picked at her food. Henry didn't touch his. He waited. He thought. Then he stood up abruptly. "Let's get out of here."

"I can't do that to Ivan."

"He'll be fine. He'll eat a nice dinner."

Henry stepped around the table and helped Costanza to her feet. He didn't quite lift her, but he gave her some guidance, gently forceful.

She let him walk her into the foyer. "Do you have comfortable shoes down here?"

She pointed to a closet. Henry opened the door. Half a dozen pairs of women's shoes were lined up on the floor. He brought her a pair that looked comfortable. Black flats. He knelt down, took off her heels, then slipped the flats on her feet.

"And a sweater, a jacket?"

"There's a jacket. Black wool."

He found it and draped it over her shoulders. She stood up. "It's not as warm in New York," she said flatly, "as it was in Italy."

"No. It's not."

When they turned toward the door, it had already been opened. By Ivan, who was standing there in silence. Costanza avoided his gaze; Henry met it.

"I'm sorry about the dinner. Mrs. Sarnoff needs some air."

Before they left, Ivan handed Henry a bag. Inside was the fruit. "It's not the sort of thing that keeps very long."

⌐

The sun is in the wrong place.

This was Costanza's first thought of the new day. She felt the sun on her back, whereas in New York the sun, in the morning, usually shone on her face. And she was on the right, not the left, side of a large empty bed. A bed that was not hers, in a room that was plainer than the one she was accustomed to waking up in, in New York. The room had beams, molding, windows with divided lights. Where pictures had once hung, silhouettes checkerboarded the walls. The floor was bare, and the window frames needed paint. The whole room did.

She was waking up in Henry's bedroom. She knew that. It was not as if she had drunk so much that she forgot. Though her sleep had eventually been leaden, she remembered walking out onto Fifth Avenue, with Henry at her side. She remembered looking at the leaves on the trees, how they fluttered as a breeze picked up. She remembered hearing a siren. And she remembered being able to breathe, and think, properly think, for the first time in a week.

She remembered having dinner with him, a picnic in his living room. Japanese food, sent in. A cold Sancerre. Cross-legged and shoeless, they sat on the floor and ate on their laps. After dinner, while Henry was clearing away the bento boxes and the empty wine bottle and all the rest, she had found her way into his bathroom and then his bedroom, where she undressed and slipped into bed. When he found her there, the look on his face was of pure joy. He shed his shirt and his pants, then he got into bed alongside her. He touched her hair and stared at her as though she were an apparition, a phantasm. She was neither. She was a woman, a real woman, who had merely sounded, and followed, or was possibly testing, her heart—it was as if the earlier part of the evening, in Morton's apartment, belonged to another strand of her life, another story. This was the story, she decided, she was meant to follow. Did the why of it matter? What mattered was the fact of it. What mattered was that she had allowed herself to slip into Henry's bed. And that she had touched her hand to his cheek, and left it there. He closed his eyes. When he opened them again, they were moist. A single tear spilled out of his right eye and left a thin damp trail along the side of his nose. She kissed it and felt a pang of tenderness for this man, for the improbability of his presence in her life, and for hers in his. She had had such a hard time in these last years with Morton, then without Morton. It had nearly consumed her—nearly. Being able to feel tenderness was helping to release her from Morton's spell. So was coming to realize that she had been afraid of Morton, whether because of his age, his accomplishment, his nature (or her nature), she wasn't sure.

Henry kissed her palm. Then he kissed her neck, her breasts. She put her hands on his back and drew him closer. She inhaled the scent of his hair. It smelled of leaves. Eucalyptus, or mint. She could feel his hardness against her thigh. She lowered her hands. She cupped his penis in its envelope of cotton. The envelope was full, warm, and pulsing. It was like holding a small bird. She reached inside. His penis was alive. When she touched it, it quivered; what an explicit, communicative thing the male organ was. With her hands moving, exploring, she guided him toward her. The last time they had made love he had been tentative at first. This time he wasn't. She felt a small flash of pain, then a flare of pleasure that built and built.

She had no further memory of being conscious again until she felt the sun on her back. It warmed her, and it woke her. She rearranged the pillows and sat up in Henry's bed. She listened to the morning. A distant steady vibration of traffic floated up from the street. Water hissed as it hurried through pipes in the wall. Someone was causing glass or china to chatter.

It was Henry. He had showered and was dressed for the workday, but he had managed to put together a breakfast tray, which he was carrying, effortfully, into the room.

On the tray was a small bowl of his fruit, expertly cut up, along with a croissant, a cup of coffee, and a pitcher of warm milk. He delivered it to her lap.

"Impressive." She added milk to the coffee and sipped it. "*And* you serve good coffee."

"For an American."

"You said that. I didn't."

"But you thought it."

She conceded with a half nod.

"I may not live on Fifth Avenue, Costanza, but I do grind my own beans."

"Ivan never understood how to make proper coffee, and Morton strictly drank tea."

Henry sat down on the edge of the bed. "Are you really going to go back there?"

"That's exactly what I've been sitting here trying to work out."

"Didn't you tell me you kept your old apartment as an office? Could you go there?"

She hesitated. "I sublet it before I left for Italy."

"What about selling Fifth Avenue and moving on? It's been a year, over a year . . ."

"This is kind of . . . private, Henry, but Morton didn't come from money, and the fact that he made a lot of it was a burden to him. I signed an agreement before we were married. If I decide to leave the apartment, it gets sold, and the proceeds are added to the trust he set up to support writers who live under governments where they aren't able to publish freely. The truth is, I'm more than ready for that to happen. The apartment—life up there—just wasn't for me. I'm much more comfortable sitting at my simple wooden desk, puzzling out words."

"You could rent something else, couldn't you? Somewhere new?"

"I could. It's just . . . it's just that I don't think I'm of a mind, yet, to make a new home for myself. Before I do that, I need to know what my next project is. When I'm working, everything else in my life tends to fall into place."

Henry ran his hand through his beard. "What about . . . what about staying here?"

She set down her coffee cup with more clatter than she intended. "Here, with you?"

"Well, not *just* with me. Justin is coming back tonight for a few days, before he returns to school. Andrew, as you know, is starting his senior year. He spends half the week and every other weekend with me, but by next fall, next year—"

"By next year you'll have a vacancy, and you're looking for a room-mate," Costanza said lightly.

"That is not at all why I'm asking you to stay. And you know it."

There was an uneasy silence. She stared into her coffee cup.

"You don't know me well enough, Henry. And I don't know you."

"It would be one way to find out. We're not children."

The light in her eyes seemed to turn inward. After several moments she said, "I would expect a breakfast tray like this every morning."

Henry's eyebrows drew together. "You're making a joke *now*?"

"Who said I was joking?"

"All right then, I will make you a breakfast tray every morning, though since several days a week I leave for work pretty early, I may have to put the coffee in a thermos. But the rest, yes, it will be like this, or close to this, every morning."

When he completed this formal little speech, Henry simply looked at her.

Costanza sat very still. The room was so silent that she could hear Henry's breathing, as he could hear hers.

Henry. Henry and Andrew. Henry and Andrew and sometimes Justin. A new world opened up, *offered* up, to her just like that. A world that had nothing to do with Morton, nothing to do with the past. A chance to escape Fifth Avenue, to start afresh.

And to see about Henry. To see if what had happened to them in bed, twice now, had legs. To see if the feelings that had stirred in her were to be trusted.

"I tell you what. How about if I agree to stay for a little while, just until I can get myself . . . sorted."

"I understand this doesn't say anything about us," Henry said cautiously.

"Well, I wouldn't say *that* . . ."

Smiling again, he took her hand. "I wish I didn't have to go to work. And that's not something I ever feel." He kissed her on the forehead. "What will you do today?"

"I'll pack some things. I'll return a call about a translating job."

"We'll have dinner together?"

"We'll have dinner together, yes. I'll prepare it. I don't expect you to feed me. Breakfast was enough—is enough." She paused. "You do know I was kidding about every morning?"

"I wasn't."

Costanza showered in Henry's shower. She dried off with Henry's towel. She made Henry's bed. All this felt oddly natural; alarmingly natural.

Afterward she picked up the breakfast tray and carried it into the kitchen, where she lowered the dishes into the sink and washed and rinsed them by hand before spreading them out neatly on the counter to dry.

As she was setting down the last coffee cup, a voice said, "When you wrote in that letter that you'd come find me in New York, this isn't exactly what I pictured."

She turned around. Andrew was standing in the doorway, watching her. He was wearing a pair of boxer shorts and flip-flops and rubbing the sleep from his eyes. Her first impression was that he wasn't the same young man she had gotten to know in Florence. Or, rather, he wasn't—and he was. Andrew's blemished skin had cleared up in the intervening months, and he seemed to have grown into himself, to inhabit his body more fully. But then again she had never seen him shirtless before. Maybe that was all it was, seeing him half-dressed.

"It wasn't what I pictured either, Andrew."

An uncomfortable silence opened up between them.

"So how are you?" she asked.

"I'm okay."

She leaned forward, waited for more.

"I'm starting senior year. In about ten minutes I'm going to start having four hours of homework a night at least, swim practice three times a week, and eleven college applications to fill out. I would say that I'm the picture of calm, a regular Buddha."

"That bad?"

"Some of my friends are applying to twenty schools."

They stood staring at each other for a moment.

"What about you?"

"I'm—I think I should just come out and say it. Your father and I appear to be—"

"Together."

"Figuring things out."

"I'm glad for you—both of you," Andrew said opaquely.

"It also means you'll be in my life. That's a bonus, to me."

Andrew didn't say anything to this.

"There's something else."

"You're going to marry Henry?" he blurted.

Her face flushed. "Well, no. I'm just getting to know him, after all."

"I'm sorry." Andrew crossed his arms. "That sounded like something a little kid would say."

"Your father—he has offered to let me stay here. Just temporarily. Until I—get my bearings."

Andrew looked away from her.

"He's helping me out. My situation at the moment—"

"I really don't need to know any more. All this is between you guys."

"Actually this part is about me. But you're right. I just wanted you to know."

Andrew looked up. "Does Justin?"

"It was decided only this morning. An hour ago."

"Justin's coming home this afternoon. I haven't seen him, or talked to him, since June."

She nodded.

"It's been a long summer. He's completely opted out around here. And there." *There* meant their mother's apartment on the West Side, indicated with a tilt of Andrew's head in that direction.

Costanza nodded again. The two of them fell silent. Kitchens, when they were silent, always felt more silent than other rooms, probably because they were such tightly wound places, always ready to spring into action.

"I'm heading home now to pick up some things. Would you like to walk me there?"

Andrew shrugged. But the shrug said yes more than no.

He struck her as altered in other ways too. It wasn't just that he seemed more open in Florence; he was more original, she couldn't help but feel. In New York he seemed gloomy or hidden; maybe it was merely hidden, and she was inventing all the rest. Or maybe he was simply mulling over the news she had just shared with him.

The two apartments were fifteen blocks, but many worlds, away. As they walked, Costanza tried to distract Andrew, and herself, by asking him what classes he was taking, which schools he was applying to, what kinds of pictures he'd been shooting.

The usual, too many to remember, only mediocre ones since summer ended.

That was about how it went. She was relieved when Fifth Avenue swung into sight.

"Swank," he said, looking over the building. "I've been reading some of Sarnoff's books. The older ones, about the young guy, Leiberman, growing up in Jersey."

"What do you think?"

"Somebody's pretty angry. I can't tell if it's Sarnoff or his character. But angry in a way you believe. At least I do."

"The character mellows later on."

"They say that happens to young people." This, at least, he offered with a curl of a smile.

Costanza's least favorite doorman was on duty. She glanced at him, then at Andrew. "Would you like to come up?" she asked—hopefully, as it would be so much easier not to have to go into the apartment alone.

He shook his head. "I'm supposed to meet my stepfather for break-fast. He wants to have a Talk. Everyone wants to have a Talk with me. This whole senior-year thing. Everyone has an opinion about how I should present myself, describe myself, write about myself. To me it's just the next thing really."

"That's one way to think about it. A good way—if you believe it."

"I half believe it." There he was. More like the Andrew she knew. "I'll be seeing you for dinner then."

"Do you like pesto?"

"Basil, pine nuts, garlic, Parmigiano, oil. What's not to like?"

"You're forgetting the salt. It can be a little flat without the salt. You can help me make it if you have time."

"My dad sends out. Don't expect to find any fancy equipment in our kitchen."

"No worries. I'll bring my own."

As soon as she stepped into the elevator, Costanza began mentally pack-ing. Clothes, jewelry and cosmetics, several key notebooks. Her laptop. Her address book, dictionaries, a few books. From the kitchen a cheese grater, a pasta pot, the mini-Cuisinart if she was going to make pesto. A garlic press; a knife or two. Her mother's olive oil. To be safe she'd take a colander too. It didn't matter that she might only end up staying a few days; she would revel in being in charge of a kitchen again, how-ever briefly.

She had it all organized before she even had her keys out of her purse. But she didn't need her keys. She had Ivan. He was standing by the open door when she stepped off the elevator, ever his immaculate waxworks self.

Costanza decided to dive in. It was like accepting Henry's offer. She was going to ride the wave as far as it would carry her before it crashed— or she did.

"When I left for Italy six months ago, Ivan," she said right there in the foyer, "I warned you that this way of life here, in the apartment, would have to come to an end. I realize it may feel abrupt to you, but six months is a very long advance notice of change."

He nodded somberly.

"I told you then that the time would come when the apartment would be put on the market to be sold."

"And I would become homeless."

Out of politeness she waited a moment before continuing. "Well, that day is coming—has come. It's today. I'm going to get in touch with Mr. Sarnoff's lawyer in a few minutes. Of course I don't expect you to leave today just because I've decided to. I think three weeks, four if you need them, is reasonable, don't you?"

"Three weeks, until the end."

"Actually I would say that the end came when Mr. Sarnoff died, wouldn't you? All the rest of this, prolonged though it has been, has been posthumous."

Ivan blinked at her. "But writers never really die, do they, Mrs. Sarnoff? With a stroke of the pen they can force back the clock, many times over."

"They live on in their work. Not in furniture. Not in places."

"Of course. But at the same time, don't you believe that a man's spirit continues on after him? Don't you feel Mr. Sarnoff's presence here with us now?"

In fact she did. And that was a large part of the problem. Though she chose to answer Ivan differently. "I think that the dead, when they continue, continue in the living, Ivan."

Ivan listened. Ivan nodded. "Do you mind if I ask about Mr. Sarnoff's papers? His manuscripts and so on. What will happen to them?"

"His executor will take good care of them, I am sure."

"There's a lot of material that a biographer might one day like to review. It's a job for someone with an archival . . . bent. I might be able to help with that."

"I'll be happy to speak to Mr. Wexler."

"But he takes his guidance from you, doesn't he? And Mr. Sarnoff's brother."

"Believe it or not, I have very little say in these matters. As for Howard, you're free to speak to him directly. He's far better informed than I am about the state of Morton's papers."

Ivan sniffed, just slightly. The sniff told her that he likely knew about the diaries.

In keeping with her decision about the day, she continued with a frontal approach. "I'm referring to Mr. Sarnoff's diaries, naturally."

"They will be widely read, I believe, when they're published." So Ivan knew about their publication too. "There are many readers who will be very curious to know him as we did."

"And you believe the diaries show him as we knew him?" Costanza asked, she thought slyly.

But Ivan wasn't biting. "As a reader, I'm always eager to know how the writers I admire think and live. How they write, when they write for themselves. And besides, Mr. Sarnoff had many fans who would be interested in reading *any*thing he wrote."

"That's what Howard feels."

"And you, if I may ask? What do you feel?"

"I feel, quite honestly, that it's a little soon to be putting them into the world."

Costanza was determined for their conversation to end on a civilized note. As warmly as she could under the circumstances, she added, "I know Mr. Sarnoff meant a lot to you. I've told you before how much you meant to him. He often said to me that he would never have recovered from his first illness without you. Even the money he left you cannot repay that kindness. Only there's nowhere to go from here but forward. For both of us, Ivan, it's time."

Costanza went upstairs, left a message for Howard, and e-mailed Morton's lawyer. She committed to a new translating job. She assembled a stack of the books that she knew she would need in the coming weeks. She sorted through her clothes, packing half of them in a large box she would eventually take to her studio downtown.

When she went to pack the other half in her large suitcase, she found Morton's diary, still there where she had stashed it all those months ago in Florence. It had followed her to Liguria and back to New York. She had not once felt like looking at it again. She didn't feel much—at all—like looking at it now either. Yet it seemed almost to vibrate with the pent-up energy of words unread, a voice unacknowledged, a command, Morton's command, unheeded. Not EAT ME, not DRINK ME, but HEAR ME; only Costanza was determined not to go down this rabbit hole, not on this morning of all mornings. She tucked the package into the box that was earmarked for downtown and kept moving forward.

By noon she had left her suitcase and a canvas bag with kitchen implements on Sixty-Ninth Street, with Henry's doorman. Then she headed off to Union Square—on foot.

It had been surprisingly easy to leave her country behind, but its food was another matter. For Henry and his sons Costanza was determined to make a simple but accurate pesto, or a pesto as accurate as she could make it given that, in America, basil was grown until it was large, leggy, and bitter, whereas in Liguria it was picked young, tender, and sweet. She was lucky. She found two youngish bunches at the farmers' market that were surprisingly vital given the midday sunlight. She bought garlic there too, and bread, and greens for salad, and apples for a tart.

Walking through Union Square on market day gave Costanza the greatest happiness. The profusion of the American harvest was at its most impressive in these stalls, with their mounds of carrots and beets in yellow, orange, and purple, their stalks of tightly whorled brussels sprouts, their lettuces in every tint of green, their apples, turnips, onions, eggplants, mushrooms, pumpkins, gourds, radishes, and squash. She delighted in the beautiful incongruity of all that was delicious and perishable being laid out in a rare open space in the midst of so much stone and cement.

Her happiness accompanied her all the way to her old neighborhood, where from an Italian grocer she bought pine nuts, Parmigiano, and several bags of good pasta. For antipasto she decided on prosciutto and olives. When she finished, her bags were heavy and her stamina was beginning to flag.

For nearly two hours Costanza had concentrated on the specifics of the meal rather than the circumstances under which she was making it. Now, slowing down for a moment, she began to think about these circumstances, and she was faced with her mother. Often when Costanza moved forward in her life, she was visited by a spectral Maria Rosaria in this way: Twice in a row you dive into the unknown? Twice in a row, and at nearly forty, you conduct yourself like a girl of twenty-two?

And more: You have talent as a writer yourself, yet you turn away from it, because you're afraid of failing, and so you translate other people's work instead. Like so many women, too many women, you spend years hiding behind an Important Man. A year after Sarnoff is gone, you're still hiding. In your place, I would dare myself to write finally. I would find a nice affectionate dog for companionship. I would put myself to a *real* test.

(Maria Rosaria had said these very sentences, more or less, during Costanza's recent visit.)

But Mamma, Costanza imagined herself responding, I know what life alone feels like now. It feels empty, and anyway I refuse to become bitter about that marriage. Or: I'm entitled to be attracted to the possibility of love; is it not every human being's human right? Or: Finding love does not mean the end of work. It might mean the beginning of work, new work, a new phase in my life. It might even—who knows?—mean the beginning of a family of my own.

A family of her own?

Costanza breathed—she tried to breathe. Just as there was no point in arguing with a phantom mother, there was no point in taking on all the most daunting themes in one afternoon.

She continued along First Avenue. Soon she was within two blocks of her apartment. In front of the building she fished in her purse for her keys, let herself in, and climbed up to the fourth floor. She had not entered the place where she had begun her life in New York since just before she left for Italy. The air in the room was stale. She set down her bags and opened a window.

She told herself that she had stopped by to check on the apartment and collect a mortar and pestle, which she thought she might use to prepare the pesto. She had forgotten how heavy it was, though. She could not manage it along with her shopping bags.

It was curious about places that were lived in intermittently: they seemed to hold on to some sense, or sense memory, of where life had been left off within their four walls. One key moment where life had been left off within these four walls, for her, was that grim day some months after she and Morton had separated when her friend Annelie had quite literally had to pull her out of bed. First Maria Rosaria, now Annelie: was that, deep down, why she had come to the apartment—to take a look at herself at one of her lowest moments, to remind herself of the dangers of moving too fast, too carelessly or blindly into something unknown?

Costanza glanced at the old sofa, a thrift-store purchase that dated to her very first month in New York. She had spent a lot of hours on that sofa, reading, working, and thinking. What she found herself thinking about now was why she had told Henry a lie—a white lie—about having sublet the apartment. Her subtenant had, in fact, left at the beginning of the month, but she had not wanted to tell Henry that. She had been untruthful, moderately untruthful, because she had wanted Henry to ask her to stay with him. She knew that pretty clearly. She had wanted that extra bit of assurance, even though the moment she had awakened in his bed she had not wanted to leave.

Certainly it would be more prudent—safer and more honest—if she were to phone Henry and tell him that she had changed her mind, or (better) that her subtenant had turned out to be flexible. He had decided to move in with his girlfriend. She would therefore be able to move back into her own place. She and Henry could see each other regularly. They could come to know each other gradually, the way sensible people did. Yes, that was what they would do. Be careful, sensible.

Only sensible didn't interest her. It never had.

⇌

Andrew was right about Henry's kitchen. It was clearly not a place where many meals were prepared. The pots and pans were unmarred by use, and of poor quality. The dishes and bowls were all white, and matching. The glassware was lined up in two spare soldierlike rows. This told Costanza that Henry's wife must have emptied out the kitchen cupboards, just as she had taken the paintings off the bedroom walls. Costanza pictured Henry, newly on his own, going into one of those big generic stores and filling up a shopping cart. Perhaps his assistant accompanied him, or a friend. The shopping was done expediently. No one thought through to complicated recipes that needed specialized tools. There were eight of everything. Eight, in this context, was such a forlorn number. Eight said that there would never again in this house be a Thanksgiving, a New Year's Eve, a large gathering of any kind.

Costanza unpacked the box of kitchenware she had put together before she left the duplex. The one thing she had forgotten was a tart pan, but way back in one of Henry's cupboards she found an old cookie sheet, bent and in want of a good scrubbing. She would make a free-form tart and shape it with her hands.

She began with the pesto. Within minutes the rich sweet aroma of crushed basil was floating into the room. Preparing the quintessential dish of her place in Henry's kitchen was the ideal way to make her feel at ease. She felt happiness wash over her for the second time that day.

Also for the second time that day she looked up from a task to find that she was being observed by one of Henry's sons.

She recognized Justin from a photograph on Henry's dresser. If by any conventional measure of attractiveness Andrew was an improvement on Henry, Justin was an improvement on Andrew. He had luminous green eyes. His hair, which he wore in untended long curls, was the color of caramel and seemed almost to glow. His thin angular body was poured into a pair of narrow jeans. He wore a grubby T-shirt printed with the name of what she assumed to be a band, a wrist full of woven and leather bracelets, and an unexpected pair of loafers that appeared to be expertly made, if much scuffed.

She had no way of knowing how long he had been standing in the doorway, watching her work. As soon as she noticed him, though, he said, "And you might be . . . ?"

"Costanza. I *am* Costanza."

He was puzzled. "Costanza, the caterer? Henry must really be putting it on for my welcome-home dinner."

"No, Costanza the friend. Of your father's. Who happens to be preparing said meal."

She wiped her hand on a dish towel. She thought that he might understand and walk across the room to shake it, but he remained rooted in place.

"Friend, as in girlfriend?"

She hesitated. Then: "I suppose."

"And already you're cooking?"

"I've been cooking all my life, Justin," she said dryly.

He took a quick survey of her work so far. "It's green."

"Yes, it's pesto. A specialty of Liguria, where I'm from."

"You're Italian."

"Half."

"Well, I don't do green. My father will have forgotten to mention that, I'm sure."

She tried to work out whether he was joking. He didn't appear to be. "You haven't tasted my green. You might like it."

"I might not. But don't worry. I can always send out."

As far as first impressions went, Justin was making rather a bleak one. He approached the counter.

"So you two met where?"

"In Florence."

"The summer trip. More to it than he reported."

She wasn't sure what to say. The conversation seemed to have its own rhythm, far from pleasant. No, not its own. Justin's.

Apparently he wanted to continue their friendly talk: "Do you have extra green sauce?"

"Of course."

"I've invited a friend. What time is dinner?"

"Your father said he'd be home by seven."

"My friend's train gets in at seven fifteen. I expect you can wait."

"I expect we can, Justin, yes."

"Super." And with this he left the room.

After she finished preparing the dinner and set the table, Costanza took herself on a little tour of Henry's apartment. By any point of comparison other than Morton's, Henry's home was roomy and gracious in the best old-fashioned way. The layout—unlike that of Morton's duplex—was fairly straightforward. A large square foyer led to the right into the kitchen and straight ahead into the living room. Between the living room and the kitchen was a library that, Costanza suspected, was originally meant to be the dining room; it opened onto the living room through wide double doors. One of its walls was fitted, floor to ceiling, with bookshelves. The titles ranged beyond medicine to politics, natural history, art history, history, and some fiction; two shelves, she noted, were dedicated to the Holocaust and the Second World War alone. A drop-leaf table stood against another wall, but it seemed clear that Henry and the boys customarily ate in the kitchen. A desk sat in the alcove by the window and a pair of club chairs floated in the center of the room—and that was it. At least the living room was furnished with a sofa, another pair of chairs, and a few side tables. Henry had mentioned that his father was an upholsterer, so she wasn't surprised to see that the upholstery was pristine, yet both rooms seemed not only underfurnished but also underlit. As in the bedroom there were shadows where pictures had once hung. In the living room and the library, in addition, ghostly rectangles darkened the floors, which had evidently once been covered by rugs.

Henry and his wife had lived apart for five, six years now. How long did it take for the dark parts of the floor to catch up with the light ones? A decade? A lifetime?

Costanza returned to the foyer. The long corridor that led out of the foyer in the opposite direction of the kitchen reached all the way to Henry's bedroom at the far end. In between was a row of doors. All were dark except for the first one. She approached it and knocked.

"Come in."

Andrew was sitting at his desk, shifting folders and papers around. Stacks of photographs spread out next to him and continued in a chaotic swirl across the floor.

"I didn't even know you were here," Costanza said. "Why didn't you come say hello?"

"I didn't want to disturb the master chef."

"Well, it's not so masterful really. It's pretty basic, what I've done."

"I know, remember? Pine nuts, garlic, basil, cheese, oil—and salt."

She smiled. "It didn't seem to appeal to your brother."

"He doesn't 'do' green," Andrew said. "Wait. You met Justin? Where?"

"He popped in briefly."

"Really? What did you think of him?"

Costanza hesitated. "He seemed nice."

Andrew gave her a skeptical look.

"He seemed—surprised to find me in the kitchen."

Andrew nodded. "I bet."

On the wall above his desk hung a cork bulletin board, where dozens more of his photographs were arranged in thematic clusters. Costanza stepped toward them. "When did you start taking these?"

"About six years ago. When my mother left. In fact I took the first one the actual day."

He indicated the upper left-hand corner of the bulletin board, where a faded photograph, curling inward and slightly blurry, depicted a slipper whose cushioned interior held the imprint of a woman's foot. Costanza studied it as Andrew continued, "Over the next few months I went around taking pictures of things she left behind, either intentionally or by accident. First came the slipper, then the rest."

The rest, arranged in a long vertical line below the slipper, included a comb with a missing tooth; a pile of sweaters spilling out of a bag marked CANCER CARE THRIFT; a college psychology textbook with a round brown stain on its front cover; a silver soup ladle with an elaborate scrolling G engraved on the handle; a box of hair clips; deposit slips to a savings account printed with HENRY WEISSMAN OR JUDITH GERTZ WEISSMAN; an open drawer full of spools and scraps of ribbon; and a white wedding veil, yellowing within its sheath of dry cleaner's plastic.

Andrew followed her gaze. "She took, or maybe got rid of, the dress but left the veil. I could never figure that out."

To the right of the photographs relating to Andrew's mother were a number of views from windows that had been arranged in thematic groups. The ones from Florence Costanza recognized, but there were other windows, apparently New York windows, as well. In one extended series an older woman, photographed in profile, was sitting on her couch. There were about twenty pictures of her, in her pajamas, her bathrobe, her bra, in a summer shift, in a turtleneck sweater. In every single photograph save one she was reading.

"And these?" Costanza glanced up at his window. "They're not taken here."

"On the West Side. I photographed her for almost two years, across the courtyard from our kitchen. Ninety percent of the time she was sitting in the same place, on the same blue sofa. And she was almost always reading. She reminded me of Charlotte and her family. I liked the way she repeated, every day, the exact same thing."

"But presumably she wasn't reading the same thing, so every day—every minute really—was different, to her."

Andrew took this in. "Maybe that's why she looks slightly different in every photograph." He paused. "Earlier this summer, before we left for Italy, her apartment was dark for several days. You can see it in the last pictures. I photographed the darkness. When we got back, it was empty. Just a white box. A dingy white box. I think she must have died."

"She might have moved."

"If she'd moved, I'd have seen her packing. Or dismantling things."

Costanza looked around at the room. "Like you're doing now."

"Believe it or not, this is me organizing. My stepfather suggested I put together a portfolio of my photographs. He said it might be smart to send them around with my applications. Something 'extra' to show how special I am."

Costanza brushed past the sarcasm. She looked at the photographs scattered on Andrew's desk. One in particular drew her attention. In it a debonair middle-aged man stood in a street where the buildings looked decidedly Italian. His face radiated an odd equanimity. She picked it up. "He seems familiar."

"This is one of the photographs I don't really understand. He's a colleague of my father's. We ran into him in Florence and I felt, I don't know, that I just had to take his picture."

She recognized him now. "He's Dr. Schoenfeld, isn't he? I consulted him once. Morton and I did."

Andrew nodded. "I intended to shoot him as he was walking away. From behind. I like to photograph people from behind. But then he turned around. It was as if he knew I was looking at him. He waited for me to take his picture. Posed, almost."

Costanza continued to study the image.

"If you and your husband went to see a doctor like Schoenfeld, then you must have been pretty serious about trying to have a baby."

"I was, but Morton . . ." She put the photograph down. "Let's just say the timing wasn't right."

"People say that, but I'm not sure what it really means."

"It means that things happen, or they don't, for a reason. If they happen, they were probably meant to all along. If they don't . . ." Costanza looked away.

"Would you say you were meant to move in with my father all along? When you only met him three months ago?"

Now it was Andrew's turn to look away, to look anywhere but at Costanza.

"I would say . . . I would say that your father and I were meant to find out what we're finding out. And besides, Andrew, I'm not moving in. I'm just staying here for a little while."

Back in the kitchen, Costanza turned the flame on low under the pasta water. Then she found a bowl and started to assemble the salad. The evening was gradually beginning to take on some of the grit, and a little of the gloom, of the real. Prickly Justin . . . complicated Andrew. Was there no perfection to be had, even in a single meal? Probably the mistake was seeking perfection in the first place. She had wanted to mark the evening, but what it was to her, or to her and Henry, was going to be different from what it was to Andrew and to Justin. Happiness, she knew, was not a particularly insightful state of mind. It had been so long since she had even had a taste of happiness that she had forgotten how blinding it could be.

When Henry walked into the kitchen just after seven o'clock, Costanza took one look at his face and sensed that something wasn't right. Maybe it was his habit to come home every day from seeing patients with this same air of worried abstraction. His work was often upsetting, surely. But he didn't even take in her preparations. The food, the scents, the table, entirely passed him by. He said merely, and with exasperation, a single word: "Justin."

For a moment that seemed to be all Henry was going to say. But he went on, "He just texted. He's bringing someone to dinner."

"I know. He was here briefly earlier. You seem disappointed."

"I had hoped to have him to myself—I hoped *we* could have him to ourselves. It's been so long. More than two months."

"But he's in town through the weekend, isn't he?"

"The days will fly. They always do. He'll find excuses to go out . . ." Henry seemed to catch himself, or to listen to himself. "I haven't even said a proper hello." Then he kissed her.

"That was proper."

He smiled finally. He looked around. "You've been busy. I don't think there's been such a nice table set in this house for years. It's only missing one thing."

He slipped into the hall and returned with a bouquet of flowers. They weren't precious hothouse flowers but wildflowers, grown outdoors somewhere in a field. Black-eyed Susans, deep gold with black centers, autumnal and spirited. "It's been a long time since I've had anyone to give flowers to."

"It's been a long time since I've been given any." She smiled.

He reached up to a high cupboard, brought down a glass vase clouded with dust, and rinsed it.

"Tell me." Henry handed her the clean vase. "Tell me everything you did since we parted this morning."

As she unwrapped and arranged the flowers, she gave him an abbreviated version: the phone calls, the packing up; the food shopping downtown; then cooking, meeting Justin.

"And did you get a sense of him?"

"He was just here for a few minutes," she said diplomatically.

"I hope he wasn't in one of his surly moods."

Her silence prompted Henry to explain, "That's all just cover. It's his way when he's uncomfortable."

"Well, we all have a way when we're uncomfortable."

"It'll take time, but you'll see what a great kid he is."

Justin liked green after all. And he could be charming. After a small assessing bite he dug into his bowl of *linguine al pesto* with appetite. He praised Costanza's cooking and announced to the table in general, "What a really nice dinner this is."

He had returned from the train station in a more buoyant mood, moving through the apartment with a proprietary air, opening and pouring wine as though he were the host. He was helpful, charming, a different Justin—Henry's Justin? Closer, for sure.

"Ah, yes," Henry said when Justin introduced his friend David.

David, six or seven years older than Justin, had been his TA at Bard. A wiry, ethereal young man in the obligatory battered jeans, David had prominent cheekbones, hard gemlike blue-green eyes, and a mouth that might have been appealing if it hadn't been so busy delivering opinions and pronouncements.

David liked the pesto too. David knew all about pesto. "It's the classic dish of Liguria," he told the table. "It comes out of a tradition of *cucina povera*, humble local ingredients resourcefully combined. Food that was once devised out of necessity is now considered a regional delicacy." Henry raised his eyebrows at Costanza at the idea of David, in front of Costanza, holding forth on the gastronomy of Liguria, but at least he had his facts straight. He had been to Genoa, and down all along the coast. He had even visited Recco. He knew the *focaccia al formaggio*, and he had swum in the pool where the famous water-polo team practiced. He had hiked into the hills too, as Costanza had many times, over many years. "That little church, a thousand years old and halfway down the hill toward Punta Chiappa—remind me of its name?"

"San Nicolò," she said.

"Correct." (*Correct*—as though she were a student of his.) "There's a little square, you can't even call it that, a little *pad* out front, paved with a design of gray and white pebbles, the kind you find on the beaches nearby. It's like the pesto, everything very much of the place."

And what place was *he* of? It was not easy to determine.

"We should go there sometime, Justin," David added, holding out his wineglass, which Justin promptly replenished. "The swimming is terrific. You see all kinds of fish . . ."

Henry, who had been holding back and observing more than participating, now said, "Justin's never been that much of a swimmer. Andrew is the swimmer in the family."

"I've been swimming," Justin said. "David and I have, a lot this summer. We found a lake outside of town. A hidden lake, clear as glass. We've been sneaking in." Justin turned to Andrew. "I guess I've sneaked in on your turf, Baby B."

"I don't own swimming," Andrew said.

"You *are* brown," Henry said. "It's not how I'm used to seeing you."

"What my father means," Justin explained to David, "is that I spent most of my high school years doing math and playing music. I rarely left the house. I was like a ghost."

"A studious ghost," said Henry. "A gifted ghost."

"But still a ghost, Dad. And a ghost is not enough. Not anymore, not for me."

The temperature in the room seemed to drop abruptly.

"Are you saying you regret the math workshops?" Henry said. "The music lessons? The fact that we encouraged you to practice?"

"I don't regret the work. I regret not having had a life to go with it."
Justin drank some wine. "Now that you have one again"—he glanced
at Costanza—"maybe you understand better."

Barbed though this remark was, Justin delivered it airily. But Henry
didn't bite, at least not in the way Justin seemed to expect. Instead Henry
sat back in his chair and said, "Tell me more about the lake. Clear as
glass, you said. Sneaking in."

Justin looked off into the distance. "They were just about the best
afternoons ever. This place, you have to drive about twenty minutes
from campus, along a back road. You park in a little clearing and walk
through the woods another ten minutes or so."

"Closer to fifteen, I'd say," said David.

Justin smiled at David. "Fifteen, right. There's a dirt path, so your
steps are very quiet, muffled. And you feel completely on your own.
That's the best part. Away from people, traffic. It smells of summer.
You know that smell? All the plants and trees are lush and green, full
of juice. And the air has a sound, it almost, I don't know, *hums*. From
the bees and the crickets and—and it's like you can hear the plants
growing. That's their music. They stretch, they reach for the sunlight.
They become stronger. That's what I felt I did with my summer. I
stretched, I—I felt things." Justin glanced at David nervously. "All
kinds of new things."

"For David," Henry half said and half asked. It was a leap, but if he
was right—and he was nearly sure he was—he wanted to get ahead of
this situation. He didn't want to give Justin any more reason to withdraw from him, from them. And his love for his son was deep enough,
unconditional enough, to withstand anything—anyone—Justin might
turn out to be.

In Justin's face: surprise, then confusion followed by curiosity. "How
did you . . . ?"

"Well, I *am* your father, Justin, and I . . . I did some thinking while
we were away this summer and you weren't with us. I noticed that
David has been coming up a lot in conversation. And then, seeing you
two together. It was just a feeling."

Justin nodded. Henry had the impression that his nodding was a
way of biding time, of giving himself a moment to reset his thinking,
since the conversation didn't seem to be going the way he'd anticipated.

"David and I are together," Justin said finally. "We have been since the summer. Since the lake." He looked at David, then at the others. "Though for the record, I don't identify as gay. Not yet."

"For the record," David said, "I do—in case you need to know that."

Henry stroked his beard. "You know, Justin—and David—I see lesbian couples and help them to have children through insemination. I see gay male couples who have children through a surrogate. I was one of the first practitioners in New York to address the fertility issues, and needs, of this population. They make up an increasingly significant part of my practice."

"That's very interesting, Henry"—David smiled—"but Justin and I aren't thinking about having kids *quite* yet."

"He was just trying to make us comfortable," Justin said to David. "Weren't you, Dad?"

Henry nodded. "Yes, Justin, that's exactly what I was trying to do."

Justin sat back in his chair. "That was a lot easier than I thought," he said, as if to the whole table. "Any follow-up questions?"

There was a moment of silence. Then Andrew raised his hand.

"Yes . . . Baby B," Justin said, in the mock tone of a teacher calling on a student.

"Do you think anyone really cares who you're sleeping with?"

The question seemed to sober Justin up, a little. "Actually, yes."

"Well, I'm not one of them. What matters to me is what kind of a brother you are, and for a while now—just for the record—you've been a selfish and pretty shitty one."

Andrew walked in squares. That was what you did in Manhattan; you obeyed the geometry. You allowed its orderly grid to curb a ranging or troubled mind. Though Andrew wasn't troubled so much as rattled. Once again, yet again, the focus had been all on his big brother. *He* was the one applying for school. *He* had spent the summer father-sitting Henry. *He* was the son with a broken, or fragmented, or anyway aching, heart. He would have appreciated a drop of his family's attention to have been focused on *him*; instead, as usual, Justin was the magnet.

Justin and his food likes and dislikes; Justin and his revelations; Justin and that dick he'd brought home.

After a few minutes Andrew broke free of the squares and walked west. He was conditioned never to walk into Central Park at night, certainly never alone, but tonight he didn't give a damn. He walked forward, and at a healthy pace. The deeper he went into the park, the fewer people he saw and the less traffic he heard. Instead there were footsteps, there was rustling in the shrubbery. A whoosh overhead, followed by a handful of leaves fluttering down out of the sky, told him that a bird was on the move. On the path ahead of him an older mustached man was leaning against a tree, smoking. He was wearing a tweed hat and wire-rimmed eyeglasses and his hand was buried in his pocket, buried and rooting around. Only it wasn't in his pocket, Andrew realized as he came closer. The man's hand was thrust into his pants, which were halfway unzipped. He was playing with himself while smoking, which was a little dexterous and a lot creepy, since his eyes clung to, it seemed, Andrew's every step.

Andrew felt sweat lacquering his forehead. He sped up and made his way to the reservoir. In all the years he had jogged around the reservoir, he had never run at night. It didn't matter that he was bundled up or wearing jeans. He increased his speed again, fell in with the few intrepid joggers who were out late, and began circling the inky water counterclockwise.

As he circled around the north side of the reservoir, it dawned on Andrew that he might not have headed into the park entirely by accident. He had likely sought out the park because it would lead him to the West Side, and on the West Side, just now swinging into view, was the El Dorado, the building where Charlotte lived.

He supposed it would be better if he didn't turn up sweaty. It was strange enough that he was thinking of appearing there in the first place. So he slowed down and cooled off before heading toward the building's heavy bronze-and-glass doors.

Carlos, the doorman on duty behind the desk, recognized Andrew and greeted him with a genial smile that hardened into some kind of official doorman pleasantry after he phoned upstairs. "She said she'll be down in a few minutes."

"Down?"

"She asked you to wait in the north lobby."

Carlos pointed the house phone leftward before replacing it in its cradle.

Andrew hesitated for a moment, then headed for the north lobby. On his way he glanced at the mural that represented the legend of El Dorado. Depicted in—what else?—gold paint, a party of explorers were crossing a bridge into the golden land, a place of abundant wealth and (in some tellings—he and Charlotte had read up about them one evening) true love and happiness as well.

He fell into a rust-colored armchair. Its fabric felt as unpleasant as it looked. Andrew fought the impulse to run out the door, back into the park, around the Reservoir, and home.

"This is a surprise." The voice came from over his shoulder.

He turned around, then stood up awkwardly. "I wanted to see you before you left for school. I guess I wanted to say goodbye."

"Well, you're seeing me."

He was seeing her, yes. He was seeing how different she looked. The long locks that Charlotte used to wrap around her index finger, or chew on when she was reading, were gone. A close, severe auburn frame now set off her face. It was still her face, still wide and freckled, yet a hardness had crept into it. Or had been put into it. For his benefit, or distress.

Charlotte dropped into the companion chair to the one he had just stood up out of.

He sat back down. "If we had our books, it would be just like upstairs."

"I'm not reading so much these days."

It was not an easy conversation to get going.

"You seem different."

"I just chopped off my hair." She checked him out. "You're the one who seems different. More—grown-up. More *manly*."

"So why aren't you reading?"

"I'm taking a break from Literature. I'm thinking of doing something wild and crazy at college."

"Like what?"

"Studying pre-law."

"I didn't think you could study pre-law."

"Well, whatever it is you need to know to go to law school."

"That doesn't sound like you."

"I'm breaking free."

"Breaking free means becoming a lawyer?"

"Breaking free means doing something, anything, different from my parents."

Andrew gave her a look in which puzzlement competed with upset. "What happened to you this summer?"

"*To* me? Nothing."

He nodded skeptically.

"My sister almost OD'd. Did you know that?"

"Emily does drugs?"

"She's in a place in Minnesota now, undoing them." Charlotte paused. "I told you that you romanticized my family, Andrew. You thought it was perfect just because my parents were together and no one bothered you when you came over."

Andrew silently disagreed. Then: "Well, Justin says he's gay."

"So?"

"And my father has a girlfriend. Everything's falling apart. Everything and everyone."

"Oh, don't be so dramatic. Justin's not falling apart just because he says he's gay. Emily's being put back together in Minnesota. A girlfriend is exactly what your father needs—that's what you always said. And you and I are not falling apart."

"Speak for yourself."

She picked a piece of lint off the armchair. "You're here, I'm going to guess, because you didn't like the way we ended things."

"I'm here because I didn't like the way *you* ended things."

"The thing is, Andrew, you just . . ." She flicked the lint away. "You just liked me too much."

"Sure I did."

"I'm serious. You did. And I didn't want to be liked so much."

"That's sick. No. That's sad."

"It is what it is." Then: "I've discovered that I like nastier boys."

"That *is* sick."

"All right, guys who hold back more."

He crossed his arms across his chest. "Why?"

"You really want to know?"

"Sure I do," he said, even though he wasn't.

"They turn me on."

Nasty guys turned Charlotte on? Really? How was it possible to be so close to someone, then discover she wasn't the person you thought she was? "You're not the girl I used to like so much."

"See, everything worked out okay then."

Andrew sat back and studied her face. It was as though the front door to a house had been closed while he stood on the porch, trying to peer in. He thought back to what Costanza had said to him in Florence, when he told her about Charlotte. "Are you sure you weren't afraid?"

"Of what?"

"The—feeling. Between us. There was a lot of feeling there, for a while."

"You're going to be a psychologist now like your mother?"

He held her gaze. "I don't think so."

Andrew took a taxi home. The apartment was dark and quiet. In the kitchen, replacing the aroma of cooking, a trace scent of soap and scouring powder lingered in the air the way it did on the days after Hilda came. It was as though the dinner had never happened.

At the end of the hallway a band of light spilled out from under his father's door. Justin's room was dark. Andrew went into his own room, took one look at its chaos, and for a moment contemplated putting everything in order. But he was so tired his limbs felt as if they were made of iron.

He took off his pants, dropped onto his bed, and slept solidly for several hours. Then at about one in the morning his eyes sprang open. He lay awake with a painfully full bladder, paralyzed. It took a while before he could hoist himself up. Finally he went into the bathroom he shared with Justin and peed.

Back in the hall, he stopped to listen. He detected faint sounds from behind both his father's and his brother's doors. He stepped closer to his brother's. What he heard was unmistakable. It was the sound of two people giving each other pleasure. Whether the intermittent muffled moans came from David or Justin or both, he couldn't be sure. It was a song; their song.

At his father's door he heard a murmur of conversation, back and forth. The last conversation he remembered hearing from behind that door was agitated, fiery; it came out in short spurts, like gunshot. This was different, low in tone, tender. It too was a song. Everyone in the house was singing except for Andrew.

⇌

Each morning for the remainder of the week, Henry scrambled to put together a breakfast tray for Costanza, as he'd promised. He wasn't satisfied with any of them until the weekend rolled around, when on Saturday morning, before she was awake, he had the chance to slip out for provisions. He came home and set up a tray as though he were getting ready for surgery. He opened and seeded a cantaloupe and sliced off three perfect half-moons of fruit, then topped them with a scattering of raspberries. He toasted bread and in a separate dish arranged a slice of butter and a dollop of gleaming apricot jam. He placed a mug of coffee and a pitcher of warmed milk in the upper right-hand corner and next to it a glass of sparkling water—Costanza had mentioned that she liked the way, in Naples, they always gave you a glass of sparkling water before you drank coffee.

As he walked down the hall with his carefully appointed tray, Henry remembered a scene from a foreign movie he and Judith had seen together. He no longer recalled its name, but he could still clearly see the long shot that followed a young woman who was nervous and, as Henry recalled it, in love as she carried a tray full of champagne glasses through an ornate large apartment, on her way to meet her lover. Her hands were trembling, and the trembling caused the wineglasses on the tray to touch each other and make a tinkling, chattering sound. The sound both underlined her agitation and was strangely piercing and beautiful.

As Henry carried his tray down the long hall to his bedroom, nothing on it chattered. He didn't splash a single drop of coffee or water or milk. Yet as he walked, he felt an approximation of what that young woman appeared to be feeling in the movie. He was excited to be greeting Costanza for the first time that day; he felt the excitement in his chest, his steady hands. It was the first time that they were going to spend an entire day together. The fact that it was a Saturday was even more delicious. Henry loved Saturdays. He had loved them ever since he had wrested them back from the strict Sabbath restrictions of his childhood. He might do anything and everything with a Saturday . . . and *this* Saturday, well, *this* was a downright magical Saturday. This Saturday the fates, whoever they were, had delivered the spectacular Costanza Ansaldo into his life. She was sitting up and waiting for her coffee in his bed; waiting, he hoped, to see what they might do together, with their Saturday.

Henry had left the door ajar earlier, so that he might push it open with his foot when he arrived with the tray. He did this now, then stepped into the room. The bedcovers were pulled back, the bed empty. For a moment Henry thought Costanza had vanished. Not just from his bed but from his life. Just like that, as mysteriously as she had first appeared in it.

But she had only gone into the bathroom to brush her teeth. He heard the water running, he heard her spitting. What a lovely sound spitting could be, under the right circumstances.

He set the tray down on the bed. The bed was saturated with a scent that came toward him strongly. It was stronger even than the coffee, the toast, and the fruit combined, a sweet floral scent, perfume and soap undercut by a whiff of sweat. The scent of a woman; the scent of this woman, and in the bed, and room, where the only body he had heard or smelled in the past six years had been his own.

"You've really outdone yourself this morning, Henry." Costanza, returning from the bathroom, spoke words that, because of where Henry's attention had turned, seemed to have come from far away.

"Well, I had the time . . ."

"I've always been fond of Saturdays."

"Me too." Henry paused. "I probably should mention that my father is coming in tonight. The visit was scheduled a long time ago, so that he could see Justin before he goes back to school. I'd like you to meet him, of course, but there's no obligation for you to be here."

"I would love to meet your father, Henry. I'd be happy to cook for him."

"I appreciate the offer, but no one ever cooks for Leopold, because he keeps strictly kosher, which means that we either go to the one French bistro on the Upper East Side that he somehow believes, without a shred of evidence, follows obscure four-thousand-year-old dietary laws to the letter, or else we send out for deli. Given that I can't be sure when the boys will turn up and that my father is very particular, as well, about the hour at which he sits down to eat, which is always seven sharp, the safest bet is deli, trust me."

"I happen to love pastrami."

Henry smiled. "Those words seem downright exotic coming out of your mouth."

"And pickles. Sour pickles."

He smiled. "It's settled then. That leaves us ten unstructured, unspoken-for hours. What shall we do?"

"Actually, I have an idea . . ."

The rugs were arranged in separate waist-high stacks. There must have been fifty different islands of pattern and color colonizing a vast loft space in a former manufacturing building in the Flatiron District. There were old rugs and new rugs, subtle rugs and garish rugs, rugs with thick pile and others with a thin flat weave. Costanza was so evidently in her element, waiting with such patience as the rug handlers peeled back example after example for them to review, that Henry smiled in easy agreement. Whatever she liked, he liked. It was that simple because it was true.

She had taken him by surprise, at first and just a little. Over coffee she had asked him, sensitively, if he was happy with the way "things" were in his house. For a moment he thought she intended the state of his family. But that was not what she was asking about; she was asking about the condition of the apartment. He knew what she meant. The place looked like Judith had walked out with half the stuff six days instead of six years earlier. The upholstery aside, Henry's apartment was shabby and uninviting. She didn't use these words; she didn't need to.

"What do you think," she'd said, "if we spend some time today just gathering ideas for a little refurbishment? It's something I like to do, fix places up."

Henry thought it was an auspicious sign that Costanza looked at the apartment as a place to refurbish. She couldn't mean to be leaving so quickly, he reasoned, if she was concerned about the lack of rugs and lamps. "Why just gather ideas?" he had said. "Let's get whatever you think it needs."

As he stood there amid the stacks of rugs, Henry felt a stab of nostalgia for the days when he and Judith were setting up their household together and used to spend a Saturday doing just this sort of thing. At the same time he was grateful to be with Costanza, in this place, on this day. He was grateful to be parting with several thousand dollars so that he might buy the rugs she chose. And he was grateful that, for the first time in six years, he would be able to walk around his apartment in winter in bare feet.

Costanza was a much more decisive shopper than Judith had been. In under an hour she had narrowed the choices down to four possibilities for the living room and two for the library. She had assessed the colors and patterns on the sofa and chairs, and she had taken into account the wall color, even as she hinted that it might be time to repaint.

The carpet handlers moved off to work with another customer while Henry and Costanza sifted through the subset of possibilities. They were all fairly neutral, and mostly geometric. Henry would have been happy with any of them, he told Costanza. He fully expected them to go on having this lightweight conversation about decoration until he heard himself say to her, "There's something I've been wondering . . ."

"All this pattern is going to be too busy against those chairs of yours? I know it's a concern. But I think it'll work."

"It's not about the rugs."

She leaned against one of the stacks.

"I've been wondering whether you've given up wanting to have a baby or whether you still—whether it is something you still think about."

Several reactions passed across Costanza's face in rapid succession. Surprise; then confusion; then something that looked like pain. That was what Henry thought he saw anyway. For a moment he wished he hadn't asked her so directly, but it wasn't his nature to sit on certain questions when they occurred to him. He needed to know what he needed to know when he needed to know it.

When she didn't answer, he added, "I hope I haven't offended you by asking."

"You haven't offended me, Henry," she said slowly. "But I am curious why you're asking me this *now*."

"Maybe I started at the wrong place. Maybe what I should have said first—what I should have said first is that I love you."

She waited for him to continue, since he appeared to have more to say.

"I cannot stop thinking about you. The more time I spend with you, the more human I feel. The more—hopeful. I feel—I feel that, with you, I have a chance to be alive in a way that stopped, for me, a long time ago, probably farther back in my marriage than it's easy for me to admit." He ran his fingers through his hair. "I've been having these feelings pretty much since I met you, and I've been trying to understand them for myself and communicate them to you, even as I've been aware that it may be too soon, that we don't know each other so very well at all. But I just can't reconcile that worry with what I'm experiencing. What I'm feeling—for you."

He paused. "The only constant I've had in these past years has been the clinic and my kids. I've let my friendships go, my house . . . and I want more now. I want to *live*. Don't you?"

She seemed to have been holding her breath as she listened. Breathing now, she said, "Of course I do, Henry."

After a moment she added, "But you assume that, when I met you, I had not been living."

"Is that so wrong?"

She didn't answer him at first. Then: "No. Not entirely."

"I want to be with you, Costanza. And if being with you means making a family with you, then I want you to know that I'm open to that too. I think it's important to establish that from the get-go."

Costanza looked at him with shining eyes, and she nodded.

"I wish I knew what that nod meant. What your eyes . . ."

"It means that I hear what you're saying. It means—I want to make sure I understand. You're asking if I want to have a baby—with you."

"Yes, with me. Of course with me."

"Isn't it a little—a lot—too soon?"

"I'm only asking you to think about it. To think, maybe, possibly, eventually, about trying. I'm sure I don't need to tell you that time is against you—against us."

"No," Costanza said softly. "You don't need to tell me that."

Costanza looked down at a rug as if some kind of hieroglyphic were woven into it that it was important for her to decipher or translate yet was beyond—way beyond—her skill set.

"And if we tried . . . and failed . . . ?" Naturally her mind went there, first of all. To that place; that experience. That unhealed wound.

"Then you would come in, obviously, and let me run some tests."

"And if those showed—if they showed, definitively, that I couldn't have a baby, what then? You wouldn't want to be with me?"

"You can't have truly heard what I just said if you're asking me that."

She flushed. "I'm sorry. I did hear you, and what you said was moving. It's just that it's all a little confusing. The speed with which you think . . . and act."

"I'm a man, Costanza, but I'm also a physician who specializes in issues of fertility. It may be clumsy of me to merge the two, but what can I say, this is how I'm made."

Her chest tightened. It was easier to nod than to speak.

"Biology, in these matters, has a certain degree of control over destiny, but biology can be more malleable than you expect. As long as you know what you're doing, and do it early enough. Personally I believe that it's best to decide your own life when you can, rather than having it be decided for you. Which is basically what happens to so many of the women I see."

She was listening closely. "Henry, I feel . . . I feel that this is too—"

"Too fast," he said, deflating.

"Too much. I don't know. And at the same time not enough."

"What do you mean, not enough?"

"Isn't it a little—strange—yes—strange to open up this kind of conversation without our first having—"

"Committed to each other."

She nodded.

"There's something else I've been wanting to ask you. I almost asked you in bed last night." Henry's face turned subtly pink. "All morning I've been hoping that by suggesting we come here you were thinking along the same lines, thinking that it didn't make sense for you to move back downtown but to stay with me. To live with me. To give us a proper chance."

Costanza thought about the intensity of feeling that passed between them in the last few evenings, when the boys had left and they lingered over their wine. And the talk that continued long after they went to bed.

And the lovemaking that followed. She was so unused to things in her life aligning that she had to review them to assure herself that they were true.

"This is a question I can answer more easily. And it's yes. Yes, Henry, I will live with you and I will give us a proper chance. I will do that much. Yes, I will."

Despite her minimal experience of what life was like in Henry's household, Costanza sensed a distinct change in the atmosphere about an hour before Leopold Weissman was due to arrive for dinner with his caregiver, a Jamaican woman named Lorna. Costanza was sitting in the living room, trying to read but instead thinking, still thinking, about the conversation she and Henry had had that morning at the rug store, when she perceived a tautness in the air, a palpable sense of anticipation that was broken, in spurts, by flurries of activity: two showers running in close succession and then some harried banging around. Between Henry and one of the boys—Costanza couldn't be sure which—several heated words were exchanged.

At about six thirty Henry emerged. His beard was newly trimmed and he was wearing a freshly laundered shirt. He asked Costanza if she would help him set up the table. Set up, not set. What this meant was moving into the center of the library the drop-leaf table that Costanza had previously noticed and wondered about. Afterward, from a cupboard she had not seen in her earlier survey, Henry retrieved a linen cloth and matching set of napkins, china with a delicate pattern of garlands and flowers, footed crystal glasses, silver flatware and candlesticks: so it was possible for Henry to have more than eight people over, after all.

He explained that the china, glasses, and linen were gifts from his parents, and that Leopold liked Henry to use them when he came to dinner, even if the meal was ordered in from a deli on Second Avenue. "It's a kind of re-creation," he said. "This is how the table was set when my father was a child. It's how my grandmother's house was run, and it's how he feels houses should still be run half a century later and half a planet away." Henry lit a match to soften the bottom of a taper, something Costanza's grandmother used to do. "It's easy to please Leopold in such small matters. The large ones—less so."

By a quarter to seven Henry, Justin, and Andrew had gathered in the living room. The boys were freshly showered and newly shaved, their hair combed, their jeans traded for khakis. Henry and his sons sat in a line on the sofa, one two three. It was the most like a family that they had seemed to Costanza since she'd seen them together.

The house phone rang. The boys sat up straight; Henry stepped into the hall. When he came back, he said, "The deli's coming up."

The deli came up. Henry tipped the deliveryman and left two warm, aromatic bags on the kitchen counter. He turned down Costanza's offer of help. "Later," he said, as he resumed his place on the sofa.

"Did you order his cream soda?" Andrew asked his father.

"I ordered the cream soda," Henry answered.

The three continued to sit in their silent line. Henry glanced at his watch. "Maybe the car was running late."

"You called the usual service?" asked Justin.

Henry nodded. "Why don't you play something for us? You know how much I hate waiting around."

Justin retrieved his violin from his bedroom. In a single flourish he had it balanced between his chin and shoulder. Two quick adjustments to the tuning pegs, and he was off, just like that producing a sound of such depth and ease that it seemed to originate as much from somewhere in his body as from the instrument in his hands. The music—Bach—was tender, far more tender than Costanza expected it to be. She was impressed by the speed with which Justin became so decidedly at one with the sound he was making; but almost as notable was the way Henry watched his older son, the way he looked at him as if he were hearing him play for the first time.

The bell rang again before Justin had finished the piece. As abruptly as he began, he stopped. "Ugh."

"That was exquisite, Justin," Costanza said. "From one of the partitas?"

"Number two and about a million miles from exquisite. Maybe I'll try again after dinner."

"You're too hard on yourself, Justin," Henry said as he headed toward the entry hall. "You always have been."

"My numero uno fan," Justin said.

Through the arched opening between the two rooms, Costanza

watched Henry open the door and then stand there, as though at attention.

The boys shuffled over to join their father. A minute later a gravelly voice could be heard saying firmly, "I prefer to do it on my own."

Do it meant walk into the apartment. On his own Leopold somewhat unsteadily came through the door and stopped to be kissed on his right cheek, first by Henry, then by Justin, then by Andrew.

Costanza saw him in profile first. The profile was bold, with a high forehead, a sharp nose that evoked Henry's, and a solid chin. Something about the shape of Leopold's head, or his bearing, or both, was regal, almost aquiline. It wouldn't have surprised Costanza to see a plume of feathers cascading down the back of the old man's skull. Instead he had hair; silver and abundant, neatly combed, parted, and tucked behind his ears.

Costanza didn't see Leopold's eyes until he had turned around to face her. By then he had been followed into the apartment by a refined-looking older woman with rich dark skin and hair through which, here and there, white strands twisted and turned: Lorna; "our godsend," Henry had called her.

Lorna, their godsend, was holding Leopold's cane. Once he had entered on his own, he was apparently willing to take it back. He pivoted toward the living room and looked Costanza over with icy dark eyes. "I am Leopold, and you are Costanza. I will be just a moment."

He stepped into the powder room and closed the door.

"He always washes his hands as soon as he arrives," Henry explained to Costanza. "It's left over from the camps."

"They were pestilential places," Costanza said.

Henry shook his head. "The water was filthy. It wasn't about cleanliness. It was about holding on to civilized habits."

Everyone stood waiting for Leopold, with his civilized habits, to wash his hands and emerge from the powder room.

When he reappeared, Leopold said to Henry, "You got deli?"

Henry nodded. "I got deli, Father. Yes."

"And my cream soda?"

Henry nodded again. "Would you like it now?"

"In a minute."

Leopold turned to Justin. "Your father says you have something to discuss with me."

Justin shot a dark glance at Henry.

"I thought it would be easier if I prepared him," Henry said.

Leopold said to Henry, "I think I'll have the soda now, after all. Maybe Lorna can help you unpack the dinner."

As soon as Henry and Lorna disappeared into the kitchen, Leopold said to Justin, "I'm not blind, you know. Two years you don't have a girlfriend—and look at you. They should be taking numbers." He looked around the apartment. "So where is he, this young gentleman?"

"He might stop by later. I think you'll like him. He's an excellent musician."

"What instrument?"

"Violin, like me. Some piano."

"You make music together then!"

Justin reddened.

"Well, I can't like someone I haven't met, now can I?" Leopold leaned forward on his cane. "In the building across the street from me in Warsaw there lived my friend Mendel, a dancer. A very good dancer. We sat in the first row at his recitals, I could see the perspiration flying off him like sparks." Leopold's fogged eyes looked off into the distance. "A *fagele* and a Jew. That was a bad combination in my time."

"This time could be considered your time too, Grandpa," Justin said.

"Possibly, but not by me." Leopold turned to Andrew, his face brightening. "And you, *boychik*, what news?"

"No news."

"I've decided which class you should take for your elective next semester."

"Let me guess. Twentieth-century history. The Second World War, maybe?"

"No. Fifteenth century. The Wars of the Roses." Then: "Of course twentieth-century history. What else?" Then: "Girls?"

Andrew shook his head.

"You're not a *fagele* too, are you?"

"I don't think so, Grandpa, but the way things are going . . ."

"Oh, come on now. The one with the glasses, the librarian—gone for good?"

"It seems so."

Leopold produced a sound. In English it might have been some-thing like *blech*; but it wasn't English.

"What about you, Grandpa?"

"What about what about me?"

"Any girls?"

"Ha." Then: "Go, both of you, help Lorna and your father," he said to the boys. "Make sure he puts out the mustard. He always forgets the mustard."

The boys obediently headed toward the kitchen. "Not Dijon—French's," Leopold called after them.

He turned to Costanza. "Funny, isn't it? Dijon is French, but French's is American. Let's sit."

She offered him her arm. Surprisingly he took it. When she looped his arm through hers, she found herself looking, as how could she not, at a patch of his forearm where the skin differed in color and texture from the rest.

Leopold noted her glance. "I was awake when they went on. And I was awake when they came off."

In the living room he indicated one of the easy chairs. Costanza walked him toward it. Before he sat down, he used the tip of his cane to whack the skirting, which was folded back over one corner, into place.

It was a simple chair, but Leopold sat on it as though it were a throne.

He pointed to the left end of the sofa. "This way you'll be on my good side." Then, appearing to understand that the sentence could be taken in more than one way, he clarified, "For my hearing."

It was not as though Costanza thought that getting on Leopold's good side was going to be quite that easy.

She sat down where he indicated. He focused his slate-colored eyes on her. He seemed to be reading her, her face and her body, more than looking at her. "You are not Jewish."

"No. I'm not."

"You're Italian."

"Half."

"Which half?"

She gave him the facts.

"But you're light."

"Yes."

"That's your natural hair color."

"Yes."

He looked her over once more. "No children?"

She shook her head.

"Do you want children?"

First the son, now the father. "I don't know. It depends." As the boys were still in the kitchen, she decided to add, "I might try."

"My son tries. Every day. He tries to replace what they took away." Leopold paused. "I know what you're thinking. He does not make Jewish babies alone. But a lot of them he makes. Thirty, forty percent. This is New York. Manhattan. He takes care of his people. And not just his people—twenty percent pro bono too. Women with no means also have a right to reproduce. No one knows about that. Henry is a good man. Responsible. He has helped all people and he has helped in particular his people. A *bisl*." He paused. "It means a 'little.'"

"*Yo, ikh vays.*"

"You speak Yiddish?"

"A *bisl*. My husband was Jewish. And anyway I translate. I pick up languages. Bits and pieces."

He gestured at the room. "Translate this."

"What do you mean?"

"What went on, in this house. Put it in plain English."

She shook her head. She wasn't following him.

"The wife, venomous. Sneaking around with another man under my son's nose, then bloodying him in a fight for the boys. Not how a Jewish woman should act. She broke him. Broke his spirit. Took the wedding china, the rugs, and the *tchotchkes* too. But not my dishes and silver, not my furniture. My furniture she did not touch."

He tapped against the chair with his cane. "So what do you make of it?"

The question was easy enough; it was the answering that was hard.

"I think it was very difficult. Very sad for everyone. She must have been very—unhappy. In herself."

"A translator and a diplomat too. They should pay you double."

She smiled.

"Of course my son comes up with you. Literate, a thinker—I can tell. Gentile, European, so different. Serene—on the outside. Inside, who knows. But clearly not like Her Whose Name Shall Not Be Spoken. The opposite. That is what men do, when they have been broken."

He waited.

"I don't know what to say to this, Leopold."

"Who asked for commentary? It is what it is."

Again, further, the icy eyes worked over her body, her face. She could almost feel them lowering the temperature of her skin.

"This husband of yours. What was his name?"

She told him.

"*The* Morton Sarnoff?"

"You've read him?"

"Who hasn't read Sarnoff? Bitter, sarcastic books. But also in places very funny. Delightful."

"Sometimes, yes."

"His shortcoming was his women. Too many frail waifs. In my personal experience, women are ten times stronger than men."

"But the last novel—"

"Was not his best, even if he put a woman—three women—at its center." Leopold smiled. "You didn't mark me as a reader."

Was something showing through on her face? "I didn't mark you at all. I'm simply getting to know you."

"We can exchange reading lists."

"I'd like that."

"Do you have a book club?"

She shook her head.

"I do. Me and seven ladies. At the synagogue. We meet Tuesday evenings in the Community Room. Some of them have big brains. They've spent entire lifetimes with their noses in books. Right now we're reading a new biography of Primo Levi."

"What do you think?"

"For me Primo Levi poses a problem. The books, especially the one he wrote after the war, the one no one wanted at first, they are more like the actual experience of being in the camps than anything else I have come across. But I will never read them again. I even put them back to front on my shelf. The man who wrote that sentence—I knew it by heart once, how does it go?—'The business of living is the best weapon we have against death'—no, the best *defense*, that's it—'the best defense against death'—in the end chose to close up shop. He himself chose death instead."

"Isn't it more correct to say that he *seemed* to choose death?" Costanza asked gently.

"Really? How did he end up at the bottom of that stairwell then? Why, afterward, did his wife say he'd done what he'd always said he'd do?"

Costanza thought for a moment. "No one knows for sure what happened that day. It's possible that he fell. He left no note. He'd been taking medicine that made him dizzy. From my reading of him, it just didn't seem—in character. It doesn't *feel* like a suicide."

Leopold gave her an inquisitive look, which she correctly interpreted. "My father," she said.

"I regret to hear that. How old were you?"

"Fourteen."

"Even more regrettable." He paused. "And what about your husband?"

"Cancer."

"Like my wife."

"I'm sorry." He put a small silence, a bracket, around that exchange; then he was off again. "Now you are available. Do you love my son?"

"We haven't known each other very long."

"What does time have to do with it, my dear? It's gut. Gut and gonads."

"If those are the measures, then, yes, I do love your son. I haven't felt this much—this much hope in years."

"You wouldn't say this to humor an old man."

"No."

"Love." Leopold's eyes lit up. "Ha!"

Costanza found it difficult to work out whether Leopold was a little bit, or more than a little bit, off or whether his curious directness was a result of what he had lived and survived or whether age might have unleashed in him, as it sometimes did in the old, a frankness that would have seemed rude or confounding in a younger person. Obviously she did not know him well enough, after just half an hour, to decide—and why did she need to? She didn't need to understand him to feel for him, to feel for his life, his lucky, fierce endurance. That, all that, was enough for the moment.

Over dinner Leopold asked Henry a number of questions about his practice. He was interested, in particular, in what he kept calling "the figures": how many women were cycling, how many had recently had a positive pregnancy test, how many were carrying multiples. He especially liked the multiples. *"Gut, gut."*

Henry and Lorna had arranged the cold cuts on a platter and served them alongside rye bread, pickles, onions, sliced tomatoes, coleslaw, and mustard (the American French's). Henry, Lorna, and the boys made themselves thick sandwiches; Leopold, like Costanza, ate his pastrami with a knife and a fork.

"We two are the Europeans at the table," Leopold said gaily, tossing a nod in Costanza's direction. "These Americans . . ."

"Grandpa," said Justin. "Lorna is from Jamaica. The last time I looked at a map, Jamaica was not part of America."

"Thank you for the geography lesson, Justin."

"And what's wrong with a sandwich anyway?" Justin added sourly. Ever since Leopold had used the word *fagele*, a scowl had stamped itself on Justin's face and had shown no sign of lifting.

"Did I say something was *wrong* with a sandwich? I simply said that this young lady and I have a different style at the table."

"But you implied—"

"I hear that the French eat their ice cream with a fork," Lorna piped up cheerfully. "Can you imagine?"

"I never noticed that," said Justin. "We were in France last year."

"Did we eat ice cream?" asked Andrew.

"Of course we ate ice cream," Henry said. "At Berthillon. I had *framboise.*"

"That's raspberry," Lorna said. "*Fraise* is strawberry and *citron* is lemon."

"We tacky Americans," said Justin. "We didn't use a fork, did we?"

"Very likely there was a spoon involved," said Henry.

A silence fell over the table as everyone dug into their ice cream. Henry was looking at Lorna, thinking . . .

"Why all this interest in things French, Lorna, if I may ask?" he said after a moment.

"Well"—Lorna smiled—"I'm going on an extended visit to Paris."

Henry turned to Leopold. "Please don't tell me you fired her. Please, Father."

"In fact, Lorna's position with me has been terminated, effective last week."

"I begged you, Leopold." *Leopold* was for when Henry was exasperated. "And you promised me."

Leopold reached over and put his hand on Lorna's. "Lorna and I would like to announce to you all that we . . . are a we."

Henry swallowed his breath. "You are a we. With Lorna."

To the table Leopold said, "He still has his hearing. That's good. He won't end up like me." He paused. "I don't want to know what you feel if it's anything other than happy. Nina has been dead for eight years. Lorna has had no husband for nearly twelve. We are discussing the possibility of her converting, but if she doesn't, that's her business. I will not leave her all of my money, if you need to know that."

"I'm not interested in your money," said Henry. "And, Father, I *am* happy for you. I'm just—surprised."

"You're not the only one," said Lorna. "I've done this work for forty years. I've never before had feelings for anyone the way I do for Leopold."

"Boys," said Leopold. "Have you nothing to say?"

"*Félicitations?*" Andrew said, with a discernible question mark in his voice.

Justin asked more ambiguously, "When do you leave?"

"We travel Wednesday night," answered Leopold. "By Thursday we'll be having ice cream on the rue de Rivoli."

"And we'll be eating it," Lorna said, beaming, "with our forks."

⇌

On Monday morning, the day after Justin returned to college and the day before Andrew was to begin his senior year in high school, he woke to the sound of something shattering. He slowly hauled himself out of bed and into the living room, where Costanza was sweeping up the shards of

a yellow ceramic lamp. The room was entirely unmade. Chairs and tables
had been moved to the periphery. So had the sofa. Leaning against it was
the apparent culprit: a large rug, rolled up and tied with rope.

"It didn't look particularly valuable. I hope your father won't
mind . . ."

Andrew stepped over to the rug and peeled back one corner.

"What do you think?"

"It's okay. It's just—" He looked around the room. "It's just that it's
been like this ever since my mother left."

"She made a new home for herself, didn't she?" Costanza said logically. "And for you boys."

They stood together in silence, each seeing the room through different eyes.

"So will you give me a hand?" she asked as she finished sweeping.

What Costanza said made sense, but still it felt as if she were tres-
passing on a place, or a time, that was objectively no longer relevant but
seemed surprisingly important, to him.

She picked up one end of the rug. When he hesitated, she put it
down again. "It's all right. I can wait for your father."

"No, it's okay."

Together they wrestled the rug into place. Then they shifted some
of the furniture around on top of it, in an arrangement Costanza pro-
posed that was different from the one there before.

"Well?"

Andrew shrugged. "Not bad. I have to admit."

Costanza put her hands on her hips and assessed. "This always happens when you bring in a new piece."

"What always happens?"

"It shows you everything else that needs doing."

At the other end of the day Henry looked in on Andrew, who was again
deep into the work of sorting through his photographs.

"I understand you helped Costanza lay down our new rug this
morning."

Andrew nodded but didn't say anything.

"I didn't know you cared so much about interior décor."

"I care about change. At least I thought I did."

Andrew's bed was covered with nearly as many photographs as the desk and the floor. Henry shifted several aside without looking at them. He sat down and rested his palms on his knees. "I might as well just say what's on my mind. I've been wondering what you would think about spending some more time at your mother's."

Andrew moved a photograph from one stack to another without looking at his father.

"I don't expect you to be able to understand this, Andrew, but starting a new relationship when you're my age—and Costanza's—isn't so easy. It can help to create a . . . little air around things, that's all."

"I take up so much of it?"

"It's not that *exactly* . . ."

Andrew turned to face his father now and crossed his arms in front of his chest. "All those years you spent battling Mom about sharing us fifty-fifty, down to the last day, the last *hour* sometimes. The time you made us go in—do you remember?—to talk to the judge ourselves, to tell him how much *we* wanted to have equal time with both of you?" Andrew gestured at his neck. "I was just a kid. I had to put on a tie. I hate ties."

"It would just be for a month or two, until things fall into place here. You'd still have one set night and alternating weekends. And of course you could always come back here if things on the West Side became complicated."

"Things on the West Side are always complicated."

"Consider it a special favor to me, will you, Andrew? Please?"

The next day, Costanza brought another suitcase and a box of books to Henry's apartment and arranged to have the rest of her things from Morton's moved downtown. After she returned from doing her food shopping later that evening, she glanced into Andrew's room, where she saw at once that he had organized and filed away his piles of photographs. He had sorted through all his books too and arranged them neatly, with all their spines lined up at the edge of the shelves. He had tidied his desk and made his bed. He had even emptied his wastepaper basket.

As she was moving in he appeared to be moving, or thinning, out. But why?

Only a single photograph remained on the bulletin board, one Costanza had not seen before. Andrew had taken a picture of her from behind as she left him that day in Florence after they had gone to the Mercato Centrale. She was wearing a white linen dress, which she later stained with wine and abandoned at her mother's. Receding into the crowd, she looked like a shadow, a white shadow, of herself.

She leaned against Andrew's desk and studied the picture.

Henry found her there several minutes later. He stood beside her and followed her gaze to the bulletin board.

"It's from the first day we met," Costanza said.

Henry nodded.

"We'd gone to buy mushrooms."

They both examined the photograph in silence.

"It almost feels like Andrew has moved out." Costanza turned to Henry. "Why would he do that?"

"Did he say anything to you?" Henry asked evasively.

She shook her head.

"My understanding is that he's going to be spending a little more time at Judith's."

"Why all of a sudden?"

"Well, he's got all his applications to tackle, and Judith has the time to help him with them. He's also got extra swim practice, since his meets are coming up, and her apartment is closer to the pool . . ."

Henry's explanation had an overly logical quality that wasn't quite convincing.

"It's not because of me, is it?"

"Andrew wants you to feel comfortable here as much as I do."

That sounded less convincing still; but what was she to do? She couldn't simply drop into a family and understand overnight how it worked. Or over several nights, or months, or years even.

Henry distracted her by kissing her on the back of her neck. She closed her eyes.

⇌

Their conversations went on for hours, often deep into the night. Over and over she asked him a variation on the same question: How could two people who knew each other for such a brief time decide to have a baby together, just like that? Because time isn't as important as tim*ing*, Henry kept saying. Because there are some situations in life where you have to follow your heart. Because, in trying to make a baby together, we will come to know each other well, to see each other clearly.

But what if we don't like what we see?

"Quite honestly the possibility doesn't even occur to me," he said.

Allowing the idea of having a baby to rise up in her again made Costanza feel like someone who had been traumatized, a survivor of a car accident who moved tentatively and vulnerably through space. Space and time. She felt fragile, uncertain, wary. But her wariness had gaps. Gaps that let in air, light. Gradually the accumulated normality of her days and nights with Henry began to have an effect. They made room for different sorts of feelings to surface. She allowed herself to taste, just taste, a bit of her old yearning. She allowed herself to think *what if*.

Once she opened herself to the yearning, it returned, spilling, then gushing, into an old channel that appeared to have been waiting all along to receive it.

She woke up one morning feeling deeply rested, the way she felt after having had a fever or a flu. Everything seemed put back, put right. And clear. Beautifully clear. She showered and washed her hair, then she threw away the birth control pills she had begun taking soon after she moved into Henry's apartment. After sitting at her desk and working for several hours, she went out and bought a kit to track her ovulation. That night, when she told Henry what she had done, he opened a bottle of champagne.

For two months Costanza and Henry tried to conceive a baby together. In the days leading up to Costanza's ovulation they made love every night. Henry came to know her body's calendar better than she did. In bed he was giving. He was not always passionate, but who would be under the circumstances? He never flagged or hesitated, and he never failed. He did not have a stitch of Morton's ambiguity or tortured ambivalence. He was so clear about what he wanted and what he hoped for that at moments Costanza wondered whether this quest was somehow more about Henry, Henry and Judith, Henry and the boys, Henry and Leopold maybe, or Henry and the world—showing the world that he could start his life over. She decided that if this was, in part, what was driving him, it was okay. At least his need of her and her need of him dovetailed, and in a way that might well lead to a new life. A baby; their baby.

When Costanza's period started, Henry seemed unsurprised, almost disengaged: "It's as expected. We're simply falling in with the statistics." Later: "It's as I thought." And: "You know what I think. You should come in and let me see what we can do."

Nevertheless after the second month she failed to become pregnant, Costanza couldn't quite bring herself to go into Henry's office. She asked Henry if they could continue to try for another two months on their own, and he showed his impatience with her for the first time. "When you turn forty, the numbers are more steeply against you. It seems like an arbitrary thing, just another birthday, and it's true that not every woman's ovarian reserve drops at the same moment, but still, statistically speaking, once you cross that line, you start off in a far more challenging reproductive field."

It didn't help that he was already talking to her as though she were a patient.

"What if we try for just one more month? I think I'll be ready after another month. I hope I'll be ready."

"What makes you say that?"

"I don't know, Henry. It's just a feeling I have."

"Thinking, hoping, feeling. None of this is very scientific."

A few days after her period began in that second month Costanza opened the Sunday *Times* and, as often, turned first to the *Book Review*. There, on the cover, was Morton staring out from the Avedon photograph, staring—she immediately felt—at her. The merciless focus, the plain white background: Sarnoff (she could not think of him as Morton in this context), battered. Sarnoff, lined and liver-spotted. Sarnoff with those sly piercing eyes. She'd seen the picture a hundred times, but on the hundred and first it still made her jump.

She read the headline: "Sarnoff's Secret."

Sarnoff's *what?* And published *already?* That could only mean that the project had been well underway by the time Howard sent it to her in Florence, or else (or in addition) that it had been hurried into print.

> From what we've known up to now about the elusive writer Morton Sarnoff, he would seem the least likely author of one of the most personally revealing diaries to be published in recent years, but Sarnoff's intimacies are just one among many surprises to be found in the aptly titled "Last Words: Diaries, 2007–2013," which has been edited down from the nearly five hundred (manuscript) pages found among the writer's papers by his brother, Howard, and Ivan Ellison, a poet who worked as Sarnoff's personal assistant in the last years of his life.
>
>   It is nearly impossible to have followed the unfolding story of late twentieth-century American letters without being aware of Sarnoff's famous reclusiveness—

Yes, yes, Costanza thought. *All that again.* With a thumping heart she hurried ahead:

> —but as any close reader of Sarnoff's fiction knows, in even the most circumscribed lives there are always revelations or denouements—

Why not just come out and say it? Because that wasn't the reviewer's mandate, was why.

> Along with Sarnoff's dying—and I will return to those anguished, meticulously anatomized entries in a moment—the writer's courtship of, marriage to, and separation from the translator Costanza Ansaldo provide the greatest suspense and drama in "Last Words." They are also the source of the diary's deepest heartache and—eventually—biggest dilemma: Should the writer, in his sixties and convinced he is in declining health, commit to bringing new life into the world?

Costanza's heart tightened as she skipped ahead one more time:

> While it's true there are qualities in all the best diarists that
> make us cringe—Pepys's blithe infidelities and Virginia Woolf's
> barbed cruelty and anti-Semitism are two examples that leap
> to mind—we do not read a diary as we do a novel. We read a
> diary to know the inner life of a man who, because of his work,
> accomplishments, or personal story, makes us curious to know
> his most private thoughts.
>
> As a reviewer, I've debated whether to lay out what "Last
> Words" helps us to see about Morton Sarnoff, but as this par-
> ticular information is now on the page and soon, doubtless,
> will be disseminated in the press, I've decided to report that I
> was surprised, as many readers are also likely to be, to learn
> that Sarnoff, for all his tortured deliberation about parenting,
> was already a father—to a child he chose not to own.
>
> And so here it is: Sarnoff's secret. He confesses it to his di-
> ary one evening soon after he and Ms. Ansaldo separate, when
> he opens a bottle of bourbon and in rushed staccato prose tells
> the story of the affair he had with his longtime Guatemalan
> housekeeper in Columbia County; pseudonymously named
> here Maria Hernandez, she gave birth to a baby boy just before
> Sarnoff published "The Life to Come" and returned (one might
> now posit, fled) to Manhattan. Sarnoff never even saw the child,
> though in exchange for this woman's silence, he provided . . .

Here Costanza stopped reading. She could no longer see the print
through the blur of her raging sobs.

Columbia County in winter was a bleak place. The skeletal trees, the
brown fields wearing a thin crust of blue-tinged frost, the clouds hanging low overhead: everything about it struck Costanza as leaden and
dull. She preferred an open sweep of sky or water—water most of all.
This landlocked countryside was where Morton had exiled himself for
nearly twenty years: crumbling farms, roadside diners, gas stations and
beauty salons and tattoo parlors. How did he not find it all insuperably

grim? She tried to imagine it all under a warming sun, a blue sky . . .
cows nibbling in green fields . . . birdsong. Maybe in summer, yes, it
was bearable, but there would still be those low confining hills, that
long belt of highway laid down among them like a gash.

An endless unfurling landscape for a man with a life—an afterlife—
that didn't seem to end: looked at that way, he belonged. If elusive
Morton Sarnoff belonged anywhere—and she wasn't sure that he did—
he belonged to his fiction, to his words. His words with their secrets, his
words with their ability to send out one last lash from beyond the grave.

And his actions? A sharper lash still. A lash, a kick. In her stomach—
her womb. Yes, her womb.

The missing piece of information clarified so much. Its simplicity
had a certain beauty. She and Morton had tried to conceive for a year
and a half, and failed. He and his housekeeper had a baby together after
a "brief" affair. Now she had tried with Henry, already a proven father,
and she had failed with him too. What that added up to, for Costanza,
was a problem. Her problem. And she was going to deal with it head-
on. She was going to tell Henry that she wanted to come to his clinic
for treatment, and as soon as possible.

But she had to do one thing first.

Ivan had moved to Brooklyn, Cobble Hill. He sent her a change-of-
address card, printed and impersonal, which she had tucked into her
phone book. He lived on the third floor of a medium-size brown brick
apartment house off a commercial street. She waited outside for twenty
minutes, until a neighbor arrived, then she slipped in behind her and
made her way upstairs. She didn't want to risk buzzing and being
turned away without seeing him, face-to-face.

As she raised her hand to knock on the door, she had a vision of
herself from behind—standing there, her dirty hair tucked under a hat
of Henry's she'd grabbed from the closet, a short jacket thrown over a
long sweater, her shoulders, her whole body, tautly curled in on itself. It
wasn't a pretty picture.

Ivan didn't seem that surprised to see her. Even though he wasn't
wearing one of his trademark gray suits, he still gave her a little bow,
ever the majordomo, and asked her in. The neat, clipped way he stood

aside as she walked by was enough to remind her how relieved she was not to have him in her life any longer.

The apartment was pristine. In the background a table was set for dinner—for one, Costanza thought, until she stepped farther into the room and saw that another place was set, with a person sitting at it, a small whippet of a man who looked oddly like Ivan. Somehow that made sense, another piece falling into place.

"Kevin, would you give us a moment," Ivan said to the man at the table.

"Of course."

After he left the room Ivan said, "My brother comes to dinner once a week."

So much for pieces falling into place.

"I have a feeling I know why you're here," Ivan said. "It's about Ricardo, isn't it?"

Ivan said the boy's real name in such a familiar way that it made Costanza flush.

"Yes."

He blinked at her. "You never liked me much, did you, Mrs. Sarnoff?"

Before she could reply he added, "Answer truthfully."

"No, Ivan. Not so much."

Who smiled at an answer like that? Ivan did. That was who.

"Ricardo means powerful and brave ruler. Mr. Sarnoff liked the name. We looked it up together. 'May he be all of those things,' he said when I told him what it meant."

She refrained from saying, much as she would have liked to, *Save it for his Boswell.*

"He had nothing to do with choosing the name, in case you wanted to know."

Costanza nodded. "Is it true that Morton never met . . . Ricardo?"

"He preferred not to."

"He preferred not to see his own son."

How she loathed having to come to this man for information about her husband.

"He saw photographs. Several, over the years."

The *years.* She tried to imagine how Ivan filed away those photographs and the letters, because surely letters accompanied them, among Morton's compendious papers. Under "Sarnoff: son"? "Sarnoff: bastard"? "Secrets Morton Sarnoff Is Keeping from His Wife Who Yearns to Have a Child of Her Own"?

"Ricardo knows nothing about his father. That was part of the agreement. Obviously the names in the published version of the diaries have been changed."

"Obviously."

Costanza had not even thought to buy a copy. Would she ever? She wasn't sure. She was so *through* with Morton Sarnoff. Except for this last—what?—coda. This last image. She had to have the image of the boy's face. She had to see him for herself.

Ivan went over to his bookshelves and took down a book: *The Life to Come.* "Mr. Sarnoff inscribed this to me after I'd been working for him for a month. I asked him to. It was my own copy. That's why it's so beat-up. I used to take it everywhere with me."

He opened the book and read, "'For Ivan Ellison, at the beginning of what is sure to be a memorable relationship.'"

Then he flipped through the pages and extracted a tiny sheet of paper. He looked down at it for a moment.

"You know how Mr. Sarnoff liked to say that he never read the reviews of his own books? Well, that wasn't quite true. There was one he mentioned to me often. The reviewer—a woman, a novelist herself—said that, insightful though he was about human nature, and accurately though he wrote about all kinds of people, Mr. Sarnoff had one great shortcoming. Having never been a father, he did not portray parental love very convincingly. Mr. Sarnoff was troubled by that. I think it, more than anything else, drove him to write the last novel. 'A writer must be a shape-shifter, Ivan,' he used to say to me. 'He must be able to become *any*one, he must be able to feel *any*thing . . .'"

Ivan unfolded the paper. "It wasn't my place to disagree with Mr. Sarnoff while he was alive. But I did have my own—take. Yes, that's it. My own take. On things. My own ideas about what was right and what wasn't. I grew up—well, let's just say, I grew up, Kevin and I both did, in an unhappy situation. And I think that when people have children, they should really *want* them. Be interested in them. Otherwise they are burdened . . . well, they *are* burdened. Let's leave it at that."

Again he looked down at the paper. "Of course I knew what you two were trying to do, hoping to do. There was very little I *didn't* know really. I have to say this was the one time I was disappointed in Mr. Sarnoff. I felt it wasn't fair to—"

He hesitated. "When I imagined saying this to you one day, it didn't come out so tangled up."

He handed her the paper. On it was a name and an address in Hudson, New York.

Costanza looked at the piece of paper for a moment. "Thank you, Ivan. I don't know—"

He put up a long thin hand. "Don't say anything, please. And whatever you do, please don't start liking me. Not now."

⇉

At least Hudson, the town, had water, a stripe of river at the far end of the main street, beyond a steep embankment: the Hudson itself, gray, slow-moving, but moving nevertheless. A few boats bobbed sleepily midriver. And ducks—not many—floated by.

She had gone to seek out the river first, just to get her bearings. The town must once have turned all of its attention riverward; now it turned in on itself, on its shops. They weren't what she expected, row upon row of storefronts displaying expensive antiques, gleaming, gracious objects. There were art galleries and jewelry stores too, and restaurants that looked as if they had been transplanted from Tribeca or the Village.

That was the main street. But the address Ivan had given her was on a street two blocks north, an entirely different world. The spruced-up storefronts were replaced by bedraggled houses with sagging porches and flaking paint. Even the pavement was made of a different, more faded asphalt. Instead of French fauteuils there were bodegas with neon signs pushing lottery tickets and beer.

The house she was looking for stood a distance away from the river end of town. The small attached wood-frame building, like the others nearby, was in disrepair. But at least it was tidy. The garden hedge was trimmed if dormant. On the porch a pair of plastic chairs were drawn up to a small round table. The table and chairs struck Costanza as a hopeful sign, a sign that, in summer anyway, people sat and ate there,

or visited there, or from there sat and watched the boy—Ricardo—play
in the yard.

She remained in her rental car and surveyed the scene. The street
was quiet. A garbage truck rolled by but did not stop to pick up any garbage. A woman two houses down came outside to collect her mail.

As she sat in the car, Costanza thought about the last chapter of
Morton's life, which looked very different to her now that she had this
new piece of information about him. She thought in particular about
the afternoon about four months into their separation, when her
Swedish translator friend Annelie found her paralyzed in bed in her
apartment and surmised that she had been lying there for days. Annelie
had her own set of keys because she had been using the place as an
occasional office ever since Costanza had moved in with Morton, and
when Costanza failed to show up for their yoga class, Annelie showed
up at Costanza's place instead.

"You must never let a man do this to you," Annelie said in that firm
Swedish way of hers. Then she pretty much hoisted Costanza out of bed
and threw her into the shower.

Annelie, Costanza knew, was no fan of Morton's. "He reeks of ego,"
she said of him soon after they first met. "He gives you the feeling he's
always stripping you in his mind. Not like other men, because he wants
you physically, but because he wants to use you. Your story."

Sitting at her small table, where Annelie had somehow made a sandwich materialize out of the bare cupboards, Costanza said, "You don't
know what it's like to try to conceive a child, the pressure it puts on
your intimate life . . ."

"Having trouble screwing on schedule doesn't justify summarily
ending a marriage. Not even if you're the great Sarnoff."

"You haven't lived through what I have, Annelie."

"Which means what, exactly, in this context?"

Costanza remembered almost to the word what she had said to
Annelie because she had said it, thought it, several times to herself
before—and since: "I believe it's because of my father, because of what
happened. When I let myself become interested in a man, the regular
checklist isn't so meaningful to me. I don't feel I have to look for this or
that quality in a companion. He can be married. Older. Younger. Difficult. 'Unsuitable.' None of it matters. When the father you grow up

loving can extinguish all that love just like that, what do you have to gain by being cautious or careful? Nothing."

"If all this is true," Annelie said when she had finished, "then why did I find you nearly catatonic in bed this morning?"

This question wasn't as easy for Costanza to answer. "My reasoning doesn't make me *happy*. And besides, I'm tired. Deeply tired."

"Quite honestly, this doesn't look like fatigue to me."

"What does it look like?"

Annelie merely gave Costanza a look. The look had such heart in it, and such concern, that tears flooded into Costanza's eyes.

Annelie took Costanza into her arms. "Sadness is good, but personally I think anger would serve you better."

Anger: Where had it gone, what had she done with it? Costanza had buried it. That's what she'd done. She'd buried it when Morton suggested they move from separation to divorce. She'd buried it when he encouraged her to make a plan to return to Italy for a while. She'd buried it when, after Morton called to tell her that he had been diagnosed with pancreatic cancer, she unmade that plan. And she buried it when, at his request, she'd moved back in to see him through to the end.

She had not thought long or hard about the decision: that too was part of dispensing with the regular checklist. She saw him through because it was the right thing to do and because, despite everything, she still loved him. When near the end he said to her, "I made a terrible mistake, I wish we'd tried harder to make a baby together," she let him say it. She even let him believe it was still possible, and with great effort, they made love for the first time in a long time, and the last. Afterward in a quiet and sadly confused voice he said, "Did I come? I couldn't even tell." "You came," she lied. He asked what day it was in her cycle, and she said, "It's day thirteen. I expect to ovulate at any moment."

It was in fact only day five. But these words appeared to bring him some peace.

Three weeks later he died.

He died with his secret intact and unshared. He'd died without telling her that he knew he could conceive a child, which meant that possibly—probably—the issue was at her end. He died as selfishly as he had lived.

•

After forty-five minutes the front door opened. A seven-year-old boy in a red hooded parka stepped out onto the porch. He was holding a soccer ball. He bounced the ball down the steps alongside him. The ball beat him into the yard and skidded across the patch of wintry lawn. The boy followed the ball and began kicking it and chasing it around.

Now and then he looked back over his shoulder to see if anyone was standing in the open doorway, watching him. No one was.

Costanza had not thought about what she would do if he never came outside or wasn't home. Sit there all day, all night? Very possibly.

But there he was, and there she was, slowly getting out of the car. When she exhaled, her breath marked the air with thin white plumes that quickly disappeared. Her heart was racing. She had a bag with her—not candy, though she had thought of that, but apples. She had stopped at a roadside stand outside town, where at this time of year they sold only jars of jam, some tired-looking cabbage and potatoes, and apples. At the moment it had felt like a charming idea; now as she carried the bag, she could only think of the poisoned apples in fairy tales, fruit delivered by murderous stepmothers. A stepmother—though not murderous—is technically what she would have been to this little boy, if everything had been . . . everything it wasn't.

There was something else about fairy tales. They were full of barren couples, or couples who had to wait years and years to have a child, who, as soon as she—almost always she—was born, was menaced or stolen or was expected to be handed over to a resentful harridan or a fiendish old man who had some kind of hideous leverage over the new parents. This thought occurred to Costanza, then vanished like one of her breath plumes.

She approached the fence, she and her witch's offering.

The boy, Ricardo, took a break from his kicking to scratch his right ear. Morton used to do that, when he was writing. He always scratched his right ear too. It made her heart stop: a gesture so characteristic of that difficult, self-enclosed, maddening man, reproduced so precisely in miniature in this child. His child.

She looked at the child who had come from Morton Sarnoff, a child like, and utterly unlike, the one he would not allow her to go the distance to try to conceive. Wasn't it enough, merely to have seen him? What was she going to say to him, anyway?

She lingered at the fence for another moment, then started to walk back toward the car. She hung the bag of apples off one of the fence posts: an offering, or trash. Either way, a mystery.

At dinner that evening she told Henry about her day and she told him that she had decided: she was ready to come in for treatment now. He listened closely, then said, "Part of me hates Sarnoff for keeping this secret from you, and part of me wants to thank him for his inadvertent help." He pushed himself back from the table. "Though . . . though if I'm going to be totally honest, Costanza, I guess I wish you could have come to this on your own, without needing this—this push, this prod or whatever from the past."

Or whatever? It was hardly that, far from that, to *her*, but she had no idea how she was to convey, to someone who had not experienced it, what it felt like to have lived with Morton, to have tried for more than a year to conceive a baby with a man who knew that he was fertile but withheld that knowledge from her, and therefore consigned her, however unintentionally (but was it unintentional? Was it not, despite that moment when he was dying, the great egoist's last great act of egoism?), to a period of sustained doubt and anguish about what her body could, or more accurately couldn't, do. The anguish part Henry could no doubt understand, since he was faced with it, as he himself had told her, nearly every day at work, but the deception was altogether different.

"I'm sorry," she said, "but I needed clarity—more clarity. And now I have it."

"And I'm glad that you do."

"So? Where do we begin?"

"You make an appointment to come in—well, I make an appointment for you."

"I can do it myself. As far as possible, I would like to be treated like anyone else."

"Anyone else," Henry said dryly, "would have to wait three months to see me for the first time."

"I'm going to see *you*?" Costanza fought, and failed, to keep the emphasis off that one word.

"Well, if not me, who then? I mean, if you want the best treatment, the best eyes on the situation . . . ?"

The situation. "Yes, but . . . but would you treat your own sister?"

"I wouldn't be trying to conceive a baby with my sister, now would I?"

"You know what I mean. Don't physicians, typically, refuse to turn family members—and close friends—or girlfriends—into patients?"

"Typically, yes. But fertility is not typical medicine."

Costanza took this information in and tucked it away for further review. "There's something else. I'd prefer it if nobody in your office knew about us."

"But why?"

"I don't want the eyes of the world, your world, on me. It's going to be hard enough for me as it is."

Henry considered for a moment. "We can arrange that, if you insist."

"I do."

⌐

On one matter at least Costanza capitulated and let Henry set up the appointment, which he did, for eight o'clock on the following Monday morning. She had no way of knowing how unusual it was to have an initial evaluation with Dr. Henry Weissman at that hour. Mornings were when he saw cycling patients, not new ones. The fact that Henry had had her slotted into the morning schedule set Costanza apart—but in a way that, at least for the moment, would be evident to only a few members of his staff.

At eight o'clock in the morning Henry's waiting room was packed almost to the last seat. Costanza had to stand in a line, a long line, before she could check in. Afterward she was given an eight-page questionnaire to fill out.

When she finally sat down, Costanza surveyed the room. Most of these women were on one side or the other of forty, as she was. Nearly all of them had buried themselves in reading material or in their devices, thirty—more—self-contained islands on a sea of muted, deliberately soothing gray-green carpet. Judging from their clothes, they appeared to be largely professional, or in any event sufficiently well-off to afford the cost of infertility treatment. These women were used to being in charge of their lives, or being under the illusion that they were in charge, but in Henry's waiting room, in Henry's clinic, they had come to a place where both that fact and that illusion were taken away, completely. It was like sitting in a hall of mirrors: these women didn't look up because they were afraid of seeing their yearning, also maybe their fear, reflected back at them. It was much easier simply not to engage.

Costanza didn't see herself belonging to this sisterhood—and yet here she was. A series of bad, or unconscious, or half-conscious decisions brought her here, though they didn't always feel like decisions in the moment so much as life unfolding, life carrying her on its current, away from her father's death, away from her mother's tentacles, away from Genoa, away (eventually) from Italy itself. So many things made more sense to her now, looking back. It made sense that, losing her father at fourteen, and losing him the way she had, she would be drawn to older men (Stefano, Morton . . . Henry, though of all of them he was closest in age, at fifty-five, to her). It made sense that, for years, she poured herself into her work, protected herself with her work, so that she wouldn't have to test (or expose, or risk) herself in other areas of her life. Convincing herself for years that she didn't want to have a child even made sense, a certain sense, until all of a sudden it didn't.

Costanza wondered if all these other women in the waiting room had gotten themselves as wrong as she had gotten herself. What if, instead of reading, or texting, or hiding behind their earphones, they all started speaking, what a conversation that would be, what a chorus of regret and anguish! And anger, probably that too. And heartache. Not a chorus; an opera.

She turned her attention to the forms. The first questions she answered easily. She had had none of the illnesses listed. Heart, lungs, kidneys, liver, bladder—all fine. Medicines: vitamins, aspirin for headaches, sleeping pills for the worst insomniac nights. She had never had surgery, unless you counted wisdom teeth. Her menstrual cycle was regular. She moved on to her family history. Her mother had a variety of age-appropriate ailments; Costanza named them as best she could. Maria Rosaria had been fertile, yes, and had in fact had Costanza when in her late thirties, which was considered a seriously advanced age at that time.

The next questions concerned her father. They were easier to answer

than those concerning her mother, since he had been physically robust
until he died, and nowhere was she asked about his mental health. As
such forms tended to, however, it did ask if he was alive or, if dead, at
what age he had died and of what cause. Generally when Costanza came
upon this question she would write *car accident* or *plane crash*—people
didn't often ask follow-up questions when you said that your father died in
a gruesome way. For some reason, however, on Henry's form, in Henry's
clinic, her first impulse was to write down the truth: that one searing
word. *Suicide. Suicidio.* It was no more palatable in Italian. She got as far
as the *s*, then stopped. She thought of several reasons it might not be prudent to tell the truth. What if she went ahead with the in vitro treatment
and took the drugs that, she knew from her reading on the subject, might
color her emotions and moods? If she reacted strongly, might people
(Henry's colleagues, Henry himself) think that it was her father coming
out in her, a genetic instability, instead of the drugs? Might they adjust
them downward as a consequence or offer her lesser alternatives that
would reduce her chance of becoming pregnant?

Swimming *accident*, she wrote. He had been swimming off the
Punta with his eyes closed, plowing ahead, unaware that he was on a
collision course with one of those jagged, just-submerged rocks. He hit
the rock, and the impact knocked him out instantly. Or maybe—more
plausibly—he had swum out too far and a fishing boat had sped by and
failed to see him skimming along the surface of the water. That had
happened to a woman from Milan three or four summers back. Her
body parts washed up as far north as Sori.

"Costanza Ansaldo?"

Costanza had not noticed the nurse. Tall, and with short silver hair,
she had approached from a hallway on the left. "The doctor is ready to
see you now."

Henry was standing behind the desk, his shirt and well-knotted tie
covered by a crisp white jacket. "Ms. Ansaldo, I'm Dr. Weissman.
Won't you sit down?"

She sat. Henry sat. Susan, the nurse, sat in the subordinate's chair
to his right. They both uncapped their pens at the same time.

"What brings you in to see us today?"

It was she, after all, who had asked him not to tell anyone about their connection. She hadn't imagined he'd be able to act so credibly.

"I suppose I want some information. I want to explore how I—how I—"

"Might become a mother."

She nodded. "Yes." She hastily added, "My—my partner, he is—at a work conference this week. He regrets not being able to be here. Deeply."

So she could act too.

He nodded. "Today is about figuring out how best to proceed. Costanza—may I call you Costanza?"

"If I may call you Henry."

"Of course." Indicating with his head, he said, "Susan is my oldest nurse. I mean the nurse of the longest standing here."

"Oldest on both counts," Susan said, without looking up from her notepad.

"We go back to the beginning of my practice, just about. She'll stay with us while we talk now, and afterward, during our exam."

"You're going to *examine* me?"

She must have put too much vocal stress on that *examine*, the way she did on that *you* when Henry first brought up the subject, because a wrinkle appeared in Susan's forehead.

"Well, yes, of course."

Costanza sat back in her chair, a gesture of submission.

"Tell me how long you've been trying to become pregnant."

"In my current . . . relationship, a few months. With my late husband, much longer."

"How long exactly?"

"A year . . . more. There were months we may have mistimed."

"You tracked your ovulation."

"By temperature at the beginning. Then with the kits."

"Which one did you use?"

She told him. He made a note.

"Was your husband ever checked out? For his sperm count? Motility, morphology?"

"My husband, my late husband, fathered a child when he was in his fifties." She flashed on the moment when she'd showed Henry the review of Morton's book and had burst into tears. "I—I have come to believe that the problem lies with me."

"Why do you say that?"

"My present—partner, he also has fathered a child. Two children."

Did Nurse Susan's forehead wrinkle again, or was that Costanza's imagination?

"But you say you have only been trying for a few months."

She nodded.

"At thirty-nine, do you know how long, on average, it takes a woman to conceive naturally?"

She shook her head.

"Between a year and a year and a half. So until we examine you and run some basic tests, I wouldn't leap to any conclusions. I would assume, in fact, that it's merely your age. We can help with that."

"You can make me younger?" she said wryly.

"In a manner of speaking—yes." Then: "When are you expecting your next period?"

"Wednesday. Possibly Thursday."

"Your cycle is consistent?"

"Twenty-eight, sometimes twenty-nine days. It's in the questionnaire."

"I like to ask for myself." Henry made another note.

Unless they found something out of the ordinary through tests and on physical exam, he explained, on the third day of her next period, with the "day" beginning anytime before midnight, she would come into the office for blood work. The results would give them her random day-three levels for FSH, or follicle stimulating hormone; LH, or luteinizing hormone; and estradiol, or estrogen. They were looking for figures below a certain number, eleven or twelve at the most, since the opposite, elevated figures, would suggest a decreased ovarian reserve, which was a strong predictor of egg quality. These figures and the results from the exam and the ultrasound he planned to do would likely indicate whether she should go straight to an IVF cycle or possibly have an IUI, or insemination, first.

As Costanza listened, she tried not to think how many women, and couples, had sat where she was sitting, hearing the same plain, detached presentation. Perhaps it was extra detached, on account of her—of them. Or because of the charade she had insisted on.

"There are other things to look for, as I say," Henry continued, "but assuming that everything checks out, this is the most pertinent information we need. Do you have any questions?"

"I'd like to know what would happen next."

"On day two of your subsequent cycle we begin an IUI or a round of IVF treatment. Most likely, given your age, the latter."

"Just like that?"

"Naturally there's a whole protocol of drug treatments, ultrasounds, and other procedures, but you'll learn about all this in time."

She had had to beg Morton, and here was Henry offering to make life with her—for her, potentially. She felt . . . what *did* she feel? As if her body were floating over the chair rather than sitting on it—and as if she weren't quite inhabiting that body either.

"Anything else?"

She shook her head.

"Then Susan will show you to the examining room."

The floating, the bodilessness, were actually a help. It made the prospect of Henry examining her almost palatable.

Costanza changed out of her clothes into a shapeless robe. She sat in a chair rather than climbing onto the examining table. She sat and she waited. She waited and she wished that she had some work with her, instead of a magazine she could not bring herself to focus on, or something to do with her hands, such as knit. She wished that this were a robe that kept her warm, instead of offering no protection against the overly chilled air. She wished that the windows were cleaner, and that the clock on the wall wouldn't tick so loudly. Ticking clocks irritated Costanza, but a ticking clock in a room frequented by women whose biological clocks were ticking cacophonously was too much to bear.

But she bore it. Even if she did imagine herself asking Henry, quietly and in another context, if he had ever given any thought to what it felt like for the patient to sit in these soulless rooms and wait.

And wait.

And wait.

Eight minutes . . . eleven. Did they think it took a woman in the twenty-first century longer than two minutes to step out of her slacks, sweater, and panties?

Thirteen. Window washers, on a regular contract; an abstract print; a flowering plant; a book of poetry, sensitively chosen. Or a collection of travel essays, inviting the patient to wander somewhere, anywhere, else. Color on the walls. Why was there never any color on the walls in these godforsaken places?

Fourteen. Sixteen.

After sixteen and a half minutes—the clock had an additional diabolical hand that swept around its face, wiping away time down to the second too—Susan opened the door. To her credit she apologized for taking so long, explaining that Dr. Weissman had had to answer an emergency call. She hoped Costanza could understand.

Costanza said that, yes, she could understand.

Susan weighed her and measured her height. She took her blood pressure, her temperature.

"He likes to start from scratch," Susan said as she made notes on Costanza's chart.

"You've known Dr. Weissman a long time."

"Twenty-eight years."

"You must have quite a good sense of him by now."

Susan placed the chest piece of her stethoscope over Costanza's heart. "Quite."

"You think he's a good man—a good physician, I mean?"

Susan answered as she listened to Costanza's heart. "Both."

"But you couldn't really answer that differently."

"I *could*, but I wouldn't. Mainly because it's true."

"Mainly."

"Twenty-eight years is a lifetime. It's like a marriage."

"It's longer than most marriages."

"Well, it's longer than all three of mine put together."

Costanza smiled.

Susan took off the stethoscope and draped it around her neck. "And you two. Have you known each other long?"

"What do you mean?"

"Like I said, twenty-eight years is a lifetime." Susan looked Costanza in the eye and waited.

Costanza's cheeks reddened. "We met earlier this year."

"In Italy."

Costanza nodded.

"That explains the notable improvement in his mood."

"Does he need to know that you've figured it out?"

"But why the—pretense? The double pretense, that is?"

"I think I may still be trying to act as though none of this is happening."

This Susan seemed to understand. "A lot of women find it difficult to give up control over their bodies, even if it's only temporary."

"So I am trying to exert it somewhere else? Is that what you're saying?"

"Pretty much."

After five minutes the door opened again. Susan returned with Henry. He washed his hands, palpated Costanza's thyroid, and listened to her heart for himself as Susan looked on silently.

Then he instructed Costanza to lie on her back and insert her legs into the stirrups.

Susan gestured first at Henry, then at Costanza. "So, Henry, what exactly is the plan here?"

Henry glanced at Costanza and understood.

"I'm sorry," Susan said to Costanza. "But after thirty years, you stop holding your tongue."

"You stopped holding yours after about thirty minutes, if I recall correctly," Henry said. "The plan, *my* plan, is to help the woman I love to conceive a child. Usually treatment begins with an exam."

"Yes, but this is a most unusual situation," Susan said.

Costanza crossed her arms. "Henry wants me to have the best possible chance at succeeding," she said, defending an approach that a few days earlier she was still questioning herself.

"We all do." Susan turned to Henry. "I can get Woo in here in three minutes. You can supervise. You do half the time already anyway. I'll manage the story, but really I do think it's the smartest thing for both of you—and for all of us."

Henry again glanced at Costanza, who nodded at him. "Fine," he said.

After Susan left, Henry said, "She's looking out for me."

"I did raise the concern myself, you remember."

"I remember." Henry sighed.

Susan returned, as promised, in three minutes. Fewer. She was accompanied by a young doctor, Felicity Woo, who didn't strike Costanza as a particularly felicitous person. She was small and brisk. Costanza had no idea what Susan had told her but decided that she could trust Susan, and so she decided to trust this Dr. Woo as well.

Dr. Woo introduced herself as she wriggled into a pair of sterile gloves. Then her hands disappeared under Costanza's robe. Henry looked on impatiently as Dr. Woo felt and prodded. She was not especially tender. A pain shot through Costanza, and she winced. Dr. Woo apologized but didn't stop. She explained that she was looking to see if on physical exam she might find any polyps or fibroids, any growths or abnormalities that might impede implantation in her uterine cavity.

She probed for several long seconds. "All clear."

Then the younger doctor nodded at Susan, who, having unwrapped a condom, slid it over the ultrasound wand and applied a generous squirt of lubricating jelly to cover its surface.

(Condoms in a place where women were trying to get pregnant? It seemed as problematic to Costanza as that loudly ticking wall clock.)

Dr. Woo angled the wand first one way, then another, at intervals freezing and retaining images. She gazed at the screen calmly and thoughtfully, apparently impervious to Henry's monitoring gaze. Their joint silence worried Costanza. She imagined that they were seeing problems, growths; polyps or cysts of unwieldy dimensions. Tumors; horrors. She kept raising her head awkwardly, dividing her attention between the screen, where she understood nothing, and Henry's face, where nothing was understandable.

Finally Dr. Woo turned to her. "There's no sign of fibroids, polyps, or cysts. The lining is thin, the antral follicle count reasonable at three. You're in good shape."

"Good shape?"

Henry dived in. "She means there's nothing on exam or ultrasound that would impede your moving on to a cycle of IVF. Depending on your blood work, naturally. For that, as I told you earlier, we'll have to wait until your next period."

Costanza was so relieved that for a moment she seemed to stop breathing.

Dr. Woo made a note in Costanza's chart.

Henry turned to Susan. "Where next?"

"Three."

Examining room three, Susan meant. He was moving on with his day. His hand reached for the doorknob, and the next minute, with the briefest and most distant of goodbyes—a goodbye he'd give to any other patient—he was gone.

Much of the rest of Costanza's day was spent working on the new translating project she had accepted, a strange and original book called *Honey from a Weed* by Patience Gray. It was (and wasn't) a cookbook. It wasn't (and was) a memoir. The book captivated Costanza in part because it was so difficult to categorize, but largely because it spoke to her in a way that felt both personal and—given where her life was at the moment—necessary.

Gray was an English food writer and, for a while, a jewelry maker whose companion ("The Sculptor," otherwise unnamed) worked in marble. His quest for materials took them to Carrara, Catalonia, Naxos, and Puglia to live for long periods, often plainly, so plainly that they didn't always have electricity. Gray's approach was to adapt: to learn from local traditions and local women (and men), to follow the seasons, to appreciate bounty but also to accommodate deprivation. As a writer and a cook she moved nimbly between asceticism and sensuality. She was an early forager, a diligent researcher, a skilled listener, and her prose had a measured, elegiac quality that derived from her awareness that she had landed in places where the old traditions were dying out. In one passage she likened herself to a student of music who recorded songs that were no longer sung and would soon vanish.

The reawakened cook in Costanza appreciated Gray's culinary guidance—in that sense the project couldn't have been better timed—but what moved her, truly moved her, was the way the Englishwoman gave herself completely to wherever she was living, and under whatever conditions. If there was no running water, she filled her pots at the local stream. If there were no vegetables in the garden, she headed into the forest to gather weeds. She faced each new circumstance, each new experience, with a curiosity that Costanza found enviable.

As a translator, Costanza was herself used to doing a good deal of adapting. For several months at a time she traveled outside of her life and into someone else's. It was as if she had spent years now living in a series of borrowed apartments, moving in for a season or two, wearing her host's clothes, absorbing the relevant specialized information in the books on her shelves, peeking into her medicine cabinet, and sleeping in her bed, all the while forcing herself to become as invisible as possible, since as she well knew a translator should be heard but never seen. It was a particular experience, writing a story (or capturing an idea, or expressing a feeling) without digging it out of yourself, playing ventriloquist's dummy—if the dummy could read and write—to another human being's consciousness; and yet it was in that in-between space that she often felt most comfortable, in her work and (she had come to understand) often in her life as well.

Around five o'clock Costanza took a break and checked the messages on her cell phone. Henry had called to let her know that he would probably be home around eight that evening. He said that if she needed him to stop for anything, she should leave him a message on his cell phone, or with Wanda.

That was it: nothing about the appointment, or Susan, or Dr. Woo—or her.

Costanza packed up her manuscript and her notes and made her way back to Henry's apartment, picking up the makings for a zucchini frittata and a green salad as she went. Foraging like Patience Gray? Not really, no.

Back at the apartment Costanza found Andrew in the kitchen, rooting around in the refrigerator. She hadn't seen him for two weeks. "It's Monday, of course," she said—Monday being the fixed night he had been spending on the East Side. Quickly recalibrating her meal plans, she added, "I was about to run out for more provisions. How do you feel about lamb chops?"

"I'm not doing so much meat these days." He bit into an apple he had extracted from the fruit bin.

"What if I throw together a pasta with *funghi porcini*? I still have some of our mushrooms left from Florence . . ." The *our* leaped up out of the sentence awkwardly.

"Sounds great. But not tonight. I've got swim practice."

"And if you skip it?"

Andrew closed the refrigerator door. "One: at the beginning of the year we sign a contract saying that we won't miss a single practice— even if we're not feeling well, we have to sit there and observe. Two: if I don't swim or run every day right now, I might lose my mind. I'm going to guess that it's been a while since you've been a senior at a New York City private school."

"Love the sarcasm, Andrew. But not counting these friendly stop-bys, you've missed three out of the last six Mondays."

"Are you sure you aren't Jewish?"

"My paternal grandfather was, but I never met him. Why?"

"You've got the guilt thing down."

"I wasn't trying to make you feel guilty. It's just that we've—I've— missed you."

"*I've* is probably more truthful."

She was determined not to be upset by two Weissman men in the same day. "All right then. *I've.*"

He tossed the apple core into the garbage. She opened a carton of eggs. "You don't have anything to say to that?"

He shook his head.

"Well, the way you're just standing there makes me uncomfortable. Why don't you at least help me by cracking some of these into a bowl?" She produced a bowl, a whisk. "You can beat them too."

"How many?"

"Eight. But only six whites."

"You're pushing me to the edge of my culinary abilities."

"I think you can handle it."

But he couldn't. Andrew tried, and failed, to separate the yolk from the white.

"Here. Let me show you."

She took the oozing, half-cracked egg out of Andrew's hand and

demonstrated how he should let the white dribble into the bowl by pouring the yolk back and forth into the two halves of the shell. Then she
gave him another egg to try on his own. As she did, Costanza thought
how curious it was that she was making an egg-based dinner for Henry
after a day on which she had begun the process by which *her* eggs would
be submitted to his treatment.

"Can I ask you a question?"

Andrew was concentrating on his task. He nodded absently.

"What was it like, for you, to have a doctor for a father?"

"Well, he's never treated me for fertility issues."

"You know what I mean."

Andrew cracked and separated another egg, more adroitly this
time. "We could never be sick, really, growing up. 'These things are all
self-limiting'—that was Henry's standard phrase, every scrape, every
wipeout on our bikes. Every bug. Ice packs? He never heard of them.
Sugary chewable aspirins? A placebo. Cool Spider-Man Band-Aids like
other kids? He swiped plain old ones from the office and only let us
wear them for an hour or two at most before he'd rip them off. 'Fresh
air is best.'"

Andrew began beating the eggs. "When I first started swimming—
he and Mom were already apart by then—I slipped and fell getting out
of a cab on my way to a meet one winter. It was kind of excruciating,
but with self-limiting and all, my father was convinced it was just a
sprain or a torn tendon, so I went to practice anyway. He did suggest
an ice pack. The next day I couldn't really tie my shoe, so I wore it un-
laced. That night was a West Side night. My mother took one look at
my foot and ten minutes later we were at the ER. The doctor spoke to
her like he was ready to call child protective services. 'You waited *how*
long . . . ?' Oh, Henry and Judith had a *big* fight after that. The next
time I saw Henry, he apologized to me. It was one of the only times I've
ever heard him say he was sorry."

"After that things were different?"

"Well, I never broke my foot again."

It was almost as if Henry had eavesdropped on their conversation or
had spent some time reviewing the way the morning had unfolded: he

came home with pastry, a crusty bread, and a good bottle of white wine. It made Costanza feel briefly ashamed of her spare meal.

As soon as the wine was poured and sipped, he asked Costanza how she thought it all went.

"You mean after Susan outed us?"

"Isn't it more like she gave us a chance to rethink what we were doing?" Henry said.

"We . . . ?"

Henry looked at her. "Okay. *I*. Other than that, I felt it went fine. Didn't you?"

"You just—flew out of there. At the end."

"I had another eight patients before lunch. Nine, maybe."

"To me that was some—significant news. To know that I checked out all right."

"It's a little soon to celebrate."

She slipped the frittata under the broiler. She wanted to be sure to speak carefully, neutrally. "I know that . . . but are you always so—so remote with your patients, or is it just the ones you're involved with?"

Henry smoothed his beard. "I treated you the way I would most anyone else. I've been at this a lot of years, Costanza. You can't expect me—"

"To make an exception?"

"To change my ways."

"But we're thinking of making a baby together."

"I'm infinitely aware of that."

"On the basis of a relatively shallow knowledge of each other."

"Well, it's becoming deeper," Henry said lightly.

"What does that mean?"

"It's merely a statement of fact. As is this: you're nearly forty, remember."

When she didn't say anything, he added, "And I love you."

"So you keep saying. But the more you say it, the less I believe it. I'm beginning to think it's an idea—a notion—maybe a longing—in you, rather than an experience between us."

Again he studied her face. Whatever he was looking for there, clearly he was not finding. "Why are you trying to hurt me?"

"How do you know that's not what love is, some kind of . . . delusion."

"Because I believe that something so strong *has* to be shared between two people. Also because I'm listening to my own heart. And trusting it."

In a softer voice she said, "The situation *is* unusual, Henry, you must concede."

"I do. This is hardly familiar ground for me. I'm just feeling my way. I'm bound to make mistakes. We both are."

"No. Just you." She smiled. The atmosphere lightened.

He put his arm around her. "Would it help if we got married? If I asked you to marry me?"

"Where is this coming from?"

"My heart. Where else?" He paused. "I realize it isn't very romantic, the way I said it. But if you would have me, I would marry you tomorrow."

Costanza turned her beautiful, unreadable face to Henry. "And if there's no baby . . . ?"

"Then we have each other."

She opened the oven and took out the frittata.

"You haven't answered my question, Costanza."

"Right now I can't even *think* about answering your question. I'm not ready to. But I am ready to eat."

On Thursday, her period began. She returned to Henry's office for a blood test three days later. He brought the results home with him. Her random day-three FSH was thirteen. Thirteen put her slightly on the high side of the cusp: she could try an insemination or move directly into a cycle of IVF. His feeling was that she would do better with IVF, so she decided to do that. Just like that, she decided. After so much doubt, hearing that number, having a hard fact finally, anchored Costanza in the pragmatic. If an objective lab test suggested that her egg quality was beginning to deteriorate, then the time had come to sign on.

The following week she received a phone call from one of Henry's nurses, Sandra, who said that she was reviewing Costanza's records and noticed she had yet to register for what she called (oddly, Costanza thought) a "teach class," an evening in which she would be instructed in how to prepare and perform the injections, what to expect during the cycle, where to go on the day of retrieval, and other details related to her treatment.

That Thursday, Costanza went to the hospital to listen to this nurse, Sandra, describe a typical cycle, from the very first blood test to the transfer of an embryo and the pregnancy test that would follow two weeks later. By the time she stumbled out of the room nearly two hours later, she was numb.

Henry had gone to a lecture that evening and was not due back before ten o'clock. Costanza poured herself a generous glass of red wine, then in the dark, which in New York was never so very dark, found her way to the living room. She sat down in one of the chairs that faced the windows and sipped. As she sipped, a memory came. Out of nowhere, or so it seemed at first, her mind turned to the day when a line was drawn between childhood and what was to follow, between thinking she understood and understanding she didn't, between feeling at home in her home and feeling truly at home nowhere ever again.

It's a Saturday in April, and she is in the garden at Recco, which is in lavish early spring bloom, the roses competing with jasmine and wisteria to sweeten the air. She is sitting at the round table under the grape arbor, doing her homework; trying to do her homework. Her father has been gone—only not gone, but missing—for two days. He's away on an unexpected research trip, her mother has tried to tell her, unconvincingly, because for months now Alan hasn't been doing any research, he hasn't been going into Genoa to teach his classes, he hasn't been reading (he who was never without a book in his bag, under his arm, in his lap, by his chair), he hasn't even been out of bed for more than an hour or so at a time. At the bottom of the stairs that lead from the garden down to the street, the metallic clang of the lid on the letterbox announces the delivery of the morning mail, and a moment later Maria Rosaria comes flying out of the house, and flying is just what it seems like too, since her mother is still in her white nightgown, which swells and billows out behind her like a sail as she hurries out the front door and into the garden, past the arbor and the table where Costanza is sitting, through the gate at the top of the stairs, and down the stairs to the street. A second, gentler clang of the letterbox and then a long, excruciating silence follow. Costanza waits and waits. Five minutes, ten. In her memory she waits, it seems, for an hour, though she knows it cannot have been an hour, maybe it wasn't even ten minutes, or five. Eventually she hears her mother's footsteps, heavy, struggling, suffering footsteps that hoist her body back up the stairs. First a tip of her appears, a thatch of dark hair, then the rest of her, in profile, her features frozen, her shoulders and arms slack, her hands holding the mail where among the bills and magazines are two letters from her father, one for Maria Rosaria, the other for Costanza. One is open, the other still sealed. Two envelopes, two stamps, two sheets of paper, two lives never again what they were.

How many times over the years has she gone back to that moment, or has it come back to her? Sometimes it acted like a drug, inoculating her with a dose of its toxicity as a way of resetting her perspective. She had a feeling that was what was going on now. *Toughen up, girl*, it was saying, or something in that vein. But tough was the last thing she was feeling.

Costanza was still sitting in Henry's half-empty living room, sipping her wine and studying the dreary décor, when he returned an hour later. He switched on the light, and she turned to face him, squinting. "Why are you sitting in the dark?"

She shrugged.

He sat down in the chair that paired with hers. "How did it go?"

"It went."

"Sandra knows her stuff."

Costanza nodded.

"Are you okay?"

"I will be." It wasn't clear whom she was trying to assure with those unconvincing words.

"You're not having second thoughts?"

"Third, fourth, fifth—but not second."

"I wish I knew what that meant."

"It means . . . that I am going to go ahead. But I think you might have to help me learn how to do the shots. Knowledgeable though Sandra was, I'm not sure I followed so well."

"No problem."

"And, Henry?"

"Yes . . . ?"

"What would you think if we had this room painted? And the library too?"

He looked as though he expected something more relevant; more momentous, even. "Of course not. Just choose the color, and I'll get the super in here. He does that kind of job with his cousin."

"It would be good for me to take on a project like this right now. And I believe it would make me feel more at home."

"Nesting. Let's get on it."

⇄

The next morning Costanza made a beeline for the sample chips at the closest hardware store. It was like falling into a sea of color, gently graduated by tone. She went for the yellows first. Golden Honey. Good Vibrations. Candlelit Dinner. Who came up with these names, anyway? Shooting Star. Lightning Bolt. Little Angel. Sunny-Side Up. Could she live in a room whose paint color was called Cheerful, or Pure Joy? That was asking a lot. Perhaps she would be more comfortable with the grays or the greens. Vale Mist. Paris Rain. Nimbus. Inner Balance.

She took a dozen different samples back to Henry's apartment. Please, nothing too dark was all he said. Other than that he trusted her to choose the color herself.

She taped up the sample chips in the living room and stood back to study them. She had always loved refurbishing projects. As a girl she liked to play house with her mother, which didn't mean rearranging doll furniture but real tables and chairs and paintings. Once she was grown up, playing house—though it wasn't exactly playing then—helped her to make a new place feel like her own. (One of the reasons she had never felt at home in Morton's penthouse was that it was such a closed system—in many ways, just like him.) When Costanza wrote a story she always began by thinking about the setting, then the people, then what happened to the people in that setting. Before she could imagine, she had to visualize, everything from the carpet to the lighting to the view out the window. She approached her translations the same way. She always mapped out the locations in the book first. If it was nonfiction, or fiction set in a verifiable street or town, she would zoom in on Google maps, so that if the writer described a character going up or down a street, or turning right or left, she could follow along. While working on certain novels she had even been known to draw a sketch of the interiors of rooms or to block out the floorplan of houses that she put together from clues she extracted from the text and accumulated in a little notebook while she was reading. She was convinced that these exercises allowed her to inhabit these other worlds more fully and made her a closer reader and a more accurate, even a more imaginative, translator.

Now here she was, living—starting—a new story herself. Of course she had to put her mark on Henry's apartment.

Since the living room windows faced north, and admitted a rather cool, almost gray-tinged light, Costanza decided on a yellow that was essentially an amped-up cream: Pale Straw. The color was pretty (but not too pretty), the name palatable. The super was coming at eight o'clock on Saturday morning, which gave her half a day to get the place ready.

She dived in. After rolling up the new rug that she and Henry had bought, she removed the few remaining pictures from the walls, emptied the bookshelves, and stacked up the books in the middle of the room. Under the bookshelves was a row of cabinets with raised-panel doors. They were packed. If she was going to do the job, she decided, she would do it properly. Evidently no one had organized these cupboards in a long time, probably not since Judith left. Costanza found notebooks, files, old cameras, chipped clay pots made by the boys. The typewriter ribbons alone were evidence that this was a highly outdated corner of Henry's world. She spread everything questionable out on the drop-leaf table for him to review.

In the last cupboard she came across a box of photographs. So far, she had resisted the temptation to do any sleuthing. She believed that people's stories came out over time, and what's more, having decided to go forward with Henry and the treatment, she was curbing her impulse to find reasons not to. But photographs? How could she not, at least, peek?

Because the photographs had been tossed into the box as they accrued, she found herself surveying Henry's life in reverse order. He became younger, thinner, with a beard that grew bushier, then more close-cropped, then bushy again; interestingly, there wasn't a single picture of him barefaced in the lot. Costanza noted a hardness in his face that relaxed as she dug deeper. It was a most poignant reversal: the joyless Henry was replaced by a joyful one as a family divided turned back into a family intact. The sober single father became paired again with his wife, smiling again at dinners, parties, beaches, touching Judith, holding her, holding their boys.

Not just Henry but the whole family traveled through time like this, magically substituting their past selves for their future ones. Where else, except in memory, could Justin and Andrew shrink back down through adolescence to boyhood, then toddlerhood, and then infancy? Before that, they were captured in utero, as someone, Henry presumably, photographed Judith in a series of shots where she raised her shirt and stood in profile against a dark background as her large melon-shaped belly grew smaller and smaller still.

The bottom of the box was all smiles, parties, and play. A young couple, a new couple, on vacation. At dinners. At picnics. Dancing. Skiing. At a baseball game. At someone's wedding. Touching—kissing—happy. Costanza could feel the sex, she could almost smell it. Even, maybe especially, when the pictures were of Judith alone: in a bikini by a beach or, once, lying in a rumpled bed, alongside a breakfast tray (had Henry recycled this knack of his for her?).

Costanza had dropped all the pictures into her lap, facedown, carefully preserving their order. She leaned forward and was just about to tip them back into the box when she heard someone in the hall. Startled, she turned around and sent them scattering.

It was Henry's longtime housekeeper, Hilda. "I didn't mean to scare you, Señora Costanza." She looked around at the disassembled rooms.

Costanza explained about the painters, then Costanza gathered up Henry's now-scrambled life and put it back in the box. "They were just so—beautiful," she said with a sigh.

Hilda glanced at a photograph of Judith pregnant. "Yes. A beautiful family. A nice family. I was here, you know, before the boys."

"That's a long time."

"Oh, I was here before Señora Judith too . . ." She paused. "Dr. Weissman, he has been good to me, to my family. *Mire.*" Hilda had found a picture of herself, holding one of the boys—baby Justin—in her arms.

At last all but a handful of pictures were back in the box. Costanza lingered over one in particular: a photograph of two couples, sitting at a dinner table. Henry and Judith she recognized. The other two she did not.

Or did she? The couples sat at a table in what looked like an old-fashioned New York chophouse, all dark walls and red leather upholstery. They were drinking martinis. That didn't seem at all like Henry, or the Henry she knew. But then this picture was taken decades ago. Before children, Costanza surmised from the haircuts and Henry's and

Judith's youthful faces. The men were sitting on one side of the table, the women on the other. A waiter must have taken the picture. They were all looking straight at the camera, and grinning. Henry had his arm around the shoulder of this other man. That too didn't seem like Henry. She couldn't imagine him, today, sitting at a table with his arm around another man, conveying such open affection. And grinning. And the other fellow also, a handsome man whose oval face had a patrician air, as did his thick hair, his eyes that were like that stone. Which? Obsidian. Yes, that was it. That was how such eyes were described. In books anyway; it was a little bit cliché. Costanza felt she had seen these obsidian eyes before; she had seen him before, somewhere. But where?

"I feel like I know this man," Costanza said, as if to herself.

"That is Dr. Isaac and Señora Eileen. He used to work with Dr. Henry."

Dr. Isaac—Isaac Schoenfeld? She remembered the photograph she'd seen on Andrew's desk, the one he'd taken in Florence, and she remembered Schoenfeld from the time she and Morton had consulted him in his office. He was a good deal younger in this photograph, naturally.

"They are old friends, he and Henry?"

"They were at school together. Afterward they worked together, for a while. Dr. Isaac used to stay here sometimes. They were like brothers."

"Were?"

Hilda flushed. "These things I don't know so well. Only after Andrew was born, they stopped working together. Dr. Isaac had his office and Dr. Henry had his."

Costanza nodded. She wondered what it meant that when she'd told Henry that she and Morton had consulted Schoenfeld, Henry hadn't mentioned their connection. Probably there was some bitterness about business. She started to put the photograph back into the box, but there was something about it. She slipped it into the pocket of the apron she'd put on to protect her clothes when she started prepping for the paint job, then continued with her work.

As she came closer to starting her IVF cycle, Costanza alternated between losing track of entire days and feeling others inch by. She knew she'd been busy because the pages of her translation were accruing during the long days she'd been putting in at a café around the corner while the super and his cousin extended the painting project beyond the living room and the library to the foyer, and Henry's (now their) bedroom and bath.

During the evening and on the weekend Costanza assigned chores to Henry: trips to the hardware store or tasks such as weeding through and organizing his books. They were living together and sleeping alongside each other, yet for days on end they scarcely had a conversation of any substance. Nesting *vincit omnia* was all Henry could think, but not unhappily.

Henry disposed of a formidable quantity of things that he didn't even know he had and shed books he hadn't opened in decades. They ate their way through three weeks of alternating Chinese-Thai-Japanese-Turkish-pizza takeout. At the end of the second week he went to work on a Friday morning. At about five o'clock he received a message from Costanza asking him to pick up a bottle of prosecco on his way home. When he let himself into the apartment, he saw books on the shelves, rugs open across the floor. In the living room were flowers, candles, bright new pillows, several new lamps. Over the lingering smell of fresh paint and furniture polish he detected garlic; something was cooking.

Costanza met him with a platter of antipasti, beaming. "It's still a little bare, but we can change that with time."

We. Time. How Henry loved hearing those words come out of her mouth. He now understood what these weeks had been for her, for them. It was their first shared domestic project, the first time in years he didn't have to look at those depressing shadows on the walls and be reminded of his ex-wife's angry departure.

Henry put his arm around Costanza. "This is really fantastic. It's like starting over in a new place, only without the headache of having to move. How often do you get to start over in life?"

"Not often, in my experience."

"In mine, never—until now."

There was an ardor to Henry and Costanza's lovemaking that night that took Costanza back to their very first time at the Ricci. The experience had been so mysterious to her, unfamiliar and also, yes, wonderful.

And frightening. It was less frightening now, to feel how much she wanted Henry, in her mouth, deep inside her, lying close to her when they were finished. And she didn't need to send him off afterward, as she had in Florence. That time wasn't so very long ago, but it felt like it belonged to a different part of her life entirely.

Only later, as she was falling asleep, did Costanza realize that she had not been tracking her ovulation. Between refurbishing the apartment and anticipating the in vitro (*between*—as though there were no connection), she had not been paying attention to the calendar. That was probably why she felt so free in bed. Trying to become pregnant was not going to be up to her, not up to her body alone. Because the in vitro would permit them to bypass long months of timed intercourse, she believed that her physical relationship with Henry wasn't likely to deteriorate as irreparably as hers with Morton had. It might be tested, but she did not think it would be compromised.

She woke the next morning, Saturday, to one of Henry's breakfast trays, which he left by the bed before he went into the shower. He had taken extra care, making fresh orange juice and scrambled eggs, a frothy mound of them. Costanza tried not to think of the photograph of Judith in bed with her tray. That was years ago, decades now. And besides, he had not scrambled eggs for *her*.

When Henry emerged from the bathroom, he asked her whether she had any ideas about the day, if, that is, they were free to do things that weren't related to putting the apartment into shape. They were free, she said. Yes. They traded suggestions for which museum they might visit, or whether they might take a walk in the park instead. How delightful this kind of easygoing scheduling conversation could be.

Henry dropped his towel and opened his dresser drawer, took out a pair of clean shorts, and stepped into them. Costanza enjoyed watching the naked Henry disappear into his clothes. A T-shirt came next, then socks. Then he stopped. He stopped because he had glanced at the top of the bureau, where the night before, as Costanza was changing out of her work apron for dinner, she had emptied her pockets. Among the rags and picture hooks was the photograph of Henry and Judith with Schoenfeld and his wife.

She watched Henry pick up the photograph. One of its corners was bent, and both sides curled inward. Costanza was so focused on the change in its condition that she thought at first that was why Henry was saying to her in such an altered voice, "Where did this come from?"

"The library cupboards. I think I told you that I glanced through that box of your photographs . . ." Glanced. "I set that one aside because I was curious to ask you about it. I wanted to know why, when I told you that Morton and I had been to see Dr. Schoenfeld, you never mentioned you were friends."

He looked at her in silence for a moment, then tossed the picture into the wastebasket. Afterward he went back to dressing. For the pants he had to step into the closet. When he returned, more than just his body seemed covered up.

"Are you going to tell me why you threw that picture away?"

"Costanza, we haven't talked about anything other than domestic matters in weeks. I don't want our first conversation after all this time to be about trivia. Now: MoMA or the Met?"

They sounded like pills. Punishments. "Trivia?"

She was out of bed now, belting her robe tight.

"I was once better friends with that man," Henry said neutrally.

That was it. He turned to the mirror and started combing his hair. "That man?"

He returned the comb to his top dresser drawer.

"There's so little I know about your past, Henry. Please."

Henry looked into the mirror for a moment. Then he turned around to face her. "Schoenfeld and I were in the same class in medical school. We were fellows together in Peter Harris's clinic, and we worked for him afterward. Later on we went into practice together ourselves. We lost a good deal of money at first. Judith's father helped us out, and Judith had a good head for business, but it wasn't enough. Schoenfeld's parents put up a lot more. They had deeper pockets. I wanted to keep things equal, even so. I felt our work and our ideas were where the value was, not in who contributed this many or that many dollars. Schoenfeld, or his family, I never really understood, disagreed. They had a lawyer draw up a document. That's where it all started to unravel. We didn't even really have a chance to get our practice going, not properly." He paused. "Satisfied?"

"You felt Schoenfeld should have stood up to his parents more? Taken more of a stand?"

"Yes."

"So he disappointed you."

"Yes."

"Well, money can have a very—a very particular effect on people."

"Indeed," he said. "I really thought we were onto something."

"And you were."

"*Now* it looks that way. But now is a different story. In the early years, it would have been easier to endure all the disappointments, all the challenges, with a partner. Someone to share all the hard times with." Again he paused. "Okay? Enough?"

Vuillard et Waroquy, a rectangular canvas of about six by eight feet, hung in one of the smaller rooms that extended the Met's story of Impressionism. Henry led Costanza to the picture, then took a step to one side, presenting it to her as a child might a prized toy. Rendered in a limited palette of grays, browns, and watery greens, it was a double portrait of the artist and his friend. Vuillard was standing in the foreground, with Waroquy just behind him, and they were looking into a mirror, which was actually the canvas, or what the canvas was pretending to be—only a bottle (of wine, or liquor) in the lower right-hand corner, reflected in the mirror/canvas, gave away the trick.

"Fantastic, isn't?" Henry said. "He's painting a painting of himself painting a painting of himself, while his friend watches. It's almost like it's happening in real time."

"Fantastic, yes." Costanza studied the painting. "Very imaginative. But . . ."

"Go on."

"Quite honestly, something else stands out to me. This morning you talked about Isaac Schoenfeld. You gave the impression that it was a friendship that you're still haunted by. Then you bring me to see this painting of two male friends looking at us—trying to say something to us—across time. Don't you think that's—curious?"

"Honestly, it never occurred to me."

"But it seems so obvious."

"Is this how it always is with you?" Henry asked lightly. "This constant *examining*?"

"Pretty much, yes."

"You want to know how I feel about that?"

She nodded.

"Excited." He kissed her on the neck.

"Thank you, Henry, but I feel that you're deflecting me."

"Not at all. For years Judith didn't seem interested in listening to me or understanding me. Now I *want* to be listened to, I want to be known. Especially by you."

"Then you have to answer me. You have to show yourself to me."

He looked back at the canvas. "Maybe bringing you to see this picture *is* a way of revealing something I myself don't understand, how much this part of my past still—troubles me. There. Is that what you're looking for?"

"What I'm looking for, Henry, is the truth."

"I believe that *is* the truth. I'm just seeing it now . . ." He studied the painting for a few moments, then faced her. "Your turn. What is it that *you're* not showing *me*?"

"That's easy. How lost I feel."

"Still, even now?" As he said this, he gestured, indicating himself, then her.

"Especially now. Questioning, or doubting things—it's how I was born, Henry. And also, I'm afraid."

"Of the cycle?"

She nodded. "From your point of view, I know, it's routine. But not for me. I don't know what it will feel like, whether it will work—even you can't know that. I don't know whether you and I will survive it. The quest for a baby finished off my marriage to Morton, you see."

"But surely it wasn't only that," Henry said soberly.

"Not only. But mostly. At least that's how I've come to think about it. Also I worry that if the treatment doesn't work, I may fall into—into a state of mind, a darkness, like my father's. He's been on my mind a lot right now." She looked back at the painting. "How come he didn't have a friend to look over his shoulder, to watch over him—to help him?"

Henry took her hand. Tenderly he said, "From my own experience, Costanza, I've learned that when you have a child, when you grow and rear a new being, it lightens the weight of the past. My own father was an enormous burden to me, right up until Justin was born. This is not to say I've shaken completely free of Leopold. But it's not as it was. Not nearly. And even though the circumstances with your father are different, I believe that something similar will happen to you. In fact, I'm sure of it."

○

On Thursday at just about noon, after putting in three hours on her translation, Costanza went to the bathroom to pee. When she wiped herself, the toilet paper was bright red. As she'd been instructed, she left a message with the nurses at Henry's office.

She arrived at the clinic at eight o'clock the next day. Costanza was no longer the outsider now, observing from a cool distance. She was one of the women who put their names on the sign-in sheet and with that one simple act set the whole experience in motion. She was one of the women who sat down and raised a magazine shield, then peered over its edge to survey the waiting room. And she was one of the women who, hearing her name called from a doorway, leaped up to flee that waiting room as fast as she could. She followed a nurse, JASMINE, it said on her name tag, into a room divided by half walls into cubicles. She sat down, and Jasmine drew her blood. Afterward she led Costanza into an examining room and instructed her to undress. Costanza undressed, climbed up onto the table, and covered herself up. Sometimes it was almost a relief to follow directions.

Within minutes there was a burst of light, noise, warm air. A young doctor stood before her. His ears branched out from his head like handles on a pitcher; he looked as if he should be studying for his biology final in high school.

"Good morning, Costanza. I'm Dr. Sommers, a fellow here at the clinic, and I'm going to do your baseline ultrasound this morning."

Jasmine, who had returned with him, began entering information into the computer.

"If you're Dr. Sommers," Costanza said crisply, "then I'm Ms. Ansaldo."

"Well, if you're Ms. Ansaldo, then I'm Dan." He smiled at her. "Your first time?"

She nodded.

"Any questions I can answer before we get started?"

"How about this: Can you tell who's going to succeed?"

"Scientifically? No."

"Unscientifically?"

"The right attitude helps. I've only been here a year, but it has really stood out to me. IVF works best for women who are confident—and stay confident even when there are bumps."

Bumps?

"A canceled cycle. A failed cycle."

"I didn't know they could be canceled."

"*Converted* is the more commonly used term. We won't let you go to retrieval with fewer than three viable eggs; we'll do an insemination instead." He looked at her properly. "You strike me as one of the confident ones," he said encouragingly.

"That's just because I wouldn't let you call me by my first name, Dan."

Jasmine handed him the ultrasound wand. "Can I get you to scoot back a bit?"

She scooted. Just then the door opened, and Henry stepped in. He gave Costanza a private nod. He said nothing to the fellow, who underwent a sudden physical transformation. His shoulders slackened, his face inclined toward the computer screen, and his hand—was it possible?—almost imperceptibly shook as it guided the ultrasound wand. Henry examined the screen over Sommers's shoulder and didn't even wait until the junior physician had finished before declaring, "Lining highly appropriate." Then, as abruptly as Henry appeared, he was gone.

At six o'clock that evening a nurse phoned to say that Costanza was to inject herself with 150 units each of Menopur and Follistim at any time before midnight that night and the one following, and that she was to come in again on Sunday morning for blood work.

Even though Costanza knew that Henry would double-check everything she did, she asked the nurse to repeat the dose and wrote it down on a scratch pad by the kitchen phone.

Then she poured herself a small glass of wine. She had been advised against immoderate drinking during the cycle, but she didn't see how she would make it through these first days without a small easing sip now and then.

She had almost emptied the glass when she heard the front door open. In the entry hall she found Andrew dropping a small bag by the door. "This is unexpected."

"I've missed so many Mondays I thought I'd have a makeup day, and besides, my mom is away this weekend." He paused. "You don't seem too happy about it."

"I'm just a little surprised to see you, that's all. And I haven't thought about dinner."

He pushed his hair back off his face, as though to take a clearer look at her. "I'm not here for dinner. I'm just leaving some stuff for later . . ."

But Andrew's attention was drawn elsewhere—behind her, to the living room. "You really went the distance with the house thing."

"Well, what do you think?"

"The color's . . . cheery." He stepped into the room and looked around. "The pictures are in different places, the books . . . wow."

"Well, we painted the shelves too. Everything came down and got cleaned and organized. Your father thinks I should keep going."

Andrew fussed with his hair again. "You mean like with the bedrooms?"

"I'd never touch yours without your permission, Andrew. I remember how you feel about change."

When Henry returned from work around seven thirty, he joined Costanza in the bathroom, where he gently showed her how to draw up the medicine, swap out the needles, and sterilize her abdomen. He advised her not to wind up—she wasn't throwing a dart—but to keep the needle perpendicular to her skin, and to insert it quickly. "The less thinking, the better."

It was much easier than she imagined it would be. She felt a sharp pinch as the needle went in and, after that, a tolerable burning that subsided after a minute or two. Afterward she breathed audibly. Like so many things in her life, it was the buildup—the anticipation—that set her churning.

"Are you all right?" Henry asked.

"I'm just waiting to feel something. Like Dr. Jekyll, or the monster in Frankenstein."

"It's nothing so drastic. The effects are cumulative. You'll see. Or maybe you won't. Everyone's different."

After he filled a bowl with cereal and fruit the next morning, Andrew opened the cutlery drawer to look for a spoon. The cutlery drawer was directly under the kitchen phone. By the phone was a scratch pad. He glanced at it: *Menopur, Follistim—150 units.*

Clearly legible, evenly spaced, vaguely European-style letters: not his father's writing. Menopur and Follistim, Andrew knew, were fertility drugs that were given to stimulate women at the beginning of an IVF cycle.

Costanza stepped into the kitchen just then, wiping sleep from her eyes. Andrew looked again at the pad. She followed his gaze. Instantly her cheeks flushed.

"So it is you," he said with a slight crack in his voice. "It is for you."

A flicker of hesitation, then: "Yes."

"You're taking—those drugs. My father is—treating you. You're trying to—" He stopped there.

Costanza placed her hand on the kitchen counter. "Yes, he is. Yes, we are. Trying to have a baby together."

Andrew took a moment to absorb this news. "That's big."

Costanza had not imagined—but how hadn't she?—having to explain herself to Andrew. "Your father and I have been trying by regular means for a while to—" She hesitated. "I don't know why I'm telling you this, really."

"Uh, because you should?"

She wished she had coffee in her already, sharpening her brain, giving her whole being more muscle, more *control,* but she had awakened before Henry that morning. "I do want to be open with you, Andrew. Yet at the same time . . ."

"That's not why you wanted to redo my room, is it? For a baby?"

"I never considered redoing your room. I told you that, remember?"

"Well, if you need a room, take Justin's."

There were instances when Andrew's mind still worked like a younger kid's.

"It seems odd, to focus on—lodging. When this is still just an idea. A hope."

When he didn't say anything, she continued, "Have you thought, if it works, that you would be an older brother? I think you would be a *terrific* older brother."

"The idea hasn't been floated long enough for me to think. I don't understand why you didn't just come out and tell me. Why I just had to find out . . . by accident."

"I—we—would have told you, in time. And anyway, I'm telling you now." It became easier the further along she went. "As of last night we officially began an IVF cycle. There. Now you know everything there is to know."

Andrew scratched his head. "But isn't it a little . . . soon to start IVF?"

Costanza tightened the belt of her bathrobe. "I have reason to believe that when my husband and I failed to conceive a baby, I was the one with the problem."

"You're referring to his child, aren't you, the one he had with his housekeeper?"

Costanza's eyes turned glassy. "Yes, Andrew, that is what I am referring to."

She couldn't help herself. No degree of bathrobe tightening, no pausing, could thwart the feeling that began to rise up in her. "I'm sorry." Her voice cracked. "I shouldn't—"

"No, *I'm* sorry." Andrew stepped toward her and set his hand on her shoulder. Her shoulder was warm, and he could feel it. And she could feel him feeling it. They stood there a moment in charged silence.

They were still standing there when Henry walked into the kitchen. His eyes shot immediately to Andrew's hand, which Andrew gently lowered.

"I've been telling Andrew about the cycle."

Henry's eyes darkened. "Before you and I spoke?"

Costanza explained about the notepad.

"I might have wanted to say something to my son."

"You still can," Andrew said evenly.

Henry smoothed his beard. "I'd just like to make sure you understand that your place in my life isn't—"

"Going to change just because you're planning on having another family?"

"Well, I don't think of it as another so much as a larger one. I think of it as building on."

"Building on what, Dad?"

When Henry didn't answer, Andrew said, "Justin is gone—pretty much for good, I think we can safely say. I've been reduced to one night a week. That's not much to build on, is it?"

Costanza looked at Henry. "Reduced?"

Color came into Henry's face. "I thought we should have some space. Just for a while."

"Isn't *that* something we should have spoken about first?" Costanza asked him.

"Honestly?" He took one look at Costanza's face, then judiciously changed his tone. "Maybe."

"That means maybe not."

"Costanza, please. Not now. Not in front—"

"Don't say anything the children shouldn't hear," said Andrew. "I guess he can't say it to you in Yiddish, the way he used to, to my mother. Or Leopold. *Red nisht, di kinder darfn nisht hern.* Well, you don't have to worry about this *kind.* I'm going to be late for school."

With this, Andrew was off, leaving a big smoky silence behind him.

"I'm surprised he knows that *kind* is the singular of *kinder,*" Henry said after a pause.

Costanza crossed her arms. "Do you realize how hard you are on him? You're always building Justin up and bringing Andrew down."

"Well, you help balance all that out, don't you, my love?"

"What does that mean?"

"Just what it says. You and Andrew have an understanding. A rapport."

"Is that so wrong?"

"Maybe I'm envious. Maybe I'd like to have an easier time with him, myself."

Her ovaries began to hurt. She had never even been aware of them before; now she felt as if she were walking around with a pair of golf balls lodged in her loins. After she showered in the morning she stood in front of a full-length mirror and examined her body, to see if it was visibly altered or misshapen; but she saw nothing, only her long, slender, familiar self.

Well, maybe her face had changed. It looked harder, with the skin drawn more tightly over her bones. From the drugs or from the waiting. It had begun to feel as if all she were doing was waiting—for appointments, injections, phone calls. Everything else in her day was tightly wrapped around these focal events; nothing else mattered nearly as much. Not even her work.

On Thursday morning, nearly a week into the cycle, Costanza had her third ultrasound, this time with Dr. Woo and again watched over by Henry. They counted at least thirteen follicles, eight on the right, five on the left. The follicles measured between ten and twelve millimeters, appropriate sizes for that point in the cycle. Thirteen follicles, Henry cautioned, didn't automatically translate into thirteen eggs, as some could be immature or even missing, but it was a good sign.

He flashed her a smile before disappearing into his day.

After this auspicious ultrasound Costanza floated out of the building. Thirteen? She was growing a village's worth of eggs in her body, her formerly barren body. If only half of them were viable—half of half—she'd be ahead of the game. Even half of half of half: after all, it only took one.

Jasmine phoned that night and instructed her to add to her cocktail 250 micrograms of ganirelix, the drug that would prevent her from surging and ovulating before the eggs were retrieved. Starting with the next morning and continuing until retrieval, there would be daily appointments, with daily ultrasounds. "It's looking good going into the big week," she said.

Henry was working late that evening, but Costanza felt confident enough by now to draw up the medicines and give herself the injections, all three of them. She had grown accustomed to the burning and the puffiness of her abdomen, and she knew to try to find a fresh patch amid the constellation of irritated red dots and bruises that was beginning to populate her skin. After a week, what had at first been daunting was now almost (almost) routine.

Afterward she treated herself to a small glass of a good Chianti that she had bought for Henry's dinner. She ate a bowl of pasta followed by an orange and was asleep before nine.

At midnight she was up with a restless mind. Across the bed Henry was sleeping on his side, snoring. She had not heard him come in. She had not heard him climb into bed. Now she was awake, vividly awake, taking an unbidden tour of some of the most disturbing moments in her life. She zigzagged from that awful day during her separation from Morton when Annelie had to pull her out of bed, to the morning her mother came up the stairs in Recco, holding the suicide notes her father had mailed from the hotel where he had gone to end his life. She swooped over to Stefano's office at the university, where a month short of three years into their relationship she had opened the door that afternoon to find Anna Carini licking his penis; then came the hospital bed she woke up in the next morning, after having fallen (she still believed . . . or hoped) off that terrace.

Costanza knew all about the middle of the night. You woke up and believed you could see through things, to their very essence. No time felt clearer. Also nothing, usually, was darker—or gave rise to darker interpretations. She knew these middle-of-the-night reflections were unreliable, but she was powerless to stop herself from having them.

The alarm broke into her thick, sticky, dreamless sleep. She opened her eyes to dread. Dread at the day; dread at having to haul herself out of bed and into the shower. Dread at having to fly out of the apartment by seven thirty, so that she would arrive at the clinic before eight o'clock for her blood work and ultrasound. Dread at having to turn in a draft of the translation by the end of the next month. Dread, beyond that, that she could not account for, but could feel deep within herself, in her very flesh.

Costanza was not normally a morning person. She liked to read or work in bed, and to make her way into her day slowly and with a generous amount of coffee clarifying her mind. She could do nothing about the hour these days, but the coffee, at least, was usually there waiting for her on the breakfast tray that Henry continued to prepare for her most every morning. Often its aroma woke her before the alarm and started her day on a pleasing note.

This morning it wasn't the coffee, though. It was the high squeal of the alarm, followed by the dread, followed by a glance out the window, where she saw a flat, leaden, wintry sky.

She reached for the mug. It was lukewarm. The toast was more wood than bread. Even the orange slices were mushy and full of pits.

Henry was just wrapping up his own morning routine. He emerged from the bathroom groomed and suited up for his day.

"Really, I don't know why you bother to make me breakfast if you're going to do such an abysmal job of it," she said sourly.

He looked at her. "I'm sorry. I have an early meeting."

"On days like this I'd rather make my own coffee."

"All right then. We can phase out this little tradition of ours."

"Oh, so I offer one criticism, and you pack up your toys and run away."

"I'm just responding to what you're saying, Costanza."

"No, you're *exaggerating* what I'm saying. You're *escalating* it. You're taking it to a different level."

"Actually I'm not taking it anywhere." He sighed. "Would you like me to make you another cup?" He glanced at his wristwatch.

"I don't want you to do me any favors, Doctor. And *I* don't have that much time. I have to be at your clinic in half an hour. As you well know."

In a soft tone Henry merely said, "Costanza."

"What?" she barked.

He picked up the mug of coffee. "Why don't you let me at least heat this up?"

"Coffee? Reheated *bad* coffee? Which I probably shouldn't be drinking in the first place? Are you trying to poison me?"

She started to push the coffee away, but the gesture was a little too vigorous, and the liquid splashed onto Henry's immaculate suit and beyond, onto her new paint job.

Costanza gaped at the dripping fabric, the brown liquid spattering the cream walls. Henry said nothing but stepped into the bathroom and returned with a damp hand towel. He wiped the wall as clean as he could. Then he disappeared into his closet to change his clothes. When he returned, Costanza was in the shower, sobbing.

In the examining room Henry again slipped in at the last minute to observe the ultrasound, which was being done by Dr. Sommers. There were still thirteen follicles, but only eight or maybe nine of them were maturing in tandem; the others were lagging behind. Henry said that this often happened, that she still had a good number of eggs, and that they were at an appropriate size. He told Costanza he anticipated she would be taking the HCG shot either that evening or the next; definitive word would come at the end of the day, after the team had reviewed all her data.

"Dr. Weissman," she said when he had finished. "May I speak to you for a moment alone?"

Henry nodded at Sommers and the nurse, who left the room. As soon as the door closed, Costanza said, "I want to apologize . . . about this morning . . . I was—"

"You were upset."

"I wasn't thinking clearly. I wasn't myself."

He put his hand on her. "It's the drugs. I told you. Some women can become not themselves or more—"

"More?"

He hesitated. "More emotional than normal."

Her tone sharpened abruptly. "Do you know how much a woman hates being told that? How invalidating that is?"

"Costanza, I don't really have time for—"

"You don't really have time for me? You're putting my body through hell, you're telling me that these drugs are making me crazy . . ."

"You have a sensitive system. Everything will become better with time."

She was to receive her HCG injection at eleven thirty on Saturday evening. That meant she would be among the first women to have her retrieval on Monday morning. More would be known after the retrieval, and a lot more by the following day, when the eggs would have been fertilized and, ideally, begun to divide.

She and Henry went out to a late dinner. Their conversation was stilted and quickly petered out into silence.

"This is hard for me too, Costanza. Not like for you. But I too—I too want the treatment to succeed. I too want—" He started again. "Last night I dreamt I was holding a baby. A newborn. *Our* newborn. It was thrilling."

What Henry said made her shiver. "Was it a boy or a girl or couldn't you tell?"

"The baby was wearing pink."

Costanza shivered again. "I've lost sight of you. Of you in all this. I'm sorry." She thought for a moment. "You know, Henry, I used to be— I *am*—about so much more than this . . . quest. Sometimes I forget that. It feels like the IVF has obliterated the rest of me. It's a body snatcher, a mind snatcher. It's taken over my waking life, my dreaming life, *your* dreaming life . . ."

"I see this kind of thing often. Difficult though it is, it's finite. You have to remember that. You're in it now, but you won't be for much longer."

HCG was given by intramuscular injection. On Saturday night at eleven twenty Henry drew up the medicine, tapped it to dissolve air bubbles, and changed the needle. They came to the moment when Costanza had to lower her skirt and underwear to expose the upper outside quadrant of her buttocks, where the injection had to be administered. It wasn't as though Henry hadn't seen her naked. It wasn't as though he hadn't touched, caressed, even kissed her backside; but still—still Costanza hesitated for a moment before undressing. Then she closed her eyes. She felt the mild sting of the alcohol wipe being drawn over her skin. Henry told her he was going to count to three, and she should remain still. At three he would insert the needle.

He counted. At three she felt a searing stab deep in her flesh.

"Shit!" This wasn't a word Costanza often used.

"I'm sorry. It's been a while since I've done this. I may have hit a nerve. But you've got to stay still. I have to pull back to check for blood."

There was no blood. He completed the injection, then withdrew the needle. Now there *was* a little blood. A ruby drop formed on her white skin. Henry reached for a tissue. "There's a little blood at the site. It's normal. I'm applying pressure. It'll stop in a minute."

In the papers she was given and from the doctor who performed her preoperative ultrasound, Costanza was reminded that retrieval was surgery, and that, as it took place in a hospital and anesthetic was admin- istered, she would not be discharged if she was alone. It was striking how a line on a medical form could make her feel such a pang of long- ing for Annelie, who had moved back to Sweden six months after Morton died. There was simply no one else in New York she felt com- fortable inviting into this most private moment in her life.

A solution occurred to her as soon as she unlocked the door to Henry's apartment and heard the gentle pleasing hum of a vacuum being drawn across the living room rug. She would ask Hilda to accom- pany her. She genuinely liked Hilda. Hilda would sit with her patiently and quietly. Hilda would have no agenda of her own.

Yes, of course, Hilda said when Costanza asked her, and it didn't feel like an obligatory yes either. Hilda did not seem surprised when Costanza explained what was going on and asked for this favor. "I work for Dr. Weissman a long time. I understand."

Hilda arrived at the apartment at eight o'clock the next day; by eight thirty she and Costanza were in a cab. Only then did Costanza feel the experience was happening, finally. After these long two weeks, there was nothing more to do, to hope for, worry over, or try to control. It was all in the hands of the doctors now. Or the fates. *And* the fates.

At the hospital Costanza and Hilda rode the elevator to the sixth floor. When they stepped into the hallway, Costanza's eyes immediately landed on a bulletin board opposite them, which was covered with an- nouncements seeking participants in research studies, the sorts of pages that end in a fringe of phone numbers that people were meant to tear off and slip into their pockets. One study was offering help for anorexia, another for panic attacks: "If you have physical symptoms such as pound- ing heart, dizziness, nausea, or trouble breathing, we will exchange 24 sessions of free therapy for . . ."

It was the only announcement that had all but one of its tabs missing.

Hilda watched Costanza staring at the notice. She set her hand on Costanza's shoulder. "You're not going to feel any of those things, Señora Costanza. You must not worry. It's not so bad. I remember."

Costanza turned to Hilda, confused. "You remember?"

"From before. With Señora Judith." Hilda flushed. "Señora Judith—she needed also Dr. Weissman's medicines. To help make the boys. You knew that?"

"Of course I knew that," Costanza said as evenly as she could. "I think it's this way. Yes. See—over there."

Over there, where the words IN VITRO FERTILIZATION were mounted above a corridor. Whose idea was it to put the words up there like that, and in garish brass letters, so that everyone would know exactly why a woman had come to this wing of this floor of the hospital? Was it Henry's? It didn't seem like Henry. But how did she know what seemed like Henry? It would have seemed like Henry to have mentioned to her that Judith had also undergone IVF, would it not? To help make the boys, both boys, plural. When she was a young woman, younger than Costanza by far.

Judith had had IVF too—and Costanza was only finding this out *now*? And from Hilda? Her mind—she could feel it, animal-like, rearing up, *gearing* up, primed to dive into a whole new dimension of worry and fear. She took a deep breath, forced herself to pause, and experimented with something she'd read about once in a book on meditation but had never implemented before. She visualized herself standing in an open doorway as Demon Worry began to approach. She wasn't going to pretend he wasn't there, but she wasn't going to invite him inside, and she wasn't going to sit down with him. Not at the moment, with the drugs in her body and Henry's semen in her purse, a small vial of possibility tucked in among her wallet and her sunglasses, and with her hopes raised the way they had been in these past weeks. No, not now. Not yet. Instead, Costanza stepped through the glass door and checked in with the receptionist. And just like that it began.

A nurse called her into a back room. The first thing she did was take Henry's specimen out of her bag and give it to her. Henry didn't think it was appropriate for him to be seen sitting in that waiting room alongside his patients and their husbands, so he took an option the clinic offered and produced a semen sample that morning in the bathroom at home, using a kit (sanitizing soap, a sealed plastic container, and envelope) that he had brought back from the office for that purpose earlier in the week.

To Costanza it seemed momentous to hand over that vial of milky liquid, which determined—in part determined—what her body might or might not do in the next few hours and days; but for the nurse, Costanza was merely another patient with merely another vial of semen. Merely another woman changing into a gown and having an IV line set. Merely another woman rejoining the other women—couples—in the waiting room.

Soon the men began to be called, one at a time. A nurse would lead a man out a different door, and he would return fifteen, twenty minutes later, wearing a face that was trying hard to look like an ordinary face. There would be a glance, in one case an eyebrow raised, at the wife, or partner. The men had gone to one of the specimen rooms. She had asked Henry to describe them to her—she had wanted to know everything about this process. Tiny and furnished with a large reclining chair, these rooms were stocked with erotic magazines, a DVD player, and a drawer full of movies with titles like *Seasoned Players* and *Fun Amanda 3*. The men would look at the magazines or watch the movies until they were sufficiently aroused. Then they would masturbate and ejaculate into a cup.

Had Henry played a movie that morning (how? On his phone?) or opened a magazine? (If so, where did he keep such a thing?) Did he undress entirely or just take off his pants, or not even? Had he thought of her? Someone else? What kind of orgasm did he have after washing his genitals with antibiotic soap and masturbating while sitting on the toilet? Maybe he stood. Or sat (or stretched out?) on the floor . . .

The male wiring: it was just so other. On the face of it, so much simpler. Imagine being able to come at the pop of a lid on a plastic cup.

Two of the men had gone and returned when she heard her name called again. A different nurse took her now to a different, smaller waiting room.

Eighteen excruciating minutes passed before a doctor, dressed in green surgical scrubs, dropped down into a chair across from her. His mask, at least, was lowered off his face. He introduced himself as the anesthesiologist, Dr. Milliken. He explained that in about five minutes a nurse would bring her into the operating room, where he would give her a modest cocktail of drugs that would cause her to fall asleep completely and quickly. When she woke up, the retrieval would be over.

The nurse returned with an empty gurney and asked Costanza to climb up on top of it. Then she pushed Costanza ahead, through a pair of swinging doors and into the operating room. Costanza slid onto a large bedlike table. At its foot there were two stirrups. The nurse helped fit Costanza's feet into them. "Dr. Rogers is doing the retrievals today," the nurse said. "He'll be here in a minute. Good luck to you, *mi amor.*"

This was one time when a minute was as described. Rogers, clean-shaven and nearly bald, came in through a different door. *His* mask was still over his mouth. He did not bother to lower it as he briefly described how he was going to aspirate the eggs from her ovaries. When she awoke, she would be told how many were retrieved and how they looked under the microscope. He asked her if she understood what was about to happen to her. She answered that she did. He had her sign one last form. The anesthesiologist materialized and began injecting liquid into her IV line. "It shouldn't be very long now," he said.

"Are you going to ask me to count backwards? I can do it in five lang—"

When she opened her eyes, Henry was sitting by her bed, holding her hand.

"I came over to check on you. It's done. It's over. You know that, right?"

She wasn't certain what she knew. But she nodded all the same. "You wonderful man. You look so—marvelous. Everyone's in white today. You match the clouds." He was wearing his white doctor's coat, over a shirt and tie. "I love you."

"I love you too," he said, but he didn't look so happy.

With great effort she organized her thoughts, her words. It was like setting a heavy, complicated machine in motion. "How many?"

That was the key question. That much she knew. How many eggs did they retrieve? She was pleased with herself for getting that question up and out.

"Five. Three are clearly mature. The others they're looking at."

So his face was dour because of the results. "Looking at?"

"Measuring. Waiting on. They can continue to grow in vitro."

"Not a village at all."

"A village?"

"Not at all"—she tried to speak more clearly, more logically—"what you hoped for."

"It's definitely something to work with. It only takes one viable egg, remember."

"I'm sorry."

"It's nobody's fault. You try one combination of drugs the first time. You change it the next."

He was already talking about a next time?

"Kiss me."

He kissed her. A whisper of a kiss.

The pain was like menstrual cramps. Bad but not incapacitating menstrual cramps. They started in the cab. As soon as she returned to the apartment, she took two Tylenol and went directly to bed.

She felt empty. She *was* empty. Her ovaries had been stimulated, swollen, and suctioned clean. Human reproduction, this essential act of nature, was happening outside her body, in a petri dish behind closed (indeed locked, and highly monitored) doors on the sixth floor of a hospital on the Upper East Side of the island of Manhattan. There was nothing she could do, yet again, but wait. Wait and sleep.

The sound of china pinging woke her. China pinging against china, on a tray. A teacup, a teapot, a little pitcher of warmed milk. Fruit, pastries.

With great concentration Andrew was carrying the tray, keeping it level. He lowered it down onto the bed next to her.

"Oh, Andrew. What a nice surprise."

"How do you feel?"

"Wiped out."

"Did it go . . . as you hoped?"

"Not entirely. But we'll know more in a day. When we hear what—takes." Her eyes filled up. "I promise not to cry."

"You can cry."

So she did. "I had no idea it would all be this intense."

"It's a big deal."

"Thank you for thinking of me." She pulled herself up, blew her nose.

From the other end of the apartment came the sound of a raised, peeved voice: Henry's. Amid this distant muttering a few phrases cohered: "where did I put" and "not where it belongs" and "I give up!"

Henry appeared in the doorway. He was carrying a different pastry, on a plain white plate.

"Ah, *there* it is. I've been looking for that tray all over the place." He glanced at Andrew. "I see you're all—set." Then: "How are you doing? Do you have any fever?"

"I don't think so."

He placed his palm on her forehead. "Cramping?"

"Less now."

He nodded. "You've been sleeping."

"I just woke up when Andrew came in."

"The anesthesia can take some time to work out of your system. And you didn't sleep so much last night, after all." He paused. "I'll let you rest."

He started to go. When Andrew didn't show any sign of joining him, Henry added, "*We'll* let you rest."

Andrew said goodbye. Henry waited until he left the room, then closed the door behind them and followed his son into the foyer.

"Were you thinking of staying over this evening, Andrew?"

"It's Monday, isn't it?"

"Yes. About that. I'm sure you understand that this is a—a complicated time for Costanza. For both of us. And I think—well, I know— that we could really use a bit of space. Costanza and I. Just until the transfer and the waiting period are over."

"Are you reducing me *further*? From once a week to nunce?"

"*Nunce?*"

"You know what I mean. *Gornisht.*"

"What's with the Yiddish?"

"I've been having dinner with Grandpa. On the nights I used to be here."

"I'm speaking about a very temporary arrangement. For a few weeks. I think it would just be simpler for everyone all around."

"Everyone—or you?"

"This is something I need right now. Something Costanza and I need."

"*You* need is more correct."

"Okay then. Something *I* need. What do you say?"

"Do I have any choice?"

Henry sighed. "Not really."

The embryologist phoned Henry early the following morning. Just three of Costanza's eggs had turned out to be mature. Two of the three had fertilized. They were at two and three cells in size. Still viable, but slow. The next twenty-four hours would be critical.

Costanza was still half-asleep when she heard Henry answer his cell phone and step into the bathroom. When she finally got up to have dinner the night before, she had had her first real glass of wine (actually two glasses, moderate ones) since she began the treatment. The alcohol, the anesthesia, the painkillers, the enormity of the day—all this combined to send her into an early, deep, and dreamless sleep, but she came out of it quickly enough when she heard Henry's murmuring.

It was a few moments before he stepped out of the bathroom. By then she was sitting upright in bed. After he imparted the facts, she said, "So it's bad."

"I would say it's average. The results are average." His voice, like his face, gave away nothing. His whole demeanor was professional, neutral.

"Can you put a number to them? To my chances of success?"

"I'm not a statistician, Costanza."

"But you are."

He hesitated. "Thirty percent. Twenty. Somewhere in there. It's not exact."

"It's not exact," she echoed bitterly.

"Your chances are much higher than they would be if we were having timed intercourse. As I've told you, the first round is often about gathering information. We'll alter the protocol the next time around. There are several options—"

"I wish you would stop talking about the next time so soon. This has been very hard for me. To sit here, to be waiting, preparing my body, my *mind* . . ."

"It's the physician in me. I cannot stop him—it."

"It?"

He simply looked at her somberly.

"I am too much of a patient now for you to take my hand? Or maybe I'm merely too much of a disappointment. Maybe that's it."

"I'm sorry, Costanza." He sat down on the edge of the bed. "You're not the disappointment. If anyone is, I am. The process is. Its unpredictability is regrettable."

He put his hand on hers. She was not comforted. She looked toward the windows. The blackout shades, still drawn, were framed in halos of bright morning sunlight. "There's something on my mind."

He waited for her to continue.

"I discovered yesterday, I was surprised to discover yesterday, I should say, that Judith had also undergone IVF. To have the boys."

He cocked his head.

"Hilda. She made a reference in passing, by accident. She didn't do anything wrong. It just slipped out."

He nodded slowly.

"You never thought to mention this to me before?"

"It felt like Judith's business. Her story."

"Which you were part of. A big part of. Come on."

Henry didn't say anything.

"Are you not going to tell me *why* Judith had IVF?"

Costanza saw clearly that Henry would have preferred not to have this conversation; but they were going to have it. Boy, were they.

Henry appeared to choose his words more carefully than usual. "We'd been trying to conceive for a while. A year. More. It's not that we were impatient so much as worried. Maybe we moved on to IVF faster than other people would have, on account of my work, also my bias, my nature. And Judith's. We were both solution seekers, problem solvers."

"But what was the problem exactly? Not her age."

"No. Not her age."

Henry took a moment to answer Costanza's question. The moment felt strangely long, and charged.

"It was my problem."

"It was your problem. What do you mean?"

"The obvious. My sperm count was not high. It was on the low side. Quite low."

"Your sperm count was not high. It was on the low side. Quite low." She repeated his words to understand them, to keep her anxiety from spiking. "You tell me this *now?*"

"Yes, I tell you this now. Now it no longer matters. It did then." His face reddened. He spoke rapidly. "We didn't have ICSI in those days. We couldn't extract a healthy sperm, wash it, and inject it into the mature egg. Today we can."

"I understand what ICSI is, Henry," she said sharply.

It was her turn to pause, to try to absorb—parse—the information Henry had just given her. "So plain old IVF worked for Judith?"

"Yes. We were lucky."

"It worked right away?"

"Two tries with Justin. Just one with Andrew. Judith was quite young."

"She produced many eggs. Many more than me."

He nodded.

"Forgive me if I need to review. You're saying that both boys were conceived through IVF."

"Yes."

He looked away from her. What did it mean that he looked away from her? "We were lucky, as I say."

"I see." But she didn't, exactly. "Have you tested your sperm since then? Since we decided to—to put ourselves through all this?"

Ourselves. What she meant was *herself. Myself.*

"ICSI renders sperm count essentially irrelevant. And anyway, Costanza, you have two fertilized eggs, both reasonably sized. You see that my sperm is viable. You see that what we do works."

"Thus far."

"Which is as far as we've come."

Her mind was working, churning. "Do the boys know?"

"What makes you ask that?"

The conversation was beginning to feel like a minefield. But why? "It seems like something they would know—should know."

"I've never told them. Judith may have."

"Why not?"

"I never thought of it."

"Just like you never thought to tell me?"

"I wouldn't put it that way."

"How would you put it then?"

"I never saw the need. It never came up."

"Your sons were born because of the science that has been your life's work, and you've never seen the need to tell them?"

"That's correct."

"If I'm lucky enough to become pregnant and grow and deliver and raise this baby, would you not tell her, or him?"

"I can see it's something we'd have to discuss."

"It is indeed," she said with a flash of anger.

In his calm—or was it placating?—doctor voice Henry said, "You might try seeing this from my point of view, Costanza. I oversee hundreds of cycles of in vitro a year. Low sperm count no longer registers as an especially concerning factor. Our clinic has one of the highest success rates in the country. Two years ago the ten-thousandth baby to be conceived through us was born. Ten thousand babies. That's what *I* think about—not all this."

She looked at Henry. "You reason your way around everything, don't you?"

"Reason around?"

"You resolve all possible concerns, all possible fears. You have a way of making me sound illogical, overly worried. Overemotional."

"I don't mean to do that."

"I think you do, as it happens. And I think it's a very male, a classically male, thing to do too. I don't know how comfortable you are with the paradox of human—human feeling. *My* feeling. And with the way that feeling might get to its own truth, by channels other than your logic. In Italy you seemed more—well, of course I did not know you so well then." She paused. "I'm not crazy, Henry. These drugs may make me more heightened than usual, but they don't make me crazy."

"That's your word. Not mine."

"Yes, my words, my feelings, my doubts—and my body." She swung her legs over the edge of the bed. "Did your embryologist say when she thought the transfer would be?"

"Tomorrow, as predicted. A nurse will call with the time. It's usually in the early afternoon."

She had waited through the first two weeks, to see how her body would perform under stimulation. She had waited through the last beastly day, and night, to see how her eggs would fertilize. After the transfer she would be waiting for another two weeks to see if she would become pregnant. On this, her one day free from waiting, Costanza put her conversation with Henry out of her mind—for the moment. Something in it, several things, were unsettling and not easily parsed, but she knew herself. She knew when she had to shut down a certain way of thinking, or else it would threaten to consume her. She knew that if she started to pick apart his responses to her questions about how Justin and Andrew had been conceived, and what they didn't know about their conception, and why they didn't know it, she would likely not think of anything else. For her peace of mind—more important, her peace of *body*—she couldn't allow that to happen now.

Instead she showered, dressed, made her own coffee and breakfast, and sat down with her translation. What a relief it was to lose herself in someone else's story, someone else's language and rhythms. It was one of the great pleasures of translating, for her, to be able to slip outside her brain and into another person's; to be thinking, actively thinking, but not to be bound by her own worries and obsessions, her own mental kinks. It was like travel; better than travel. For the remainder of the day she remained blessedly elsewhere. She almost forgot what she and her body were going through. Almost.

A new day, a new disappointment: one of the embryos had not grown beyond four cells and appeared to have a good deal of fragmentation. The other had reached eight cells and had moderate fragmentation. Costanza was to return to the hospital at two o'clock for the transfer of one or both, depending on how they looked as the day unfolded.

•

At ten minutes to two Costanza presented herself at the hospital. This time she sat quietly, read through the most recent pages of her translation, and observed the other women. This wasn't a day for the men. This wasn't a day with anesthesia in it, or enormous suspense. They were there because they had at least one or two viable embryos to transfer. They were there because, thus far, the in vitro was working to whatever extent. The women sat calmly reading or quietly chatting. Costanza realized this was the first time she had heard any of these women speak to one another.

She was soon sent off to change, then she was led into the same inner waiting room as before, and, after that, the transfer room. Within minutes a doctor came in and introduced herself as Dr. Trager.

"Everything is happening so much faster this time," Costanza said.

"Well, it's a lot simpler today." Dr. Trager tapped a few keys on a nearby computer. "You have a single embryo. Nine cells. You can take a look."

An image appeared on a screen that was hung on the wall across from Costanza. It looked like a tiny collection of bubbles, something at the end of a child's wand after it had been dipped in a bottle of soap and glycerin. This was her embryo. Her nine-cell embryo, a union of her egg and Henry's sperm, combined and fertilized through intracytoplasmic sperm injection and grown these past three days in a warmed broth of fertilization medium, an act of human ingenuity that was utterly mysterious. Miraculous, even.

"Can you show me the fragmentation?"

If Dr. Trager was surprised that Costanza knew what fragmentation was, or that her embryo was fragmented, she didn't show it. Instead she dragged the cursor over to some of the bubbles that seemed imperfect in shape, overlapping and messy. "It's about twenty percent. It's not that bad."

Not that bad. "The embryo looks like it's breaking down."

"You might put it that way, but it doesn't always matter. Very often these embryos turn into—"

"Yes, I know, perfectly healthy babies," Costanza said brusquely.

The doctor nodded.

"Don't you people ever give a bad report?"

"Well, we don't transfer when the embryo is clearly not viable."

"And unclearly not viable? Ambiguously not viable?"

Dr. Trager looked at her. "Ms. Ansaldo, it's our job to make life. That means we push for every single opportunity we get."

⇌

Adapting to the rhythms of his parents' divorce had been a major challenge for Andrew when he was younger. It wasn't just the logistical confusion (though there was plenty of that; for years he left things at one apartment when he needed them in the other); it was being expected to check seamlessly out of one world, one sensibility, and into another according to a calendar he could almost never negotiate. There was such a marked difference between waking up as Judith's son and waking up as Henry's that he used to linger in bed on a changeover morning, reminding himself whether it was okay to be more outspoken (Judith), or less (Henry); whether his shifts in mood, which spiked unpredictably during his early adolescence, were likely to incite a reaction (Judith, of course) or be overlooked (of course Henry); and where it was wiser to be open or more self-editing about certain aspects of his personal life (mainly of late Charlotte). He had to pay attention even to such basic details as which parent cared whether he hung up his clothes (Judith) and which didn't (Henry, usually).

All this had settled into a pattern that Andrew didn't have to think so hard about anymore—until his recent, and presumably temporary, banishment to the West Side. Waking up at the start of a week without the prospect of the pendulum swinging him between Henry and Judith, Upper East and Upper West, Andrew felt an unease that took him a few days to recognize for what it was: he felt, he admitted to himself, a little trapped—with his own mother. (Well, to be fair, also with his stepfather.) Before, when Andrew bristled at Henry's overbearing nature, Andrew knew that after a few days he would be treated to Judith's curiosity and concern; likewise, when it began to feel that Judith was asking too many questions, worrying over too many small details, and getting too involved in his schoolwork and social life, there was Henry's bracing focus on bigger, or anyway different, matters.

Now it was Judith, every morning, and again every evening, asking how he was doing, and in a way that always seemed to expect him to answer that something was wrong. She was the kind of parent who liked a problem; liked to sit with it, tease it out, and find a solution. How much of this had to do with her being a psychologist and how much of it just had to do with her being Judith, he would never know. It almost didn't matter how he answered; still she probed, still she sought to expose, parse, and dissect. It didn't matter if he told her that he was fine; she seemed almost determined to hear that he was unhappy (much as she was the opposite) about his exile to the Upper West Side, but the truth of his feelings wasn't that simple. He was unhappy, yet he kind of understood, because he sensed that Henry had never totally gotten over the fact that Costanza and Andrew had met each other and become friends first. He understood because, of all people, weirdly Judith helped him to understand. "You remember when Charlie and I first moved in together?" she said to Andrew at breakfast on the first extra morning he had stayed with her. "It was that summer when your father took you boys to France. Charlie and I seized that opportunity to get used to each other. After a certain age, it's not that easy to combine your life with someone new, even someone you love as much as I loved Charlie."

It had been a long time since Judith had tried to help Andrew sort out a matter related to Henry; but then, when he thought about it, she was also speaking about herself. Herself and Charlie.

Andrew considered for a moment before saying, "I kind of wish I'd known that before. I thought Charlie moved in while we were away so that we couldn't have a chance to object."

"Well, that was probably part of it too." Judith tilted her head back, studied her son for a moment. "But you don't object to Costanza, do you? My impression is the opposite."

Andrew tried to put on as neutral a face as possible, which was often difficult around Judith. What she didn't perceive, she guessed at, and she was more often right than wrong. He had told her almost nothing about Costanza, both out of his own sense of protectiveness and, more specifically, because Henry had asked him before if he would agree not to mention to Judith that Costanza was doing a cycle of IVF. Instead he was to say (echoing Judith as it turned out) that moving in together was stressful and that the pair needed some privacy. Fertility treatment, Henry pointed out, was one of the most difficult things that could ever come at a couple, and having outside eyes on the experience as it was unfolding only made matters more anxious. Judith, for all her expertise at figuring people out, had no idea about any of that, but she did, it seemed pretty clear, sense that Costanza and Andrew shared some kind of affinity.

"You don't object to Costanza," Judith repeated.

"No. I like her."

"Justin told me that you met her before Henry did."

Andrew nodded. He wondered how much of a nod was too much. With most people, it wouldn't matter, but his mother wasn't most people.

"I'm kind of curious about how all that happened. How you met her, how they got together."

"Mom, you know Henry wouldn't want me to talk about any of that with you, just as you wouldn't—"

"With me and Charlie there was nothing to hide. Almost from the very beginning, for better or worse, we were open, as you well know."

"I'm not saying there's anything to hide. I'm just saying . . ." What *was* he saying? He felt his cheeks grow warm.

"You like her, don't you? You care for her."

"For Costanza."

"Yes, Andrew, for Costanza."

He shrugged. The shrug was like the nod earlier. He worried his muscles had a little too much activation. He could almost feel the assessing going on behind Judith's dark brown eyes, the way it did, or so he imagined, with her patients, and it made him uncomfortable.

"Sure I care for her. I think she's a good fit for Henry."

"I see." Judith's tone suggested she saw more, or intuited more, than she was choosing to let on.

Costanza was pregnant. She was convinced.

Her breasts were tender, and their areolae had changed shape. They were leaking darker, redder pigment out of their normally circumscribed circles. A classic symptom. She had read about it.

She was nauseated too. The idea of certain foods repulsed her. Cream cheese, for instance, which Henry brought home with bagels for Sunday brunch. Mint jelly. Kiwi. Just touching it, feeling the fuzzy texture of its skin, made her throat constrict.

Also there were these odd—vibrations. She didn't know what else to call them. Little twinges, echoes deep within her body, as though it were busy making life.

She didn't say anything to Henry. She didn't want him to know how utterly obsessed she was. She waited for him to leave for work before she took off her clothes and stood naked in front of the mirror, first frontally, then in profile. Of course there was nothing to see, but she had to look.

She didn't know when she had last so enjoyed looking at herself in the mirror. *My body*, she thought. *It can do this.*

The next morning she again stood naked in front of the mirror. Her breasts were not tender. The areolas were pink again. On her toast she ate cream cheese *and* mint jelly, just to see. She couldn't face the kiwi, though.

Henry had glimpsed her palpating her breasts, cupping them from below, to see if they felt different, heavier. He said, "Just so you know, for lots of women the progesterone can mimic the symptoms of pregnancy. I've seen patients set themselves up for a great letdown."

The progesterone, which was meant to help the embryo stick, and which he was injecting into her buttocks every night at ten o'clock, a shot so painful that afterward she had to ice her backside. So it was the drugs, not her body, after all.

"I know the waiting isn't easy," he said.

"It's excruciating."

On another day she felt, and heard, a gurgling in her abdomen. She had eaten a simple lunch. It wasn't indigestion. She could feel her womb working. Her breasts were tender again.

Later that same day, just before dinner, she went to pee and found a spot of blood in her underwear. Implantation bleeding! She had read about this too. A message from deep within the body.

Her breasts were tender. She was convinced again.

Some mornings Costanza woke up and in those first few moments of consciousness forgot what she was waiting for, what was going on in her life. She felt a sense of liberation in that interstice between sleeping and waking that was beyond physical. She wasn't confined to a woman's body that was medicated and forbidden from exercising and drinking; she was free. Free from the needs, the mechanics, the tricks (the trickiness) of the flesh: freed from carnality; free from being obsessed with her reproductive system; free from eating, digesting, farting, shitting, menstruating; free from bathing, moisturizing, putting on and taking off makeup and washing, cutting, and combing her hair; free from stink, free from perfume; free from panties, panty liners, tampons, bras, T-shirts, blouses, skirts, pants, dresses, sweaters; free from *coats* (God how she hated a heavy winter coat), stockings, socks, shoes, hats, scarves, and gloves; free from jewelry; free from having to blow her nose, floss and clean her teeth, harvest the wax from her ears; free from having to clip her fingernails and her toenails, shape her eyebrows, shave her underarms, wipe her ass.

It was bliss. To be free; to forget.

But then she remembered. After seconds, minutes—it was not easy to tell how long it took for the mind to fly, then land. With a thud. And it hurt. As if she'd been struck. Lashed. She was still trapped in her body and she was still waiting.

When Andrew hadn't shown up at Henry's for more than a week, she called him to ask why. Swim practice, he said. Homework. An overnight to Haverford, where his cousin Sophie was a junior.

The progesterone seemed to have trimmed Costanza's reserves of patience. "It sounds like you're making an excuse," she said bluntly.

"Honestly, I've just been crazy busy."

"Don't say *honestly* when you're not being honest. It's better to say nothing."

There was a long silence at the other end of the phone line.

"Andrew?"

"You said it was better to say nothing."

"Tell me the real reason."

Another silence.

"Tell me."

Another silence, shorter this time. "Henry asked me to give you two some space."

"Ah."

"He said that this was a complicated time for you."

Complicated. What an interesting word. What a telling and not-telling word. The son was threatened by the father, and now the father was threatened by the son. Threatened? Was that even right, or was she, or were the drugs, inventing it?

"Your father is only trying to help," Costanza said, even if she only half believed it.

"We could always meet out—for one of our walks, if you like. Or a coffee. Or you could come to one of my practices. There's one on Monday after school up at Asphalt Green."

"I don't know, Andrew. Maybe it's better for us to wait."

"For what?"

"For all this to be over. Either way, I'll know in about a week."

It was the slowest week she could remember living. When she opened up a book, her eyes blurred. The pixels on the computer screen felt like pins pricking her eyeballs. She was uninterested in cooking. She was hot, then cold, then hot. She had so much energy that she imagined taking apart Henry's kitchen and painting it herself in a single morning (wisely, she didn't); she was so exhausted that after breakfast she felt she could go right back to bed (wisely, she did).

All day long Costanza kept looping back to one state of mind, one state of being, a clear unrelenting consciousness of what she was doing, which was waiting. *To wait*: surely it was one of the most painful verbs in the English language. *Aspettare*: with that harsh *p*, even in Italian it was an ungainly word.

On Monday she set out for a walk. It was a frigid January afternoon, but she felt drawn to the park, to the thin frosting of snow that made the leafless trees look like intricately branched candelabra stuck into a vast white cake. She noted the way the bright wintry New York light, reflected and amplified by the snow, made her eyes ache. She noted the way she moved in her own portable cloud of breath that replenished itself over and over.

For twenty minutes she stopped thinking about the embryo and her body; the embryo *in* her body. Instead she thought of the scattering of birds—sparrows?—busy searching for morsels to eat. She thought of the bulbs, buried under the snow, that in a few months would spring to life again with the longer days and the new season.

Just when her mind was about to deliver her back at the threshold of her bodily worries, Costanza remembered that Andrew had invited her to his swim practice that afternoon. Had this been why she felt drawn out of the house and had been strolling toward the north end of the park? Asphalt Green was north, and quite a lot farther east. His practice began in half an hour. She could watch for a bit and afterward she could visit with Andrew. She would again be taken out of herself, or possibly be made to feel more at ease *in* herself.

She could smell the chlorine from half a block away. She followed her nose to the pool, where she took off her hat, gloves, scarf, and coat and sat down in the bleachers. The water was alive with dozens of swimmers doing the butterfly, one after the next making vigorous arcs. She tried to pick Andrew out among them, but all she saw was a rapidly flashing film strip of shoulders, backs, and heads in tight bright yellow swim caps. She listened to the hands and the bodies slice through water. It was a calming, lulling sound. The sound, along with the heat and humidity of the room, made her feel woozy. She closed her eyes and listened to the water frothing, the coach blowing his whistle and barking his corrections. When she next opened her eyes, she saw a line of young men standing at the deep end. Long, thin, muscled young men with milky pink skin, dripping statues in royal blue Speedos. The coach blew his whistle, and the first six dived into the water; another whistle, another six. Andrew was among the third group. His eyes were obscured by tinted goggles, and he, like all the other swimmers, was concentrating on the timing of his dive, so she didn't think he saw her. But she saw him, strikingly muscled and effortlessly agile as he raised his arms in sync with five of his fellow swimmers. At the coach's whistle, the six of them sprang into the air and made beautiful arcing shapes followed by precise splashes. Once in the water they rose up and began a classic free stroke, whisking the water into a bubbling, hissing foam.

Just as Andrew and his team began their fourth lap, she was seized by a hot flash. The air, the damp, the drugs, her doubled-up sweaters—surely. Or mostly? Partly? She was aware of the intensity of her watching now. She was watching Andrew, all these young men, with some—yes—pleasure. It unsettled her. She wished she had brought a bottle of water; she wished she could have a gulp, just a single gulp, of cold water or cold air to clear her mind.

She could. All she had to do was stand up and leave. She stood up shakily, and she left.

At four o'clock the next morning she was awake, consulting the bedside clock. Did four o'clock count as morning? It was dark outside. The streets were quiet. Henry was sleeping with one arm folded winglike and tucked under his head. Four o'clock was not morning.

At five forty-five she was up again. Henry, though apparently still asleep, had set the palm of his hand protectively on her belly. She was convinced that in his sleep, in his dreams, he was trying to communicate with their embryo. Maybe his touch, his physician's touch, would will it to live; live and grow.

She waited until he had left for work, then she hobbled into the bathroom with a full bladder. She opened the pregnancy test she had tucked in her bathrobe the night before and peed on the stick. Then she waited. Three minutes, the package said. Three long minutes.

It was unmistakable. It was mistakable. There was a hint of a second line. She held the test up to the light. Then again to the window. It was like chasing a mirage; the more she looked, the less she saw.

After ten minutes, Costanza threw the test away. Summoning a discipline that was amazing to her, she showered, then sat down to work on her translation. She worked past lunch. Afterward she went for one of her walks. Normally she would then have shopped for dinner, but she had no interest in food. When Henry came home they sent out for pizza.

"It gets harder the closer you come to the twenty-eighth day, doesn't it?" Henry said when they sat down and he studied her face. "But think of this. It's only two more days."

On her way home from her walk that afternoon Costanza stopped at a drugstore. She had vowed to herself that she would wait until the blood test; it was the only definitive way to know, Henry had warned her more than once. But that was before the drugstore positioned itself right in her path, before she came across, for the first time, First Response Gold, a *gilded* incarnation of the regular First Response test. And digital too. What would they think of next? Verbal? Imagine a tiny machine speaking the news from a computer chip: "Madam, we would like to inform you . . ." Madam? Miss? *Ms.?*

Costanza bought a box. As before she hid the test in the pocket of her bathrobe. She and Henry went to sleep as soon as they tidied up after dinner. He slept through the night. She woke again at four, again at five-something. At a quarter past six she slipped out of bed and into the bathroom, closing the door quietly behind her. On the twenty-seventh day, the pregnancy test was something like ninety-five, ninety-eight percent accurate. That was good enough for her. She peed on the stick and waited. In the window of the test a tiny icon of a clock blinked and blinked. *Be patient*, this meant. *I'm doing my job. Your heart is racing, your neck is damp with sweat, you're determined to know your fate, and I'm looking for traces of HCG in your urine . . .*

The tiny clock blinked. Behind her the door opened. Henry padded into the room, squinting. He looked at the test, then Costanza. "How long has it been?"

"Two minutes."

He hadn't put on his bathrobe. He was shivering.

She kept her eyes locked on the results window. He kept his eyes locked on the results window.

The clock blinked and blinked. The last minute felt like an hour.

Finally the window went blank. Then a word appeared on the screen:

No.

No?

NO.

She looked at Henry; Henry looked at her. It was as though a current whipped between them with a zap. She felt it, but remained frozen, incredulous. Henry too seemed paralyzed at first, but then, and to her surprise, he emitted a single aching sound, half moan, half sob.

⇌

The last time Andrew walked out of school in the afternoon and saw his father waiting for him was when his grandmother died, and Henry had come to tell him in person. That was eight years earlier, when

Andrew was in fourth grade. He remembered with great clarity coming out through the main doors of the school with his friend Kevin. They were talking about the kind of skateboards they wanted to buy when they had saved up enough money. The inanity of that conversation would remain forever after frozen in time for Andrew, who had looked up and noticed Henry but was so confused by the incongruity of his father's appearance at school at that hour that he didn't stop talking or walking. At first he wasn't even sure Henry *was* Henry. Then after a moment he understood that something had to be wrong. Very wrong, for Henry to be there. Then time slowed down, and it took him, it seemed, many minutes instead of a few seconds to reach his father and hear what he had to say.

Now Andrew was a senior in high school, and Henry had come to tell him that Leopold's turn had come.

"It's Grandpa. Something happened," Andrew said anxiously.

"To Leopold?" Henry was confused. "Nothing has happened to Leopold. Nothing *else*."

"Is it Mom? Justin? Why aren't you at work?"

"It's nothing like that. I just wanted to talk to you. Can we . . . ?" Henry indicated the sidewalk ahead, away from Andrew's classmates.

Andrew and Henry stepped off to the side of the street. "Actually, I've come about Costanza."

Andrew's stomach tightened. "Is she all right?"

"Physically she's fine. But mentally . . . mentally she's rather . . . low. The cycle didn't work, and she's coming off the drugs, and quite honestly, I'm finding her a little unreachable right now. Well, quite a lot unreachable. She's very low. I said that. Very, very low."

Andrew noticed that Henry's skin had a gray, almost sickly cast, and that his eyes seemed tired and distant under heavy lids. "And you have come to tell me this because . . ."

"You're her friend. And because you care for her. I thought that maybe . . . maybe you could go see her."

Andrew nodded slowly. "I care for Costanza and I'm her friend, yet when it was inconvenient for you, you asked me to stay away. Now that things have changed, now that she's low, very, very low, you're asking me to come back."

"Yes, now I am asking you to come back." Henry's mouth puckered,

as though the words had a sour taste. "Please. She's having trouble—
and I think you—I think that she might like to see you."

Andrew nodded again. He was aware of his head bobbing rhythmi-
cally as he absorbed what Henry was saying. Absorbed just how selfish
a man his father was turning out to be.

"I'll have to think about it," Andrew said finally.

"You'll have to think about it? What does that mean?"

"It means I have to think about it."

"You can be mad at me for all kinds of things, but please don't take
it out on Costanza."

Andrew considered for a moment. "If I agree, can we consider
this ban on my coming home lifted? I can come and go again the way
I used to?"

"Yes, yes, anything you want. So you'll go see her? You'll go today,
Andy?"

Andy? Things must have been very difficult for Henry to reach back
for that old nickname.

"I'll think about it, Dad," Andrew repeated evenly.

In the Manhattan equivalent of coming home to find the locks on the
front door had been changed, Andrew stepped into the lobby on the East
Side and saw that Joe, the midweek doorman, had a substitute—LEWIS,
it said on his name tag. Lewis intercepted Andrew before he could head
for the elevator.

When Andrew explained that he was going up to apartment 9E, *his*
apartment, Lewis said, "Oh, you're Dr. Weissman's son. The younger
one. Your father said I should be on the lookout for you. Jeremy is your
brother."

Andrew didn't correct him. The idea of Justin one day being greeted
as Jeremy was just too sweet.

The apartment was dark and quiet. Andrew called out, "Hello?" But
the question floated off into all the new interior décor.

He went into the kitchen and opened the refrigerator. The refrigerator was as good a reflection as any of Costanza's state of mind. Other
than condiments and a carton of milk, there was nothing but a chunk
of Parmigiano, a few lemons, and a bunch of limp greens.

He made his way to the back of the apartment. A narrow band of light was shining out from the bottom of Henry's bedroom door. Andrew stepped toward it and knocked.

Costanza, if she was there, didn't answer.

He knocked again and waited.

Finally there was a faint "Yes?"

He opened the door. Costanza was lying in bed, or rather *on* it, fully dressed. She was even wearing her shoes. Her eyes were pink and dim. Her hair was spread out on the pillow.

"Oh, Andrew," she said in a low, flat, faraway voice. "I wasn't expecting you."

"I left you a message on your cell phone. I said I was coming by around seven."

"Is it seven already?" She propped herself up to look at the bedside clock, then dropped back down again. "I haven't been—engaging with the phone."

"Henry told me about the cycle. I'm sorry."

She shrugged. Her jaw quivered.

"Is my father coming home soon?"

"I honestly don't remember."

"Would you like me to order out, or even make some dinner? I think you should eat. I know I should."

"Dinner?" Costanza looked at the clock again. "Let's order in."

"But doesn't cooking usually . . . make you feel better?"

"Usually—but not tonight."

"Do you want to talk about the cycle?"

"It failed. What else is there to say?"

"Are you going to try again?"

"I can't think about that right now, Andrew. I need to get back to myself first."

"What's going to help you do that?"

"Time."

They both fell silent.

"My birthday's a week from Saturday. And so is Grandpa's."

"Your father said something about a dinner. He said Justin might be coming in as it's also Presidents' Day weekend."

"An extra special birthday treat," Andrew said flatly.

"What do you usually do?"

"We bring in deli, of course. Sometimes Henry remembers to buy a cake."

Costanza thought for a moment. "If I'm up to it, maybe we can do something a little more creative."

"I don't know if Grandpa will go for that. But after all it's my birthday too, right?"

As soon as she stepped into the Greek market that was just a few blocks away from the Thirtieth Avenue subway stop in Astoria, Costanza felt her heaviness of being lift for the first time in weeks. She felt as if she had traveled somewhere far from her regular life. All the usual markers were different: the scale of the buildings; the look and bearing of the people; the scents; the words, in this case also in places the alphabet, on signs and packages; and especially the food. There were dozens of different kinds of olives in open containers; enormous bricks of feta that looked like blocks of snow; bunches of fragrant dried oregano; spanakopita just out of the oven, flaky, crisp, and oozing spinach and cheese. An aisle along the front window was filled with religious candles, soap scented with lavender or rosemary, worry beads, mugs printed with images of ancient Greek statuary, and blue glass eyes that were meant to bring luck.

Costanza fingered one of these for a moment, before reminding herself that she didn't believe in such talismans. Actually, in talismans of any kind.

She and Andrew filled a shopping cart nearly to the top, then arranged for their bags to be held while they went to have coffee in a café next door.

"Coming out here makes me think of our walks in Florence," Andrew said when they were out on the street. "Maybe we could do more of that kind of thing here . . ."

"Maybe," she said, but in a tone that suggested the opposite.

"You know, my father seems to feel it's okay for me to be around again now."

"That was something he and I never discussed, just for the record."

They walked on in silence. After a moment Andrew said, "You came to my practice the other day. Why didn't you stay?"

Costanza flushed. "I didn't think you saw me. I wasn't myself, with all the drugs. It was so warm in there . . ."

"I see."

His *I see* was like her *maybe* earlier. Deliberately untruthful, or imperfectly truthful.

"You swim gracefully, Andrew. You *are* graceful, in so many ways. You're a very caring young man. So patient with me, and so thoughtful. One day I think you will make a wonderful partner to a very lucky girl—woman."

"I appreciate the nice words, Costanza. But it feels like you're speaking from some distance. Like you're a remote grown-up."

"I hope I'm not remote. But I am a grown-up, or trying to be."

"Trying . . . ?"

She looked at him. "You know that you and your father share a certain . . . insistence?"

"No, we don't. He insists. I just think aloud, sometimes."

Costanza produced a small smile. "Henry is not always the easiest person. I recognize that, from my own experience now and of course from the way you speak about him. But you have to understand, he is— this is—my path, my life."

They had reached the café, which was helpful, as the atmosphere between them had become uncomfortable. They sat down and ordered coffee and a plate of baklava.

"We haven't really had a chance to talk about your news."

"Well, it's not exactly news anymore. I do think Penn will be a good fit for me. I got lucky with the early decision—I just wish I hadn't put so much time in on all the other applications, but my mother and Charlie insisted."

Costanza took a sip of coffee. "My own feeling, and this may come from having grown up where I did, is that all this to-do about where you go to college is kind of out of proportion to what really matters, which is what you make of wherever you land, and I have a feeling you'll make a lot of it."

"I'll try."

She sat back in her chair. "Has anyone caught your interest at school, or not at school?"

"You mean, I'm guessing, girls-wise?"

"Yes, that's what I mean."

He shook his head.

"Have you heard from Charlotte?"

"Not a word."

"There comes a time, you know, when you just have to let go. When I was near the end of the longest relationship of my younger life, the man I was involved with, and still cared for deeply, said something to me that I have never forgotten: 'You cannot make someone love you.'"

Andrew studied Costanza's face closely. "That must have hurt coming from someone *you* loved."

"Hugely. And it seemed so unfeeling as to be cruel. But I have come to see that he was wise, in his way."

"You cannot make someone love you."

"No. You cannot."

On the afternoon of Leopold and Andrew's shared birthday dinner Henry was called to the hospital, where one of his patients, six weeks into her pregnancy, was having a complication. He returned close to six o'clock, drained and irritable.

"This was not an easy day," he said to Costanza as he took off his jacket. "I think I might need to move up the cocktail hour." He uncorked a bottle of wine. "I assume you got my message and the deli is all sorted out."

Costanza explained about her adventure in Astoria with Andrew, and the menu the two of them had planned.

"The two of you? Don't you think it would have been more appropriate for it to have been decided by the two of *us*?"

"Well, it *is* Andrew's birthday as well as Leopold's."

"Yes, but what's my father going to eat?"

"I made a substantial salad," Costanza said with forced brightness. "There are all kinds of different dishes to try. I'm sure he'll find something he likes."

"I wonder if it's too late to call over there." Henry reached for the phone. Costanza, offended, hurried out of the room. Henry put the phone down and turned to follow her, but stopped when he saw that they had an audience.

"Going out to Queens really helped take Costanza's mind off things,"

Andrew said. "And anyway I picked up a pastrami sandwich for Grandpa just in case."

Henry just glared at his son.

"She worked hard to put this meal together. She was trying to be creative, different. It's what makes her Costanza."

"I don't need you to tell me what makes Costanza Costanza."

Henry found Costanza and apologized. "The food doesn't matter," Henry said as he stepped into the shower. Costanza, for her part, said, "I know I'm extra sensitive right now. It won't last forever. I *hope* it won't last forever."

Henry was still getting dressed when the house phone rang, so Costanza alone greeted Leopold at the front door.

"Leopold," she said, after kissing him on both cheeks, "happy birthday to you. You look wonderful."

"You are charming, my dear. A charming liar. The lady"—he stepped aside so that Lorna could precede him—"now *she* looks wonderful. I look as I am, fatigued."

Lorna did look wonderful, in a pretty green blouse and with her black and silver hair pulled into a chic bun. She and Costanza exchanged an embrace before Lorna, indicating a bag, said that she had a few things to take into the kitchen.

"You'll wait for me just a minute?" Leopold asked Costanza.

As last time, he headed straight to the bathroom to wash his hands. When he emerged, she could smell the scent of lavender, from a bar of the Greek soap she had bought that afternoon.

"I have some things for you," he announced. "Shall we sit?"

They headed for the living room.

"But wait? What happened here?"

Costanza explained about her refurbishing project. Leopold inspected. Leopold absorbed. "No more trace of Her Whose Name I Do Not Speak. And such a good color sense too."

"Thank you, Leopold."

"An auspicious sign."

She pointedly did not ask him of what. He told her anyway: "I know from *ferpitzing* the house. In my business, it meant something when a couple came in to select fabric together."

As they sat down, Leopold reached into his pocket and handed

Costanza a burgundy leather jewelry box. It was old and worn around the edges.

"You bring me a present on *your* birthday? Isn't it supposed to be the other way around?"

"It's much nicer to give than to get."

Costanza pressed a small brass button at the front of the box to unlock a padded, silk-lined interior stamped with the name of a long-vanished Viennese jeweler. Resting against the padding was a pair of dangling rose-gold earrings set with modest emeralds. "They belonged to Nina's mother," Leopold said. "She had given them for safekeeping to a neighbor, a goy. They found us afterward, a strange stroke of luck. 'The jewelry could survive, but not the woman,' Nina used to say. 'Explain that.' She wore them for fancy. She loved that she could touch something her mother had touched."

"They're beautiful, Leopold. But shouldn't you save them for one of the boys? For their wives, or maybe one day their daughters?"

"You think I'll live long enough to meet their wives? And what are we saying, *their*? I don't think Justin will have much use for his great-grandmama's baubles. And as for the other, he'll be having his heart broken another fifteen times before he settles down. No, I want you to have them."

"I don't know what to say."

"How about thank you?"

She thanked him. She embraced him.

"There's something else." Leopold reached into the breast pocket of his jacket and handed her a small cloth pouch. "It too was Nina's."

Inside the pouch was a yellow Star of David. The fabric was so thin that in places Costanza could see where the warp and weft came together, and just barely at that.

"Leopold. I—"

"It's a little unusual maybe. But you see I have given one to Henry, one to each of the boys. I have two left. Just one now."

"But why me?"

"Because you are with my son, and—" Leopold stopped. "You see I, Nina and I, we could only bring into the world the one child. We were so—so beat up after the war. We had to start our lives again from *zilch*.

There was too little time, too little money. Nina lost several pregnancies before Henry . . ." He paused. "Well, it was not to be."

She touched the star gingerly.

"The science is quite miraculous now. The way they can help nature. ICSI is the one that gets me. Injecting a single sperm into an egg—this is impressive. This is a way of beating fate." His old fogged eyes fixed on her. "As maybe you can imagine, I like the idea of beating fate."

She understood what he was getting at now. "I gather you know then, Leopold."

He hesitated—but only briefly—before nodding.

"But for all the science, all the miracles, we didn't beat fate, did we?"

"This time." Leopold paused. "You must try again. You must try until you cannot try anymore."

A few minutes before seven o'clock the front door opened. "Jeremy has arrived," Justin called into the library-cum-dining-room, where everyone was already sitting at the table, which had again been elegantly set to Leopold's standard. "I hope you haven't started yet."

Leopold leaned into Lorna. "What did he say?"

"It's Justin. But he said Jeremy has arrived."

"Who's Jeremy? Another boyfriend?"

She answered with a shrug just as Justin stepped into the room. "It appears I have a new name."

A thin waif of a girl in tight jeans and a flowing white blouse trailed in after Justin. "Someone called Lewis just baptized him," she said.

Leopold turned to look at her. "Baptized Justin? What?"

"It's just a manner of speech, Grandpa." Justin planted a kiss on top of his grandfather's head. "This is Zoë. She's *always* been Zoë, right?"

"Right . . . Jeremy."

He laughed. She laughed.

Henry stood up. "I'm sorry." He extended his hand to the girl. "We didn't expect . . ."

"It's all right. I'm macrobiotic. I'll just have a glass of wine. I'll sit on the floor if you don't have a chair."

"We have a chair," said Costanza. She went off to find a chair, also a plate, cutlery, a glass, and a napkin.

"Is wine macrobiotic?" Andrew asked.

"My little brother, Andrew, the nutritionist." Justin went on to introduce the others. Then he dropped into the open chair next to his grandfather.

"So what happened to the *fagele*?" Leopold asked with his usual bluntness.

"He has another *fagele* now."

"Pity."

"Yes and no." Justin smiled at Zoë.

Leopold said, "I don't mind if you like the boys, Justin. Just so you know. I've been reflecting. The world is a looser place than when I grew up. I mean, think of what my people would have said"—he glanced at Lorna—"a fellow like me with a lady like her."

"Because she's black, you mean."

Leopold said unhesitatingly, "Yes, that's what I mean."

"Well, I'm with Zoë now."

"I see," Leopold said. Then: "Actually, I don't see."

"I like girls *and* boys, Grandpa."

"I like boys *and* girls," said Zoë.

"Kismet," said Henry from the head of the table.

"Where does that word come from, anyway?" said Andrew.

"I believe it's Arabic," said Henry. "It has something to do with the will of Allah."

"First baptism, then Allah," Leopold said. "What's next?"

"Dinner," said Costanza.

The salad, the spinach pie, the stuffed grape leaves, the olives, the Greek cheeses Costanza had paired with pears, apples, and quince paste—all of it was light, bright, and disappeared so quickly that she had to replenish the bowls and platters twice from the ample provisions she and Andrew had brought back from Astoria. Leopold never opened his deli sandwich. Zoë the macrobioticist suspended her rules beyond just the wine and dug in with appetite. Without David there, Justin seemed more relaxed, much more himself. And Andrew retreated into high observing mode, as though he were making photographs just by looking around the room.

For Costanza, the evening had the feeling of a turning point. The ordeal of the past month seemed on its way to coalescing into an experience that would situate itself in her past. It would be the cycle that she had tried, a trial that had failed, the failure that, in time, she would learn to live with. Despite Leopold, she did not yet know what she would do next. What she and Henry would do next. But the fact that her mind could expand to accommodate the mere idea of next was a sign that something was shifting.

Only when Costanza started to clear away the dinner dishes did Henry notice, and comment on, something that Costanza had observed much earlier in the evening: Lorna was wearing a bright diamond on the ring finger of her left hand.

"Father, is there something you and Lorna have to tell us?"

"I wondered when you'd ask." Leopold took Lorna's hand in his. "And, yes, it means exactly what you think it does. Exactly what such rings always mean."

The old man was beaming and flushed. "Lorna and I hope that you will be free on the second night of Passover, which is a Saturday this year. Saturday the fourth of April."

"Saturday is the fifth," Lorna corrected him gently.

"The fifth then. Rabbi Mendelstein is coming after sundown, and there will be music. A trio, I heard them at the senior center. And— despite tonight, which has been delicious—deli. I like the idea of deli at a wedding instead of at a shivah."

"I'm baking the cookies myself," Lorna said. "I'm starting way ahead."

"The freezer's so full we had to toss out all the ice!" Leopold said gleefully.

"Is this where you're meant to say *mazel tov*?" asked Zoë.

"Exactly where," said Justin.

"If only we had some champagne," said Costanza.

Lorna said, "I put two bottles in the refrigerator when we arrived."

After Andrew and Lorna retrieved the bottles and glasses, Henry raised his glass to the new couple. His toast seemed genuine and also a little wistful. (He couldn't help but wonder, *Shouldn't I be the one getting married?*)

Afterward, and with some difficulty, Leopold stood up. "I too have a toast. To this lovely family of mine. And also, to all the splendid women here tonight, Mademoiselle Zoë and *la bella* Costanza." He turned to

Andrew. "Not to worry, birthday *boychik*, your day will come." Then: "And of course to Lorna, who has brought so much light back into my life."

Glasses touched; champagne was sipped. Leopold teetered slightly, then dropped back down into his chair.

"Father, are you all right?"

"I'm fine." But Leopold didn't look fine. His face, flushed earlier, was now beaded with sweat. "It's just kind of warm in this hotel. Maybe we could open a window."

All eyes were on the old man. "What is it?"

"Hotel?" asked Andrew.

"What hotel?" Leopold turned to Lorna. "My dear, may I have some of those things in the bowl?"

"What things, Leopold?"

"The things to put in my thing. My receptacle. Because it is so *hot* now. The cold things. You know."

"The ice cubes?"

"Yes, those things. *Les glaces*—no. *Les glaçons*. To put in my thing."

"To put in your water?"

He nodded. Lorna started to pick up two ice cubes with the tongs that were hanging over the rim of the bowl. Leopold, bypassing her, reached over and with great concentration managed to pick up a single cube and drop it into his glass. It was the only sound in the room. Ice against glass. Ping—and then silence.

"What's wrong with everyone?" Leopold asked.

"Nothing," said Henry in an artificially calm voice.

Leopold reached for a second ice cube. This time he missed the glass entirely. The cube skittered across the table and dropped on the floor. He looked up. "An old man losing his aim. It happens."

"Father," Henry said. "Can you tell me what month it is?"

"Well, it's April, of course. 'Chestnuts in blossom,'" he sang. "'Holiday tables under the trees . . .'" Leopold looked up. "But where are the trees?"

Henry disappeared from the table and returned with a thermometer.

"I don't need that."

"With all due respect, Father, yes, you do. Open up." Henry inserted it into Leopold's mouth, felt his forehead, and waited.

A minute passed. Everyone at the table was still and silent.

The thermometer made a high-pitched beep. Henry took it out of Leopold's mouth. "103.2. Where's my phone?"

⇌

The next morning, on five hours—fewer—of sleep, Andrew splashed cold water on his face, pulled on his running clothes, and headed over to the park. He circled the reservoir four times, coming in and out of awareness of the sparkling February morning, the slowly rotating panorama of park and city, the steely-gray water. He had a single goal: he wanted to stop wondering whether his grandfather was about to die.

Leopold hadn't died—yet. In the ER they'd given him Tylenol and oxygen, and within half an hour his temperature had come down, he'd stopped sweating, and his mind cleared. When a chest X-ray came back showing probable pneumonia, they hooked him up to an IV, gave him antibiotics, and admitted him. Henry, Costanza, and the boys went home; Lorna chose to sleep in the reclining chair by his bed.

By seven o'clock that morning Lorna called Henry with a report: Leopold had slept well; his temperature had stabilized at around 99.5; there was no further sign of delirium; he'd fallen back asleep and was sleeping still. All this Henry had written in a note and left in the kitchen before going back to sleep.

Toward the end of his fourth lap, Andrew slowed down to cool off. Although he was calmer now, the run and the minimal sleep and lack of breakfast were combining to make him feel light-headed—so light-headed that he thought the young woman walking toward him, in a plaid jacket and red knit cap, was a carbon copy of Charlotte.

But no carbon, and no copy either. It was Charlotte herself, in town, like Justin presumably, for the long weekend. They exchanged a formal hug, a few pleasantries.

Andrew noted that her hair had grown out and that she had added a second piercing to her left ear. She was very, maybe even problematically, thin, and to him, as ever, lovely; but it was impressive what some time and distance could do. At first it felt almost (almost) like catching up with an acquaintance, not his former girlfriend of nearly a year.

But something altered when he told her about Leopold. Her face softened and she listened carefully before saying, "Leopold is incredibly special to you. Losing him is going to be hard."

Andrew willed himself not to tear up. Becoming emotional in front of Charlotte was the last thing he wanted to do. "He's not dying. I refuse to believe he's dying."

"Well, maybe not now . . ."

"Not ever, would be my first choice . . ."

She touched him gently on the shoulder. Despite himself, he registered her touch. And Charlotte registered him registering it.

"You know, Andrew, I'd really like it if we could find a way to be friends. I value you a lot, as a person."

"When a girl says that it's deadly."

"Not this girl. I've learned, I think from going away to school, that it's important to hold on to the best of our past."

"There're a lot of guys who might say, uh, 'fuck you' to that."

"Yes, but you're not one of them."

Andrew was beginning to shiver. He rubbed his arms to try to warm himself up. "If I'm the past, then is there a present that you want to tell me about?"

"Only if you'll tell me too."

"There's no one yet."

Her turn. "We met at school. He reminds me a little of you."

"So you're over your mean period."

"It looks that way. I think you'd like him."

"Yeah, right. Of course I would."

She slipped her hands into her pockets. "There's a party at his place tonight. You should come."

"I don't think so, Charlotte."

"He has nice friends. There'll be some girls . . ."

"Please."

"I don't know what else I can do." She paused. "I'll text you. Anytime from eight o'clock on. And when you see your grandfather, please give him a huge hug for me."

At home Andrew stood under a long scalding shower and then took himself to his favorite East Side diner, his longtime refuge from all things upsetting, and ordered a mound of scrambled eggs and a cup of coffee.

He thought about all the meals he'd eaten in this diner and its cousin on the West Side and how they shared a common theme of escape: from overbearing Henry, from probing Judith and snarky Justin and, now, ailing Leopold and—how to think of her? Rejecting? Love retracting?—Charlotte. What an odd, but also quintessentially New York, practice it was to have to nurse one's hurts in a public place, and in this particular sort of public place, with its greasy booths, chipped linoleum tables, and cartoon mosaic of the Parthenon.

Andrew was not naïve. He knew Leopold was old and that his time was finite, but knowing that in an abstract way was very different from stepping into the hospital room and seeing his grandfather lying in bed, his round white head nesting in a pillow, his mouth hidden behind an oxygen mask, a snakelike IV biting into his forearm. Wisps of oxygen, escaping from the sides of his mask, sent tiny translucent question marks into the air and made it seem as though Leopold were secretly cadging a cigarette. Smoking had in fact some years back, before Nina died, been his secret vice, but Leopold was well beyond that kind of thing now. Now he looked like a noble old tree that had been felled. The bones in his face seemed highlighted, something out of a sketch drawn by one of those sidewalk caricaturists who go for the bold, vicious, or summarizing stroke. His pallor was awful. Twenty hours earlier Leopold had been singing about Paris; a night in the hospital had transformed him into a preview of the corpse he would one day become.

Andrew lingered for a moment in the doorway, then stepped into the room where Lorna too was horizontal, or nearly horizontal, in a big tub of a vinyl chair that reclined to provide her with an approximation of a bed. When she saw Andrew, she pulled herself upright and stretched.

"How's he doing?"

"*Comme ci, comme ça.*" She made a little accompanying gesture with her hand.

"Any developments since last night?"

She shook her head.

"And you? How are you doing?"

"I'm fine. Well, truthfully, I'm feeling a little claustrophobic." She glanced at Leopold. "It's not because of him, mind you. But this place. You see I nursed my mama through a long—a long time."

"Why don't you go out for some fresh air? I'll sit with him for a while."

Lorna brightened. "I'd like to buy him—us—some fruit. And maybe a few cookies to have with tea this afternoon." She glanced over at Leopold. "He likes oatmeal chocolate chip." On her way out the door Lorna said, "Don't pay any attention if he calls the nurse and asks to go home."

Andrew sat down in Lorna's chair and experimented with its reclining feature. It was surprisingly comfortable. His brain told his hands that he ought to bring himself upright again, but his hands disobeyed. Within minutes he was asleep.

"Boychik!"

Andrew's shirt made a tearing sound as it peeled off the vinyl upholstery. He looked around, disoriented.

"You come to visit me and you pass out. Be careful, they'll shove an IV into *you*."

Leopold was sitting up in his bed. He had put on his glasses. He looked more like himself.

"Sorry, Grandpa," Andrew said groggily. "I was up late last night, remember?"

"No, I don't remember. Or, rather, I choose not to." Leopold paused. "Lorna tells me I thought I was in a hotel and I sang like an off-tune Frank Sinatra."

"It was a nice song . . . ," Andrew said consolingly.

"Such a *gute neshoma* you are."

"I'm sorry. I don't know that one."

"Look it up."

Andrew patted his thighs. "I seem to have left my Yiddish-English pocket dictionary in my other jeans."

"It means 'good soul.'"

Andrew smiled at his grandfather and felt his heart constricting. "They explained to you why you were like that? That it was the fever that made your brain not—work so well."

"Yah, yah. It was the behavior of someone else. A me I don't know—a me I don't want to live long enough to know."

"Please don't say that."

"It's the truth. You must not be afraid of the truth. If my mind goes . . ." Leopold shaped his hand into a gun and held it to his temple.

"You don't own a gun, Grandpa."

"This is America. You can buy one easy as a pack of chewing gum."

Andrew obliged his grandfather with a laugh.

"You know, your father will be the one in charge, when the moment comes. He's a very *commanding* sort of person."

"This is news?" It was curious how readily Andrew could take on Leopold's Yiddish-infused lilt.

"So you can make a joke," Leopold observed.

"In the right circumstances."

"Another. Ha."

A small silence opened up between them. "Sometimes I wish I took after him more," Andrew said pensively, "in that way."

"You want to command, join the army."

"I mean, take charge more, be more . . . I don't know . . . forceful."

"But you are not like him, in that way."

"And many others."

Leopold's head tilted to an angle. He looked busy. Busy thinking. He straightened his glasses. "With fathers and sons—I well know—it is not always easy."

"I don't know when it has ever been *easy*. Not for me."

Another silence opened up between them. After a moment Leopold said, "Minnie, one of the ladies in my book club, told me a good one last week. Do you know why grandparents and grandchildren get along so well?"

Andrew shook his head.

"They share a common enemy."

Andrew laughed ruefully.

Leopold looked at his grandson through a pair of dirty lenses. "Something particular has got you down, I sense."

"I went for a run this morning. I ran into Charlotte."

"The reader."

"She doesn't read anymore, but anyway, yes."

"She's back?" Leopold said almost hopefully.

"Oh, sure. She's back. Back in New York, torturing me on her way to hang out with her new boyfriend. She's even invited me to a party at his house."

"Ach." Then: "You should go."

"Why should I go?"

"To show how fine you are without her."

"But I'm not."

"Fake it."

"I think it may be too late for that."

"Then you show her there's been a change."

"Since this morning?"

"Change is not about putting in time. Change is about understanding. Insight."

Andrew sat back in his chair. "Where did you learn to be so smart about girls?"

"What girls? I had two before your grandmother. Belle Levitsky, whose papa hated me, and Rose Cohen, who preferred my best friend. Then I married Nina and now comes Lorna. That's not much of a school."

"You did okay."

"It's the women. They made it okay. They made me the best that I could be." Leopold paused. "Did the reader do that for you?"

"Honestly I don't know anymore."

"Well, think about it."

Andrew nodded.

"And, *boychik?*"

Andrew nodded again.

"At least run a comb through that hair of yours before you go to the party. Better still, a nice shampoo."

1040 Park Avenue, 10A, Charlotte texted. *After 8:00. Please come.*

At nine twenty that evening Andrew found himself standing at the corner of Park Avenue and Eighty-Sixth Street. Because he hated to be hot, he often misjudged the temperature, and he was shivering in a thin cotton sweater as he waited to see if he would in fact cross the street.

He shivered. He crossed. He shivered some more.

In the way of a native New Yorker he made a quick assessment: prewar, interior garden, lobby clearly renovated in the past few years. Someone had made or inherited a lot of money or bought years back.

"Ten A?" asked the doorman, who had made a quick assessment of his own.

Andrew nodded and was directed to the appropriate elevator. He heard the party even before its doors opened and he stepped into the hall. Music; voices; laughter; a flare of indignation, which must have been feigned or exaggerated, because it was followed by more laughter still.

What had he been thinking? Under normal circumstances he felt out of place at a party like this. And these weren't normal circumstances. Nevertheless Andrew pushed the door open and stepped inside. Across the foyer a large living room was packed with bodies. Young bodies; his peers. Some were standing in clusters and talking, with beer bottles in hand. A few were sitting on sofas; *draped* was a better word for one or two of the girls. The scene was, to Andrew, impenetrable.

The apartment was stiflingly hot. He took off his sweater.

"Hey." A thin young woman with red hair was standing to his left. "Let me help you with that." He gave her his sweater; she tossed it on a mountain of outerwear piled every which way on a bench. "Benjamin's put me in charge of the drinks too. What's your poison?"

He wanted to say seltzer, but knew better than that. "I'm okay."

"Oh, come on. It's a party." She sized him up. "You look like a Stella guy to me."

"What does a Stella guy look like?"

"Cute, a little nerdy. Expensive Italian shoes."

My father made me buy them, he did not say. "And what kind of girl are you?"

"You tell me."

He looked her over. "Red hair, two tattoos, and—let me guess—a vintage dress. Anchor Steam?"

"Not bad. Except I've got three tattoos and it's some kind of craft beer I've never heard of."

She whirled around to a table full of bottles and glasses, plucked out a beer, and had it open and in Andrew's hand in a flash. "If you're wondering where the third one is, come find me later."

Andrew took a sip of beer. "I'll do that."

He raised his bottle to her and took another sip. So he did know how to flirt, a bit. All you had to do was pretend you were on TV.

This exchange gave him the courage to approach the living room. It was even larger than it looked, once he was in it. The furniture was spare and made of steel, leather, marble, and glass. Some impressive-seeming abstract paintings hung on one wall, big splotches of saturated color. Another wall was lined with books.

Andrew tried hard not to look like he was looking for Charlotte, even though he was. Then, because he couldn't think of anything lamer than standing in a room where everyone else was talking or dancing, he wandered over to the bookshelves.

The books were alphabetized. There was a lot of history, organized, it seemed, by period. Many of the jackets were wrapped in plastic sheaths.

"Pretty compulsive, huh?" It wasn't a girl this time, but a guy. Thick-set, round tortoiseshell glasses, navy blue polo.

"You could say that."

"It's Benj's dad. He's pretty precise."

Benj.

"I've seen someone take a book down to look at something and put it back in the wrong spot. He'll just be walking by, he'll see it and reshelve it."

"Crazy."

"Yeah."

"You know Benj a long time?" Andrew had to refrain from putting quotation marks around that *Benj*.

"Since sixth grade at Dalton. I started in kindergarten. A lifer."

Andrew nodded.

"You want some?" The guy lifted up his hand. Only then did Andrew notice that he was holding a lit joint.

Andrew had tried pot two times in his life, a record low, he was nearly certain, for his age group. He hadn't cared for it much on either occasion. He shrugged, hoping the shrug would be taken as a no.

The guy handed over the joint. Andrew hesitated, took it, then inhaled. His lungs burned, but he tried not to cough. After a few seconds he sent two thin plumes streaming out of his nostrils.

"What about you? You know Benj a long time?"

"Never met him."

"Oh?"

"I'm a friend of Charlotte's."

"Oh."

"I'm her ex-boyfriend actually."

"Oh. Wow."

Andrew shrugged nonchalantly. "It's okay. We're friends now."

"Cool. Or is that, *cool* question mark?"

"*Cool* period works."

Andrew's new friend offered him the joint again, and again he took a hit. This time, when the burning in his mouth and chest receded, he felt oddly happified. That was just the word for it too. As though something outside of him was working on his mood.

"Good stuff." Was that the kind of thing he was supposed to say? It sounded imbecilic.

By the time Charlotte found Andrew, he was in the middle of the dance floor, which was the dining room with its rug rolled up and the table moved to one side. He and two girls were dancing in a small raggedy circle when Charlotte came walking toward him in a short lilac-colored dress. A guy was following her, lagging behind by a few steps.

Raising her voice over the music, Charlotte said, "Andrew, this is Ben."

Ben, not Benj.

A hand came out to pump Andrew's with a little too much muscle. Andrew grasped it dutifully and with muscle raised (he hoped) to a parallel pitch.

It took a moment for Andrew, his focus a little bit askew from the pot, to take the guy in. When he looked, really looked, at Ben/Benj/Benjamin, he felt instantly off in his stomach, as though it had shifted places in his abdomen.

"Hey."

"Hey."

The two of them stood staring at each other for a minute. It wasn't entirely because of Charlotte.

"Well, this is a little awkward," Benjamin said. That *was* because of Charlotte.

Standing there looking at them, first one, then the other, she was the first to say it: "You guys kind of look alike."

"We do?" they both said at almost the same time.

Benjamin was taller than Andrew, but they had a similar narrow build, a similar well-made nose, similar long silky hair that was at that moment running to a similarly untended length.

"You do," Charlotte declared. "It's weird."

"That must be why." Andrew gestured at Charlotte, trying to make a joke.

There was a beat, long and uncomfortable.

"Must be," Benjamin said.

"Okay, time for a beer run," said Charlotte.

"Coward," Benjamin said after she disappeared.

He could say that. Andrew, at this juncture, could not. Much as he agreed. The music changed.

"I kind of don't know what to say," Benjamin said.

"Ditto."

There was a pause. A long one. Where was Charlotte?

The music started up. "Come on," Benjamin said.

They rejoined the dancers. Benjamin danced and Andrew danced. They danced face-to-face, each on his own spot and at his own rhythm. Now and then one, then the other, would close his eyes, but they both peeked. They were both curious.

It had to be the pot. The pot and the beer. The pot and the beer and the day and the dancing. Andrew felt the room destabilizing. He kept looking, and not looking, then looking at Benjamin, who kept looking, and not looking, then looking at Andrew. This went on for several minutes. Then out of nowhere Benjamin reached over and placed his right hand on Andrew's left shoulder. *What the fuck?* Andrew thought. But then he found himself mirroring Benjamin. He put his right hand on Benjamin's left shoulder. They stood there linked like this, sort of dancing and sort of pushing or holding on to each other for several beats.

They both looked up and held each other's gaze. A shiver whipped through Andrew's entire body, from his feet to his knees to his balls, which rustled in his shorts, to his stomach, chest, and neck. What was this? *His* homo moment? His palm was so sweaty he was afraid it was going to leave a handprint on Benjamin's shirt, but he didn't let go, and nor did Benjamin.

After the shiver came a feeling he could identify only as a combination of nausea and pleasure. As though a pod, tight and closed, had popped open inside him. *What the—?* The two of them continued like this for several bars, dancing and looking, looking and dancing.

Finally Charlotte returned. "Cute," she said, before distributing the beers.

Andrew danced with a few different girls. He shared another joint. By the time he found the redheaded girl again—Allison—he felt bold enough to ask her to dance, and then, when he was invited, he guessed that her third tattoo was on her left thigh.

"It's on the right. Now guess what it's of."

"A serpent?" It was late. He was drunk. She was drunk.

"A lizard."

"Well, I was right about the reptile part."

Andrew drew her toward him. They danced. They kissed. The room began to spin. All those patches of bright color on the walls began to move and recombine like chips of glass in a kaleidoscope, and then Andrew felt his stomach rebel. "I'm sorry, I think I'm going to be sick." As graciously as he could, he disengaged himself and hurried off to find a bathroom.

Afterward he washed his hands and face and shoved his hair back behind his ears. Instead of rejoining the party, he looked for his sweater in the mountain of clothing. Either it was too deeply buried or someone had taken it by accident or snitched it. He'd never liked that sweater anyway. It was one of his father's choices from some expensive Parisian shop. He headed for the door in his clammy T-shirt.

When he opened it, a man and a woman were standing there, he with his key in hand, she with a worried expression on her face, her ear cocked. The parents, presumably. But not just any parents. Parents, or at least one of whom—the father—Andrew recognized. He lowered his head and tried to slip away.

The woman had already stepped inside. "I'm going straight to bed. If I walk into the living room, I might have a nervous breakdown."

The father, looking Andrew over, said, "Wait a minute there. I know you."

Andrew nodded.

"From where? Not here."

"No."

"Are you a friend of Benjy's?"

"A friend of a friend."

"You're Henry's son."

"You're Benjamin's father."

They both nodded.

"We met in Florence," Isaac Schoenfeld said. "At Zubarelli. The shirtmaker."

Andrew nodded.

"You're Andrew, the second one."

He nodded again.

"You're not wearing your shirt."

"No." He looked at Schoenfeld. "But you are."

Schoenfeld glanced down. "I am." Then: "Are you going out in the cold like that?"

"I had a sweater, but it's gone."

Schoenfeld nodded. "Wait here a minute."

"Really, I'm—"

Schoenfeld put up his hand. The gesture had the force of a command. Andrew stayed put while Schoenfeld went inside. He returned after a minute with a thick gray cardigan with leather buttons. "Put this on."

"But I—"

"Cashmere doesn't suit you? I remember that you had strong sartorial opinions."

"It's very kind of you."

"Just put it on."

Andrew put the sweater on. It was soft.

"Are you all right? You look a little green."

"Too much party for me."

"You're not a drinker."

"No."

"My son isn't either—but he gets swept up in the moment."

Andrew didn't know what to say to this. Schoenfeld peered over Andrew's shoulder. "Benjy has trained us not to ask what happens at these gatherings of his."

That's wise, Andrew thought. "I'll return this to you tomorrow."

"Don't worry about returning it. Just be warm. And take two aspirin when you get home with several glasses of water." Schoenfeld sounded like the physician he was. Then he put out his hand. Andrew shook it and left.

⇌

Costanza was only half-awake when she shifted in bed and felt a gumminess between her legs. An exploratory finger into her underwear came up red. Her second period since the failed cycle. And what a period too. She had bled into her underwear and beyond, into, and nearly through, her nightgown. She discovered all this only after she pushed herself out of bed and into the bathroom. She wouldn't even bother washing her panties; she preferred to throw them out and start fresh. She showered, inserted a tampon, put on clean underwear, dark jeans, a sweater. At seven in the morning she was ready for her day.

But what was her day to be? The apartment was quiet. Henry was horizontal. Andrew's door was closed; if he had come home at all the night before, he had come home late and was still asleep. Justin's door was open and his bed was empty; he was off at school, but even when he was gone he was still there somehow, in Henry's thoughts, on Andrew's mind. She envied them: they had each other. At least they could keep disappointing or surprising each other; at least they could keep going back for another round and another after that.

What did she have? No father, no baby; no prospect of a baby. She didn't even have her rage anymore. She had had that—for days—after the blood test confirmed what the golden pregnancy test had already prepared her for. As she came off the progesterone, she felt her whole body, her whole self, turn into a geyser of raw anger, most of which she directed at Henry. It didn't take much to set her off. One evening when he came home with a nice bottle of wine and, after looking—she saw it as pawing—through a few drawers, asked her where the corkscrew was, she lit into him. The corkscrew was where the corkscrew went, she railed, in the second drawer in the butler's pantry, which was where she had found it when she first got to know the kitchen, and which was likely where Judith, who so easily became pregnant through IVF, *that* Judith, had originally put it. Henry stared at her and said "Right" with such evenness, such *calm*, that she felt an even hotter wave of anger rise up in her; it was so powerful and so luscious that when Henry poured her a glass of wine, she just let go of the glass and watched it drop to the ground and shatter and, what's more, enjoyed watching it drop to the ground and shatter.

For several mornings after that, Henry set off earlier than usual for work and returned well after dinner.

Costanza was all over the place. One day she called up Alitalia and booked a ticket on a flight for Milan that left at eight o'clock that evening; an hour later she called back and had the money refunded to her credit card. (The twenty-four-hour grace period was a godsend to such a state of mind.)

The following morning she packed a large suitcase, hailed a cab, and headed down to her old apartment. She had dived into Henry's world too hastily. She knew that for certain now. The time had come to move out, slow things down. She was going to let herself cool off, recuperate in her own surroundings.

When the cab became stuck in midtown traffic, she thought she would jump out of her skin. She had the driver leave her at the corner. She wheeled her suitcase over to the curb and stood there at the intersection of Park and Sixty-First not knowing, until she stepped onto the sidewalk, whether she would head downtown or back to Henry's.

She headed back to Henry's. On foot.

That night she made a bouillabaisse. Not a simple dish; not a dish for someone as unraveled as Costanza was. Halfway through her preparations she looked around at the kitchen, wondering how she had possibly dirtied so many bowls and plates and utensils, and how those driblets of stock had ended up on the cabinets, and why the sink smelled so strongly of rot, and a moment later she found herself crumpled on the floor, hugging her knees to her chest and listening to the pilots on the stove breathe out their gassy blue exhalations.

Henry praised the dish lavishly. He said it was the best he had ever tasted. Her eyes filled up in gratitude. She felt in sync with the world again. "I love you," she said.

He smiled at her. He breathed. He ground fresh pepper into his bowl and ate some more.

As she watched him, the forgiving, adoring expression on her face turned fierce. "You don't say you love me back?"

"I love you back, Costanza," he said affectionately.

"But you need a prompt."

He started to speak—then elected not to.

"Why do you need a prompt?"

"I just—I think we could say that it has more often been the other way around, more you who needed—"

He ducked to dodge the soup ladle. It flew across the room, trailing a shower of tiny drops of bouillabaisse. They both listened to it clatter to the floor. Henry remained silent. Costanza stood up, retrieved the ladle, and put it in the sink.

She sat down again and stared at him.

Henry sat back in his chair. "What can I say? That I know you're coming down off some awfully powerful drugs? That you've been through an ordeal? That your behavior isn't, just now, that of the woman I know, respect, and, yes, love? Is that what you'd like to hear?"

"I'd like to hear that you're sorry."

"Okay. I'm sorry."

"You don't even know what you're sorry for."

"The cycle? Its failure? Doing the wrong thing, or not doing enough of the right one?"

"Putting pepper in a perfectly spiced stew."

By the time Henry padded into the kitchen just after nine o'clock, a rare late waking time for him, she had formulated a question, but she waited to ask it until he had his coffee and was sitting with a steaming cup between his hands.

"So what, exactly, is involved in my doing another cycle?"

She watched as his morning grogginess gave way to surprise. "You want to try again? Really?"

"I do." She added after a beat, "Really."

She wasn't entirely sure what she meant to do until she said the words. Once she said them, though, she was sure. Or nearly sure. That was the attraction of language: you could test your feelings against the words. There would always be a chance later on to revise, revisit, or simply retract.

She did not think she would retract. This last month had hardened her resolve.

"Wow," Henry said, "I didn't expect this."

"You don't sound so happy to hear me say it."

"I am. It just seems so—"

"Improbable?"

He refrained from saying anything to that.

"You yourself said, Henry, that there were a lot of crazy-making hormones pumping through me. Things feel different now. *I* feel different now. And there's your father in the hospital . . . I guess I'm feeling time, concerned about time. I guess that's it."

He nodded. He sighed a long sigh.

She told him about her period, then asked how soon she could start again.

"Well, with your next cycle, I suppose, at the end of March."

"That's when my mother plans to visit."

"Right about then, yes."

"But I don't want her to know."

"Why not?"

"I probably don't need to tell you that in Italy many people still aren't as open to fertility treatment as they are here. Some women are *still* going off to places like Croatia and Spain to try to conceive, and if you're gay or need a surrogate or a donor egg, forget about it. My mother is in many ways a rational person and a modern woman, but she is also Catholic, and of a certain generation, and I'd just prefer not to talk to her about what we're doing, that's all."

"I'm well aware of the history of that punitive Law Forty, Costanza, and I'm up to date on all of the changes that have been made to it in recent years. I just didn't realize, after all the time you've lived here, that such an attitude would be so—so relevant to you."

"I've lived a long time in America, Henry, but my mother, remember, has not."

"Okay, I get it."

She studied Henry for a moment. This was the most easygoing conversation they had had in days.

"If my mother does end up coming, how can I possibly explain to her why I have doctors' appointments every day at seven in the morning?"

He took out his phone and brought up a calendar. He counted the days several times, then said, "Why don't you have her come around the twenty-first. If you have to go in before that week, it would most likely be once, if that. We'll tell her that I have a conference in Toronto if she tries to come any later. There are always conferences in Toronto."

Andrew kept reaching for Isaac Schoenfeld's sweater, even though it was too big on him and not really his style. It had traces of Schoenfeld's scent on it, something herbal crossed with something vaguely antiseptic. He wore it to school. He wore it when he went to visit Leopold in the hospital. He wore it at home.

Home: which was again where Andrew chose it to be, and when.

Henry, looking in on him one evening while Andrew was working on a paper, noticed the sweater right away. "Is that something your mother bought you?"

Andrew explained that he had lost his sweater at a party and that the father of the guy who was hosting it loaned, or maybe gave, him this one to wear home.

Henry seemed baffled.

"Actually you know him. The father. Isaac Schoenfeld."

Henry's eyebrows drew together. "Isaac gave you his sweater? You met Benjy? How?"

Henry knew Benjamin? And was of the "Benjy" school?

"He's . . . a friend of Charlotte's."

"I didn't think you were still a friend of Charlotte's."

Andrew looked up from his computer screen. "Yes, I am still a *friend* of Charlotte's."

"Where did this meeting take place?"

"At their apartment."

"On Park Avenue?" Henry was speaking slowly, as though he needed to deconstruct the logic of the conversation.

Andrew noted his father's confusion. "Yes, at a party at Dr. Schoenfeld's. On Park Avenue."

"What was Isaac doing at a party for people your age?"

"He came home at the end."

"Did he ask about me?"

"Dr. Schoenfeld?"

"Yes, Andrew. Who else?"

"No. Why would he?"

Andrew waited for Henry to answer.

"I've told you before. We have history."

"But why do you care about him after all these years? Your practice is a huge success."

Henry sighed. "I suppose I'm not someone who lets go of things easily."

"I've noticed, Dad."

Henry smiled. The atmosphere in the room shifted. "The reason I stopped by was to see if you wanted to go with me to visit your grandfather."

"I went today after school. I've got to finish this history paper now."

"Tomorrow then."

Leopold had been in the hospital for more than ten days. Every time he was about to be discharged, he spiked a new fever, and Henry insisted on further tests, another round of antibiotics. He refused to send him back to Brooklyn until he was sure—of what? That Leopold was himself again. But would Leopold ever again be himself? The hospital had weakened him and diminished him. For the first time he seemed truly, incontrovertibly old.

Henry observed his father for a moment from the doorway. Leopold was upright, with the *Times* in his lap open to the crossword. Upright—but not right. Not quite dozing, but drifting. His gaze was distant, silvery. Elsewhere.

Henry would never be ready for the end of Leopold. He could not see any way of "preparing." His father was bone, tree trunk, rock. Leopold was his duelist, his life opponent, his life giver, his frame—and his framework. He had survived, phoenixlike, the fires of Hitler's hell. Such a man could not allow a case of pneumonia to bring him down. No.

"Father, how are you feeling this evening?"

Leopold looked up at Henry and, clearly, maybe because he wasn't expecting him, did not at first know who he was. The moment went on for no more than a few seconds, but they were excruciating. Then: "Ah, Henry. I was just thinking about you."

"Oh, yes?" Henry lowered himself into the chair by Leopold's bed.

"I was thinking about the day those test scores came in the mail and you decided to apply to medical school. Your mother and I knew what the envelope was, but we didn't open it. We put it out on the kitchen table for you to see. We leaned it up against the saltshaker. Do you remember?"

"Of course."

"And they were very high, those scores. And that was when we knew you could do it."

"We."

"You say that as though there were something wrong with that."

Henry paused. It was a judicious pause. "Not at all. You, you and Mother, were most—supportive—yes—at a time when I probably needed it."

"Not probably. Definitely."

Henry's face hardened. "All my life, Father, you pushed me. To take science classes. To go to medical school. To specialize in assisted reproduction. To start my own practice . . . and stick with it."

"Was all that so mistaken?"

"I don't really know anymore."

"I prefer to think of it as encouraged. I knew you were a smart boy, a gifted boy. Also, yes, I wanted revenge—through you. I didn't expect it to work so brilliantly. You took the encouragement and went from there. It has been the greatest gratification of my life, after I saw so much death, and lost so many people I loved, to see you make so much life. So much of it, I will also say, Jewish. But even so, you have made life for many people who would not have had life, period. That is an accomplishment beyond all else, to me. And it has made me a very proud father. The proudest."

Henry softened. "Well, thank you, Father. For saying that."

"But there is one thing, one area, of which I am not so proud, not so pleased." Leopold went on, uninvited, "I think you should tell the boys."

"Please, not that. Not now."

Leopold clasped his hands. "'The truth will out.'"

Henry produced a formidable sigh. "Papa, you're layering on Shakespeare?"

"You haven't called me that in years. Since you were small."

"Papa . . . ," Henry repeated, as though he were trying the word out again, curious to see what memories, what feelings, it might bring back.

"'It is a wise father that knows his own son.'"

Henry was perplexed.

"Also from *Merchant*. Do you remember how I used to learn all that Shakespeare by heart? After work, after all that deadening time in the shop. I came alive at night, with my reading."

"I don't know how you got up the next morning, you stayed up so late."

"I loved the smell of those books. I can smell them now. The old paper. It had a special mustiness, like tea leaves. Tea leaves closed up in an old tin. How I loved to stretch out on the sofa, the one with the striped linen. Belgian linen, quality cloth. With you asleep and your mother asleep, or knitting quietly in her chair. All the work of the day completed, set aside. A good meal in me. Your mother always made sure of that. A glass of schnapps after. A bright light over my shoulder. It was in that room, on that sofa, that I felt it most acutely: I had come out on the other side of something that, at one point in my life, I never thought . . ." Leopold paused. "And then . . . and then you add Shakespeare on top of that. And Dostoyevsky. And Hardy. Schiller. Proust. *Mein Gott*."

Henry could almost hear the sound of pages turning; of Leopold, a younger, more vigorous Leopold, lifting and separating them between his thumb and index finger, one after another after another, passing this too on to his son: a love of reading, an appetite for knowledge, both unbridled.

"I have no idea if I tell them what might unravel."

"What does Costanza say?"

Henry looked into his lap.

Leopold scanned the whole of his son's face. "You trust her with your seed—but not your life?"

Henry took this in. He took Leopold in. Old, faded Leopold, still fierce, penetrating, and regal. His was a small kingdom, but he still asserted his power over it.

"I believe it is the right thing to do. I believe you know it is the right thing to do."

Henry sat back in his chair. "This is beginning to sound awfully like a deathbed conversation."

"Well, that I can't know. But it's one I've been wanting us to have for a while." Leopold directed his gray eyes at Henry. "I won't ask you to promise. *That* is a deathbed conversation. But I will ask you to think. In the middle of the night. Or some morning. Somewhere undistracted and quiet. I know you have so much on your mind. So many people depending on you, so many patients. It's a more open world now, Henry. Open yourself up with it."

"What if they use this as a reason to—" Henry stopped there.

"To what?"

"Give up on me."

"Give up on you—or give you up?"

Henry's eyes narrowed. "Give me up."

"They could have done that with the divorce, no? Gone to live with Judith only. They elected not to. Both of them, independently. And in court. Remember?"

Leopold and his piercing, clarifying logic. Leopold and his pushing. Leopold and his authority.

Leopold.

The evening following Henry's visit, Lorna tried to cheer Leopold up by bringing in a picnic, French in theme. Two cheeses, a baguette, pears, for Lorna half a bottle of Sancerre. Afterward there was pastry, which they never got to. Leopold ate in birdlike portions. He told Lorna that he did not feel unwell, but he did not feel quite right either—in his body. In his heart, he told her, he felt a sense of relief. He used those very words but did not explain. He fell asleep holding her hand.

At three that morning she heard him call out. A word, several words, that she could not understand. "Nina" might have been one of them, but then again it might as well have been "need" or "knee." He reached out for a glass of water and knocked over the plastic pitcher on the over-bed table.

When she was sopping up the water, Lorna touched Leopold on the arm. She knew at once that he had a fever. A high fever, it turned out, after she called the nurse. Over 103 degrees again.

The nurse gave him extra Tylenol. She called the physician on duty, and he said that, as Leopold was already receiving a cycle of antibiotics, all there was to do at that hour was monitor the fever and check his oxygen levels. In the morning, the doctor said, he would order a new set of X-rays.

Later—it was still dark—Leopold called out again. This time what he said didn't seem to be in English. It was in Yiddish maybe, or maybe even French. Lorna had no idea. She heard him babble, but as she was in a deep sleep herself, she wasn't sure. The language sounded as though it came from a faraway time and place in Leopold's brain, and life.

As the sun rose, he woke her with the gurgling sound, a wet, raspy, choking sound that wasn't coming from his throat so much as deep down from inside his lungs. Lorna called Henry, and he hurried over to the hospital. He met with the attending physician, who ordered yet another round of X-rays and blood tests. A picture fairly quickly took shape: Leopold's pneumonia had developed into congestive heart failure. His right lung, scarred and weakened from years of cigarette smoking and a touch of emphysema, was in danger of shutting down. They suctioned his lungs, put him on diuretics, changed and amped up his antibiotics. Rendered effectively mute, or at least noncommunicative, by his oxygen mask, or his fever, or his exhaustion, Leopold seemed significantly further away, and further gone, than he had just a day before.

Henry didn't see the point of calling Justin back from school. There was no way to predict how long this would go on or where it was going.

Andrew and Henry alternated sitting by Leopold's bed, holding his hand, sitting him up, then laying him down again. He used the last of his severely diminished energies to try to hock, spit, spew, cough, and growl his way back to breath and to life. On the third day, the hideous sounds disappeared. Leopold's silence was far more ominous than his fight had been, and it meant exactly what it appeared to mean: while Andrew was at swim practice and Henry had stepped out of Leopold's room to check in with Wanda at the office, Leopold turned his head toward the window and quietly died.

⇌

Leopold's life ended late on a Tuesday afternoon. Justin came home from school on Wednesday evening, and Leopold was underground by Thursday before lunch. Henry invited only family to the burial; afterward he opened up his house to any of Leopold's friends who wished to pay their respects. Henry refused to use the word, let alone sit, shivah. No mirrors were draped nor cloth rent, though Leopold might have liked both. Henry organized the rabbi, the service, the food and drink. So it happened that deli was served at Leopold's funeral and not his wedding, after all.

Costanza, observing Henry in action—hyperaction, almost—wondered what had happened to him. His control over every detail, everything, including his feelings, was magisterial—at least in the moment. In the days and weeks that followed, she watched him turn inward. A blankness crept into his eyes. He sat for hours in silence, his back rounded. He showed no interest in food. He didn't touch her.

Early one evening, just as she was beginning to cook, he walked slowly through the door, a weary bear—bear hide—of a man. He asked her when she thought they would sit down to eat, then he went to take a bath. Henry never took baths. He disappeared for an hour; longer. The water must have turned ice-cold. She did not hear him refilling it from the tap, as she would have. Eventually she knocked on the door and asked if he was all right.

"All right?" he said, as if trying to figure out what such words could possibly mean.

She opened the door and stepped inside. "Is it Leopold? Is that where you've gone, Henry?"

"Gone?"

"You seem so absent. I don't mean just tonight. Since your father died. If it's grief—that I can understand. Of course I can understand."

"You're asking if I've disappeared into my grief."

"Yes, that's what I am asking."

His skin, under the waterline, had acquired a greenish tinge. "No."

"Is it about the cycle?"

When he didn't answer right away, she continued, "Because if you've changed your mind, you must tell me, and soon, before I gear up again mentally. Once I start with the drugs, and the ultrasounds, if I hear there are a number of eggs, I know, even after last time, that my mind is going to go very far, very fast."

"All that is typical. And, no, I've not changed my mind. Not in the least." He made sure that she saw his face, and his eyes, when he said this last part.

"Well, what is it then?"

"It's nothing."

That Sunday, Henry went out to Brooklyn to his father's apartment. Costanza asked if she might come to help, but Henry said he preferred to go on his own. He had grown up in the apartment and fled from it when he went to college. Everything in it felt confining to him and was saturated with memories he preferred not to dwell on. He intended to be in and out fast.

And he was. He gave most everything to Lorna, who under Leopold's will, recently revised, was left the apartment for her lifetime. After she died, it was to be sold and the money was to be added to the boys' inheritance. Except for an old peacoat Andrew had asked for and a watch that was intended for Justin and a few other bits and pieces that even unsentimental Henry thought his sons might like to have, Henry gave Leopold's clothes to his synagogue's thrift shop. His books went to Henry, but Henry left them behind. He would look through them one day, he told Lorna. The only thing he brought back from Brooklyn was a box of photographs and the silver candlesticks his mother used on Friday nights.

He put the candlesticks away in the cupboard where he kept Leopold's china. The photographs he set down on the drop-leaf table in the library. For several weeks he didn't even glance at them. To Costanza the box seemed to vibrate. She didn't understand how he could keep from looking at them—she had pored over pictures of her father after he died, seeking consolation but also an answer, a fragment of an answer. Leopold obviously did not leave quite such an enigma behind; but still.

When Henry did finally open the box one evening after dinner it was well into March. Costanza was nearly finished with her translation, and she was tensely anticipating both her mother's visit and the next cycle of IVF. She felt a strong sense of being at a pause, at that moment before the tide pulled back to form the next wave. She would have liked to find peace in this interlude but felt the pull of the undertow instead. Having Leopold die had not helped. Having Henry withdraw and turn so remote had not helped. What helped was when, for the first time since Leopold's death, Henry sought her out and said, "Shall we take a look at these photographs together? Would you mind?"

"The opposite," Costanza said, as she sat down next to him on the sofa.

Henry uncorked a bottle of wine and poured two glasses. Then he opened the box and took out several albums. Costanza found herself thinking back to the mass of loose pictures she'd come across when she was preparing to paint Henry's apartment. They had presented the story of his life in reverse. These pictures instead told it in a forward direction. They were meticulously pasted into volumes of now-flaking black paper, mostly black-and-white images with tiny gummed corners holding them down onto the page.

The albums were all about Henry. He began as a smiley baby, swaddled tight, held tight, by a stolid-looking woman—Nina. Or balanced in the lap of a clearly delighted man—Leopold. Henry was photographed on a lambskin rug, naked. He was photographed in his bathtub, in his high chair, being fed, being walked along a gravel path in a park. There were birthday parties with tiny pointed caps and homemade cakes and a clutch of freckled boys in attendance. In several photographs Henry played doctor with equipment that over the years became increasingly realistic. "Leopold was not exactly subtle about his vision for me," Henry said when they came to the fourth iteration of the young doctor in training. "This one was a real stethoscope. He asked Dr. Marx, our family physician, to order it from a medical supplier as a birthday present. I was nine. Nine!"

Henry present peered at Henry past. "I'd just like to know how it would have felt to have come to doctoring more on my own."

"Would you have?"

"That's the million-dollar question, isn't it? Many things interest me, as you know. Left to my own devices, who knows what forks in the road I would have followed. What mistakes—what interesting mistakes—I might have made."

They moved on to the next album. Henry at his bar mitzvah. Henry at a picnic. Henry playing tennis. Henry at his senior prom.

"Henry, Henry, Henry," said Henry.

"Well, you were an only child."

"Yes, but there are so few pictures of me with other people, or of us together as a family. Or even of my parents before I came along. Most people hand cameras off, you know. To friends or relatives—and we did have one or two who survived. Just to—just to broaden the subject. To vary it. But not Leopold."

"He loved you."

"Yes . . ."

"You sound doubtful."

"One thing Leopold certainly did was love me. In his way and on his terms."

"Isn't that how we all love, and are loved, typically?"

Henry, sipping his wine, retreated again. But not so much away from Costanza as to somewhere private. Somewhere down deep with Leopold's love, and all it meant to him.

"He told me what a fine person he thought you were," he said after a moment.

"Your father and I, we had some—exchanges of substance," Costanza said with feeling. "He was someone I wish I could have known for a longer time. But I feel lucky to have met him. To have met him was to know you better. To know where you come from."

"Where I come from . . . Where I come from is a very forceful, dominating, clear-thinking man who had, or thought he had, all the answers, when I was young. What I would do when I grew up. How much schooling I would need to get there. What kind of sports I should play. What I should believe: 'Despite everything, in this family we believe in God,' he once said to me, when I questioned—well, when

I questioned. *We?* Did I have a choice? About God? About religious school, keeping kosher, being bar mitzvahed, attending every Friday-night and Saturday-morning service for most of my childhood and adolescence? Or about being kept inside on the Sabbath, doing nothing? All I wanted was to be out in the world, getting some *air*, seeing some other *kids*. Do you know that until I was sixteen years old my father made me wear a T-shirt all year long, July and August included? I didn't even have a choice about my *under*clothes."

"Was it all bad?"

"Of course not. But there were times, many times, when I felt imprisoned by Leopold's authority. I mean, what do you say to a man who lived through what he did? 'I'd prefer not to attend *shul* this week, Father. I'd rather go see a movie.'"

Costanza took Henry's hand. They sat in silence for a moment. "It seems like Leopold was the opposite of my father. My father saw nuance and complication everywhere. The depression made it difficult for him to make up his mind about anything, including staying alive."

"Actually he *did* make up his mind about that, didn't he?"

"Well, yes—in the end."

Costanza came to a photograph of Judith. Wearing a short skirt and carrying a bouquet of zinnias, she was standing in front of the entrance to Leopold's building in Brooklyn.

"They were a gift for my mother. It was the first time they met, a Sunday in mid-July. My mother made a pot roast—in the summer. My parents preferred to eat early, so that my father's evenings could be free for reading."

"How did it go?"

Henry shrugged. "I thought fine. Judith said Leopold disliked her. She maintained that never changed, all through our marriage."

Costanza turned the page. The next one was blank, all the others too. "The story ends here?"

"It continues elsewhere."

Costanza picked flecks of black paper off her lap and set them in a little pile on the coffee table in front of them. "You know, it was Leopold who tipped me over into deciding about this next cycle."

A line appeared in Henry's forehead. "I didn't know you two ever discussed . . ."

"Well, we did. He did. He and you did too, obviously."

Henry inhaled deeply, as though he were about to apologize, or explain.

"That's all right. It was helpful. Leopold gave me a nudge."

"He was big on nudging." Then: "I guess there are surprises, even after the end."

"In my experience, the surprises never stop, Henry. It's like the understanding. It goes on pretty much forever."

⇌

And then there she was: her mother, Maria Rosaria, sitting in an Upper East Side hotel lobby, absorbed in the *Times*.

She sat, as ever, with perfect old-school posture, erect and with one leg neatly crossed over the other just above the knee. She was wearing a smart tweed suit, an ivory silk blouse, and on her right wrist a chunky gold bracelet that had belonged to Costanza's grandmother. A trench coat was draped over the arm of her chair, a pair of reading glasses balanced at the tip of her tiny nose. All of this was familiar to Costanza; she recognized it as her mother's city look, the sort of outfit she wore and the carriage she adopted when she went into Genoa or traveled to European cities. Yet something else was different, disconcertingly so. What? Her hair. That was it. Her mother's thick silver hair had been given a crisp new cut. It made her look years younger.

Costanza approached her mother, who stood up with energy. They embraced, and Costanza remarked on her haircut, and asked about her flight and if she wanted to have a rest.

"I've been resting for eight hours. I've come here to see and do. So let's go see, let's go do."

She was thin as ever and, on those hill-toughened Ligurian legs, stockinged and shod in low-heeled pumps, ready to march across Manhattan. Jet lag, she declared, was a state of mind, and one she chose to have nothing to do with. She adored the bustle of New York. She found the clothes in shop windows enchanting. For once in her life, she appeared not to care about money. She had gotten her first ATM card and delighted in taking dollars out of "the wall," as she put it. She did not once complain of being hot or cold or tired or disappointed by whatever Costanza showed her. Her attention span was fierce, which wasn't much of a surprise, but her eagerness to taste new food was. "There's only so much pasta one can eat in a lifetime," she said gaily, as they sat down to an early spicy Vietnamese dinner. "I think if you ever moved home again, you would be bored by our repetitive habits."

Lo vedo ora, ora lo capisco: she saw, she understood, she appeared not to judge. Had Maria Rosaria undergone a late-in-life softening? It was known to happen. Henry had more than once told Costanza that the Leopold she met, and liked, was not half as fierce as he used to be. As some people aged, they lost their tooth, their bite. Was her mother among them?

Morton hadn't been so tolerant of Maria Rosaria. "Too judgy," he said after the first time they met. She reminded him of his New Jersey aunts, the kind of hard, critical, unforgiving Jewish women he had so witheringly captured in his early novels. Henry, by contrast, was graciousness incarnate. He left work early the following evening, and he and Costanza walked to Maria Rosaria's hotel hand in hand. He assured Costanza everything would go well: "Just leave it to me."

When Maria Rosaria joined them in the lobby, he drew the old lady into his arms with commanding warmth. He turned on the Henry charm, which could be formidable, and kept it going all through dinner. He had been to Genoa to give a lecture once and drew on his memories and his reading (both also formidable) to reminisce about the port, the *caruggi*, the mysterious inward-facing palazzi, and via Garibaldi, "the one Rubens called the most handsome street in all of Europe, yes?"

Maria Rosaria melted. "You visited so many years ago, you remember so much."

In truth he had given himself a quick Google refresher during his lunch break.

"I remember all the Van Dycks in the museums, and that stunning black-and-white-striped cathedral—San Lorenzo, right? And the cemetery. Staglieno. All those Victorian portrait statues covered in soot, and then rained on, so that the faces appear to be weeping. I've never seen a cemetery like that anywhere. It goes on for miles and miles."

The old lady had many other passions, but none went quite as deep as her passion for the place she came from, Genoa and the patch of

Ligurian coast south of the city where her family had lived forever. "If you visit, I will show you the hill that belonged to my grandfather," Maria Rosaria told Henry. "He had his olives there, his grapes. It's all divided up and mostly sold off now, but whenever I look at it, I see the place as it was when I was a girl and my grandfather would invite me to walk the hills with him and he would say to me, 'Remember to stay close to the land, remember it is important to have a piece of earth that is entirely your own.'"

"A Ligurian Scarlett O'Hara!" Henry exclaimed with delight. In exchange he described Leopold to her, if in a capsule version. Henry told her about his sons and where they were in their lives. Because she asked, he told her about his work, this too in abbreviated form. As she listened, Maria Rosaria fell (to Costanza's mind) worryingly quiet before saying, "You have to realize that we are still a very Catholic country at heart. For worse or for better the Church's opinion on such matters has a powerful effect on the thinking of ordinary people like me."

Because Costanza knew her mother, she knew how clever she was to speak of her country's attitude and not her own. And because Costanza knew Henry, she knew how hard he was refraining from saying what he thought about the Church and its "powerful effect" on assisted reproduction. He merely nodded and said, "That's what makes it all—interesting, doesn't it? To explore different points of view."

Henry's sidestepping was a work of art, a debonair little Van Dyck of phrasing unto itself. As he delivered it, Costanza's heart swelled with love for him, for the skill with which he seemed to grasp Maria Rosaria and modulated his normally vivid outspoken self. Maybe spending a lifetime as Leopold's son had prepared him for parents of a certain alpha cast. However he got there, Costanza was grateful, and told him so.

"I like a tough old bird," Henry said. "And you may have trouble seeing it sometimes, but your mother has a big heart."

Costanza often had trouble seeing her mother's heart, whatever its size, but this wasn't one of those times. In these first few days she was aware of Maria Rosaria's tenderness and something else, something unfamiliar: her sensitivity. At more than one juncture her mother held her tongue or softened one of her involuntary assessments with a little self-deprecating joke. If Costanza didn't know better, she would have thought Maria Rosaria had had some therapy. Maybe it was simply that she missed her daughter and was enjoying this taste of a world quite a bit wider than the rather limited points on her regular compass. At eighty she couldn't have that many more ambitious trips in her, after all.

Maria Rosaria had brought Costanza a large container of pesto wrapped in bubble paper, a package of *trofie*, and a brick of Parmigiano, and on her second night in New York she and Costanza prepared dinner together for Henry and Andrew. The pesto in particular, which had been made by Ines, Maria Rosaria's housekeeper, had decidedly transporting powers: one whiff and Costanza knew, from years of experience, that the basil had been picked when the leaves were small and soft, the pine nuts had likely come from Pisa, and the oil from her mother's own olive trees—the handful of them that were still in the family. The pesto Costanza had made for Henry and the boys the fall before was a pale approximation of this one, which released a scent that acted as a kind of magical potion. As she tossed the sauce on the warm pasta, Costanza closed her eyes, inhaled the fragrant steam, and was in an instant transported.

Maria Rosaria observed her. "So it still pleases you, this humble aroma of ours?"

"Of course it still pleases me, Mamma. There's nothing like pesto from home. You can't make it here. I've tried. It just doesn't come out the same."

"You must use *basilico di prà*. I know from when I lived in Palermo. I could never get it to come out right there either." Maria Rosaria paused. "I am pleased to see that home stays with you."

"Mamma, I dream of home all the time. In my . . . thoughtful moments, do you know where I go?"

"The Punta."

"How did you guess?"

"Because it is the most special place. Because you and your father loved to swim there." Then: "I'm sorry to hear that you have so many down moments."

Costanza bristled. "I said 'thoughtful.'"

"Yes, but you *meant* down."

She had lowered her guard and her mother had jumped right in, as ever.

Maria Rosaria changed direction. "I wish I had the legs to do the walk. I retrace it sometimes in my mind, when I have trouble falling asleep. Certain details I don't remember so well. There is an abandoned house, yes? Just after the church at San Nicolò?"

This drew Costanza in. "The chimney is still standing. I saw it last summer. You can tell where the kitchen was. There are tiles like ours, blue dots on a white ground, only charred."

"And your name? Is it still in the cement near the *fontanella*? Your father was so delighted when we came upon the wet cement that day. You must have been seven or eight."

"I was eight. We were walking to lunch."

"Yes, I remember now. Your eighth birthday."

The two women fell silent.

"I hope to bring Henry next year. You could come by boat. We could swim, have lunch at Drin."

"I would like that very much."

Over dinner at Henry's apartment the ballet continued: a careful choreography of good behavior and safe talk. Andrew, joining them briefly, was even more reserved than usual. Maria Rosaria asked him what he would be studying at college; his answers were abbreviated and noncommittal but polite. Later he told Costanza that the way she kept looking at Henry, then Costanza, then at him, one-two-three, as if her eyes were moving around some kind of private pinball machine, made him want to run and hide.

"Imagine that kind of assessing eye on you all through your childhood and teens and beyond," Costanza said. "No hiding, no running—unless you run *away*."

After dinner Andrew excused himself, saying that he had a paper to finish for English. The others retreated to the living room to finish their wine. Maria Rosaria, scanning the spines of Henry's books, remarked on the wide range of his interests, at least as reflected in the accidental accumulation of his library.

"By calling it accidental you deduce—correctly—that I am not really a book person. I go through many books, but they don't always end up on my shelves."

"Costanza's father was the same. Everything stayed up here." Maria Rosaria tapped her head. "I'm different. I keep most of my books, and in fairly good order."

"She has them alphabetized by room," Costanza said. "*A* to *F* is in the front bedroom, *G* to *L* is in the hall . . ."

Maria Rosaria smiled. "Well, I have time in my life for such things. The doctor has more important matters on his mind." She moved on to the desk in the window. "This room is very *accogliente*—I've always had trouble with that word in English."

"It doesn't really exist," said Costanza. "*Inviting* comes close. *Cozy.*"

"Cozy."

"That's thanks to your daughter," Henry said. "The apartment was kind of . . . neglected, before she gave me a hand with it."

"She's always liked to fix up places. Even as a girl." Maria Rosaria indicated the desk. "And is this where you work?"

"Yes," Costanza said.

"You're able to concentrate here?"

"Quite well."

"When there's so much distraction? All these windows to peer into?"

"It gives me something to look at when I'm struggling with a word or phrase."

"And also you cook, I imagine, while you work."

Costanza heard a criticism in that sentence that she knew Henry missed. Her mother's remarks, on the surface merely observational, often contained such hidden barbs.

"Yes, I do."

"My daughter is a very good cook, you know," Maria Rosaria said to Henry.

"And I am the beneficiary." Henry patted his stomach.

"It can be quite time-consuming, to cook well. To cook well means always keeping a train of thought on what's going on in the kitchen."

"Well, I, for one, envy her," Henry said. "I've always found that I do my best thinking when I step away from a problem and do something unrelated for a while."

But Maria Rosaria would not be deflected. "There's another way to look at it. Women, I hardly need to tell you, no matter how intellectual or professional, have always been tugged into the duties of the household. I felt it myself when Costanza's father was alive, and of course afterward, when there was only me and I was teaching full time and at home had to try to do everything, be everything, to my daughter. Running a home well can take you very far from your work."

"But, Mamma, I don't *run* this home. Henry has a housekeeper, a wonderful woman who has been with him for years. I cook because I love it. And I am at my desk almost every day."

"I had hoped you would start writing for yourself again, that's all."

This was new information to Henry. He looked with puzzlement at Costanza, who said, "In Italy, before Morton came into my life, I published some poetry and maybe a dozen stories. But it wasn't so easy to write when I was married to *him*."

"So you see," said Maria Rosaria. "Less stirring and more typing, please."

Even after this exchange, Costanza couldn't get Henry to understand. Wasn't that how it always was with a parent who had the ability to unhinge a grown child with criticisms and recriminations, however subtle or suggested? The web was often secretly claustrophobic. "She wants you to be the best you can be," Henry said as they went to bed that night. "It's what all parents want for their children. You'll see—I mean, let's hope you'll see."

"My mother always puts her finger on the thing that's missing. If you tidy up a room, she finds the pair of shoes you left out. If you give her your most recent translation, she draws up a detailed list of the inaccuracies and fails to comment on all the rest. Instead of seeing that I have a good life here, she looks for what I don't have, what I'm not doing. Even after all these years she still makes me feel so *small*."

Yet it was manageable, mostly manageable, until mother and daughter went to see the Vermeers at the Frick.

Costanza was familiar with these paintings. She had always thought that their theme was time. Time, stopped in paint. Time expressed through light, caught on a sleeve, a sheet of paper, a face. Maria Rosaria, advancing her theme from the night before, had a different idea. She contended that they were all about the confining or limiting of women. Standing in front of *Girl Interrupted at Her Music*, she chewed her lip for a moment, then said, "Do you honestly think this young girl will continue to study her music once that fellow comes into her life?"

This personalizing of the paintings irritated Costanza—and was surprisingly transparent besides. Maybe her mother *was* showing her age. "I sense you have something on your mind, Mamma."

"Since you ask, well, yes, as it happens I do." Maria Rosaria turned her sharp eyes away from the paintings and toward her daughter. "I think the doctor is an attractive man. A man of substance."

"I do too."

"But, *amore mio*, you have known him so briefly. How can you move into the house of a man in winter when you only met him the summer before?"

"It was fall when I moved in, Mamma. In some ways I scarcely knew him at all." Costanza said this almost provokingly. Triumphantly.

"All the more so. And this is not for the first time. You dove in with Sarnoff too."

"That's right."

"You remember how miserable he made you."

"And also how happy, ridiculously happy, for a time."

"You didn't get out of bed for days. You told me yourself."

"That was at the end."

"Before that there was the professor. And you remember what happened there . . ."

"Actually, I don't. But, Mamma, quite honestly, who are you to pronounce on whom I should choose to love? What makes you such an expert judge of who will make a lasting companion?"

Maria Rosaria didn't flinch. "I married the sunny exchange student who loved me from afar for ten years and with whom I had a beautiful ten years after that. The man who took his own life emerged later on. We've been over this many times before."

There was simply no winning with Maria Rosaria. No reasoning, no give-and-take. It was her point of view, only. "When you first arrived, you were so careful. I was so full of love for you. I thought you had changed."

"I *was* careful. I wanted to see with my own eyes how you were. I didn't want to jump in. I'm not a fool. I know I have strong opinions. I know, because you've made me see, that they are not always easy for you to hear."

"So why are you saying all this now? What's different?"

"My plane. It leaves in two days." She set her hand on Costanza's.

"Do you never think of coming home to Genoa, where you belong? With your people, who love you?"

"The Genovesi are not my people, Mamma. I've always been an outsider, because of Papa."

"Are you one of them here, then?"

"That's just it. There is no 'them' to be one of. That's the beauty of New York. Of America."

Maria Rosaria turned again to the painting of the young woman looking up from her music. "There's something else."

"Yes?"

"I wonder if you have realized that the boy is infatuated with you."

"Andrew?" Costanza's face colored. "He and I are friends."

"Have you noticed the way he looks at you? Follows you at the table, listens to what you have to say? Watches as you eat and drink?"

"Mamma, Andrew is in love with a girl his own age called Charlotte, who does not love him back. It's a sad story."

Maria Rosaria fixed her eyes on her daughter. "How old am I, Costanza? You should trust me sometimes, trust what I see."

Costanza emitted a long slow sigh.

"And one more thing. I'm just curious."

"Don't hold back at this point," Costanza said acidly.

"Why always the Jews?"

This she did not expect. "Do you have something against Jews?"

"No. But I have been wondering. First Sarnoff, now the doctor."

"I suppose they remind me of Papa. There is a strength, a kindness. An intelligence."

"But your father was not Jewish, and Sarnoff was not especially kind."

"Morton had his moments. And Papa had a grandfather who was Jewish."

"Who died before he was born. What does that mean? Nothing."

"To you it means nothing. To me it is a connection. Slight, but there."

"Your whole life has been too much about your father's death, Costanza. Still after twenty-five years you live in the past."

"The truth, Mamma," Costanza said with a flare of temper, "is that right now my life is very much about *life*. It's not about the past. It's about the *future*."

"Oh? How so?"

So it happened that, reactively and with a trace of defiance in her voice, and not at all the way she intended to, she told her mother about the first failed cycle of IVF and the next one coming up.

It was not easy to reduce Maria Rosaria to silence. Costanza's erect, fierce, formidable mother softened her posture and looked away.

"That is your response? You turn away from me?"

"I'm happy for you?"

"I hear the question mark. I know it's not what you feel."

"Quite honestly, it's alien to me. This whole meddling with biology."

"*Meddling?*" Costanza's voice rose. Fortunately, at eleven o'clock in the morning the museum was nearly empty. "What Henry and his colleagues do is alter people's *fates*. They change their *lives*. Do you know what my chances are of conceiving a child on my own? A healthy child? And besides, I love this man! And he loves me!"

In a more moderate voice Maria Rosaria said, "I must think about all this. Really you have taken me by surprise. I thought—"

"You thought I no longer wanted a child or a family of my own."

Her mother nodded.

"It is what I most desperately want. You think my life has been too much about Papa's death? Maybe there's some truth in that. Do you know what would make my life about something else—something more? This. A baby. A child. A chance to express all the love that I have in me—a chance to turn my heart away from the grief."

"You don't think that being expected to cure your grief is a terrible burden to place on a child?"

Costanza stepped into the adjacent gallery and lowered herself onto a bench. She felt weak, spent. Analyzed, assessed, doubted down to exhaustion.

Maria Rosaria joined her after a moment.

"I haven't spoken to you this openly in years," Costanza said. "Even this you judge, you criticize. I don't see how you can. I just don't see . . ." She trailed off into silence.

"I had you late in life, as you know. There are things I understand that you cannot. How altered your life becomes. How difficult the experience can be, physically. How much time you lose . . ."

Costanza had heard objections like these before, from Morton—

but from her own mother? What mother didn't want her daughter to become a parent? "Your pregnancy was miraculously lucky and, I realize now, probably not intended either."

"It doesn't mean I love you any the less. It's simply the truth. I don't regret—"

"You don't regret having me? Is that what you were about to say?"

"By the time I became pregnant, I knew your father very well, Costanza."

"Did you really?"

Her mother's face darkened. "Well, I thought I did. No, certainly I did. Know him then. In that period, before he became sick. Because that is how I have to see the sadness that seized your father in the last years of his life. He was a different man then. He—" She stopped, put herself back on course. "Do you know the doctor well? Do you truly, honestly believe that?"

"I wish you would stop calling him the doctor. Yes, I do know Henry. I know him well."

"*Henry* is a very clever man. Educated. Charismatic. Clearly in possession of a nimble mind, a wonderful memory—Rubens and the weeping statues and all that. Charming with us old ladies but, even so, I think, ultimately hidden."

"What makes you say that?"

"My experience of life. My intuition."

"Your suspicious nature is closer to the truth."

"It's a feeling I have, Costanza. I watch people and I think about them. I'm simply offering you my impression, unfiltered."

"And unasked for."

"I'm nearly eighty. You can't expect me to change, now after all these years to begin holding my tongue. And why should I, when I feel something so strongly? You are my child . . ."

"Mamma, your feelings are judgments. Call them what they are, please. You never embrace anyone, or anything, outright. You are cautious, critical. It's not how I want to live my life. I want to be free. I want to be open to possibility, *this* possibility."

"You are very passionate, my daughter."

"And you, Mamma, are very hard. So very hard on *me*. Why?"

Maria Rosaria didn't say anything. She looked across the room at a painting without, it seemed, quite taking it in. A glaze thickened over her eyes—not tears. Costanza couldn't remember when she had last seen Maria Rosaria cry. But even a misty eye, from her mother, was noteworthy.

Then it struck Costanza. It was like a curtain being drawn from across a window, and a view opening up. "You're mad at me for leaving, aren't you?"

Maria Rosaria didn't answer.

"Are you, Mamma? Angry at me? For going to live far away?" Costanza sat back. "How can I never have seen that before?"

On the day of Maria Rosaria's departure, Costanza accompanied her mother to the airport. It rained heavily, which seemed fitting, and for most of the taxi ride the two women discussed the weather, the things they'd seen during the week, and old family recipes that Costanza wanted to make sure she knew: safe topics, topics without land mines lurking in them.

When the first signs for JFK appeared, Maria Rosaria said, "If you truly love the doc—Henry, then you should marry him."

This Costanza did not expect to hear. "But why do you say this *now*?"

"I've given it a good deal of thought. I think that if you are really determined to go ahead with this treatment, then you should do it out of the deepest commitment a man and a woman can make to each other. If you're married, who knows, maybe this time it will work."

"That's not very scientific of you, Mamma."

"Possibly not, yet . . ."

So her mother was still capable of surprises. She was still capable, possibly, also of insights.

"Do you want to marry him?"

"I do. I would."

"You do. You *would*. I see. And Henry?"

"He wanted to."

"So what's the problem?"

"After Morton, I'm hesitant."

"No two marriages are alike, just as no two people are alike. Here too, as you know, I speak from experience."

They pulled up in front of the terminal. "I'm not exactly angry that you left," Maria Rosaria said when the taxi pulled over. "But I am sometimes sad. It's not very pleasant to be sad and alone, all alone, at the end of your life, or in view of the end. It's natural to want to be together."

Maria Rosaria opened the car door. "I prefer to go in by myself. I'll wait for you, you and Henry, to visit this summer. We'll go to the Punta, you will swim, and we'll eat at Drin. Before then, you'll send me news. I hope it is the news you want. Truly I do."

Costanza got out of the car with her mother. The driver unloaded Maria Rosaria's suitcase from the trunk. It came with a sturdy handle and was compact like her.

"It doesn't have to be a production, Costanza. You're both grown-ups. You can do what you did with Sarnoff. I'll give you a dinner when you come to Italy. You can have your grandmother's ring. I have no use for diamonds anymore."

On her way to her second City Hall marriage, Costanza couldn't help but think of her first. With Sarnoff her trips downtown had been especially joyous. "Trips" because New York State law mandated a waiting period of twenty-four hours between obtaining a marriage license and having the actual ceremony, even if the ceremony was only a handful of words spoken by a civil servant in a shabby little wedding chapel next to the city clerk's office, where the rug was frayed and the roses, she well remembered, were made of plastic. Sarnoff regarded this cooling-off period with wry delight. He said, "I wonder how many people change their minds. Imagine the dramas. Well, *we* won't forget these twenty-four hours"—and he made sure of that. He hired a navy blue Rolls-Royce to chauffeur them downtown to take care of the license. Afterward the driver waited for them while they had a Chinese lunch in a restaurant on Mott Street where the menu was entirely written in Mandarin. They had no idea what they were ordering and only maybe half an idea what they were eating once it came. Sarnoff had brought a magnum of champagne; their fellow diners applauded when the cork popped, and Sarnoff asked their waiter to pour a glass for everyone in the place. Between the appetizers and the main course he gave Costanza a delicate Edwardian necklace set with topazes, which he had chosen because topazes represent fidelity and love. After lunch they climbed back into the car to go shopping for whatever Costanza wanted or needed for their trip to Paris. "I don't want anything, I don't need anything," she said, "other than this." This: their shared adventure, the luxuriously hermetic silence of the car—and each other. But Morton insisted: "A coat, a bag, *something*. Lingerie. Socks. Come on." Socks it was, for each of them, half a dozen pairs in bright colors, pink and orange and lime green, bought at Barneys and, back in the car, put on to cascades of mutual laughter while they drove around the whole of the island of Manhattan, as close to the water as they could go, a loop of a drive for a loopy day.

The next afternoon the car was back, waiting for them downstairs. The driver whisked them and Howard, their witness, back downtown, where the city clerk mumbled fewer than fifty words alongside those dreary but now also somehow endearing red plastic flowers and made them officially husband and wife. Within two hours they were on their way to Paris, where Costanza spent the sweetest ten days of her life.

She was surprised that her memory could revive the sweetness even after everything that followed. It was strange how places, or paths, could hold feelings or bring them back with uncanny acuity. Here she was re-tracing steps she had taken all those years earlier, and finding them so real and so present that she could have taken them seven minutes instead of seven years ago.

All this when both her frame of mind and the circumstances were so different. Henry had had to ask Wanda to find an hour and a half in his schedule when he could leave his patients and meet Costanza to fill out the license; he had to be back at the hospital immediately afterward. That was on Monday. He had no opening in his schedule again until Thursday, when Wanda blocked out two hours during which Henry and Susan, their witness, would be able to meet Costanza downtown. If they didn't have to wait in too long a line, Henry might be able to eat a bowl of soup and a sandwich with her afterward, before hurrying back to the hospital for his three o'clock patient. This, in its entirety, was the wedding they had designed.

The details didn't matter to Costanza. What mattered was what had happened after Maria Rosaria left and Costanza told Henry what her mother had said and she watched his features arrange themselves in an expression of joy. "I didn't think, I didn't expect—" His voice choked.

"Are you telling me this because you agree with your mother—?" he tried again, and again choked up. When she nodded, and when her tears came, she knew that she was making a good decision, a hopeful decision.

Layering on one more large, though hardly unexpected, life theme, Costanza's period came on time, and she was started on the drug protocol, at doses nearly fifty percent higher than before.

So Costanza's decision to walk from the Upper East Side to lower Manhattan was as much about calming her body as her mind. The drugs were already making her feel jittery and heightened. The heightening wasn't *all* bad—she was working with unusual focus—but she knew from her previous experience that it was not to be trusted. She knew that the downs were not to be trusted either.

No one who observed her striding along Madison Avenue in her simple wool skirt, beige sweater, and spring coat would have guessed what she was doing with her afternoon. She made only one concession to the day: in the Flower District she stopped to buy some butter-yellow tulips with a splash of pink at the tips of their petals that had been forced in some faraway greenhouse or field, flown to New York, trucked to Manhattan, and displayed in utilitarian but nevertheless luscious mounds at a wholesaler's warehouse on Twenty-Eighth Street. Costanza was obliged to buy the tulips in bunches of ten, a dozen bunches minimum: what a picture she must have been, she thought as she resumed her walk downtown, her arms cradling a hundred and twenty yellow tulips, a paper cone filled with light like sunlight itself.

She arrived downtown at ten to one. Henry and Susan were already there, waiting for her. They smiled in unison, then laughed at the lavish flowers, half of which Costanza separated and gave to Susan. Costanza and Henry kissed. Costanza and Susan embraced. Costanza changed her shoes right there on the sidewalk. There were no topazes, no limousine, no magnum of champagne, no prospect of Paris, and no socks, just a proliferation of tulips, a grinning Henry, and her own beating heart.

"This feels right," she said aloud—as much to herself as to either of them.

"Yes, it does," said Henry.

And in they went.

•

Their wedding dinner was Japanese takeout, deliberately chosen by Costanza because it made such a nice bookend to the first meal they ate together in Henry's apartment. As they had that first time, they sat on the floor and ate off the living room coffee table. They shared a bottle of red wine, which Costanza, because of the fertility drugs, drank sparingly, and afterward devoured a box of berry tarts she had bought at a French patisserie on Madison.

The tulips, arranged in various vases and pitchers and jars throughout the apartment, were droopy but still festive.

Henry was not a natural sprawler, but he stretched himself out comfortably on the living room rug, his back propped up against the sofa. He said one word: "Happiness."

He reached over and stroked Costanza's leg. She smiled at him.

"But I do also want us to have a proper celebration," Henry added. "A dinner, a party. I want to be able to show the world—my world—what a lucky man I am."

"We can celebrate later. After the cycle. Maybe it will be a double celebration. We could do something when school finishes."

A shadow crossed Henry's face.

"You have told the boys about today? You did call them?"

"It's been such a whirlwind . . ."

"Oh, Henry." She sat up. "Justin could pop down anytime. Andrew could wander in tonight. They can't just walk through the door and find everything *changed*."

"But what will have changed for them? Justin doesn't live here anymore. Andrew will be going off to Philadelphia in the fall. They're launched, nearly launched, in their own lives. I thought I'd tell them, *we'd* tell them, when we see them. In person."

"It's not right. Obviously I don't have as good a sense of Justin as I do of Andrew, but Andrew . . . I knew Andrew . . ."

"Before you knew me." Whether Henry said this lightly, or with a forced lightness, wasn't quite clear. "How about if I send them an e-mail?"

"E-mail? Isn't that a little—remote?"

"Well, no one sends telegrams anymore. A text maybe . . ."

"Henry!"

"Okay. I'll call them. Tomorrow. Tonight I just want . . ." He leaned over to kiss her.

Costanza put up her hand. "We can't. You know that better than I do."

"We can't kiss? I can't kiss you?"

She hesitated for a moment. "Yes, you can kiss me."

⇌

Costanza was no longer a first-timer in Henry's waiting room; she had stepped across the invisible divide and was experienced now. She was no longer particularly interested in the other patients. All she cared about was having her blood drawn, hearing about the number and size of her follicles, and getting out fast. The tension in the room that had seemed so palpable on her first round now seemed more distant—not less present, which was something quite different, but less infectious, to her. She kept her largest, darkest glasses on the whole time.

This was her fourth morning appointment, which put her about halfway through the first part of the cycle. They had been increasing her drugs every two days. She didn't know if this was a good or a bad sign, and she elected not to ask. One change she had insisted on was having a doctor other than Henry supervise her treatment. She didn't want him slipping into the exam rooms as before. She didn't want to have to observe his work persona or try to decode the truth from his face. She wanted to make these weeks as normal as she possibly could. She never forgot what Dr. Sommers, Henry's fellow, had said to her at the beginning of the previous cycle, about how women with a steady confident attitude tended to have the highest rates of success. She had asked for Dr. Sommers to be in charge of her treatment, but he had left the clinic, Henry told her. A personality conflict. With which other personality? It was not hard to guess.

Susan arranged for her to see Dr. Woo. She wasn't the warmest physician Costanza had ever met, but she had Henry's endorsement, and she was familiar with Costanza's body.

Costanza drew on her full powers to keep from succumbing to the mental dance. She had learned how pointless it was to try to calculate

her chances. There was nothing to be done but endure the experience. So she endured the experience. She read; she meditated; she
breathed. She remained calm until she was horizontal and the ultrasound wand was about to reveal its all-important information—then
she felt she might jump out of her body, waiting for Dr. Woo to convey
the news.

At the first appointment she had had nine follicles on the left, six
follicles on the right.

At the second: seven follicles on the left, six on the right.

At this, her third appointment, she was down to six follicles on the
left, five on the right.

In the clearest sign of her accumulated knowledge, Costanza didn't
ask to have the information interpreted. What Dr. Woo said at this
one appointment could be invalid by the next. The follicles measured
between ten and twelve millimeters. They were growing perhaps a
bit too quickly, which was why, as before, Henry's team was adding
ganirelix, the drug that suppressed ovulation. Every night she injected
herself; every day, from this appointment forward, she would return to
Henry's clinic. During the intervals she would wait.

Costanza had never quite got used to the way, in these transitional weeks
before the weather warmed decisively, the buildings held on to the damp
and the cold. The drugs weren't helping. At times she couldn't layer on
enough clothing; yet at other times, particularly in the evenings after
her nightly injections, she felt her body had caught fire. More than once
she'd taken her temperature only to find it register normal. What a treatment: it played with the body; it played with the mind; it gave the soul
scarcely five minutes of peace a day . . .

She was wilting some greens in olive oil and garlic—cooking as
therapy—when she lifted off the shiny stainless-steel lid to the saucepan and saw a shadowy figure reflected in its convex surface. She turned
around abruptly and saw Andrew standing there, watching her.

"You know I don't like it when you make those catlike appearances
of yours, Andrew." She touched her hand to her chest. "You really scared
me this time."

"I didn't mean to. I just like to see people before they see me. See
who they are privately."

"That might work when you're taking pictures, but in real life it can be kind of . . . rude." She returned her attention to the stove. She could feel him watching her again. It felt as if her body temperature was rising. The drugs, surely. The drugs, *please*. "Do you want to tell me what you saw, in my case?"

"If you insist."

"I did ask."

He paused. "A secret keeper."

She turned to face him. "Well, your eyes deceived you. There's no secret."

"My father calls me up and leaves a message on my cell. 'I thought you'd like to know that Costanza and I went downtown yesterday. We're married now. We'll celebrate the next time we can all be together. Bye.'" Andrew waited a beat. "I'm not sure about the 'bye' part." He reached into his pocket, pulled out his phone, and thrust it in her direction. "Want to listen?"

She was relieved to have the greens to keep stirring. After a moment she said, "I'm sorry about the way you heard. It's not how I would have done it. But, truly, it was decided only a few days ago."

"You have my phone number."

It seemed impossible to ignore his tone. "Andrew, what is it? Why don't you just tell me what's on your mind."

"My grandfather hasn't been dead a month." His voice cracked. "It just feels—wrong, disrespectful."

The atmosphere felt as sharp as a blade. "You're sure it's Leopold? You're sure that's why you're reacting like this?"

He nodded unconvincingly.

"There *is* a reason, Andrew, why your father and I decided to get married so quickly."

"You're doing another cycle."

"Yes."

He nodded again, but remained silent. Too silent, for too long.

"You can't just hear this and say nothing."

He looked at her squarely. "You used to tolerate silence before. You're beginning to take on some of Henry's habits. He can't bear when there are gaps in the conversation. I didn't think you were so easily influenced."

She put down her spoon, crossed her arms, and stared at him as the kitchen filled with the mild hissing of *broccoletti* giving up their juices in a partly covered saucepan.

Henry wasn't like Andrew. He didn't make catlike entrances, normally. He came home bustling, dropping keys, bag, coat. The door usually closed behind him with an emphatic bang. But on this evening he stepped into the apartment more quietly than usual, then made his way toward the kitchen. There, before they saw him, he saw Costanza and Andrew standing across from each other, staring at each other—staring each other *down*. Costanza's back was to the stove, where thin wisps of garlicky steam were rising into the air. Andrew's hands were shoved into his pockets. Something awkward or uncomfortable had been said, Henry sensed at once. The connection shared between Andrew and Costanza—his wife—continued to disconcert him, he was surprised to discover. He had not understood it in Florence, or since. For all the talking he and Costanza did, Henry knew that when Costanza and Andrew spoke, their conversation had a different quality. And not just their conversation: even the silence between them could seem charged, more than the sum of its individual parts.

Henry broke into their wordless vignette. "Andy!" He encircled the boy in a hearty bear hug. "What do you think about our news?"

Andrew accepted Henry's embrace without reciprocating it, and he did not offer his opinion on the news. Instead he turned to his father and said, "It seems like I've missed a lot in the few days I've been on the West Side."

Costanza said, "I told Andrew about the new cycle."

Henry believed he understood now why he sensed such a strong feeling between them. "I would have told you myself, but . . ."

"But what?"

"But Costanza and I hadn't yet discussed whether we were going to talk about it this time."

"*You* didn't talk to me about it last time either."

Henry didn't know what to say to this. "I'm sure I don't have to tell you that you and your brother will always—"

"That sounds like the beginning of another platitude, Dad," Andrew said. "Don't bother." Then, not for the first time when a conversation turned uncomfortable, Andrew left the room.

Five minutes after Henry sat down at his desk on Friday morning, Wanda buzzed to tell him that a woman named Lorna Walker was waiting to see him. "She's not a patient," Wanda added unnecessarily.

Lorna and Henry had spoken regularly since Leopold's funeral, mostly on administrative matters, though Henry had also called several times just to see how she was doing; not very well, she inevitably answered. He had been hesitant to tell her about his marriage to Costanza, but he did, near the end of a brief call they had only a day before; she congratulated him warmly and said that Leopold had told her more than once he hoped the two of them would marry, and sooner rather than later.

In person she seemed fine. She was dressed in a formal outfit that he had not seen her in before, a skirt and jacket and sturdy black shoes, newly polished. It was as though she had come into town to conduct business, as apparently she had.

She sat down in the chair across from Henry's rather commanding desk. "This is just such a big, big sadness for me," she said when Henry again asked her how she was doing. Then her hands, which had been clasping a stiff black pocketbook, opened and reached into it. She produced a sealed envelope.

"I'm here on Leopold's behalf."

Henry looked at her inquisitively.

"He wrote out some letters for you and asked me to deliver them in person at the beginning of each month, for as long as was necessary."

"I see." Henry's stomach tightened.

"Though I'm not sure how I'm going to know when it's no longer necessary . . ."

"Without knowing—" Henry changed direction. "I'll probably be able to figure that out."

He watched as she set the letter onto his desk with great care, almost as though it were made of glass. "Are there many of them?" Henry asked.

"Leopold told me not to answer that question."

"There must be, if that is your response."

Lorna was fulfilling her duty impeccably. Her face gave nothing away.

"Out of curiosity, can you tell me when Leopold wrote these letters? Was it while he was in the hospital?"

She hesitated. "Yes."

"You had to think."

"I had to figure out if that was something I was supposed, or not supposed, to tell you."

Henry sighed. "My father . . ."

"Your father." She stood up more lightly than she had sat down.

Henry remained at his desk, staring at the envelope. On the outside, in his shaky old-world European handwriting, Leopold had written, "For my son, Henry"—as though there were any other. In the lower right-hand corner, in small block letters and twice underscored, was the word APRIL.

Henry considered leaving the envelope where it was, propped up on his desk, or slipping it into his drawer. He could even throw it away. What was to stop him? Leopold? No one. Nothing. He was an adult, an orphan. He was a grown-up; he was free. He could do whatever he wanted.

A single gesture: that was all it would take. In a single gesture he could pick up the envelope, tear it in half, and toss it into the wastebasket. It would take two, maybe three seconds, at most.

What a beautiful expression of free will that would be. Henry would proceed with his day. He would see patients; at one o'clock he would have a tuna fish sandwich and a cup of soup; afterward he would see more patients. At seven, if the day's appointments moved along smoothly, he would go home, where another delightful, Costanza-prepared meal would be waiting for him.

Henry took a moment to revel in this fantasy of who he might be if he hadn't been who he was—then he ripped open the envelope.

Inside was a single sheet of ordinary white paper on which Leopold had written, "Have you done what I asked?"

Henry, sighing, answered aloud, "No, Father, I have not spoken to the boys."

Now he was free to throw the envelope away, and its contents too. Henry crumpled the paper into a tight ball and hurled it across the room.

Leopold, honestly. Leopold, please.

Costanza's morning ultrasound produced a mixed report: her follicle census had diminished further to seven total (four right, three left), though their sizes (fifteen to seventeen millimeters) were "decently" on target for day eleven. Chances were good, Dr. Woo told her, that Costanza would be receiving her HCG shot that night or the one following.

"I bet you'll be glad to be over this first big hurdle," Dr. Woo said, "and to have a break from the drugs for a few days."

"I'd much rather have the hope—the possibility—of the situation improving. I'd be willing to take the drugs much longer if I thought it would do any good."

"But it wouldn't," Dr. Woo said matter-of-factly.

"Yes. I'm aware of that."

Costanza had made her peace with the plain-speaking Dr. Woo. She could do nothing for Costanza anyway. There was nothing anyone could do. She was yet again in the land of waiting, that diabolical no-man's-land. If her life were like a diary (there was Morton, unbidden yet again), she would flip the pages forward and know what would happen. But life was not like that. Life was a flypaper present, a shape-shifting past, a future that forever held answers tantalizingly just out of sight . . .

Costanza was smart enough to have organized a plan for her day. She was going to see the insect displays at the Museum of Natural History, specifically those related to ants. She had received an e-mail from an editor about the possibility of her translating a coming-of-age memoir by an entomologist whose specialty was ant colonies, and she wanted to try to figure out if she had any affinity for the science parts.

As she made her way up the museum steps, Costanza was transported back in time, back, deeply back, into her life. This had never before happened to her with quite such a visceral jolt. She approached the main doors as a nearly forty-year-old woman and at the same instant as an eleven-year-old girl, walking hand in hand with her father

on one of the few visits they made to New York together. Was it the
cant of the stairs, the cut of the stone? The distinctive timbre and level
of noise in the great hall, with all those chattering children? However
it happened, thirty years dissolved in a moment, and she was there with
Alan, the two of them alone together staring at the barosaurus skeleton
presiding over that enormous room in all of its improbability as he said
to her, "Piggles"—this just one of her ever-morphing nicknames—"do
you know what? I was about your age when I came here myself as a
kid, with my grandfather. And the place looks exactly the same." She
remembered him growing quiet—doing his own bit of time travel?—
and then adding, "He was a good friend to me, my grandfather. Sometimes when I'm feeling a bit down, I think of what a good friend he was
to me, and that makes me feel better. I wish you could have known him,
and I wish he could have known you. It's just a killer."

What was just a killer? She remembered those words so clearly, but
had no idea what he meant. It was just a killer that his grandfather died,
that the generations passed so definitively, that her father felt so much
sadness? It was just a killer that she could not ask him what was just a
killer. It was just a killer that he killed himself—oh, yes, that too. That
forever.

Costanza's original plan for after leaving the museum had been to walk
home through the park, but after spending several hours on her feet,
she was weary and in some discomfort. Her ovaries were large, hard,
and swollen, and so she fell into a cab. The ride across town was slow
and gave her time to think about how alien her body had become to
her. She wondered how those ants did it: once a queen reached matu-
rity, Costanza learned that morning, she spent the rest of her life laying eggs. When conditions were right—warm enough and humid enough
after a rain, not too wet and not too windy—sexually reproducing ants
left their parent colony and flew a long distance, and the females mated
with at least one winged male from another nest. Afterward the insemi-
nated female, a new queen, started her own colony, detached her
wings, and settled in for a lifetime of reproduction, fertilizing eggs from
the sperm cells she retained from the onetime nuptial flight. She could
live as long as thirty years and have millions of babies.

Millions of babies off a single squirt of sperm! A lifetime of fecundity! And here Costanza was, with her eked-out follicles and her amped-up hormones, feeling—out of nowhere and in a span of four minutes—a stab of pain and a flash of heat followed by a sudden chill, all these regular reminders that her body was not coasting along on its own, generating its own chemistry, but was under the control of Dr. Henry Weissman & Co.

She knew it was important not to dwell on how little control she had. On most days her mind was challenging enough to tame into a semblance of steadiness and calm; now that this other, involuntary stream of sensation was feeding her perceptions, she felt as though she were in danger, at any moment, of simply imploding. Or exploding. One more hot flash and she felt she might hop into the front seat, shove the driver aside, and gun it across Seventy-Ninth Street, mowing down a sea of yellow cabs on her way.

How she would *relish* that—the speed, the power. The freedom.

Twenty—not even—ten yards farther east, she had a different vision: of tearing off the driver's turban, releasing his soft long hair, and mounting him in the back seat of the taxi.

One problem with the drugs—one *further* problem with the drugs— was the way they made her see things more dramatically, more darkly and problematically. Over this too Costanza felt she had diminished control. "We do not see things as they are; we see them as we are," Morton loved to say—especially when her mood was black and critical, and they were circling around a fight. (He lifted the quotation, apparently Talmudic in origin and a favorite of his, from a greeting card, a provenance he tended not to disclose.)

She saw things as she was: yes—and no. Costanza let herself into the apartment and quickly took its measure. The rooms, though quiet and still, did not strike her as particularly peaceful. Something was disturbed; she felt it. Something, or someone.

She wasn't so wrong. At four o'clock in the afternoon, she found Andrew in bed with the blinds drawn, lying flat on his stomach. He was wearing an old T-shirt and a pair of faded blue briefs, looking like a combination of an overgrown boy and a statue fallen off its plinth. She

saw him and then, in the next second, saw the David, Donatello's David, which they had looked at together that day in Florence. Andrew
had something of the sculpture's sinuous long grace and beauty, and he
didn't recognize it, or enjoy it, at all. What a confounding condition
young adulthood was. All that vigor and freshness, all that physical
lusciousness, and you did everything in your power not to be in the
moment, not to live. She had been like that, like Andrew. Twisted up
inside, confused, at perennial war with her mother—this even before
her father died—and afterward, oh, forget it; years just vanished into
confusion, depression, a perpetual state of holding the world at a mocking distance. She now saw all that as an expression of fear. Like Andrew,
she used to retreat to her bed. Nowhere else felt so safe or so still; so
neutral. Of course it was neutral. Nothing *happened* there. Except for
reading. Reading happened there. And waiting. For what? She no
longer remembered.

As she stood there looking at Andrew, her heart opened up to him,
to the parts of herself she saw in him, to those lost years she would never
have back, just as he would never have this time—this moment, this
day—back. Why on a free, unencumbered afternoon should he lie in a
veritable stupor? What could she say to him to make him understand?

She touched him on the leg. His skin was warm and soft.

Andrew's left eye opened, then closed. She took that to mean he
was ready for conversation. "You were out late last night."

He groaned. "Depends."

"On?"

"How you define *night*."

"I didn't think there was much room for interpretation. Sundown
to sunrise, typically."

"Then the correct response is yes, I was."

"Were you up the whole time?"

"I was out walking. I went to my mom's for a while. Then I walked
some more."

"You walked all night, in this cold?"

"I took breaks. Once for tea. Once for hot chocolate. I saw the sun
come up."

"Have you done anything with your day other than sleep?"

He answered her with a yawn.

"Why don't you come food shopping with me? We can cook together afterward. I don't know about you, but I need to keep busy."

He looked at her. "Yes, that's how you keep it together. Keep calm."

"Well, I prefer to work or keep busy rather than"—she gestured at him—"sink."

"My 'sinking' unnerves you?"

She thought. "A little."

Andrew pulled himself into a sitting position. "Well, I've also been keeping busy. I've been editing some new pictures."

He gestured at his bulletin board. The surface was covered with images of Henry, covert images taken while his attention was elsewhere. Having coffee, or speaking to Costanza, or getting dressed. They were taken through cracks in doors, from behind the backs of chairs, down long halls. Dozens of different Henrys, surreptitious Henrys, glimpsed, snatched, or stolen Henrys, were pinned to the cork.

"You're spying on your father now, the way you spied on that reader, your neighbor."

"I am trying to see him unfiltered—unaware. Without his see-ing me."

"Why?"

"I did a paper last year for my history class about the early days of photography. In the time of Nadar, when photography was the new thing in Paris, do you know what Balzac believed? He had this idea that bod-ies were made up of layers, and that every picture snatched one away."

Costanza was perplexed. "You're trying to . . . strip your father down? See his essence?"

"I've been looking at Henry all my life, yet sometimes I feel he's a complete mystery to me."

She sighed. "I don't know what to say, Andrew. I have the feeling you're asking me to explain Henry to you."

"Actually, I'm not. But it's interesting that you think you could."

Andrew swung his feet to the ground and reached for his jeans. He lingered for a moment—as if he was enjoying Costanza's eyes on him—before pulling them on.

His getting dressed changed the mood in the room. She was relieved by that.

"What are we making for dinner?"

"I was thinking fish."

"Well, we'd better buy a lot of it. Walking around all night, you work up a serious appetite."

For the second time in a week Henry came home to delicious scents, and a less than delicious scene. In the foyer he detected a strong aroma of lemon and sugar. Over that was fish, and over *that* was either garlic or onions. Henry wasn't sure which until he edged toward the door to the kitchen. It was onions, sautéing in a skillet. Andrew was standing at the kitchen counter, carefully dicing parsley. Costanza was standing next to him, trimming asparagus. They were working side by side, on two matching cutting boards. Since when did the kitchen have two matching cutting boards and two good sharp knives?

Costanza and Andrew had their backs to Henry, and he observed them for a solid minute. They didn't exchange a single word. Their cutting fell in and out of sync, like two people running or walking alongside each other, but even when it was out of sync, it wasn't, quite; the way they were standing next to each other, leaning into each other slightly though without touching, yet each with an awareness of what the other was doing, seemed to Henry to be full of silent connection.

Toward the end of Henry's long watchful minute he began to feel a tinge of shame as he stood there, spying on his wife and his son. He felt dirty too. He *was* dirty. Rather than step into the room as he had intended, he slipped down the hall and went to shower away his day.

When he returned, Andrew was setting the table, and Costanza was preparing a vegetable dish, carrots having joined the asparagus, onions, and parsley in a large low pan. There was a cheerful clatter too, as Andrew set down cutlery, glasses, and plates and Costanza stirred her vegetables and shifted the lid on a second pot.

Henry resolved to make this his official return home, and to ignore the earlier one. He saw to it that his energy picked up as he stepped in, bearing the challah and a pair of candles he had picked up on his way uptown.

He greeted Costanza with a kiss.

Andrew glanced at the bread, the candles. Instantly his face hardened. "Celebrating *Shabbos* now?"

Shabbos: he even said it with Leopold's intonation.

"I walked by a bakery." Henry shrugged. "And then I fell into a shop that sold housewares. They had beeswax candles. Real beeswax. One thing just led to the other."

Henry, unwrapping the candles, gave them a slow appreciative sniff.

Costanza asked if he wanted his mother's candlesticks. Henry nodded. She left the room.

Andrew waited for her to go before he said, "Do you know how happy it would have made Grandpa to see you light the candles just once?"

"Men don't customarily light the candles, Andrew," Henry said. "I was thinking of asking Cos—"

"Don't tell me you're planning to say kiddush over the wine as well."

"These rituals do tend to come in threes."

"You're such a hypocrite, Henry."

"I'm *Henry* now?"

"Every time we saw Grandpa on a Friday, Henry, and he said the prayers, your face would turn to stone. He dies, and you turn into Mr. Super Jew."

"That I am not."

"You're a fake. A phony."

"I don't believe I'm those things either, Andrew. I'm feeling nostalgic, I'm thinking about your grandfather. And your grandmother. Do you remember how she used to bake her own challah?" Henry indicated the loaf.

Andrew said nothing, acknowledged nothing.

"I've had a tough day, and I felt that this might be a nice thing for me, for all of us, to do."

"You despise your religion. You always have."

"Quite honestly it's a little more complicated than that."

"Enlighten me."

Henry took a deep breath, but the only word he said was "Why?" The rest of it—*should I, you little prick* or something in that vein— remained unsaid.

"You know what Grandpa called you?"

"Various things, in his day."

Costanza, returning with Leopold's candlesticks, from the doorway heard Andrew say, "A self-hating Jew. He called you a self-hating Jew."

"Never to my face," Henry said evenly.

"You think I'm making it up?"

"I didn't say that. I said I never heard your grandfather call me that." Henry paused. "Anyway this too is more complicated than you think. If you want to have a candid conversation with me on the subject, that's one thing, but to pass on a remark like that, casually, and in front of"— he glanced at Costanza—"I just don't see the point."

"I do just hate you sometimes."

"Yes, I sense that. I wish I understood why."

"Because you are—who you are. And remind me, who is that exactly?"

"Someone"—Henry poured himself a glass of wine—"who is ready for a drink, with or without the kiddush."

"That's just another bit of finessing. You deflect and try to take control of the conversation at the same time."

"Possibly." Henry raised his glass. "But I still choose to have my glass of wine."

"And I choose to leave."

"Again?" Henry said under his breath.

A moment later the sound of the front door slamming reached them in the kitchen.

Costanza looked in the direction of the foyer. "He's having a hard time, you know."

Henry took a sip of wine. "He's not the only one, my dear."

"Nevertheless . . ."

"The father should think first of the child?"

Costanza studied Henry, trying to decipher his mood.

He sipped again from his glass of wine. "Tell me about your day. Have they called yet?"

"You don't know?"

"I had to leave the office a little early. Kligerman led the meeting."

"They called, yes. The HCG is tonight. We're—*you're*—to administer it at three a.m."

Henry nodded. "I did know what your results were from this morning's blood work."

"Not great."

"But not awful."

"Is there hope?"

"There is hope, yes."

"You're not just saying that?"

"No."

Costanza disappeared into thought. "Do we understand what we're doing here, really?"

Henry let out a long impatient sigh. "You know what I notice? Sometimes when Andrew is around and being, let's just say, very Andrew, you seem to become suddenly—doubting. Of me. Of us."

Costanza ran her hand through her hair and rested it on the back of her neck. "Andrew's at an age where it's his job to be angry at his parents. I can question you, and wonder about us, and this"—she gestured at her abdomen—"all on my own. I know what you're thinking: What I'm saying is not all on my own. There are the drugs . . ."

"I was not thinking that at all."

"But you have before."

Henry's head fell to an angle.

"There are times when I quite dislike you, Henry."

Henry nodded. "Well, Andrew has company now."

"It's clear to me how much time you've spent talking to patients, placating or handling medicated or difficult women . . ."

"The men aren't always a breeze."

"You're making fun of me now?"

"I'm agreeing with you. I've had to develop a way of conducting myself with my patients. It's true. I could tell you all about it if you like, but first may I ask one small favor?"

"What?"

"Might we have dinner? It smells so good, whatever you're making."

⊇

Henry did not often eat or drink to excess. It wasn't his nature. But that evening he ate and ate, drank and drank. He wanted to alter his mind, his body, his vision. He wanted to take himself elsewhere. Mainly he wanted to silence Leopold, make him go away.

As soon as Henry hit the mattress, he passed out, but his uncon-sciousness was short-lived. Within an hour he was awake again, rico-cheting between replaying his earlier exchange with Andrew and ripping open Leopold's envelope. His mouth was stuffed with cotton; his bow-els were rumbling; and somewhere in his head a mallet was striking—but none of this drowned out the voices of his dead father and his angry son.

Henry hoisted himself out of bed and sat on the toilet. The pee gushed out of him. He drank water, chewed Rolaids, swallowed aspi-rin. He fell back onto the bed like a piece of iron.

Sleep was not there waiting for him. Sleep was nowhere. Knowing that the alarm was set for three in the morning only made him more wakeful, more alert.

A mind already sharpened and troubled, then marinated in alco-hol: it was a torment. But he was determined to fight back. He would take himself somewhere pleasant, somewhere nice and vacation-y. Only what, and where, was this place? He could summon no beach, no moun-tain or lake, that had any evocative powers that stuck. He preferred indoor attractions anyway, didn't he? The Tate, with those smoky Turn-ers. The Musée Marmottan, with its Monets . . .

The monks' cells at San Marco: that was it. He returned to the set-ting where all this began. Those breathtaking annunciations, those shimmery Madonnas with their pink-kissed cheeks, mysteriously rumi-native expressions, and thin translucent hands: Was anything more lovely? Yes, something was—someone. Costanza, that day. What was it about first impressions, first meetings? They were when actual life was most like novels or movies, or dreams. Or memories. They were the bold-stroke, big-picture moments before complication, before all the re-finement and nuance, the slog of reality and detail, followed. Without them, life was unbearable. Or, rather, life was bearable—he had borne it, for years—but it was not much more than that. In Florence, in one burst of sensation, he woke up. He had not been so knocked out by a woman since Judith, maybe ever. And how fitting that it was such a physical moment too. He hadn't seen Costanza; he had plowed into her. He had collided with this goldenness, and out flared astonishment, surprise, a heightened awareness that everything in his life could change.

And everything had changed too.

Now this woman was lying next to him with swollen ovaries containing eggs that, in a few hours, and with the help of ten thousand units of HCG, would be sent on their fateful journey. They would be extracted from her and injected with his sperm and then it would be all about waiting again: waiting to see if the sperm would take, waiting to see if this life would take *off*—and take their lives with it.

The mallet was hammering away. Henry opened one boiling eye to the face of the clock. Was it still a face, he wondered tangentially, if there were no hands, only digital numbers? And hateful numbers at that: 12:52. He felt he'd been imprisoned in that bed for a century.

Into his turmoil, a remark from across the mattress: "I know you're not asleep."

"How," he said hoarsely, "do you know that?"

"Your breathing."

Henry didn't say anything.

"What're you thinking about?"

"Many things."

"Tell me one."

"The day we met. In San Marco."

"The day you crashed into me, you mean."

"I was thinking how beautiful you were. I thought I'd dreamed you. I thought you were like—like one of those Madonnas come to life."

"A Galatea fantasy. That doesn't feel very real."

"Well, everything becomes real with time."

She rolled onto her back. "That sounds rather grim, Henry, I must say."

"Real in a good way. You can't live a dream. A dream is a fantasy. It's a postcard, when life is made of letters, chapters. Books."

"What made you think about that day?"

It came to him in a rush: "There's something I need to tell you."

He hadn't even been thinking about it—directly. But once he said the words, he knew he had been wanting to, for a long time.

"What is it?"

"It's about me. And the boys. I don't feel—I feel you should know this—before."

"Before what?"

"Tomorrow."

She was facing him now, full on. Moonlight bathed her skin. Her eyes were focused, worried. No, concerned. Worried was too strong.

He didn't want to think what her face would look like when he was finished speaking. He could well be at the end of a great period in his life, the last great period. It could all dissolve. With a few sounds, a few words. A few sentences could cause all the goodness to vaporize. And he'd be back to what? To less than before. To nothing. Not even the boys, possibly. Just himself—and what? A spruced-up empty apartment, an avalanche of take-out containers redux, and an awakened heart and body that he would have to try to put back to sleep. To put down, maybe, like an old dog.

He had no way of knowing for sure how this conversation would go, but he knew that he had to tell her. It wasn't just for Leopold—it was for himself. It was time. He did just want to remember, to savor, her face for a little while longer, just a moment or two.

How he loved her skin.

"Henry? What is it? You're scaring me."

"You're so beautiful."

"So you said."

Now worry began to seep into her face. "Is it about my body, something you know, something I should know about the cycle?"

Her question was a help. "It has nothing to do with the cycle—not directly."

He pushed the pillow up under his head, but remained horizontal. It would be easier horizontal. The conversation would feel more like sleep, more like a dream. "The boys. Andrew and Justin were not conceived with my sperm. With Judith's eggs, yes, but with another man's sperm."

Her lovely face, her lovely concerned face, vanished—his words simply wiped it away. The worry was replaced by confusion. He had seen it coming. He couldn't be that surprised.

"You're—infertile? Are you saying that you're infertile?"

"When the boys were conceived, I had male factor infertility, which in my case meant a low sperm count. I told you that already. But that was before ICSI was developed, before *we* helped develop it. It's now no longer a problem, or much of a problem, in cases like mine."

It took Costanza some time to absorb what Henry was telling her. "That must have been very painful for you."

He had not counted on her compassion. What he took to be her compassion. His eyes filled up. "Yes. Very."

"Do the boys know?"

He shook his head. "Certainly not from me."

"But why didn't you tell me before, Henry? During the last cycle? Or yesterday? Or a month ago?"

"I wasn't sure it was—relevant."

Abruptly Costanza's mood changed. She sat up—she *shot* up. "Oh, Henry, it is *very* relevant. You have misled me—deceived me."

"I don't see it that way. I have withheld some information, that's all." In his chest a fist began to clench and unclench.

"It feels like a betrayal of our trust."

"Costanza, this is something I have been struggling with, privately, all my adult life. Imagine what it feels like for me, doing what I do, not to have been able—" He paused. "Really this is about me, not us."

"I don't know how you can say that."

"You've withheld information about yourself from me."

"What kind of information?"

"About your writing. About the phantom subtenant in your apartment."

She crossed her arms in front of her chest. "What makes you think that?"

"I saw a bill on your desk. I went downtown and checked it out."

"You *what?*"

"I had a feeling. I poked around a little."

"It's hardly the equivalent, Henry."

"I didn't say it was. I just said that you withheld—"

"I would have told you about it in time. It was merely a way of giving myself—"

"An out?"

"An option. This"—she gestured at him, then at herself—"has been a rather sudden change in my life."

"As in mine."

It wasn't clear whether she heard him. She was out of bed now, her hair flying. The change in eye level was disconcerting.

"There's something else, something significant, that you never told me. About the time after your relationship with your professor—Stefano—ended. At that party. The accident."

She stood still. "Who told you about that? My mother?"

"Of course your mother."

"But why?"

"I think she might have been trying to—"

"Warn you? Discourage you from having a child with me? Making a life with me?"

"I think she was simply making sure I knew everything she thought I should know."

Costanza crossed her arms. "Well, her version of what happened is not the same as mine. I'd been drinking. I misjudged the parapet."

"To her credit she told me that you believed that too."

"A signature move. Winning you over with candor while seeding suspicions." Costanza pushed her hair away from her face. "I did not try to take my own life, Henry."

In the silence that followed Henry wondered. Costanza wondered.

"My memories of that night are somewhat—clouded. This is a longer conversation, and I am willing to have it—but not now. It's not *pertinent* now." She resumed her pacing. "I must ask you the same question I asked you earlier: What are we doing here?"

"We're doing what we were doing before I told you about this. The same exact thing."

"But everything is different."

"I chose not to tell you—for a time—something about myself. Now I have. And now that I have, there's nothing left to hide."

"I wish I could believe that."

"Can you put yourself in my place, just for a moment? You know how achingly you want a baby? A baby of your own? Well, I did too—I *do* too. A man, you know, can also yearn. Does that make sense to you? A large part of *my* being, for years, has longed for this. I am like you. I too—"

"But what are you telling me? You don't feel like the boys are yours?"

"It's not either/or. It's more a case of that—and this. I've had that experience, but now I want, I would like, to have this one."

"You you you."

"I want *us* to have this one."

The effort of thinking all this through had seized her face. "Do you know the boys' actual father?"

Henry winced. "Donor."

"Well, do you? Know the donor?"

He hesitated. "Yes."

Costanza's mind was racing. "Don't tell me. I don't need to know. I shouldn't. It doesn't matter to *me*. To them—the boys—it matters. Hugely. You're going to tell them?"

When Henry didn't immediately answer, she said, "Henry, you *are* going to tell them. It's not a question. If you heard a question mark at the end of that sentence, erase it. I'll tell you right now I won't go ahead with this cycle, I won't have the HCG shot, the retrieval, any of it, unless you promise me that you will tell Andrew and Justin everything. They need to know. Andrew especially. He senses something is not right, in himself. And between you."

"It isn't this. You said it yourself. Andrew and I are having a classic—"

"You can't definitively say what it is that he's struggling with. You hold back on some level, in some way that Andrew feels, has felt all his life from what he has told me, and that troubles him. If you know the father—the *donor*—maybe you see him in Andrew, maybe you don't like what you see of him in Andrew, maybe you don't like—who knows what you like and don't like."

Henry couldn't even allow himself to think through the layers of meaning Costanza was opening up to him. He had to stay on the surface. Only the surface was navigable.

"Andrew and I have a conflict of personality. It's come and gone over the years, long before you appeared on the scene, Costanza. It's normal."

"How can you speak with such conviction? This isn't science. This isn't a controlled experiment being conducted in a lab. You have conflicts—you also have this unspoken thing between you. And it's made worse—bigger—for being kept secret. Andrew is a young man struggling to figure out who he is, a young man who is aware, deeply aware, that something isn't right between him and his 'father.'"

"I wish you would take that word out of quotation marks. I am Andrew's father, period."

"You are Andrew's father, period, but you wish to have a different experience of fathering. You are Andrew's father, period, who has not told him a key fact of his life. The truth of his life. You will, though. You'll tell both him and Justin. I insist."

Henry couldn't remember when Costanza returned to bed. But there she was, lying next to him, her head facing the ceiling.

"Leopold knew, didn't he?"

"Yes."

"What did he think?"

"He thought the boys were a gift. A miracle."

"Yes, but what did he think about their not knowing?"

Henry paused. "He wanted me to tell them."

"And me? Did he want you to tell me?"

"Also you."

And again, half an hour later. "I need more of the details."

He told her. He explained how he and Judith had been trying for two years. He told her about the insane coincidence of his life's work coinciding with his life's need. He and Judith tried several cycles of regular IVF with his sperm before they realized that it was not going to work. With donor sperm, it went easily. Both times Judith had easily become pregnant. She was relatively young. She was vigorous. Her pregnancies were uncomplicated. But he'd been haunted all his life. All his career he'd looked for a way to help men like himself; and now he was helping himself. Treating himself.

She asked him if he felt it had affected the way he'd been a father, to Andrew and Justin.

"No." Then, with more candor: "I don't know. How can I know? I've only lived one version of this experience, one story, not the other."

It felt better—he felt better—to have told her. To have finally said it out loud.

•

An hour later:

"I don't trust you. I don't see how I can trust you."

"I see why that is. But there's nothing else to show you, to tell you. I assure you."

"I have no way of knowing what your assurances mean."

"They mean that you're seeing me naked now. There's nothing more. Nothing else."

At three o'clock the alarm went off, finally. It was a relief. A release.

He sat up and turned on the light. She looked awful—soupy eyes, mauled cheeks, hair matted with sweat.

He did not want to imagine what he looked like.

"You must give me your word that you will speak to the boys. Today."

"I give you my word."

She looked across the room, at the bag from the clinic that stood on the dresser, the bag with the syringe and the dose of HCG and the disinfectant soap and the jar for Henry's specimen that he was to use thirty-six hours later.

"You promise?"

"I promise."

Was it possible that she was making up her mind only in that moment? He would never know, just as he would never know if she was coming to her decision out of understanding, or desperation, or panic, or some combination of all three.

She decided. That was all he knew for sure.

"Then you may give me the shot."

⊐

Henry walked through the park, skirting the reservoir early on a Saturday morning. A cold wind came up off the water and scraped at his cheeks. As he walked, he rehearsed:

I want to tell you about the love. I don't know if you can dig back down, these days, to see it, to feel it. Maybe you won't ever be able to. But

I remember. I will go to my grave remembering. It tore my heart out. The way you looked up at me and said, "Dad, this is a great morning." We were out together, just the two of us, submerging pancakes in syrup. Do you remember that diner we used to go to, the one with the mosaic of the Parthenon? Do you remember Dmitri, he always brought you extra strawberries? Sunshine was streaming through the window, lighting dust motes, a galaxy of daytime stars. It was freezing outside. The pancakes were sweet, sending up little puffs of steam. The coffee—awful, delightfully awful. Another time: "Dad, did you ever notice how you eat breakfast at one end of the table and dinner at the other, but you're always the same distance from me?" Slayed—again. And I'd never noticed, either. "Dad, you're a terrible drawer, let me show you. Let me be your teacher, Dad." "Dad, let's play Concentration. Go Fish. Mario Kart." "Dad, can we go see the gems and minerals at the dinosaur museum?" "Hey, Dad, what about if you and me, just us, we watch some basketball on the sofa together." Pops too, it was, for a little while, around when you were five . . . and Scruffy, do you remember that? It started on weekends when I got lazy about trimming my beard . . .

Bottomless love, day after day, pouring out of you and Justin like breath. It made the morning worth opening my eyes to. When I tell you it's the best thing I ever did with my life, I'm speaking the truest truth I have ever spoken.

At my end—what I felt—that's the other part of the story. It takes poetry, and I don't have poetry, to get this across. I wonder if you've had this feeling yet. You may have to wait to have it until you're a father yourself. The earth, spinning through time, is holding you with its gravity so that you can come home every night and meet all that love with more love.

There is another side though—would he say this, add this?—it makes you think of death. You can't stop thinking about death: how briefly you're here, how briefly we're here together. You see life put through all these phases, in fast motion. You can't observe your own growing up like this, but your kids'—it's a devastation.

I still love you, despite—despite all the reasons you give me not to. It just doesn't work like that. Love like this never dies. I think it lives beyond us. It's the only thing that does.

●

Henry got maybe three percent of this out before he choked up. He was sitting at the foot of Andrew's bed in the room the boys shared at Judith's apartment.

"Tore my heart out . . ."

"Pancakes in syrup . . ."

"The Parthenon . . ."

These phrases he somehow managed to say, though possibly not in the most coherent order; then he lost control, and his face just liquefied.

Andrew pulled himself up in bed, groggy. "Dad, what are you doing here? Are you sick? Is it Costanza?"

Henry shook his head, mopped his face with his sleeve. He brought himself back under control by looking at his surroundings. He had not set foot in this room for five years, possibly more. His sons' parallel West Side world was fitted out with all the requisite stuff: furniture, computer, bookshelves. There were several framed professional photographs, black-and-white, of either Judith and the boys, alone, or Judith and the boys and Charlie; Henry was conspicuously absent, as though dead. And there was considerable paraphernalia of late childhood—art projects, models of motorcycles and rocket ships. What did it mean that Justin went off to college and left his things intact at Judith's, while on the East Side he purged every trace of his life?

"No one's sick."

"You seem pretty upset."

His chest felt dammed up, solid. "This is hard for me, Son."

Andrew's face, before. As with Costanza, Henry wanted to note it, to retain it. When would this young man, so handsome with his high forehead, his lush hair, and his watchful eyes, ever again look at Henry with trust or compassion? When would he ever again present such a not-knowing face to the world?

There is something—

For many years—

Maybe you have a sense—

Already Henry saw Andrew sinking deep into his body, a self turning away, inward; trying to figure it all out, to absorb, to *grasp*—a metamorphosis in the making. Henry would not have been surprised if Andrew sprouted wings or leaves, or if his fingers turned to talons or hooves before Henry's very eyes.

The dam was letting something past now. A gurgling sound. Then words. *The* words.

Andrew asked his father to repeat them. The words; the information. His face—Henry hadn't expected this—reverted in time. He didn't change into an animal or a bird or a tree. He looked like a boy, confused and innocent. "You mean to say, you're not my father?"

Was he possibly relieved? Did Henry see that too or invent it out of his worry and fear? Was it possible? Was Henry that awful, was Henry that blind to the kind of father he was, to this boy, this young man?

"Not genetically, no, but in every way that I know of, yes. Forever. Until I die."

"No part of me, though, not a gene, a single gene, is from you?"

"I think you know your biology better than that, Andrew."

He could see Andrew thinking. His eyes were busy, his brain was busy. "And Justin?"

"The same."

"Not genetic."

"No."

"The same father—donor?"

"The same *donor*, yes."

"Do you know who it is? Was? *Is?*"

Henry nodded.

"Are you going to tell me?"

"If you need to know. If you want to know."

"Yes. Everything."

Henry paused.

"Do I know him?"

Henry nodded.

Andrew sucked in a breath, and his whole face altered, as if it had been flushed by an electrical charge. "It's Isaac Schoenfeld, isn't it?"

"What makes you say that?"

"A few things. Several things. A feeling. Am I right?"

"Yes."

"Were he and Mom—"

"*No.* It was in vitro."

"Is that why you and he stopped being friends? It wasn't a business conflict, then?"

"We had a business conflict, just as I told you. But we might have worked harder to sort it out if . . ." Henry took a breath. "It was just better, I think, for our lives to be more separate."

"Does he know?

"Yes, he knows. Of course he knows."

Andrew sat back into his pillow. His T-shirt, much washed, had a scattering of tiny holes along the neck. The fabric, Henry thought darkly, had been rent.

"This is fucking with my brain, Dad. *Henry*. I don't even know what to call you."

"I'm still your father. Dad. Pops. Scruffy. Remember Scruffy?"

Andrew looked at him as though he were speaking Urdu. "I don't know what to do with this."

"In time you will. Andrew, I want you to know—" Henry's eyes filled up again. "I want you to know that you can come to me anytime, we can talk about anything you need to."

Andrew's eyes turned icy. "*Now* we can."

Henry paused. Softly he said, "Yes, now we can."

"I would have liked to know this before. A lot before." Then: "Does Justin?"

"I haven't told him. But I'm going to now. As soon as I can find him." Henry glanced at the untouched second bed. "It'll probably have to be by phone."

Again Henry could see Andrew reasoning. He could almost feel the boy's heart beating—racing. "What you're doing with Costanza, the cycle. Is it—?"

"We have new procedures now." He reminded Andrew about ICSI. He said that reproductive medicine was a different world, a world full of different possibilities. Miraculous possibilities.

"You mean if you and Mom were trying to get pregnant today, you'd be my genetic father?"

"In all probability, yes."

"I would be—" Andrew's forehead creased. "I would not be me. I may not be me now."

"Of course you're you. You're the same. It's just that your story—a part of it—is different."

"My story?"

"Your starting point. Your genetics. That's it."

"That's not a small *it*, Henry."

"I wish you wouldn't start calling me Henry just so quickly."

"That's not a small *it* . . ."

Now Henry was nameless, title-less. Stripped of his identity. It was probably inevitable that there would be some of this; a lot of this, even, for a time.

Andrew's eyes were darting, moving. "I have one more question—for now."

"Of course."

"Does Costanza know about us—Justin and me?"

"Yes."

"How long has she known?"

This Henry did not expect. A complication. A snare.

Andrew persisted: "Has she known since you started IVF, or before that? When did you tell her?"

Henry's heart began to speed up. How could he not have thought all this through? How could he not have taken the time to consider all the possibilities and ramifications, all the eventualities, so that he might be better prepared? Even after all these years he was unprepared. By pushing forward with his life, and burying this piece of it, this key piece of it, this story, he had had no practice thinking through how he might respond if—when—it became unburied, as it had now.

"Has she known all along?" Andrew asked again, more forcefully.

"Yes. Yes, she has."

Looking at Andrew's face—the darkness that rolled across it—Henry suspected he had made a mistake. He lied to protect himself, to improve his chances, on this day of all days, that Andrew would not judge him or find him wanting, a disappointment—more of a disappointment. He had been afraid of his own son, of what his own son would think of how he was conducting himself in his life now, all these years later. Probably he should have just told the truth. That's what he advised his patients to do with their children. That's what his father would have done. Leopold would have told the truth and lived with the consequences.

"And the child you have with her, if the cycle works, will be yours genetically. Yours and hers."

"If we succeed, yes."

"He will be my brother, she will be my sister?"

"In the way that I am your father. Yes."

"Not in that way, Henry. It won't be hidden, will it? Because this time there will be nothing to hide."

Costanza's pre-op appointment that morning was not at Henry's clinic but at the hospital, where the retrieval would take place the following afternoon. She presented herself at Sixty-Eighth Street and York Avenue before eight a.m., as instructed. She had slept maybe four hours—maybe—the entire night and looked it. Her eyes were red and had sunk deep into their sockets like two pebbles in wet sand. Her hair was pulled back into a sloppy ponytail. She left her dark glasses on, even as the attending physician—someone, fortunately, she had never before met—did one last ultrasound to confirm the size of her follicles. Afterward he gave her a list of postoperative instructions, a prescription for the antibiotics and painkillers. Then he asked her if she had any questions.

All this was as before. Only before, where she had said she had no questions, now, in as casual a voice as she could summon after her night, she said, "I do, actually." Then, still from behind her dark glasses, she said, "Do people ever decide not to go through with the retrieval, even after they've had their HCG shot?"

The physician—pink complexioned and seemingly young despite the scattering of gray in his hair—looked at her carefully before answering, "Yes, it has happened."

"Why does it happen, have you found?"

"Well, sometimes the patient reconsiders. In such cases typically there has been conflict between the couple. Or we reconsider, because something unusual has happened to the follicles."

"What do you do then—just give up?"

"If the couple resolved their conflict within the window"—he looked at her again closely—"then we suggest that they have timed intercourse within twenty-four hours. The sperm need to be in the fallopian tubes once the eggs are released, and the eggs are released precisely thirty-six hours after the HCG shot. Probably the best approach is to have intercourse twice within that window. This is not an assurance of anything, mind you. The chances of conceiving after ovulation has been triggered are higher than they would be without the stimulation and the HCG injection, but they are never as high as IVF would be, obviously."

"Obviously."

"Sometimes it happens that intercourse is not—successful. There is a great deal of pressure at these times. In that case, assuming a semen specimen can be produced independently, we convert to an insemination. Again it's not optimal, but it is better than nothing."

"All that high-tech medicine of yours comes down to a turkey baster."

The doctor leaned forward. "Ms. Ansaldo, is everything all right?"

"Perfectly. I'm just a—curious sort of person. I like to understand, as far as I can, the eventualities, the possibilities. I don't know if you can quite realize—it's not easy to feel so out of control of one's body, one's body's *fate*."

"In two weeks, you'll know everything."

"Everything?" she repeated with some edge. Then, catching herself, she added, "In two weeks. Yes, of course I will."

Henry bought Costanza flowers, a large bouquet of tulips close in color to the bunches she had carried downtown the day they were married. He hoped he remembered the color correctly. He hoped she would discern his intent: to try to make a loving connection. He had to do *some*thing. Best of all would have been to have found her in the apartment, back from her early appointment. He would have spoken to her, felt out her mood, her thinking. He would have taken her into his arms. He too needed some kind of gesture, some reassurance. It had not been an easy night, or morning. Far, *far* from it. But she was not there, and she did not answer her cell phone. Where was she? He had no idea. She had left no note or message.

He put the tulips in water, then set them by the bed. They seemed too funereal, too sickroom-like there, so he moved them to her desk. He wrote out a note: "I spoke to A. I'm trying to get hold of J. I'm doing what you asked. I love you. H."

Then he went to the clinic. He couldn't think where else to go, what else to do.

Andrew looked up the bus schedule to Annandale-on-Hudson. He arrived at Justin's apartment before noon. He rang three times before Justin came to the door. The way he was wearing a pair of gray sweatpants, their drawstrings dangling, suggested that they had just been pulled on.

"Andrew, what are you doing here? This can't be good."

"I just needed to talk to you. Can I come in?"

When Justin didn't step aside, Andrew glanced over his shoulder. In an alcove at the back part of the apartment was a large futon. David lay asleep there under a burgundy sheet.

"He's kind of just staying here for a few days."

"Kind of just?"

David emitted a snore. "We should probably whisper. He was up late practicing."

"Does this mean you're back together, or what?"

Justin glanced back at David. "Or what."

They went to a coffee shop around the corner. Justin placed an order for an elaborate espresso drink; anything stronger than water, Andrew felt sure, would cause his stomach to give up the last meal he'd eaten and possibly several others besides.

"I had a visit from Dad this morning—he came to find me at Mom's. Early."

"Judith must have been thrilled by that."

"She and Charlie spent the night in Jersey. They went to visit his uncle."

"I don't keep such close track of Judith's movements."

"Dad told me something pretty—big. Huge."

"Oh? What about?"

"Us. You and me."

"Let me guess. About our genes maybe? Our origins?"

The color drained out of Andrew's face. "You know?"

Justin nodded.

"Since when?"

"Judith told me in high school, at the start of senior year."

"You've known for two years, and you didn't tell me?"

"Judith asked me not to. She said she thought you still had some growing to do. Some growing into yourself, she said, that she didn't want to interrupt. I believe that was her professional take at the time."

"But I don't get it. Why you and not me? I'm a senior now . . ."

"She thought it might help with the homo thing."

"How?"

"She wasn't sure. She just 'intuited' it."

"Didn't she 'intuit' that I might need help with the hetero thing?"

"Apparently not."

Andrew paused for a moment to absorb. "What about just the human thing, the life thing? Like wanting to know where you come from, what you are made of, who made you? Wanting to understand why, all your life, you've felt your own father, on some level, hasn't quite gotten you. Or liked you."

"I suppose that wasn't on her radar, exactly."

Andrew slumped back in the booth.

"And Henry doesn't dislike you, Baby B."

"Yes, he does. Sometimes he does—lately I'd say it's been often. Even if he did tell me, in tears, about eating pancakes at the diner and feeling such love for me that it tore his heart out."

"I always thought their waffles were better. And that waiter Dmitri was hot." Andrew just stared at Justin, who changed his tone. "I'm sure he felt that, in the moment. In some rare unnarcissistic moment."

"You know what? Now that I think of it, what he actually said was that *he* felt my love for *him*, and *that* was what tore his heart out. Interesting how I got it reversed."

"Sounds more like the Henry we know."

"Though to be fair, he said he loved us a lot."

"'What's love got to do with it?'" Justin sang.

"You're mocking him—me? Now?"

"'What's love but a secondhand emotion?'"

"Justin, please."

"I've never been more serious in my life, Baby B. One thing I've learned from observing the mater and the pater is that love has a lot less to do with all this than we think."

"What does then?"

Justin shrugged. The freedom in those shrugs of Justin's, the beauty in them: Would the day ever come when Andrew would be able to shrug like Justin?

"Does Henry know you know?" Andrew asked.

"Judith may have told him. But he's never said anything to me."

"If she did . . . and if he knows, or suspects, you know . . ." Andrew's mind was flashing, connecting; *seeing*. "Do you think *that* would explain why he's been so much more into you than me? Especially since you went to school. It's like he's been trying to prove something to you, or hold on to you."

"If Henry's more into me—and I'm not saying that he is—it's probably more because he knows I don't give as much of a shit as you do."

"About what?"

"Him."

Andrew took this in. "Did Mom tell you who the father is?"

Justin shook his head.

"Are you interested in knowing?"

"Am I interested in knowing who *the* father is? Curious use of the definite article, Baby B. That would be *our* father, would it not? In some narrow biochemical sense. But—truly—I don't care whose genes are in my cells. I feel freer not knowing."

"Freer than who?"

"You, for one."

Andrew, frustrated, began to feel his temper flaring. "Aren't we in this together?"

"This? Which 'this' do you mean?"

"This—this family, I guess."

Justin leaned back. "Now what family would that be, exactly? The one Judith and Henry made and then unmade before our very eyes? That would be the legal family, the social or maybe economical arrangement that goes back millennia and was devised to preserve property, fortune, a name. That would be a resounding, um, no. The genetic family? Let's see: that one is created for the purpose of extending into distant generations the genes of a man and a woman, presumably in love, or once in love, who seek to unite their lineages through reproduction. Ding: no again. How about a looser interpretation—what shall we call it? The philosophical, the psychological, family—where two people, customarily in the olden days a man and a woman, though fortunately open to wider possibilities now, come together in an honest relationship with each other in order to create a civilized subgroup whose purpose is to rear strong children, give them a sturdy sense of self and of their place on the planet, and love them unselfishly or at least try not to play out on them all their insane animosity, egotism, neediness, pettiness, and greed, and now and then make them a decent home-cooked dinner besides? Hello? Any yeses out there in our audience?"

Justin looked around the coffee shop theatrically.

"Okay, we're *not* in this together. We're not in anything together. How's that?" Then, in Andrew's mind, a click. He stared at Justin for a moment. "I get it now. *This* is why you've been so angry at Henry. You knew, and you were mad at him, or confused or something, and you couldn't come out and say it, so you turned yourself into a real prick. And not just to him but to me and Mom and Grandpa too."

Justin started to emit one of his rapid-fire responses, but then he looked at his brother's open, hurting face. Justin drew in a long breath, as though deliberately to aerate his mind, and maybe also his stubborn heart. "Interesting hypothesis."

"Please, just for once, can you be serious."

"No, I mean it," Justin said quietly. "You've possibly got something there. Possibly you do."

The two of them sat together in silence.

"I'm sorry this is so hard for you, Andrew," Justin added after a moment. "Maybe I'm also envious—a *little* envious—of your intensity, your . . . engagement. But really I prefer it my way. I'm not happy being resentful, but I am happier not caring so much. It's harder for you, yes, but I think it also may be—I don't know—deeper."

These were some of the most genuine words Justin had said to him in a long time. Again they sat in silence. Then Justin reached over and put his hand on Andrew's. "Whatever you do, Baby B, please don't cry."

•

Andrew waited until he got back to the bus station. There, and only there, did he allow himself to burst into tears. *Five minutes of this*, he told himself. Then he upped it to ten. Where did all that freaking liquid come from anyway?

At fifteen he took out his cell phone and googled the phone number of Dr. Isaac Schoenfeld on Park Avenue in New York City.

Benjamin answered the door. Andrew's face must have showed some surprise, because Benjamin explained, "I came down for the weekend. I needed a break from school." He closed the door behind Andrew. "My father said to tell you he'll be out in a minute."

Andrew nodded. He stood in the foyer, paralyzed.

"Maybe you should take off your jacket."

Andrew took off his jacket.

"Is something wrong? You look kind of whacked. You want water or coffee or something? We just got a Nespresso machine."

Normal words, normal questions. Hospitable; affable; civilized. Andrew had to fight an image that came to him. He saw himself throwing his arms around Benjamin and saying, *Will you be my brother? Will you help? Can you?*

"I'm okay, thanks."

They both stood there looking at each other.

"There's something between our dads," Benjamin said, "isn't there? Something from the past."

Andrew didn't answer.

"And between you and my dad?"

Andrew felt color coming into his face.

"Whatever it is—no one has told me anything."

What was Andrew's heart doing up there in his throat?

Again they stood there looking at each other. Andrew had to break this excruciating silence. "How's Charlotte?" he asked with a catch in his voice.

Benjamin's hands disappeared into his pockets. "That's a good question. How is Charlotte? You're probably not the person to be saying this to, or maybe you *are* the person, I don't know. Let's just say Charlotte is in a mood. Maybe not in *the* mood is a better way to put it. She's not in the mood to continue a relationship with, and I quote, 'such a nice guy.'"

At least she hadn't entirely stopped giving the nice guys a try, Andrew thought. "I'm sorry." He had such a hunger for human connection that he was commiserating with the just-now-ex-boyfriend of his ex-girlfriend. For the second time in the space of three minutes he wanted to put his arms around this fellow and say, *Brother, I understand*. And maybe find out: Brother, do *you* understand?

But the brotherhood Andrew was fantasizing about would be founded on what? Genes? He and Benjamin shared only half their genes; Andrew and Justin shared them all. It would have to be genes—and then he'd see. He'd see if this alternative path might lead to a better world, a wider world.

Is that where this news, this truth, would lead him? To a world of more connection, deeper friendship? Would it be deeper or, well, just different? A new brother, a new . . . what would he be to Schoenfeld and Schoenfeld to him, anyway?

Schoenfeld's hair was neatly combed, his face freshly shaved. His clothes seemed deliberately chosen yet effortlessly worn. He smelled good too: of lemon, or lime. A bracing, citrusy scent that Andrew recognized from Schoenfeld's sweater, which Andrew had put on again that morning, as Schoenfeld noticed as soon as he saw Andrew. "You're getting some use out of that, I see."

"Yes." Andrew's voice was on the verge of cracking.

Schoenfeld invited Andrew into his private study, a room Andrew had not seen on his earlier visit to the apartment. There were more books, also shelved in meticulous order. A desk faced the window; a sofa and two chairs stood across the room and were covered in soft brown leather. A single, notably large painting hung over the sofa. It depicted what looked like an abstracted Cycladic figure, one of those stylized women with large hips whose head, blank of features except for a nose, tilted up to the heavens. On their visits to the classical galleries at the Met, Henry used to like to point out to Andrew these figures as among his favorites. They were believed to be fertility figures. Of course they interested Henry. It made sense that they would interest Schoenfeld too.

Andrew studied the picture. "Her hips are—impressive."

"I suppose there's a certain reverberation, professionally."

Andrew was relieved that, for a moment, there was a subject other than *the* subject. Well, *almost* another subject. "It reminds me of those small Cycladic statues at the Met."

"They are, I believe, the inspiration."

Somehow this was less offensive to Andrew than Henry's obsession with annunciations; less grandiose anyway. Schoenfeld was like Henry; he was unlike Henry. He was in control where Henry was control*ling*. He was autocratic yet thoughtful, formal yet compassionate. He had a big heart.

Did he have a big heart? What did Andrew know about him, really? In truth Andrew had no idea who he was, what his heart was like, or not like. Who he was, at least, might soon become a little clearer. If only Andrew could think how to begin.

"You wanted to speak to me."

Andrew nodded.

"Are you all right?"

Andrew shook his head.

Andrew stared at Schoenfeld. Schoenfeld stared at Andrew.

"Things right now feel very—"

An object the size of a grapefruit lodged in Andrew's mouth. It was like his heart, before. How did it get there? How had he missed all this? He and Schoenfeld had the same noses. They were built similarly. They both had long arms. The shirts, the long sleeves—at that shop in Florence. Andrew flashed on that moment, so peculiar and confusing then. So simple and obvious now.

What would it be like? Would Schoenfeld hug him? Would someone, finally, hold him and keep him from spinning, spiraling—falling?

"Things right now," he tried again, "feel very strange."

"Oh?"

Andrew blurted, "Henry finally told me. I know."

It was impossible to detect whether Schoenfeld expected this. "Ah. I see." Then: "What do you know?"

"You want to hear me say the words?"

Schoenfeld nodded.

"You are my father. My genetic father. I am your son. Your genetic son."

Schoenfeld stared at him evenly and was silent for a beat. "That is correct."

"And I have no idea what it means."

"Honestly, Andrew, I don't either." Schoenfeld paused. "I think this is something we have to find out together—or perhaps not. It's up to you."

Andrew flushed. "I don't understand. You mean, it's my . . . *problem?*"

"I mean, it's your *choice*. You choose where we go now. Forward, into knowing each other a little better. Or nowhere. We stop here."

Andrew considered for a moment. "Forward."

Schoenfeld nodded. "But, quite honestly, I think the person you might most want to go forward knowing, really knowing, is Henry."

"I know Henry."

"Do you? When did you learn—this information?"

"Today. This morning."

"So you haven't thought so much about how you know your father, with this information factored in? This new frame with which, through which, you might come to understand him? You might now understand better, or differently, what it is to be in his place. To be him."

"I barely understand what it is to be in my place. To be me."

"Small steps then."

"It's hard for me to get beyond the secrecy. The untruthfulness."

"He had his reasons, I'm sure. We all did. We're all complicit."

"You?"

"I agreed to the terms."

"Whose terms?"

"Henry's. Judith's."

"And what were they?"

"Not to tell you or your brother until it had become clear that you had been told."

"It sounds like you wish you had done it differently."

"Well, it was easier to respect until . . . until I met you again—saw you—in the summer and later this year. Then it began to feel . . ."

Andrew looked at him.

"More complicated."

A silence fell.

"This is just freaky," Andrew said. "You and I look much more alike than Henry and I do."

"Yes, I noted that instantly when we saw each other in Italy. That must have been hard on your father."

"Why do you keep thinking of him first?"

"Maybe because I am a father myself. I share his place—his position. I am not, in this, a son."

"But I'm a son—only I don't know whose. And I feel—" Andrew swallowed. "I feel awful. I feel—lost."

Schoenfeld considered for a moment. "You know, Andrew, I have lived through some quite . . . devastating experiences in my life. I watched my younger sister become ill and struggle for years and I watched her die. I was twelve, and I thought . . . I thought that was the end of me too. But I found that with time I was able to break down what happened into smaller pieces and then smaller ones still. Then I began to be able to tolerate, to absorb, more than I ever thought I could." He paused. "This has been my template for many other difficult events in life."

"But you worked this out years later, right? I'm at the beginning of all this, this—weirdness. It's all very new to me."

"That's true." Schoenfeld thought for a moment. "Tell me. How can I help?"

"I don't know. I can't figure it out. I can't figure anything out."

Schoenfeld sat back in his chair. He set his chin in his palm. "How about if we agree to a time when we can see each other? Maybe fixed times, so that we keep to them, know that they will be coming, regularly."

"Father-son dating. *Biological* father-son dating."

Schoenfeld laughed. "We could meet once a month if you like."

"What will we do? Watch sports?"

"I'm not a particular fan."

"Me neither."

"We'll go for a walk. Or a cup of coffee."

Andrew had never before understood how literal the phrase *a wave of exhaustion* could be, but he did now, because he felt it now. He felt all his energy drain out of him in a violent swoosh.

"May I—may I ask you a favor?"

"Of course."

"May I lie down for a second on this couch?"

"Of course you may."

Andrew took off his shoes and floated into a horizontal position. Schoenfeld bent over and placed his hand on Andrew's forehead, as though checking him for fever, or simply to touch him—to touch his flesh. His own flesh. Flesh to flesh, he stood there for a long moment, then left him to sleep.

What they said about homes that weren't lived in was true: over time they developed a closed, almost mortuary air. There was more to it than just the old fading spices, unvacuumed upholstery, and stagnant toilet water; there was the way such places stopped being relevant to anyone's daily life. Without food, mail, a newspaper, without curtains open to daylight, without movement and conversation, an apartment was just a moldering box.

Costanza had noticed this previously when she'd returned to her studio after long breaks, but now she was also struck by how the studio seemed to contain so much of her old unhappiness. Her unhappiness alone, before she met Morton; her unhappiness coupled, when she slipped away to try to think matters through without interference; her unhappiness when she became temporarily uncoupled from Morton; and her unhappiness when she was on her own again after he died, and she'd needed to flee Fifth Avenue.

Her unhappiness with Henry: Was that now to take its place with all these other unhappinesses? Maybe she had come down to the studio to bring her unhappiness here, to unpack it and look at it coolly, analytically. And possibly, with any hope, or luck, to leave it with its kind. Or maybe she had come down to try out what it felt like to be alone, even just for a few hours, though this was a fake aloneness, a pretend aloneness; she had come in body, but in her spirit, in her heart and in her mind, she was still caught up—deeply and intricately—with Henry.

She had entrusted not only her heart to this man, Henry Weissman, but her body also.

And who was Henry, exactly? A man who captivated and provoked

her and interested her. A man she felt compassion for and was attracted
to. A man she loved but did not at the moment entirely trust.

Why, then, had she gone ahead and allowed him to give her the injection of HCG?

The injection: that was probably the only question she could answer
with any reasonable certainty. She had felt it would have been too emotional, too impulsive and dramatic, to decide in the middle of the night,
in the aftermath of what he'd told her, to give up on this cycle. After all
those drugs and appointments, all that wear and tear on her body, all
that hope, and worry, and hope again, and worry again—not even to try?
Henry had agreed to her terms, anyway. He had said he would talk to
the boys. He would correct what was, to her mind, a grave mistake; but
this was a matter between Henry and his sons, she reminded herself. It
was their story, their problem; their challenge—not hers.

Yet how would she feel, what would she think, if this cycle also
didn't work? What if Henry had made ICSI sound more hopeful—more
probable—than it actually was, because of his yearning to have a genetic child of his own? What if, knowing the truth about his own body,
he had put his needs, his desires, before hers?

If that was the case, then he was malevolent, a demon, and she was
tragically blind and stupidly naïve.

That couldn't be right. She wasn't that woman, so he couldn't be
that man.

And what about this: What if *her* desire to have a baby was so
powerful that it had vanquished her doubts about Henry? Had she become a woman who wanted to become a mother at all costs, even by a
man she did not trust, a man who was not trustworthy?

She had come downtown to the studio to try to find clarity, but she
was finding the opposite. The aloneness, the quiet, the dust, were all
activating her worst worries.

The dust: that she could do something about. She took off her
sweater, filled a bucket with soapy water, and wiped down the counters
of her modest kitchen. Never underestimate the calming powers of
cleaning; maybe that was why she was so often on edge when she was
married to Morton. He wouldn't let her clean. Ivan wouldn't let her cook.
The interior decorator would never let her rearrange the furniture. She
had her work, her walks . . . but none of those chores that soothed an
unquiet mind.

The counters were just the beginning. She moved on to the bathroom, the windowsills. Even with the windows tightly closed, the cloth still came away black. New York could be filthy, invasively pestilential.

Suddenly she felt tired, drained. She was coming off one of the worst nights of her life, and she had just used up her last grains of energy cleaning an apartment she did not even live in.

In the kitchen cupboard was a bottle of burgundy. She knew that she was not meant to drink again until after the retrieval. She had eaten little that day and her brain was already pretty scrambled . . . but that pretty French label with its engraving of a château surrounded by formal gardens seemed to be beckoning her, saying, *Herein lies ease.* And she could do with some ease.

She found her corkscrew, rinsed out a glass, and poured herself *un'ombra*, a shadow, of wine; a safe shadow. Then she picked up a rag and a can of furniture polish and sat down at her desk.

How many hours she had sat at this desk, and how serene they had been—or seemed to have been, in retrospect. She had bought the desk at the flea market in Chelsea. The man who sold it to her said that it looked like a well-loved piece of furniture, a table with history. She had to agree. That was why she chose it. She liked to think of the desk's former life. Someone, several someones, had sat before her at this slab of walnut, thinking, working; even writing, maybe. A softening of its edge toward the left, an indentation worn down over time, led her to believe that its previous owner had been left-handed. The top drawer—she opened it to make sure—had for the longest time retained an old scent, a combination of tobacco and lavender. It still did, faintly.

In the drawer was a folder containing newspaper and magazine clippings on the subject of fertility that she had accumulated from around the time she and Morton were trying to become pregnant, and earlier. They went back years now. Several were yellowed and brittle. She turned them over, glancing at their headlines:

Picture Emerging on Genetic Risks of IVF
U.S. Panel About to Weigh In on Rules for Assisted Fertility
The Gift of Life—and Its Price: Fertility Treatments Bring More
    Twins and Premature Births

*Twenty-First-Century Babies: Painful Choices with Fertility
Treatment Lowering the Odds of Multiple Births
Life After Infertility Treatments Fail*

She had to hand it to the *Times*: they knew how to deliver a portentous headline like no one else. Where were the happy stories, the stories of dreams answered, families built out of barrenness and despair? Where were the ten thousand babies born through Henry's clinic alone? *Ten thousand.* He had reached that figure sometime before he and Costanza met. There had been a celebration in Central Park. Henry had invited all ten thousand—a whole city of Henry-fabricated lives. About fifteen percent of them had turned up, families in tow. Many of them were grown. Some had children of their own. They ate hot dogs and hamburgers, hundreds upon hundreds of them, on a balmy June day. At the end of the afternoon Leopold was given the honor of cutting a ribbon that released an enormous bouquet of pink and blue balloons into the sky. Henry told Costanza it was one of the finest days of his life.

There *had* been an article on the celebration—the *Times* wasn't one hundred percent doom and gloom, after all. Costanza had forgotten reading it and she had forgotten clipping it. But there it was, near the back of her folder: *Ten Thousand and Counting: A Fertility Doctor Throws an Unusual Anniversary Bash.*

Before she read it, she replenished her glass of wine, pouring more than a shadow now, then returning to her desk. Her eyes shot to Henry's answer to the reporter's most personal question. Did reaching this milestone, he asked, make Henry feel like some kind of omnipotent power, a wizard of reproductive fertility? Henry replied:

Come on! That's preposterous. Nature has all the power; I'm simply nature's student. My science is a tool, a quite clumsy means to a very important end. The means is not the point. The point is becoming a parent, making a family. When I look back on my life's work, I'm humbled that I have been able to help so many couples to give birth.

This didn't sound like the talk of a demon.

•

The studio had a stale, lifeless scent; Henry's apartment had an acrid one, as though something unnatural was burning. Costanza smelled it the moment she opened the door.

There *was* a fire. In the fireplace. A fire that was built of photographs. A mass of them were smoking up the living room, souring the air with who knew what kind of toxins. The photos, all the photos, were of Henry; dozens of Henrys were being licked into oblivion by crackling orange flames.

Andrew was sitting by the hearth, feeding in the pictures one by one with a pair of kitchen tongs. His gaze was so focused on what he was doing that Costanza's first impression was that he was in a trance.

"Andrew?"

He didn't look up or acknowledge her. He continued to watch the fire and drop in more photographs. After three or four had fallen into the pyre he said, "In answer to your question, I've decided that I wasn't very good at taking pictures. I knew how to look at things, but I didn't know how to see them."

She stood over him. She had not seen his face.

"That wasn't going to be my question—or my first question," she said gently.

Still he did not look at her.

"My first question was going to be 'Are you okay?'"

His answer was to show her his eyes. They were red-rimmed and distant.

After a moment she gestured at the fireplace. "Are you sure you . . . ?"

"I am fucking sure."

He stood up and walked out of the room. She followed him down the hall and into his bedroom.

Andrew had unpacked boxes and boxes of his photographs and spilled them onto the floor. He had set aside a small group, but a much larger one made up a veritable mountain of prints, apparently earmarked for the fire.

"You know that if you put all this away again, you could come back to it later, in another frame of mind. I could help you."

"I don't want your help."

She studied him for a moment. "Imagine having a conversation with a future Andrew," she persisted. "Imagine explaining to him why you gave up on all this work—and time—and creativity. Perhaps you could—"

Andrew cut her off. "Why do you care?"

"Because I'm your friend."

Andrew snorted. "That's *fantastic*. A whole new definition of friend-ship, based on, let's see, dishonesty, secrecy, the withholding of infor-mation. Betrayal. No, maybe betrayal is too strong. How about perfidy? I like that word, don't you? It was on the SATs. *Perfidy*. It's so much more—biting than *disloyalty*, wouldn't you say? Though *disloyalty* might work here too."

She felt weary, very, weary. "Andrew, I'm afraid I'm not following."

"Henry came to see me this morning at my mom's."

She nodded.

"He had a lot of *interesting* things to say."

"I know."

"Of course you know! Everyone knows the truth about my origins—my mother, who is my mother. My father, who is not my father. My brother, who is my brother but not so much my friend. Costanza, who seemed to be my friend but isn't really. Yeah, especially my *friend* Costanza."

He went on, "I talked to you more than once, about this feeling I've had, this feeling of not fitting with Henry, this feeling of not fitting with *myself*. And you *knew*. You knew and you never told me. You never got Henry to tell me." His voice was shaking with anger. "Yeah, you're my friend. Yeah, right."

It took Costanza some time to catch up—to catch on. When she did, she said, "Andrew, wait. Where did you get the idea—I have to ask you—that I knew? I only found out last night. Henry only told me for the first time last night."

Andrew stopped. "Henry only told you last night for the first time that he is not my genetic father."

"That is correct."

"I don't believe you!"

"But it's true."

"When you did a round of IVF with him before, you didn't know?"

She drew her hand through her hair. "No, I did not. Absolutely I did not."

"You didn't know that he had 'morphologically problematic' sperm?"

"I knew that, and I knew that he could get around that, but I didn't know anything else."

"That's not what Henry said. Henry said that you knew then. That you've known all along. All along, he clearly said. Since before the IVF."

The room went blurry before Costanza's eyes. "But it's not the truth, Andrew."

"So he lied."

"Yes," she said slowly, "Henry appears to have lied." Her legs went soft on her. She sat down on Andrew's bed.

Andrew sat down next to her. For several long moments they sat there in silence. Then Andrew said, "Why?"

"I don't know," Costanza said in a faraway voice.

She looked at Andrew. His eyes reddened.

"I suppose . . . I suppose he cares enough about what you think about him to want you to think that he would never have put me through IVF without first telling me what he told me far too late in this process. That was already bad enough, hard enough for me to find out last night of all nights. Now this . . ."

There's nothing else to show you, to tell you.

You're seeing me naked now.

"This makes me think I don't know your father very well at all, and that perhaps I never did."

"He's not my father," Andrew said emotionally.

A devastating clarity seized Costanza's mind. It was as though a chaotic room—after a move, or a rigorous cleaning—had been put into order. Only it wasn't a room—it wasn't a metaphor. It was her life, ordered, clarified, made logical, in a single aching vision. She saw what she had been missing, for years; perhaps forever. She saw the shape of things, their awful commonality. The pattern. First there was Morton—no, first there was her father. Because wasn't his suicide—the depth of his anguish and suffering, his hidden intentions—the original cruelly kept secret, a betrayal of her love for him, the earliest and still the deepest love she had felt for any human being on this planet? Then Stefano: three years of fidelity, intimacy, connectivity, *love*—and then, just like that, another woman. *Then* Morton, who held back part of himself from her, part of—maybe in the end *all* of—his heart, and *his* story too. And now there was Henry.

What was it about these men, whom she loved differently but profoundly, yet who remained closed to her, secretive, ultimately unknowable? And what was it with *her* that she missed all the darkest corners in the characters of the men who came into her life, the men she chose to love?

She thought she might vomit. She thought she might faint. She thought she might beat something, or someone, to a pulp.

She took a huge gulping breath into her hormonally juiced, angry, hurting body, with its strange, awful flares of emotion, its swollen stimulated follicles ready to release their eggs in less than a day, in hours . . .

She looked at Andrew. Tears were spilling down his cheeks. And now they began to spill down hers too.

Andrew turned and put his arm around her. She felt comforted. She let out a long heavy breath.

In the stillness she breathed and he breathed.

Then his grip tightened.

She wiped her eyes. She was beginning to regret drinking that wine now. The alcohol was playing with her perceptions, slowing them down, confusing her. She thought Andrew's tightening grip was drawing her closer. Was it drawing her closer? Was he?

She didn't feel so comforted now.

He leaned his forehead on hers. And left it there.

"Andrew . . ."

He didn't say anything. She tried to ease back. But he held on.

"Andrew, what are you doing?"

Forehead to forehead they sat. His eyes were closed. Hers remained open.

"I'm holding you," he said finally. "I'm holding on. I need to hold on."

A moment passed. Another. And then—and then he raised his head. He lifted up her chin, and he kissed her, on her lips. Despite herself, she felt the kiss. Simply that. She felt it—she allowed herself to feel it.

Her heart was racing. So was her mind. Every inch of her mind was saying, pause, consider, reflect. But her body—her soul—did not think the way her mind did. It did not think. It knew what it needed. It knew what it wanted. It knew.

Nine Months After That

E arly one January morning on the coast of Liguria, on a winter day so temperate it could have been claimed by spring, a brief rain washed the sky of any trace of haze. The clouds, gathering quickly, deposited their shower, and then, almost as quickly, scattered over the hills. From a bend in the road near the invisible border between the towns of Recco and Camogli, a view opened up as far as Genoa, whose lighthouse winked at distant vessels. The sea was so pristine that even from the top of the cliffs, where a bench was perfectly positioned to survey the coastline, fish could be seen darting among the rocks in the water.

Henry had never been much interested in views, but he succumbed to this one. In most every direction vividly painted old villas were tucked into steep hills and flanked by gardens that were lush even in January. Many of the surrounding slopes were terraced and planted with olives and grapes, figs and persimmons, lemons, oranges, and kumquats. But it was the sea that held Henry's attention most closely. It had more shades of blue and green in it than he could either count or name. Its constant subtle movements were hypnotic. For long stretches he gazed with absorption at this apparently infinite shelf of shivering scallops and crescents that were interrupted, here and there, by a fishing boat or a *traghetto* producing a fan-shaped wake. The sea was never still, never hewed to its pattern for more than a second; looking into the water felt to Henry like looking into time itself.

Henry was able to grasp everything up to this moment—but no further. That is, he saw himself flying from New York to Berlin, and giving a talk at a conference there, and for three days listening to talks by
other physicians and researchers. He saw himself taking a flight afterward from Berlin to Milan, where he rented a car. He saw himself driving down into Liguria and along the coast and making his way to a
sprawling old-fashioned hotel at the edge of Camogli. He saw himself
eating a lonely hotel dinner and then falling into a hard, dreamless sleep,
thickened by residual jet lag, from which he had awakened late that
morning. He saw himself ordering and then eating breakfast by his window, saw himself showering, shaving, and dressing, saw himself asking
the man behind the reception desk to direct him to a street or path that
would lead him up into the hills. He wanted to make the last part of
this journey on foot, and that is how he went, finding his way, then losing his way, and then finally coming to a cresting road that delivered
him to the bench on which he was now sitting.

He was certain it was the bench Costanza had told him about,
because it so closely fit her description. As an object it was unspectac-
ular. Its sides were made of iron, its slats of weathered wood. Its back
was canted and its seat worn smooth. The notable thing about the bench
was where it was set, just so in a widening alongside the road that could
hardly be called a piazza. The bench anchored this small level triangle
of land, which was paved with slate and planted with shrubs and trees
and edged, on the water side, with a metal railing. Beyond it the level
land fell away sharply and slid into the sea.

The water had lapped against these rocks long before Henry came
along to watch it, and it would go on lapping against them, shaping and
reshaping them, after he went away again and long after that, when he
was no more. The thought came to him easily and was a relief. A com-
fort, almost.

An old woman joined him. She was wearing a gray-and-white
housedress with a bulky cardigan buttoned over it. Her thick sturdy legs
did not seem to go with her surprisingly stylish black pumps. She was
carrying two bags of groceries, which she set down on the seat between
them.

Costanza had described the humble appearance of the bench, and
its striking position, but mainly she had told him about it because it

stood just outside her mother's house, and whenever she was feeling especially claustrophobic there, and yet not so ambitious as to want to set
off on one of her hikes through the hills, this is where she came to sit.
She had come here to sit when she had brought home her one less than
perfect grade in school and her mother's reaction had been over-the-top.
She had come here when her mother found her kissing her first boyfriend in the garden (he had joined her afterward to continue the kiss).
And she had come here the day she learned about her father's death,
fleeing down the stairs her mother had just climbed, for a few moments
breathing some air that her mother was not breathing with her. Her
own breath, her own air, her own grief.

Henry felt a deep cold ache as he reviewed these episodes: Costanza
had entrusted him with these intimate memories of hers, and then—

And then.

It didn't matter where he turned his mind: sea or no sea, the events
of April and afterward followed him like a knife; like a pocketknife
whose blade had sprung open in his pocket and threatened to stab his
flesh if he took one step too far off the course of waking, eating, shitting, showering, working, eating, sleeping, then waking to start the
cycle all over again. This was pretty much how he had endured the last
nine months of his life.

A week before he was to leave for Berlin, a card arrived in the mail.
It was the first time he had heard from Costanza in all those months.
The one-year anniversary of Leopold's death was on the horizon that
spring, she wrote, and she had learned from Morton how important it
was to acknowledge these milestones. With distance Leopold's truth-
fulness, she added, had come to resonate with her in ways that she was
only now beginning to understand.

The card arrived at the end of December. Leopold had died in early
March. Wasn't three months in advance a little too early to be remembering someone's yahrzeit? And that remark about Leopold's truthful-
ness? It felt like she was trying to communicate something to him. But
what?

Henry studied the letter as if it held some kind of encrypted clue.
On the envelope Costanza had carefully, and clearly, written a return
address, the address of her mother's house in Recco, which Henry interpreted as a signal. Even if it wasn't intended as a summons, Henry

had decided to allow himself to be summoned. He had allowed himself to travel to Italy and find his way to this bench, and now . . . now what? That was the question.

Again, yet again, he revisited that April evening. He had come home from work hoping, naïvely—stupidly he eventually saw it—to find something settled, or peaceful, or at the very least neutral or suspended, between the two of them. He had told Costanza the truth finally, and he had done what she asked. He had gone to see Andrew, and he had spoken to Justin by phone. He was so weary and so hungry that he even hoped to find one of her tasty dinners waiting for him in the kitchen. He had even—more naïvely still—allowed himself to hope that Costanza might by then have turned her attention to the remainder of the cycle, whose importance ought to have supplanted everything else.

What he found instead was a quiet, dark apartment. Costanza was not in the bedroom. Her clothes were gone. In the library her desk was cleared. In the kitchen, on the table, was a note:

> *I thought I knew you. Then I learned that I did not. I thought I knew myself. I now know I have a lot more to learn.*
>
> *If I start to speak about the drugs, the drink, my mind, the way my emotions were stirred by everything that I discovered in the middle of that brutal night, I'll try to explain myself, and I can't do that, not now.*
>
> *Nor can I see you right now, or speak to you. I have to go away. Please don't come find me. Please.*

Henry tried her cell, then Andrew's. Neither picked up. He went downtown to her apartment in the East Village—no answer. He phoned Justin, who said he had seen Andrew and described him as struggling, but Andrew had left earlier that morning and did not say where he was going.

Henry raced up to the Upper West Side, to Judith's. Her doorman told him to go upstairs. The door to the apartment stood open. He stepped through it and followed the scent of coffee down a long hall to the rear, where he found Judith in the kitchen, sitting at a round wooden table with a steaming mug in front of her. She was staring out over the rooftops.

"Sit, Henry." She calmly sipped from the mug. It was as if she were tasting those words the way she was tasting her coffee. Savoring it. Savoring the command, the tilt in her favor, for once after all these years, the knowledge she had of what had happened, because she knew, it was stamped all over her. He knew her well, too well still.

Yet her face did not seem at all calm, once he really looked into it. Instead it was rigid with upset: a mirror of what he expected his looked like.

Henry dropped into the chair. "Do you know where they are?"

"Andrew," Judith said slowly, "is staying over at his friend Kevin's for a few days."

"And Costanza?"

"I have no idea."

Judith wrapped both her hands around the mug, as though she was trying to draw the warmth out of it and into her palms. "Andrew wants to spend the rest of the school year here with me. He wants you to leave him alone while he thinks things through, sorts things out."

"But I didn't *do* anything to—"

She put up a hand. "This may come as a surprise to you, Henry, but I think it's best if I don't hear what you have to say. The truth is, you've become a memory to me, a figure from a previous chapter of my life—a previous *volume*. And I'd prefer not to change that now." She paused. "The only thing I know is that we, you and I, could have done better by the boys. We should have spoken to them—both of them—when they were younger. We should have been open. It was a grave mistake in judgment. I see that now."

Henry went home. In the cold, quiet kitchen, he picked up one of the chairs—a wooden chair—and in a rage smashed it to pieces, tearing off its legs and back and breaking its seat into two jagged wooden planks. The chair was broken and so was he. Broken, shattered—mystified. What had he done to deserve this punishment? Withheld some information from Costanza? Not told his sons the truth about their origins? Not—for the second time of his life—known the woman to whom he had entrusted his heart?

Costanza wrote that she had not known herself. Had he not known *him*self?

He had made two people close to him angry. He had disappointed them and he had hurt them. He'd made mistakes—he saw that—but did he deserve to be abandoned, to be left in the dark like this, to know nothing about his wife, their marriage, their future?

In the succeeding months Henry had had nothing else to go on. Nothing. Twice he ambushed Andrew after school; both times Andrew said he wasn't ready to see him yet, and would he please go away. When Henry pleaded with Andrew to let him know, at least, if Costanza was all right, Andrew said that she was fine. That was all he said.

Being cast into this limbo, this unending limbo, was a torture to Henry, as both Costanza and Andrew must have known. He was never given the chance to say to either of them, *I'm sorry, I shouldn't have told that one particular untruth about Costanza knowing all along about you boys—fine, not that untruth; that lie. But I was overwhelmed and afraid.* He didn't have a chance to say to them, *How could you just disappear from my life, both of you?* Or: *I understand your anger*—which he didn't, he couldn't, completely; but he was willing to try understanding on, just to see how it felt, or if it would change the way he thought, if it would stop him from waking in the middle of the night, sick and trembling with anguish and rage. He didn't have a chance to speculate, for Costanza's benefit in particular, if maybe the drugs had colored (darkened) her thinking, possibly even driven, somehow, her dramatic decision to abort the cycle and just *vanish. These hormones are powerful,* he might have said. *I once had a patient who stabbed her husband in the thigh with a dessert fork merely because he questioned whether it was too soon to pick out a color for their baby's room . . .*

He realized, as he thought this, that he might be looking to give her an out. If he gave her an out, might she see her way to giving him one? Is that what he was looking for? Not to feel guilty, not to feel responsible?

As time unspooled, Henry was willing to look back over the whole arc of his behavior to see how he might have conducted himself differently. He was willing to listen, to try to explain. Yes, he was open to that. He thought he was open to that. He also, desperately, wanted to hear what Costanza had to say. He could do none of this on his own. All he could do was suffer, and that was what he had done.

•

The woman next to him on the bench didn't even glance at him when she picked up her bags and moved on. He might as well have been invisible.

Henry went on staring at the sea. When he found himself counting the boats on the water, he recognized that he was trying to postpone the inevitable. He would have to turn around and look at the house, really look at it. It was the next step in this journey, perhaps the last one he had worked out with any certainty.

He turned around and faced the hill across the street above him. There it was. Costanza had described the house too, and she had shown him photographs of it. Large and square, it rose to four stories and had a hipped roof and a large garden. Like many of the houses in the area its detailing was rendered decoratively in paint. Bright yellow and pale green trompe l'oeil quoins delineated the corners, and painted frames outlined the windows. A band of molding with swags and leaves, also painted, divided the first and second floors. Only the shutters were three-dimensional, made of wood and colored dark green. The decoration made the house feel more like pastry than architecture; its buoyancy seemed at odds with what he knew about the lives that had been lived there.

On the second floor a small terrace projected over the vestibule that contained the front door. This floor and the ground floor below, Henry knew, belonged to Maria Rosaria. Her grandfather had built the house in 1900, and it had been divided up over the generations. A parlor, a bedroom, a dining room, and the kitchen were downstairs. A large marble staircase led up to the bedrooms. One of them opened onto the terrace, where a striped awning provided cover overhead.

A laundry rack stood in one corner. Henry squinted at it. He couldn't tell if the clothes drying on it were unusually small, or if he was just far away. He rubbed his eyes and decided they were likely an adult's socks, or underwear.

He looked at the house for the longest time. It seemed so fully *inhabited*. Costanza had spoken to him about it in so much detail that he could not regard it as a mere building. After staring at it for a few more minutes, he turned back to face the sea.

•

Half an hour later, above the birdsong, he heard a faint squeaking, followed by a gentle metallic clang. He pivoted around again and looked
at the house. No one was at the gate at the bottom of the stairs. Maybe
the sound came from another gate at the top of them, a gate Henry
could not see but deduced was there.

A twin gate, up at the other end. Installed years back maybe to keep
children, Costanza herself once, from tumbling down the steep stone
stairs.

He looked so hard at the bottom of the staircase, the three or four
steps that were visible from the bench, that the scene blurred. He blinked.
Someone was standing at the gate now. He—it was a he—pressed a button to his right. A buzzing sound followed, and the gate popped open.

Another squeaking sound, more robust this time, as the old hinges
turned, the gate opened, and Andrew stepped through it.

Henry blinked again to make sure his eyes, his eyes and his brain,
weren't playing tricks on him. They weren't. It was Andrew, incontrovertibly. He was wearing running shorts and a Penn sweatshirt and was
carrying a white plastic bag. A garbage bag. He looked in both directions to make sure that no cars were barreling around the curve, then
he crossed the road and approached.

Over a tightening chest Henry said, "Andrew, what—what are you
doing here?"

Slowly Andrew answered, "It's my winter break. I'm visiting."

"It's your winter break. You're visiting." Henry had to feed breath
into his lungs. "You're visiting . . . Costanza?"

Andrew nodded. Well, half nodded. "I arrived a week ago. I'm leaving tomorrow. I'm going to meet Ben in Sicily."

"Ben?"

"Schoenfeld."

"Your . . ." Henry could not bring himself to say the word *brother*.
His mouth simply refused to form the syllables.

"My friend."

It was Henry's turn to nod. The nod was such a neutral, noncommittal act. So open to interpretation. Why had he not spent more of his
life nodding?

Nodding and breathing—as he was now, to try to slow his heart, clear his mind. "Has Costanza been here all this time? Since April?"

"She spent a few months in Florence, at the pensione. Then she came up here."

Henry's eyes shot involuntarily back to the upstairs terrace, to the drying rack with its tiny garments.

Then his nose. It flared open. He took in the scent emanating from the bag of garbage Andrew was holding. It had the familiar acridity of—was it possible?—soiled diapers. Actually it was unmistakable, now that the thought had occurred to Henry.

His stomach, his whole body, constricted. "Is there a baby?"

Andrew looked away. Color came into his cheeks.

"But how?"

Andrew set down the garbage bag and faced Henry. "Costanza asked me to help her, and I agreed. I helped her the same way Isaac helped you and Mom all those years ago."

Henry forced his mind to slow down so that it might absorb this information.

Semen produced by Andrew, his son, had impregnated Costanza, his wife.

Andrew, his not son; Costanza, his not wife.

Suddenly everything made sense. Dreadful, frightening sense. Henry didn't know that he would ever be able to wrap his brain around this. He felt his heart. Just that. He felt his heart.

"The baby is—well? Healthy?"

"Yes, she is."

"She."

A she. A girl. A daughter. Whose?

"And Costanza?"

"She's good. She's tired. The nights . . ." Andrew stopped there. He studied his father for a moment. "What about you? How are you doing?"

"Me?" Henry seemed almost surprised that Andrew would ask. "I suppose I would say I'm not so okay really. Not at all okay."

"I'm sorry."

What did that even mean? Sorry that Henry was not okay? Sorry that Andrew had done what he had done? Sorry that they had come to—this?

Andrew pushed his hair back off his forehead. "May I ask you a question?"

Henry nodded.

"When I first held the baby, I tried to imagine how it felt for you, when you first held me. Me and Justin."

"Wonderful is how it felt," Henry said in a soft voice.

"*Wonderful* is an interesting word, isn't it? There's the sense of great, but there's this other sense too: full of wonder. Wondering at, wondering about. Did you ever sit there thinking, 'This is my child—but not really? This is Isaac Schoenfeld's flesh I am holding. Isaac's and Judith's genes, not my genes with my wife's but *his*.'"

Henry ran his hand through his beard. He knew he had to speak carefully. Everything had to be careful, much more careful, now. "Of course I had my moments. I would be lying if I didn't say that. But, Andrew, you must understand that you and Justin arrived after a lot of planning, a lot of yearning. I can tell you that with the clearest conscience. You and your brother were *wanted*—both of you most certainly and unambiguously came from love."

Andrew gazed beyond Henry, at the sea. He didn't say anything right away.

"The way this baby happened was—unusual. I recognize that. And even though I'm sure I will always know her, and do my best to love her, and tell her the truth of how she happened, I believe, and Costanza agrees, that I have to live my own life, just as she has to live hers."

Henry nodded again. That nod was proving more essential than he could ever have foreseen.

"And Costanza, what does she want? What is her plan—for herself, and her baby? Is she going to live here, with the mother she finds so difficult? Is she done with New York?"

"You have to ask her yourself."

Henry leaned heavily into the back of the bench. "How? When?"

Andrew looked up at the house. So did Henry.

"She saw you sitting here all morning."

"I feel spied on."

"Just observed. And photographed."

"So you're still taking pictures."

Andrew nodded. "I can take a break, but I can't seem to stop."

Costanza saw him all morning. What did that mean? That she was waiting to speak to him, to apologize to him, or have him apologize to her, or to tell him, or ask him, what? Did she expect him to pick up where they left off nine months earlier? Now that she had her baby, did she want Henry back, did she want to come back to Henry? Her baby: who was not his genetic offspring but who, if they found a way (what way? How?) to resume, he would be raising, as he'd raised Justin and Andrew, who were also not biologically his? Well, he would not be raising her as he'd raised Justin and Andrew, since he was no longer that father; that man.

Henry turned to look again at the sea. So did Andrew.

"It's hard to look away," Henry said. "From all this blue."

"I sat here a bunch of hours myself, when I first came."

"Between the water and . . ." Henry looked back at the house and pointed. "That's Costanza's room, with the laundry outside?"

"Yes. The terrace is off her bedroom. It gets all the sun. It's the best place to dry the baby's clothes."

The baby's clothes. Drying in the sun, the tiny strips of white cloth looked like beacons, or flags—of surrender?—flapping in the breeze.

Andrew followed his gaze. "Maria Rosaria put Lia's laundry out this morning, even though the sky was so dark when we got up. She said she knew this sky, she knew the rain would pass quickly."

"Lia." A chill came over Henry. It began in his feet and shot all the way to his scalp.

Andrew nodded. "Costanza named her for Grandpa. She said she couldn't name her for her father because he chose death. Grandpa instead, despite everything, she said, chose life."

This was such deeply, such profoundly, uncharted ground. Henry hardly knew what to think, let alone how to act. A child, named for his father, had been born to his wife but was conceived by his son. She was his child and his grandchild, legally both, but genetically neither.

For once Henry refrained from further comment. What more could he add that would matter? Andrew would live all his life with what he had done, what he and Costanza had done together, and his experience of what he had done would likely change over the years in ways that no one could predict. Henry had Andrew—and Justin—to reckon with, just as Andrew now had Lia.

After a few moments, Henry said, "I hope, Andrew, that one day you and I might start to find our way back, or forward, to being connected again. Reconnected."

"I think we already may have, Dad." Andrew picked up the trash bag.

"Where're you going?"

"I'm going to throw away the garbage. *Spazzatura*," Andrew said, carefully enunciating each syllable. "Then I'm going to run to the Punta." He gestured at the horizon. "There are these paths with stairs that rise up into the hills, then down again and along the slopes, over a footbridge and a ravine with a little stream. They lead you all the way down to the water. The whole thing takes a couple of hours. This place is . . ." He looked around. "Enchanted, like a fairy tale."

Henry had never much liked fairy tales. To him they were such bleak stories, with broken families, dead mothers, children who are lost, abandoned, stolen, or blighted—though sometimes also improbably, impossibly, lucky.

"Will I see you later?"

Andrew shrugged. "It all depends."

"On what?"

"Costanza, I guess. And you." He paused. "Dad."

"Yes?"

"I think—" Andrew hesitated. "I think she still cares for you."

He took off. He deposited the garbage bag, the *spazzatura*, in a large can farther along the street, then broke into a run. An uphill run that was steady, confident, and seemingly effortless.

Henry looked back at the water. Its blue burned into his eyes. If he could just follow one blue scallop until it floated off the scene, beyond the hill. Toward the Punta, Andrew called it. Just one crescent wave. Everything would be clear then.

Henry tried to fix his eye on a single shape, but the more he focused on it, the more elusive it became. He began again and again.

Finally he got up, crossed the street, and approached the gate.

He paused there. As he was staring at the brass nameplates and the buttons next to them, the gate buzzed, then popped open.

Henry looked beyond the open gate, and up the stairs. He could only see halfway. The stairs were old and cracked. Moss was growing in their corners. They were steep.

He tried to imagine himself climbing them. He pictured himself rising up and coming into the sunlight again, in the garden at the top of the stairs. There she would be, thicker and rounder, certainly, following the pregnancy, likely aglow in the way of new mothers. She was likely to look tired too, from the birth, and the feeding. And the nights. But, being Costanza, she was certain also to be beautiful; worn down maybe, but still radiant.

Would there be a table in the garden, and chairs, an arbor to cast some shade against all this bright winter sunlight?

Would they sit there and talk? What could she say, really?

What could he say?

What would he feel, what would he think, when he looked into the baby's face?

Henry's imagination, his anticipation, stopped there. All of his body, it seemed, was frozen, paralyzed—except for his heart. His heart was beating, pounding, away.

Then he heard a sound. A baby's cry. *This* baby's cry. He stood there listening to it as though he might listen to it for all time.

ACKNOWLEDGMENTS

In addition to the dedicatees, deepest thanks to: Elisabetta Beraldo, Sarah Boxer, Andrea Chapin, Lindsey Crittenden, Steven Frank, Merona and Marty Frank, Tamara Jenkins, Zev Rosenwaks, Jane Varkell, Ellen Williams, Sally Wofford-Girand, and—of course—Ileene Smith.

A NOTE ABOUT THE AUTHOR

MICHAEL FRANK is the author of the memoir *The Mighty Franks*, which was a Barnes & Noble Discover Great New Writers selection, one of *The Telegraph* and the *New Statesman*'s best books of 2017, and the winner of the 2018 JQ Wingate Literary Prize. He lives with his family in New York City and Liguria, Italy.